A Neighborhood. A Mob. A Girl. A
Boy. Another Girl. Another Mob.

A Hit Man. A Hit Woman. A Recession.
A Chiropractor. *And a Twist.*

BEDFELLOWS

BOB GARFIELD

THOMAS & MERCER

Text copyright ©2010 by Bob Garfield
All rights reserved.

Printed in the United States of America.

Published by Thomas & Mercer
P.O. Box 400818
Las Vegas, NV 89140

ISBN-13: 9781612183961
ISBN-10: 1612183964

Ain't That A Kick In The Head
Words by Sammy Cahn
Music by James Van Heusen
Copyright© 1961 (Renewed) Maraville Music Corp.
All Rights Reserved Used by Permission
Reprinted by Permission of Hal Leonard Corporation

Mack the Knife
English Words By Marc Blitzstein Original German Words By Bert Brecht
Music by Kurt Weill
Copyright © 1928 (Renewed) Universal Edition
© 1955 (Renewed) Weill-Brecht-Harms Co., Inc.
Renewal Rights Assigned to the Kurt Weill Foundation for Music,
Bert Brecht and The Estate of Marc Blitzstein
All Rights Administered by WB Music Corp.
All Rights Reserved   Used by Permission

Dorothy and Cliff,*

I'm sorry you

BEDFELLOWS

won't get to read this,
but you have a lovely
daughter.

Bob Barfield

* And can't reveal what
I don't know about
Brooklyn.

For my brothers

CHAPTER 1

WELCOME WAGON

"I DON'T UNDERSTAND," SAID MR. MATTRESS. OF THE TWO ENTRE-preneurs getting acquainted at the newest retail establishment in Ebbets Beach, he was the taller, strikingly becoming one. The shorter, emphatically not strikingly becoming one was making unreasonable demands and little sense.

"What don't you understand?" asked Larry Rizzo, coproprietor of nearby J&L's Subporium. He represented the neighborhood merchants and was there to welcome Mr. Mattress on the eve of his grand opening. It was the Thursday before Labor Day. On the street, the heat was oppressive; strange convections radiated from the pavement. Even at 8:00 p.m., the city baked. Inside the store, it was like the frozen desserts case at Pathmark, except with more box springs.

"Well…anything," Mattress replied. "You're saying I've got to join the Village Association even though I'm not in the Village, and, by the way, I'm not even absolutely sure what the Village is or where it begins."

How could he even guess? To Mr. Mattress, native New Yorker, a village involved cow pastures and thatched roofs. Charming rustics and inbred children. The Ebbets Beach "Village," wherever it was, was Brooklyn all the way: plate glass, grimy brick, plastic signage, and hip-hop blaring from passing cars—and as far as he could tell, 100 percent livestock-free. Yet even granting the existence of a demarcated corridor of villageness, what this Larry Rizzo character was saying was just screwy.

This Mr. Mattress proceeded to point out, "You want me to scoop snow cones Monday or something four blocks away. This would be my third day in business. My third day. And then I've got to pay off the mob, but you say it's a very nice mob. So let's start there—a *nice mob*?"

"As mobs go, oh, yeah, definitely," Larry said as he bounced on a Dream-Rite King. "I like this. Feels like a hotel bed. How come hotel beds always feel better than your own bed? Of course, I don't exactly have experience with organized crime elsewhere. Local boy made good and all that. But these guys watch our back. They're like a good neighbor. You know? Like the ad?"

Larry began to hum an insurance jingle. This was an unnecessary mnemonic prompt. Mr. Mattress was well aware of the ad—and most every other one. Could this guy somehow have sussed out his scandalous history as a mad man? No, not likely. Either way, to Mr. Mattress, whose legal name was not Mattress but Jack Schiavone, the whole conversation sounded insane.

"This whole conversation sounds insane," Mr. Mattress said. "I don't know much, but I know there's no such thing as Mr. Nice Gang."

"Brother, you'd be surprised," said Larry as the paunchy restaurateur jammed the heel of his hand into a Pillow-Quilt Royale. His fingers were stubby and yellowed from cigarettes. The thumb was thick but oddly foreshortened, the ocher nail little more than a crescent. "This is really well constructed. Soft but dense. You know,

Jack, there's a lot about this neighborhood that might surprise you. It's been kind of tough, the economy and so forth, so we try to work together."

"With the mafia."

Larry winced. "I'm not saying they're the Rotary Club, OK? But it's not like they're killers. Lately."

"*Lately*?" yelped Mr. Mattress. "Buddy, this conversation is making me extremely uncomfortable. I mean, seriously, that's just nuts. I appreciate the welcome wagon, but here's what you need to know: I am just finally pulling myself out of a hellhole like you couldn't imagine, and I have socked my last dime into this franchise. I've got no interest whatsoever in paying shakedown money to some low-rent gangsters."

"Yeah, you will," said Larry.

"No," insisted Mr. Mattress, "I won't. I mean, what is the deal here? Are you one of them? Are you shaking me down right now?"

Larry laughed. "Oh, God no. I sell sandwiches, end of story."

That was true. He and his wife had blundered into the hero industry because it both supported and complemented their Margaritaville lifestyle. Their premises were in Brooklyn; their hearts resided in a Caribbean swim-up bar. Just in case Larry's sense of personal identity might elude any customer or random stranger, he wore tropical shirts and a panama hat twelve months a year. He was wearing that getup now as he lay down testing the firmness of the Snoo-Z-Lite. After removing his hat to reveal a baldpate horseshoed by a curtain of gray hair dangling limply over his orange, red, and yellow floral collar, he lay on his left side, then his right, trying to detect the coils.

"I'm going to bring the better half in here. She's got to feel this thing," he said. "Is this pronounced Snoo-Z-*Leet* or *Light*?"

"Leet," Mattress replied. "I mean, I assume. That's how I say it."

"It's confusing," Larry said.

"I'm confused myself, I must say. Why are you running interference for criminals?"

"No need to be paranoid, brother," Larry said. "Just trying to give you the lay of the land, because when Casper eventually shows up, you'll want to know who's who."

"Casper being…"

"Casper being the individual who represents the Donato family. You'll know him right away. He looks like Bobby Kennedy."

Wait. Donato family? In his escalating annoyance, Mr. Mattress all at once felt a twinge of recognition; it was as if he had seen a sign. In fact, he *had* seen a sign, the first time he turned onto Ebbets Beach Boulevard just shy of a retail strip he now supposed constituted the Village. His store was a few blocks south, but, still, he had taken note: THIS ROAD MAINTAINED BY THE EBBETS BEACH LIONS CLUB, PARCEL PLUS, DON DONATO'S COZY NOSTRA. He had taken note because, before his humiliating excommunication, he'd once plied in the wordplay trade himself, and this particular pun was cringeworthy. Now the surreal puzzle was beginning to take shape.

"That's what the Cozy Nostra is? The mafia? Seriously? I thought it was a cocktail lounge or something."

"Really?" said Larry. "Cocktail lounge? Where'd *that* come from?"

"I don't know, really. I sure as hell didn't imagine that it had any—"

"You've got quite the imagination, all right. You know, Jack, sometimes a cigar is just a cigar. And sometimes a cocktail lounge is called Waldo's." He chuckled at his sharp riposte, for Waldo's was indeed a cocktail lounge catercorner from J&L's. "But you'll like Casper. Very nice guy. Fantastic singing voice. He sounds like Bobby Darin."

Sounds like Bobby Darin. Looks like Bobby Kennedy. And maybe commits violence with a baseball bat like the "Bobby Garfield" character in that Stephen King novel—an idle thought the mattress dealer kept to himself. He didn't really think this visitor was paying much attention to what he was hearing, or even to what he was saying. At this stage, Mr. Larry Rizzo was flat on his back, spread eagle, splayed out like a Leonardo drawing or knife thrower's assistant. "And not only Casper, either," he proceeded. "I know Big Manny personally, and he is a total gentleman."

"All right. Now you are bullshitting me. Big Manny? This is a real person? Not, like, some cartoon?"

"Real person. Impressive person." For some reason, Larry was flapping his extremities, as if to carve snow angels on the mattress.

"It sounds like a chain of muffler shops," Mr. Mattress said. "'Big savings at Big Manny's.'"

"Not a muffler shop by any manner or means. This is a man who is very bright and very generous. Not that Mr. Donato is not, but Big Manny is, in my opinion, the force behind the new Ebbets Beach. It was my privilege to work with him on the Christmas lights and the drug-awareness drive."

The mafia drug-awareness drive. This was all a little more than the new kid on the block was prepared to process. Even Larry could recognize this. Still supine but still in the mood for chatter, he decided to change the subject.

"You mentioned a hellhole. If I may ask, what kind of hellhole?"

Mr. Mattress just looked at this lunatic, still on the display bed, still scissoring his arms and legs, and wondered if this were not all someone's elaborate practical joke. But, nearly at once, he calculated the possibilities and decided, no, this bald guy was simply a pest for the ages.

"Not really eager to discuss that, Larry." Because he had lost almost anything that had ever meant anything to him, and the pain was unbearable.

"Was it one of those deals where you were imprisoned behind a false wall and sexually abused for decades?" Larry inquired.

"Huh? No! What are you talking about?"

"I saw something like that on CNN. I thought it might have been something like that. Was your identity stolen by Israeli agents to kill a terrorist mastermind?" The answer to that one was also no, to the best of Mr. Mattress's recollection. Finally, it dawned on him that Larry was not merely a world-class pest but a pest who had smoked a great deal of marijuana over a course of many decades and probably the past hour. He was twice correct.

"Larry, I've got an opening to prepare for. Let me just—"

"Mossad's a bitch. Those guys don't mess around. I hope it wasn't that." Larry gave Mr. Mattress the once over, head to toe, as if he were checking out the talent at Waldo's. "Stolen organs! Right? You were kidnapped to have your organs harvested." Though the virgin bed retailer now stared at him, his mouth actually agape, Larry seemed oblivious to the facial cues that screamed incredulity. Anyone could see that Mr. Mattress was nonplussed, yet the emissary went on as if his new neighbor were fully plussed. "So, anyway, the meeting is Saturday morning at the Parcel Plus, nine o'clock, if you want to get your Sale-a-Bration assignment and meet the other merchants."

Jack just wanted this parasite out of his store. "Sure," said the grand opener. "I'll be there. But right now, I gotta, you know..."

Larry grunted as he pulled his flabby frame off of the Snoo-Z-Lite, arranged his hat, and shook his new neighbor's hand.

"Good luck, brother. See you Saturday." Then, stepping at last outside, he ambled into a first-of-September furnace.

"Jesus Christ," Jack muttered to himself as the door swung closed. "What a freak."

He did not add, because he did not then know, "And, in a week's time, a coconspirator."

CHAPTER 2

IMPUNITY

FOR THE SORT OF PERSON WHO BELIEVES IN OMENS, AND THERE were plenty in the hall who did, it would be hard not to register the portentousness of Thursday night. Does not a pummeling in a church basement augur poorly? Our Lady of Grace hadn't seen such commotion since Rita Hayworth stood up for her godson in 1946. It was the year *Gilda* was released, and there were fistfights for standing room at the baptism.

On Thursday, when the police finally arrived to break things up, the alleged assailant had a knee against the throat of the possible victim, who was pinned to the floor, red-faced and flailing. The cops pulled her right off, but not before she got in a few more good licks. She wasn't especially strong. The woman was barely five feet tall, after all. Still, the whole neighborhood knew not to fuck with Mrs. Troncellitti, who had figured out years earlier that nobody would dare retaliate no matter how many times she poked or smacked or kicked them.

Mrs. Troncellitti was eighty-one years old. That's what they mean by the word *impunity*. Impunity is how a person can attack a two-hundred-pound off-duty police sergeant in front of sixty witnesses in a place of worship without repercussions. Even if Mike Franzetti, the fellow she was thrashing, had identified himself as a policeman to his responding colleagues—which he, of course, did not do—it is highly unlikely she would have been in any jeopardy. Mrs. Troncellitti was old and excitable, not stupid. Nobody was going to shoot her. Nobody was going to send her to jail. Therefore, nobody was going to cheat her, either. That's what they mean by the term *righteous indignation*. Righteous indignation is what makes you spit at the cops wresting you away from the cop whose throat you have your knee on. It is also what you get when somebody takes away your bingo.

"Sorry Mrs. T," Sergeant Franzetti had said to her moments before the assault. "This ain't a bingo. You markered over B-seven. It was a B-one." Then she kicked him in the balls, sending him crumpling to the floor, whereupon the angry widow dropped to her knees on top of him and commenced whaling on him. The next day, across the length and breadth of Ebbets Beach, people tried to make sense of what had taken place.

"This augurs poorly," said Father Steve to the bishop, whom he called Friday morning immediately after learning of the brawl in the church hall. "Bingo is one of the few things keeping this parish together. Most weeks it gets a better turnout than Sunday mass."

"Is she really eighty?" the bishop asked.

"I think she's eighty-one," Father Steve replied. "But spry. She looks younger. She has plenty of black hair on her head. Everyone's afraid of her."

"Why isn't she in a home?" the bishop wanted to know. "She sounds demented."

"No, Your Excellency. Just a bully. I must say, even I tread lightly around the lady. Her kids are scared of her, too."

"What will you do? Maybe you need to get a restraining order."

"We can't," sighed the pastor. "She's our organist."

That was day-after conversation at the scene of the crime. Down the boulevard at Tanning Expo—where the dominant color was teal and the dominant odor was Island Princess lotion with pomegranate mango and hearty vanilla—Sunny Kaplan heard a mouthful from her boss, Tina. Sunny was spraying Lucasol on the bed interiors, and Tina was on and off the phone confirming appointments.

"So I hear your boyfriend was assaulted in the line of duty," Tina said between calls, with a snorting laugh at the pure delicious- ness of the gossip.

"Come on," replied Sunny. "He's not my boyfriend."

"Oh, you're right. I apologize. He's a married man twice your age. He couldn't possibly be fucking you, like, twice a week."

"Teen, shut *uppppp.*" Sunny was tall, trim, and astonishingly untanned. If Tina's skin was mochaccino, Sunny's was 2-percent milk, dotted on her face and arms by tiny chocolate-chip freckles. Her hair was like perfect rings of copper wire tumbling onto her shoulders. This was the subject matter when Mike Franzetti had first hit on her, at Waldo's, where she used to tend bar. His come- on was so blindingly original, how could she not be interested?

"You know," the cop had ventured, "you look just like… whatshername…'It's a hard knock life'…whatsit…Annie."

Annie! How novel and unexpected!

"Oh, yeah?" she'd replied, as she had hundreds of times before. "You gotta thing for little girls?"

What had made her tingle was when the cop looked her straight in the eye.

"Yes," he'd said. By the end of the evening they were already on their first date, in the rear of his Crown Victoria, and somewhat to Sunny's surprise, he was fantastic. They'd remained an item now for four years, although Sunny was correct. Sergeant Mike Franzetti was not her boyfriend. He was her dildo.

Tina snorted. "Really, I'm just worried about him. It's so dangerous being a peace officer. You never know when you might be brutally attacked. Was he wearing his vest, Sun?"

"Cut it out, Teen."

"I hope he was wearing his ball vest." *Snort. Snort. Snort. Snort.*

The talk of the town did not end there, either. In the back room of Fiesta Tours, usually the province of sports chatter and shoptalk, some of the boys put aside the usual Friday-morning discussion of weekend point spreads to speculate on the significance of church bingo mutating into fifty-and-over coed mixed martial arts.

"The game must be rigged," speculated Casper the Collector as he played gin with Tony the Teeth before his Friday rounds. "That's why the old bag went nuts."

"The bingo game is not rigged," said Tony.

"Yeah, how do you know, smart guy? Who says that cop ain't fixed the game? He's probably skimming."

"The church bingo is not rigged," repeated Tony.

"But how do you know?"

"Because, Casper, we are the underworld. If the game was rigged, it would be rigged by ours truly."

"Once again, Tony, and it pains me to say this, you make an excellent point."

Casper was, indeed, pained to concede the point, because Tony the Teeth was by no means the intellectual firepower in their little crew. He was just the plain firepower, whereas Casper—twenty-eight and ambitious—was deemed a man on the way up. Or he was before the fortunes of the family, like the fortunes of the church and the fortunes of Ebbets Beach itself, began heading ominously south.

"So why don't we have a taste of that game?" Casper inquired.

Tony played a nine of hearts. "The don wants no part of it," Tony said, discarding an eight of hearts. "He says we're all part of the church family."

Casper was puzzled. "Huh?

Tony picked up the eight of diamonds he'd baited for and knocked for three.

"In other words," Tony explained, "you don't rake God."

One place where nobody was talking about bingo mayhem was a few blocks south, at the grand opening of Mr. Mattress. There, bargain hunters were too busy buying beds—and lots of them. Others came in just for the free breakfast pastry because, as Jack had asserted to his assistant, Jitnee, "The most provocative word in the English language is *free*. Truth be told, Jitnee, you wouldn't believe what even rich people will do for a freebie. Movie stars who make twenty million dollars a picture can be lured to some dumb awards show with a bag of swag worth six hundred dollars. Because Angelina soooooo needs another pair of designer sunglasses. High rollers will drop two million dollars in a weekend at the Borgata instead of the Venetian because the Borgata gave them a plane ride and an iPad. I have personally witnessed a fifteen-million-dollar-a-year CEO stuff his sixty-five-hundred-dollar suit pockets with a dollar forty worth of skewered shrimp from a cocktail party tray."

He wasn't lying about that, either. He had seen many a glittery affair, and many a perversity, in the life he'd lived before becoming the foremost bedding namesake in (almost) the Village. A lot of life experience this man had, most of it lately awful. But instructive nonetheless. Among those who seemed to prove his point about the allure of giveaways was the church organist, a tiny elderly widow named Mary Troncellitti. She had no need for a mattress of the finest materials with the industry's best warranty. Never mind twenty years, actuarially speaking, she had a reasonable chance of not living to see the free next-day delivery. This visit was about curiosity and sweets.

Alas, by a quirk of fate, just as Mrs. T approached the table bearing the coffee urn and pastry, the last of the coffee was spritzing haltingly into the white foam cup of another customer, who had, seconds before, also grabbed the last pastry, a crème-filled, honey-glazed doughnut. Jitnee, at that very moment, was in the back, arranging a fresh tray of Danishes and doughnuts, but Mrs. T did not know that. She had walked seven blocks on a scalding morning and earned a few crumbs of insult for her trouble. She scanned the room looking for an employee and fixed at once on Mr. Mattress, a handsome man with gorgeous wavy hair, at the moment brandishing an accordion-sized cross section of the Snoo-Z-Lite to illustrate the hand-tied surgical-steel springs. Mrs. T crossed the floor in his direction.

At first, Mr. Mattress did not see the woman; the store was crowded. He did, however, hear her. She had the husky voice of a life lived hard, through immigration, economic depression, tuberculosis, world war, two stillborn children, Vatican II, a phi-landering husband (God rest his soul), and the breakup of Martin and Lewis, over which sixty years later she still grieved.

"Excuse me," she said, immediately capturing the owner's attention, for her voice sounded like a bear choking on a salmon, "is there any pastries left?"

Now they made eye contact, this Adonis store owner with the generous smile and the irritable old midget.

"I am so sorry, ma'am," Mr. Mattress said. "I'm sure a new batch is on its way."

Mrs. Troncillitti took a moment to process this information. She just stood there glaring at this appallingly Danishless bed salesman who reminded her of a young Cesar Romero.

"Thank you, sir," she said. "I'll wait."

Mr. Mattress was thus perhaps spared Mike Franzetti's brand of ignominy, possibly because in his heart of hearts he knew very well that the most provocative word in the English language is not *free* at all. The most provocative word in the English language is *no*.

CHAPTER 3

BIG MANNY

FOR A HIGH-RANKING CAREER CRIMINAL, THIS UNDERBOSS WAS underbossy. Whatever brutish caricature the name *Big Manny* might conjure fit the man not at all, mainly because movies and trashy fiction don't begin to capture the true diversity of American organized crime. Yes, he looked like a bruiser, six foot four, 295, and forearms like twin *prosciutti di San Daniele*. But he was not now nor had he ever been the muscle for Don Donato or anyone else. On the contrary, he was a gentle, cerebral, churchgoing philatelist travel-agent family man.

Or at least former travel agent. Fate had thrown him together with the don in the 1970s, when a hood called Vic Donato sauntered into Holiday Supreme to buy air tickets for himself and the little woman to Palermo. The fare was $770 in 1974 dollars, which Vic paid for by peeling off eight C-notes and telling this total stranger, Emanuel Aiala, to keep the change.

"Whaddya doin', money laundering?" the travel agent had quipped, not imagining that the answer was substantially yes.

This was what you call a historical inflection point. For whatever reason, the up-and-coming mobster did not reply, "None of your fuckin' business." What he replied was, "I'm sorry, why do you ask?"

"Well," smiled Manny Aiala, riffing on his little joke, "it just occurred to me that if somebody wanted to launder dirty money, this would be just the place."

"Brooklyn?" asked Donato.

With a bemused squinching of his eyes, the travel agent's smile turned from mischievous to quizzical. Who was this Donato guy, this short little man who looked like that cartoon character, whatshisname, from Bugs Bunny? Was this little fellow that obtuse? The answer to *that* question, of course, was no. Vic the Vig wouldn't become Don Donato by not knowing when to play dumb. Equally, Manny the travel agent wouldn't become Big Manny by not understanding instinctively when opportunity was all but kicking in the door.

"No, sir," he clarified. "A travel agency. See, I'm just now thinking—because believe me I don't sit here all day dreaming up ideas to screw the IRS or nothing—but it just occurred to me, let's say you bought maybe five first-class tickets for friends or family of yours in Sicily to return to the States with you when you come home, OK? You buy them from me, for cash. And let's say you get to Palermo and discover that your family or colleagues or whatnot had an illness or something and had to cancel their trips. So you go to Alitalia yourself and get a refund for the tickets, in lira, which you just deposit in a bank in Palermo or even Zurich. You just cleaned up ten thousand dollars."

"Very interesting," said the customer.

"Yeah, it just dawned on me. I oughta take my idea to the mafia. I could make a fortune."

Victor (formerly Vitorio) Donato smiled, took his vacation tickets, and left. The next morning he returned, sat down at big Emanuel Aiala's desk, and said, "Five first-class tickets from Palermo to JFK, please." He then handed the travel agent $10,000 in cash. Now it was Manny's turn to do some rapid reckoning. It required but an instant for him to understand who, approximately, was sitting across the desk from him. He wasn't entirely surprised, but still his mind reeled, trying to recall what he'd said yesterday that could get him killed. He thought quickly, and he thought shrewdly.

"Sir, you got that kinda money sitting around in cash?" he inquired, now that the customer's cards and the equivalent of six months of travel agent salary were on the table. "With inflation at eighteen percent, might as well just take eight, nine hundreds and burn them."

Vic Donato stared hard at the enormous genius sitting across from him.

"Aiala, huh," he said. "Palermo?"

"Messina. Not me. My folks."

"You looking, by any chance, for an upgrade, jobwise?"

"Not really, Mr. Donato. I'm going to college. Pace."

"College? What are you gonna be, a doctor?"

"No, sir. Finance. I wanna work on Wall Street. I'm just doing this to work my way through."

"Wall Street, eh?" replied Vic Donato. "Well, it just so happens my employer is in the finance trade, and we have an excellent, whatyacallit, work-study program."

"Seriously?" said the travel agent. "I mean, I'm happy with my current circumstances and so forth, but you…Can I ask, in round numbers, what the salary might be for this position?"

Donato reached into his pocket for his bankroll, separated a thousand bucks in hundreds, and handed the cash to the travel agent.

"It's kind of a commission thing," he said. "But you won't believe the benefits. Only thing is, you gotta keep this job, too."

History records that Manny took Vic up on the offer and commenced his brilliant cash-management career, first hand in hand with Vic Donato for Don Greco and then, after that don's tragic passing, for the ascendant Don Donato. The "work-study" program, however, meant "work with Don Greco's outfit, study Don Greco's outfit," so the travel agent was obliged to discontinue his education at Pace University. Only later, when serving time in federal prison for a crime he did not commit, did Big Manny obtain his college degree in finance. On the outside, he required no textbooks. He had an endless appetite for learning about money in all of its forms and a preternatural gift for expropriating the principles of the free market to limit risk in the black one. As such, his career trajectory was an utter mob anomaly. Big Manny never beat anybody up. He never hijacked a truck. He never collected a payment. He never packed a gun. All he ever packed was his lunch, whenever Annabella had one of her migraines, because if he ate pasta or meatball subs with the boys every day he'd weigh four hundred—not three hundred—pounds.

They'd sit in the back room of Fiesta Tours, a business the don had eventually installed in a second-floor walkup on the boulevard, playing gin rummy and loading carbs. Big Manny would eat cottage cheese out of Tupperware and work on his stamp collection. His particular philatelic interest was the stamps of countries that no longer exist. He had specimens from Zanzibar, Czechoslovakia,

Zaire, Transjordan, Austria-Hungary, Basutoland, East Germany, Ceylon, Siam, Gran Colombia, and Rhodesia. His favorites were a 1936 Yugoslavia stamp honoring Nikola Tesla, an 1890 sheet from Abyssinia, a ten-centime Corsican issue featuring the Moorish head that was the briefly sovereign island's national symbol, and a 1971 five-rial stamp from Persia sporting the profile of Cyrus Cylinder, whoever the fuck he was.

Over the years, his colleagues treated Big Manny as a breed apart, in the manner of a monk or a two-headed goat. He was accepted without question and heeded without hesitation, even by the don. But he kept to himself and was never expected to socialize with the rest of the crew. The sole exception was the weekly *riunione*, which he never missed. In other outfits, a guy who shortcut the system, who went to mass with his nuclear family every Sunday, and who shied away from the *family* family might have aroused resentment or suspicion. Big Manny aroused none. He was beyond reproach, and if there had been any unease about him among the boys, that disappeared when he took a federal rap for Don Greco in 1981, doing four years on a phony tax beef. The Feds had trumped up the charge trying to flip Manny, but he never so much as cleared his throat for the fuckers. Any defense would have exposed the boss, so he put on a very big jumpsuit for a fifty-month holiday supreme in bucolic Allenwood, Pennsylvania.

He returned a hero, a status that rubbed off on his sponsor, Vic Donato, and together, they climbed through the ranks of the Greco family. Soon Vic was underboss and Big Manny the family's untouchable consigliere. When Manny's son came of age, he, too, joined the family—although Big Manny permitted that with only mixed emotions. He was proud that the boy wanted to follow in his father's gigantic footsteps, but he had imagined that both of his children would eschew the Life and would have been pleased if both did. His daughter, Maria, God bless her, was in college. The boy, for better or worse, worshipped him. He had grown up wanting nothing but to be Little Manny. Big Manny, who had grown up wanting nothing but to be J. P. Morgan, felt he could not in good conscience crush his son's dream.

This was the man who sat on his La-Z-Boy, early Friday morning, drinking a cup of tea. Annabella sat on the vinyl-clad sofa, telling him of the bizarre events of the previous evening, when that lunatic Mary Troncellitti kicked Mike Franzetti in the groin and spat on the cops.

"If Mike had wanted to defend himself, he mighta broke her in two. Manny, so what's he gonna do? You see what I mean? I never seen such craziness. And the worst thing is, I was just getting hot. Then—boom—that's it. The woman goes crazy and they shut down the game for the whole night. Do you believe this?"

Manny sipped his tea, trying his best to nod when nodding was appropriate and to shake his head in disbelief when Annabella expected that. She did not notice that he was barely present, much less relishing the gossip or sharing her disgust. He just wanted her to go to another room because he couldn't summon the effort to do that himself. Presently, Annabella went upstairs to dress and make the bed. That's when Big Manny began to sob.

CHAPTER 4

DROP-DEAD GORGEOUS

THE LAWYER UNLOCKED HER STOREFRONT OFFICE IN THE HEART of the Village, beneath the travel agency and directly across from Kornblitt's Jewelry. In the glass door's reflection, she saw something strange going on across the street. A man, burly and bald, was banging on the display window. A second man, also a bruiser, was hanging right alongside, sucking on his cigarette like an egg through a straw. It was 12:45, and Corny was almost certainly at J&L's wolfing down the tuna sub he ate every day of his working life. He closed the store daily at 12:30 and was always back in thirty minutes—as indicated by the plastic BE BACK SOON! sign on the door, its moveable clock hands pointing at 1:00 p.m. sharp. The bald character was now hunched over and pressing up against the window, his hand cupped over his brow against the glaring sun, and began pounding the glass again.

Angela turned to face these lugs. If she didn't know better, she would have taken them for loan sharks calling on a matter of arrears. It happened, though, that she was extremely well acquainted with the local usury industry, and this pair was definitely not on that payroll. "Yo," she hollered. "He's at lunch."

The visitors glanced back at Angela and froze in place, fixing upon her twin unblinking stares. Perhaps the men were being intimidating;

perhaps they were simply transfixed. Angela could not know, because being stared at by men was the price of being Angela. To the local riffraff in these environs, she was deemed a total babe, which was true like the Sistine Chapel is a total room. She was, in a word, exquisite. No matter how she might deglamorize herself in wardrobe and coiffure—and she tried her level best—there was no disguising Aphrodite.

As do-gooder lawyers go, Angela was simply a vision: green eyes, olive skin, dark hair like from a shampoo ad, and what her mom called "the Tripodi bone structure, back to your nana's nana." Her younger sister was blessed with the same extraordinary features, yet somehow Angela exuded a greater magnificence. This owed to her bearing. Unlike the garden-variety goddess, who can't help having her head turned by so many turning heads, Angela wasn't impressed with how impressive she was. As she had once secretly confided to a state's attorney who'd declared his utter helplessness before her, so overwhelming was her beauty, "Dude, Nefertiti was beautiful, too. So was Mata Hari. So was Joan Crawford. Three bad bets, if you ask me." The snub, of course, just made him desire her more. Only after three more polite rebuffs, a pair of impolite rebuffs, a phone call to his wife, and a restraining order did the fool finally back off. Now he's in the state legislature.

And now, in the scorching midday heat, Angela was getting a full-body scan by two piano movers or whatever, four dull eyes trained on her as if expecting an impromptu tap dance or gunplay.

"Can I help you?" she offered, loud enough to be heard from across the street, but not so loud as to sound perturbed. The bald one took a step in her direction, which did argue for the threatening end of the transfixed-intimidation continuum, but he advanced no farther. Just as quickly, the smoker had reached out to hold him in place, and after a long two seconds more of soulless staring, they turned away. Flicking his cigarette butt into the gutter, Joe Camel pointed Uncle Fester toward some destination up the boulevard and off they sauntered. So many shop windows, so little time.

Many a woman, and man, would have been reduced to a clammy sweat by such an encounter. Not Angela. As a public defender, she'd gotten her share of the fish-eye from all manner of miscreants. She could no more be bullied by eye contact than seduced by it. On the contrary, this nonsense made her feel what the self-helpsters call "empowered."

"Yo!" she called after them. "Stop back Monday. Big sale!"

They did not so much as glance backward, so she pivoted back to her door, turned the key, and entered to take care of business. This was the Legal Aid Society, and she had a full afternoon ahead of aiding society legally. In particular, she had to deal with a landlord-tenant case. That putz, Larry Rizzo, the subhuman sub shop proprietor, was trying to evict the widow Tran from her studio apartment for nonpayment of rent.

To his credit, his nine-flat building was well maintained; he was no slumlord. But he also knew that the extraordinarily hardworking Mr. Tran had died suddenly, leaving her without income pending a Social Security investigation into her immigration status. It was a complicated case; the Trans were boat people who had managed to come to the States from a refugee camp in Thailand. They were sponsored by Mr. Tran's cousin in California and eventually got green cards. But their Saigon birth records were lost in the shuffle, and their citizenship long delayed.

They had just received notice from the INS of their final eligibility when Mr. Tran was diagnosed, at the age of sixty, with lung

cancer. Within five weeks, he was dead. In view of the tragic circumstances, Rizzo had been reasonably patient for a while, but after
six months, he demanded the rent. "I'm running a business here,
sister," he'd told Angela, "not a charity." That was a sentence she'd
heard a hundred times before from a hundred creepy parasites.
Hand it to this doofus Rizzo, though. He was the only landlord
she'd ever heard of delivering free sandwiches every day to the
tenant he was trying to evict.

Angela was buried in the file when the door opened. Looking
up, she saw a familiar face. It was the mobster. He didn't enter; he
was on his rounds, so he just poked his head in the door.

"Yo, Angela," he said.

"Hello, Casper," she replied. She forced a thin smile.

"Lookit, Ange, Club Millenium tonight! Come on, you gotta
catch my act."

A kind offer, one she'd also heard a hundred times over the
last ten years. And every single time she felt the very same intense
desire. Some things, however, are not meant to be. Angela knew
that no matter how much she wished for it, Casper would not be
abducted by pirates and consigned to a lifetime at sea.

"Casper, Casper," she sighed, gesturing toward the files piled
on her desk, "I'm buried here. Tell you what, we'll see."

Casper, unmarried and childless, did not know that "we'll see"
means "no."

"Really?" he said. "Great! I'll put your name on the list!" Then
he blew her a kiss and all but skipped away.

CHAPTER 5

THE BARBER

ARTHUR DIPASQUALE, THE BARBER, LOATHED HIS WIFE.

"I hate this old cow," he muttered, under his breath, all day long. "She should be dead."

Nobody really knew why DiPasquale so detested Anna. She seemed as pleasant as anybody else. She helped at the church, baked for the school, swept the porch every day. Once upon a time she was beautiful, with large onyx eyes, womanly hips, and breasts like sacks of sugar. Naturally, over the years, she plumped up a bit, but she never stopped bleaching her lip, and she never stopped keeping herself ladylike and presentable. She favored pleated woolen skirts—the pleats of which you could slice a tomato with. DiPasquale hated her guts.

"She-devil, she belongs in hell!" he said to himself as he ran his clippers on the neck of little Anthony Vagnoni.

"What's a she-devil?" asked Anthony, who was nine. The barber stopped clipping.

"*Il mio errore*," apologized the barber. "You don't hear what you think you hear."

What the boy heard next was some indecipherable Italian mumbling amid a sudden cloud of talc. Clubman. This was, after all, no styling salon. It was a barbershop, with a cylindrical jar of

Barbicide on the counter, thick with black combs in a sea of disinfecting blue, and four Koken hydraulic chairs—the old kind, with hinged footrests, padded for ankles on one side, diamond-stamped steel on the other for shoe-sole traction. Three of the chairs were idle; times were hard. Still, DiPasquale hung on. Just as in the flush days, the striped barber's pole twirled outside, the Escher print of retail signage spiraling infinitely and impossibly from 9:00 a.m. to 6:00 p.m. every day. Only the domed cage hanging in the corner, belonging to Sophia the parrot, distinguished DiPasquale's from every barbershop you've ever seen. The bird was bright green with a white cowl on her face and a patch of red on her body beneath each wing. She looked like the Italian flag with a beak. At the moment, she was sound asleep. Like her owner, Sophia enjoyed a midday snooze.

"Tonic?" asked DiPasquale, slapping a pool of Jeris from his hands onto the boy's scalp without waiting for an answer. Then just a bit of Lilac Vegetal on his neck. Nice masculine fragrance, like a floral pesticide.

"There, son, you smell like a man. You'll have to beat the girls away with a stick."

"I hate girls," the boy replied.

DiPasquale laughed. "You say that now. You just wait. Someday you make a fool of yourself just to get a sniff. Make sure she wanna sniff you back!"

Anthony, too young to understand but too old to act squeamish, gave the barber a ten-dollar bill. DiPasquale gave him a dollar back.

"But my mom said for you to keep the change," the kid protested.

"Go buy yourself some candy," the barber said, and sent him on his way. The brass bell jingled cheerfully as the door opened and closed. DiPasquale stood for a moment with his hands on his hips smiling, then rang up the sale and commenced sweeping the floor. "This is a nice young man," he said aloud to nobody. Then he thought about his wife. "*Lei dovrebbe bruciare.*" She should burn.

"*Jingle-jingle-jingle.*" It was not the door. It was the parrot, awake and mimicking the sound she heard the most.

The barber went to the cage and tapped it. "Sophia, say, 'No, no, no.'"

The parrot said nothing.

"No, no, no," repeated the barber, slowly, pedantically.

The parrot said nothing.

"No, no, no."

Nothing.

"No, no, no. No, no, no. No, no, no."

Nothing, nothing, nothing.

DiPasquale stood again, hands on his hips, thumbs forward against his smock, puzzling over the silent bird. "No, no, no," he repeated. "No, no, no. No, no, no. No, no, no. No, no, no."

The barber was exasperated. He'd been trying to teach the bird to speak for years, and the only sound to pass her beak was the throaty avian playback of the damned entry bell. It's not as though he was asking a great deal from Sophia, who had set him back $600. He wasn't asking the parrot to memorize the Nicene Creed or the lyrics to "Volare." All he wanted was a one-syllable word, a simple affirmation of the negative. DiPasquale had spent, in the aggregate, probably three hundred hours drilling Sophia, but she was having none of it. Why wouldn't this stubborn parrot just say no? Perhaps in the tropics they are simply too agreeable.

"I don't know what is the matter with you, bird. I spend my whole life with my wife, the bitch, and it's the only word that ever come from her mouth. What kind of female are you?"

Jingle-jingle-jingle went the door.

"*Jingle-jingle-jingle*," went Sophia.

Casper had walked into the shop. Always on Fridays, early afternoon, Casper walked into the shop. Once a month, third Friday, he got himself a haircut, trimming his sideburns like dominoes and engineering his bangs across his forehead just so. Not today. This was the fourth Friday. He was here walking the length of the Village for the weekly taste. DiPasquale turned his attention from the parrot cage to regard Casper the Collector. The barber looked stricken. He was obliged to produce a hundred dollars but had nothing close to that in the till.

"Casper," he said, in barely a whisper.

"Hello, my friend," Casper said, with the kind of exaggerated chirpiness that would make most anybody in these circumstances immediately crap his pants.

"Casper, I'm a little short this week. No business. Everything so slow."

Casper raised his eyebrows in amazement. "You're short, are you? *Short…*"

It was a tense moment, and the three seconds of pregnant silence seemed to the barber like three lifetimes. Finally, the Collector spoke.

"All right, I'll get you next time! See ya, Carmine. See ya, Sophia." Casper the Collector turned around, without another word, and left.

Jingle-jingle-jingle.

"*Jingle-jingle-jingle*," the bird squawked.

The barber exhaled deeply, reaching out with his right arm to grasp the headrest of his chair. "Jesus," he said, closing his eyes.

"Jesus," the parrot squawked.

DiPasquale lifted his head, like a dog hearing the mailman. Wheeling about, he rushed to the cage, swung open the door, and reached in for the bird to perch on his finger. Withdrawing his hand, he brought the bird to his face and kissed its beak.

"Sophia!" he said. "No, no, no."

"No, no, no," the parrot replied.

The standoff with Casper, and the reprieve, were instantly forgotten. The barber was over the moon. Finally! The parrot, finally, was in working order. At long last, for those interminable gaps in his day, when the shop was empty and there was not a stray hair left to sweep, Sophia would speak to him. Another voice in the room, cheerful and dependable, would punctuate the murderous silence. Moreover, she would tell him exactly what he wanted to hear.

"No, no, no," said the barber, his heart thumping against his ribs.

"No, no, no," the parrot parroted.

"*Bella!*" he exclaimed. "OK, Sophia, my beautiful little bird, I am going to ask you a question. So when I ask you this question, you answer me with 'No, no, no.' *Capische?* Sophia, will you ever leave me?"

Would she ever leave him? No, no, no. Not like that battle-ax, that virago Anna, who six years ago cruelly consigned her husband to loneliness and heartache, forever, by selfishly dying of congestive heart failure. *La cagna.* The bitch. Parrots live a long,

long time, which is why the barber didn't purchase a hamster to keep him company. And, of course, they speak, which is why he didn't purchase a turtle. But DiPasquale longed to hear the promise from the parrot herself. He wanted the simplest conceivable answer—an affirmation via the negative—that he would not be abandoned again.

"Sophia, will you ever leave me?"

It was a perfectly reasonable question, even if, like most declarations about the future, the truth was ultimately unknowable. What the barber in his exuberance failed to consider was that birds cannot answer questions, even when furnished in advance with the answers. Because they are birds.

"Sophia, will you ever leave me?" pleaded DiPasquale.

"Leave me," said the parrot. It was quite a display for Sophia, actually. She was not giving the barber what he wanted, but she was repeating more than she had ever repeated before. Again, her beak shot open. "Leave me."

"No," said the barber. "No, no, no."

CHAPTER 6

THE ROUNDS

CASPER WAS IN A PARTICULARLY BUOYANT MOOD. DON DONATO would not be pleased to be stiffed by the barber. On the other hand, both Reyes twins came up with their end—a C-note from Famous Reyes Pizza and one from Original Reyes. Since the twins became estranged and Juan went into direct across-the-street competition with Jayson, on any given week one or the other was usually short.

Casper wondered how either of them ever came up with the cash. Famous Reyes was the first dollar-a-slice store on the boulevard, and the twins did well, about $4,000 a week in a tiny storefront. The rent was only $2,800 a month, so the don's $100 weekly end didn't sting much. Then calamity struck: Juan caught Jayson paying for a blowjob from the till. It was ugly, with words spoken neither would take back and both would regret. Juan leased the former Village Smokeshop across Ebbets and founded Original Reyes, charging 99¢ a slice. That was just the beginning of the ruinous feud. Jayson, insulted at being undersold, struck back with 98¢ a slice. Six months later, as Casper made his rounds, Famous Reyes was selling slices for 88¢ and Original Reyes 87. They'd both cut back so much on ingredients that the pizza was more like cheese-scented pita bread. Without the 5,000-percent markup on fountain drinks, neither would have been capable of filling Casper's brown bag.

On that score, at least, this week the don would be pleasantly surprised. Don Donato, of course, didn't like being brushed off. Equally, however, he didn't like getting Tony the Teeth's ulcer agitated for small potatoes—so long as the family was treated with respect. Miss a payment? Come up with his end next week, plus the juice, and we have no problems. Tony the Teeth could read the paper and chug Mylanta all day long. Mock the don, though, by trying to pull a fast one, and Tony would pay a visit. Then somebody else would be taking the medicine, if you follow.

Anyway, for Casper, this was going to be a good night. He had two sets scheduled at Club Millennium, which usually featured techno on weekends, relegating Casper to the tiny stages and indifferent audiences at Ebbets Beach House or Waldo's. So with this opportunity, he felt confident—or hopeful, anyway—that Angela would show. For ages he'd been begging her to see him sing, and, for just as long, she'd been begging off. Work, she always said, at the Legal Aid Society, trying to keep bums like him out of the slammer—the bums like him, that is, who lacked his access to sharp mob lawyers. But for whatever reason, this week, when he asked her, she did not say no. That's not quite the same as "Love to! What time?" But it's better than being dissed, which is essentially what Casper had faced for ten years, since he and Angela were at Holy Trinity, at opposite ends of the class rank but nonetheless king and queen of the prom.

So beautiful, this girl. So dark and sexy. Such cheekbones. Slender fingers, tiny frame. Tits, two. She wasn't stacked like her sister, who went with Daddy's money to Dr. Moroni for the works, but definitely in the ballpark. In Casper's eyes, she was the better looking of the twins because she wore her beauty so naturally. Angela, though she would be appalled to know it, was the main reason Casper had insinuated himself into the outfit. Of course, he enjoyed the bankroll and the status attendant to being a member of the family, and he was certainly a compliant soldier, eager to impress Don Donato, that someday he might be not merely accepted but embraced as his son-in-law. The don did indeed appreciate Casper's enthusiasm—if not his taste in music. This Bobby Darin rock-and-roll *rumore*…what was the matter with a nice, traditional song, a nice tarantella? Still, notwithstanding his ridiculous show business fixation, the boy could always be relied on to do what he was told, promptly and without complaint. Moreover, in the changed environment of mob depredation, he was a marvelous ambassador for the family. Cheerful and well liked, he was nearly as eager to please the merchants he was plundering as he was the don himself. Casper wished desperately to be cool, but that was simply not in him. He was a spaniel puppy. A Bobby Kennedy–doppelgänger spaniel puppy given every so often to slight spasms of unspeakable violence.

Now, Angela, *she* was cool. Cool like marble. What Casper most respected about her was that she, unlike most of the local pussy, did not throw herself at him. On the contrary, she behaved as if she couldn't be less interested. This drove Casper crazy—unaware as he was that she was not playing anything cool. She merely regarded him as a jackass.

Casper sauntered out of DiPasquale's and walked the pavement ten feet to the Parcel Plus. Mr. Calabrese saw him coming and, without hesitation, punched a "no sale" into the register and pulled out a crisp hundred-dollar bill. Casper walked in to find the payoff outstretched before him.

"Hey, Sam," he said. "The don thanks you."

Calabrese made a face. "Casper," he said, "tell me again what I'm getting for this?"

"Protection," Casper replied. Then he tore a piece of paper in half and handed Calabrese a stub. "And the fifty-fifty raffle. It'll have eleven hundred dollars this week."

Calabrese threw his hands up. "As if I ever win," he said.

Next stop was the dry cleaner. As Casper walked in, Mr. Kim was ready with a C-note and quick to grab his stub. Kim was always winning the raffles—eight times in the last year, $6,700 worth. It was uncanny, really. He was the only merchant in Ebbets Beach to make a profit off of the protection shakedown. Yet still he chafed at the very thought of being extorted by the Italians. He thought they were beasts and, worse than that, dumb beasts. He refused to smile at them, refused to make small talk with them, refused even to look them in the eye. He would pretend to greet them and say good-bye in Korean, but the words he spoke were these: 소의 복수형. It doesn't mean "Yo!" It means "oxen."

Today he was in a particular rage. Sales had been sliding steadily as recession gripped a neighborhood already deteriorating. The population was aging. The commercial occupancy rate was plummeting. The awnings and ironwork outside of the row houses were falling into disrepair, and this quintessential tidy neighborhood suddenly was looking slightly threadbare. Kim had not spent his life savings and thousands from his *kye*, and worked eighteen hours a day, six days a week, only to watch his livelihood gradually taken from him—especially in a brown paper bag. As

Casper the Collector turned to exit, Kim also turned. "Mr. Casper!" he shouted.

Casper abruptly looked back toward the proprietor, but, in an instant, the physical reality of the premises had changed. The afternoon sun was now reflecting off of the outside pavement so brightly and was refracted by the front window so severely that all Casper could see was glare. The dry cleaner was blackened, and all that was visible was a blinding glint off of whatever large metallic thing he waved in his hand. Casper squinted against the glare and put his left hand in front of his face as a filter. He was completely off balance and, for two or three seconds, felt the panic of a man who makes it his business never to be defenseless. Then, in but another instant, the light changed, and he was able to focus on the silvery object Mr. Kim waved before him.

"Your jacket," the Korean barked.

And so it was. Casper's silver lamé dinner jacket. The Collector owned a gold one too. "You always late picking up. Cost me money wait for you to pay."

Casper gave the Korean a quizzical look and dug into his pocket. As he paid, he calculated his withering retort for the hostile merchant, delivering it only as he finally opened the door to make his exit.

"A smile," he shot back, "uses a lot less muscles than a fucking frown."

CHAPTER 7

EBBETS BEACH

KIM SUNG JIM SEETHED. MOST OF HIS NEIGHBORS DID NOT. THEY got along. Most everybody in Ebbets Beach got along. Oh, there were squabbles and the odd robbery or violent domestic. Mainly, though, it was a peaceful stretch of Brooklyn, distinguished by two factors. The first was homogeneity. Unlike much of the sprawling borough, Ebbets Beach remained the overwhelmingly Italian enclave it had been for eighty years. There were newcomers, of course: natives of Guyana, Trinidad, Suriname, the Dominican Republic, Guatemala, Honduras, Afghanistan, Azerbaijan, Turkey, Cyprus, Nigeria, Sudan, Somalia, Ethiopia, Eritrea, South Korea, Vietnam, and Cambodia. But, altogether, even considering the Puerto Rican population, those nationalities represented a mere smattering. In terms of ethnic purity, Little Italy wasn't little Italy; Ebbets Beach was little Italy.

The second distinction, seen briefly through the five boroughs after 9/11 but receding everywhere else ever since, was a spirit of cooperation. Ebbets Boulevard ran from 59th Street to the Bay Ridge Parkway, and just inside of the neighborhood proper, where the body shops and truck-rental joints gave way to the Village, something noticeably changed. Maybe it started with the welcome sign, posted at the intersection next to Waxman's Scrap

Yard. Maybe it was just old-fashioned civic pride. For that, credit family values, the real-estate bubble, and the Federal Bureau of Investigation.

John Gotti, head of the Gambino family, died in prison. His successor and son, Peter, locked up. Carmine Persico, head of the Colombo family, locked up for life. Danny "The Lion" Leo, acting boss of the Genovese outfit, locked up. Victor Amuso, head of the Lucchese family, locked up for life. Sal "The Ironworker" Montagna, head of the Bonanno family, deported. Every one of the fabled five families was left decimated by internecine rivalries, bloody turf wars, and prosecution. These days, it was damn near impossible to run a hotel linen supply racket or a contracting company without having the RICO statutes shoved right up your ass.

That's how the don ranked as a don. Don Greco, may he rest in peace, was more like an underboss for the Genovese mob. But their grip was long gone, not merely because their power was much diminished, but because the marketplace was a shadow of its former self. You can't get blood from a stone, and you can't infinitely squeeze some Puerto Rican kid selling pizza for eighty-seven cents a slice. Even the most profitable rackets, along about 2009, suddenly began sucking wind. Loan-sharking, for instance. The global banking crash set it in flames like an insurance fire. Try commanding 12 percent a week upon threat of violence when the prime rate is 1 percent a year. Just because you are a criminal doesn't mean you're immune from market forces. Which is why, not long ago, Big Manny persuaded the don to compete with Chase and Citi on price.

"And customer service," Little Manny was encouraged to tell prospects. "Citi beats us by a point or two, but we come to your door."

The family also came to your door collecting Christmas presents for poor kids. It helped fund the Legal Aid Society, furnishing a prominent storefront to Attorney Angela Donato, rent-free. It put up the Christmas lights on the boulevard, sponsored the Little League team, kept the streets free of riffraff, and let the Our Lady of Grace bingo game rake it in week after week without skimming a dime. More impressively still, between its new policy of customer relations management and Tony the Teeth's chronic fatigue syndrome, the crew hadn't cut off a single wayward appendage or smashed a face to pulp in more than a year. A whack? Who could remember?

(All right. Everybody could remember. It was Joey Sardines. In 2003. Don Donato wasn't too exercised when Joey, his soldier, was caught with his manhood in wild Tina's well-traveled *fica*. As the Don said, philosophically, "Eh, take a number." When Joey was caught with his fingers in the numbers take, however, to the tune of six dimes, he got to play caboose water-skier. This is when you are tied by the wrists to a trailer hitch and dragged down a railroad siding until you stop screaming. Then the pulp is fed to the crabs. Tony the Teeth didn't like to talk about it because he got bursitis shoveling chunks of Joey Sardines from between the ties.)

Nothing like that could happen these days. For one thing, the numbers juice hadn't been close to $6,000 for at least two years. With the economy, most weeks the boys were lucky to bring in two grand. Medium Marco made all the calls he ever did—every bar, every street corner, every bodega, every old lady in a housecoat—and more. He started cruising the high schools, Moe Howard and Holy Trinity. He worked the senior center. He worked the hospital. Marco used to be just Marco, the pudgiest soldier, a Pillsbury Doughboy in gold neck chains, hauling in four, five dimes a week. But in the past year or two, Leonard the Calculator would say, "Marco, how is the take?" Marco would shrug and reply, "Eh, medium." A week ago, he came back with a nickel. Not even enough to pay off the cops.

There is something poignant, maybe even heartbreaking, about a continuing criminal enterprise on the wane.

Yet not all of the consequences were bad. As the mob more and more wove itself into the fabric of the community, the community more and more seemed to respond. Surely the family had always commanded respect, as only you can if you have a history of aggravated assault, arson, and murder. Yet as the violence abated and with it the fear, the crew seemed to encounter no net loss of respect. Factor out Mr. Kim. He was just a bitter and resentful man. Elsewhere on their rounds, Medium Marco and Casper were greeted with something verging on good cheer. Big Manny hadn't been handed a dinner check in anybody's memory. As for Don Donato, people would literally bow to him in the streets.

Nobody in the crew save the Teeth had the slightest trouble getting cooch, and who knew what action Tony might get if it weren't for his chronic erectile dysfunction? He was not an entirely hideous man. Somewhat big boned, yes, and a tad hirsute, but there was also that unforgettable smile. When choosing dentures, Tony had opted for pure cadmium white, a shade so brilliant as to look unnatural on a *Cosmo* cover girl, never mind the Ebbets Beach Bigfoot. His mouth was as incandescent as heaven, and he bared it as indiscriminately as an American Idol. This was all the more remarkable because Tony himself was notoriously unincandscent. His grin—which was upside down in the manner of Norma

Desmond or Wallace of *Wallace & Gromit*—was mainly out of context, neither generous nor good humored, apropos of nothing. He bared his teeth whenever he spoke, which, Tony being Tony, was mainly to complain. Yet nobody could resist staring, which is why Tony imagined his gleaming choppers to be the object of envy. He did not quite grasp that his nickname wasn't necessarily an admiring one and that his ten-thousand-watt false teeth made him that much more terrifying. But therein was yet another reason for some women theoretically to be drawn to him, because some women are fascinated with danger. Certainly no one in Ebbets Beach was more dangerous than Tony the Teeth—not counting his dick.

In short, the Ebbets Beach boys were something special. "We are like the Hezbollah," Big Manny remarked one evening. "The more we fill the needs of our community, the more power we will have." That pronouncement took place at a Saturday *riunione*. Leonard the Calculator and Little Manny understood the reference and nodded appreciatively. The others, as so often was the case, had no idea what Big Manny was talking about. Following the don's lead, however, they also nodded appreciatively. It had been at that very meal that the slogan was born. Strangely, it was Tony, the muscle, not Big Manny, the counselor, who came up with the "Cozy Nostra"—although Leonard the Calculator was the one who added the tagline "Our Thing is to Care."

CHAPTER 8

PRAYER

IF YOU THINK IT IS EASY TO BE THE DAUGHTER OF A CRIME BOSS, you are simply mistaken.

Here is the positive side: pedicures and many other goods and services are often provided at or below cost. Tina Donato's unicorn-dolphin tattoo was one such freebie, inked onto her slender left ankle by one of the guys down at Freddy's. Tina, of course, had made a show of producing her wallet, but Freddy would not take her money. The job was written off as a marketing expense, although it could easily have been booked as an insurance premium. A "win-win," they call that, and Tina liked to make winners. At this very moment, she was enjoying yet another perk, a free slice at Original Reyes, three doors down from her store on the section of the boulevard the locals called the Village.

"Lookin' good, Ms. Donato," said Juan Reyes, trying to keep his eyes off of her cleavage, for the same reason you never stare at an eclipse.

"You're sweet, Juanito," she replied, leaning forward with her knees slightly bent and her rear end thrust toward the glass door, not to create a spectacle, but to cantilever her mouth so that she didn't drip pizza grease onto either her white tank top or, presenting a larger target, her tits. Juan eyed the passersby outside, a few of whom performed vaudevillian double takes. They couldn't realize whose booty they were gawking at.

"Listen, Juan," she said, her mouth half-full of dough plus thirty or forty cheese molecules, "if anybody asks, I wasn't here. I'm supposed to be on the South Beach Diet." True enough, ordinarily Tina would have lunched hours ago on a salad or small portion of salmon, in a perfectly demure fashion. Today, though, Sunny had a doctor's appointment—or a fuck-date-turned-ball-nursing session with Mike Franzetti—so Tina had been alone in the shop tanning already swarthy people straight through lunch. Now it was after 5:00, and she was both famished and in a hurry. So she leaned and slurped.

"Looks to me like the Ebbets Beach diet," Juan replied.

"No, I'm on South Beach," repeated Tina, who occasionally was capable of making jokes but not terribly gifted at recognizing ones in her natural habitat. Further, on this afternoon, she was distracted by other thoughts. She dabbed at her mouth with a paper napkin, still bent over as if she were preparing to be paddled by Mother Superior. On the sidewalk, an incense vendor with a pristine Yankees cap, cocked to the side with a gold holographic sticker on the brim, peered into the pizza shop in lingering admiration. Then Tina stood upright, whereupon the gaper instantly recognized royalty and skittered away like a roach behind the toaster.

Yes, that was the other advantage of being a mobette. If any man disrespected you, he risked being beaten unconscious by cruel thugs wielding construction materials. This was a subject on which Tina, the younger-by-fourteen-minutes daughter of the great Don Victor Donato, was among the world's leading experts.

The world's leading expert was a young man named Fausto Pescatore, a former football star at Bay Ridge High School and friend of many an Ebbets Beach jock. He was not a boy of little substance; his father, Ernie, was a wealthy plumbing contractor and Fausto himself was a backup tailback for the University of Pennsylvania, where he was enrolled in the Wharton School of Business. He was good-looking, personable, bright, ambitious, and brutally beaten—this after Tina Donato sauntered into Waldo's past a clot of college boys and Fausto accidentally misspoke. What he perhaps should have said to his drinking buddies was, "Doesn't she go to Holy Trinity? My, what an attractive gal. I should visit Ebbets Beach more often, although I fear she is out of my league." But what somehow spilled out was, "Camel toe," and then some poorly suppressed chortling. Over the next year, the young man required three surgeries to get his face and skull approximately to where they were before he ran a gantlet of two-by-fours a few weeks later in the alley behind Club Millennium. (Happily, he eventually was able to complete his studies but for some reason decided to stay in Philadelphia working in the acquisitions unit of a large fascistic cable company.)

So, absolutely, the life of the racketeer's offspring has its benefits. Free slices and your dignity is guaranteed. Tina, however, dwelled on the downside. For one thing, no cell phone. This is like living without eyes or lip gloss, but there was no way around it. Daddy had an aversion. The other thing that bedeviled her, as she confided so often to her girlfriend Sunny, was also a direct reflection of her family position. "I can't get no fuckin' intimacy," she would slur in a jag of drunken self-pity between tequila-and-Jack shooters. "I have so much love in my heart."

Being hammered does not equal being wrong. Relationships were indeed troublesome for Tina to establish because even though the awkward Fausto Pescatore incident was ancient history—ten years ago and long before the *new* Ebbets Beach—some of the cutest men in the neighborhood genuinely shied away from her for fear of being bludgeoned. This struck Tina as ironic and unfair. She was smoking hot, an olive-skinned, raven-haired Mediterranean Venus, with pale-green eyes that glistened like opals. She was affluent. She was very, very connected. She was a good friend, an excellent listener, and if you simply treated her like a lady, she would blow you cross-eyed. Yet no matter how high her heels, no matter how many hours she shook it at the club, no matter how many Initial Shocks and Red Panties she knocked back amid hysterical, snorting laughter with her homeys, Tina Donato was the loneliest girl in Ebbets Beach.

Why did nobody take her seriously? This was the question that haunted her. Surely her twin sister Angela had no such problems. Despite dressing like a guidance counselor, Angela seemed to push men *away*, especially the adorable Casper, who was exceptionally handsome and had girls literally moaning for him at Waldo's or Millennium but still followed Angela around like a puppy and got absolutely nowhere doing it. Furthermore, Tina chafed at the deference afforded Angela just because she was a lawyer.

"Don't get me wrong," she told Sunny many a day and more or less every night, "I'm very proud of her, and I love her to death. But I didn't have no time to go to NYU because, excuse me, I happened to be building a business." That was true too. Tina Donato owned Tanning Expo on the boulevard. She outearned Angela by a factor of three. "Also, not to be mean," she'd offered more than once between shooters, "but an A-cup? I mean, seriously. She doesn't even try."

It was Friday afternoon at 5:10. Tina left the store in Sunny's hands, ducked into Original Reyes to inhale her complimentary slice, and hurried down the boulevard toward Our Lady of Grace. There, as she had daily for four months, Tina would pray.

She would pray for so many things: for the health of her family, for an end to poverty and misery in the world, to open Expo Too! for nails, to star in her own cable TV show, and, most of all, to settle down with the man she knew was her destiny. He wasn't so gorgeous, but she didn't care. He wasn't Sicilian, suggesting certain, impossible conflict on that blessed day when she would finally introduce him to the family as her intended. He wasn't even Italian. The fact is, he was Polish. But he spoke to her as no other man ever had, with tenderness and respect. His voice was so deep and self-assured, his humor so warm, his touch so gentle on her tiny bronzed hands. Tina loved him so deeply that it required her every ounce of inner strength to treat him as if he were an invisible loser, lest he should learn her secret before the time was right.

Circumstances being what they were, before Tina could even think of declaring her immortal love, first her beloved would need to need Daddy. Which was basically her plan.

At the church, as always, one vast Gothic oak door was ajar when Tina arrived at 5:25, in time for mass. Stepping into the narthex, she peered into the nave and, at first glance, spied neither Father nor any other living soul.

"Fuck me," she said, not quite under her breath. "How do they keep the fuckin' lights on?"

CHAPTER 9

CASPER THE FRIENDLY EXTORTIONIST

THE GRAND OPENING OF MR. MATTRESS WENT VERY WELL, AS JACK Schiavone had assumed it would. He knew how these things worked: At any given moment, about 2 percent of the public could use a new bed. Along comes an inventory liquidation or a grand opening, and the people in that cohort imagine that they are in luck. Just as they're in the market, a big sale! Of course, there were sales going on every week when the same people weren't in the market for a bed, but those didn't register. Those promotions were just background noise. It's the same reason pregnant women think they're all part of a gestation epidemic; they suddenly notice all the other big bellies. One way to term this phenomenon is "heightened awareness." Another way is "narcissism." Until it's about you, it doesn't exist. Jack sold twelve beds before 2:00 p.m. to folks who believed this to be their lucky day. In which case, the way he saw things, it was. They were happy. The price was significantly better than at a department store. He got his 75 percent markup. Maybe he was taking advantage of consumer ignorance and human inattentiveness, but really, who didn't come out ahead?

Of course, now he would have to stage a sale every week to eventually align with the bedding astrology of the other 98 percent of the universe. It was just a matter of time. In terms of intellectual challenge, granted, Fermat's Theorem this was not. There were no thorny communications problems to solve, no subtle psychological insights to divine, no clever messaging to craft. This was going to boil down as follows: one, show up; two, sell mattresses and box springs; and, three, deposit the checks.

Fine with him. Who said that a livelihood had to be nourishment for mind and soul? Paying the bills as an end in itself suited him just dandy. Unlike an alarming percentage of his former colleagues in the creative department of Hoffman Barol Advertising, he harbored no pseudomoral bias against commerce. They affected disdain for the artless, money-grubbing clientele; he was all for money changing hands. He was for selling stuff to people who needed, or at least wanted, the stuff for sale. He had no patience for those anticonsumptionists who wanted to decide for him whether he needed seat warmers in his Infiniti, or a flat-panel TV, or a fucking can of Coke. They claimed everything manufactured raped the earth, so we had no right to consume ecologically unsustainable goods and services. Once, at an agency retreat, he'd had to listen to an hour of that drivel from a self-righteous ozone hugger who might or might not have been Naomi Klein, but who conspicuously wasn't in bare feet and a grass skirt. If she was so pure, he'd demanded during the Q&A, why didn't she live in a hut with an earthen floor without such planet-and-soul-ravaging luxuries like central heating? And toothpaste? And chairs?

He didn't remember her answer. What he remembered was how the roomful of supposedly out-of-the-box thinkers, most of them subordinates, rolled their eyes at his challenge. They were utterly enthralled by her threadbare polemic. These were men and women who, despite earning their living in advertising, fancied themselves subversive artists who in their heart of hearts worked against, not for, The Man. Not that any of them knew the difference between a slogan and a considered judgment or bothered to venture a micron below the surface of any issue to construct an actual argument. Why weigh variables when you can save time and achieve certainty by commencing all discussions at the empty conclusion? Budweiser sucks. The media sucks. America sucks. Life sucks.

They lived in New York and didn't even read *The New York Times*, which was popularly presumed to be at all times a steno pad for the establishment, but which was mainly just too full of facts to be digested. And words. These self-styled guerillas fancied themselves writers, but they were not readers. Mostly, they looked at picture books of other advertising, but when they did affect literature, it was always countercultural. It's not so much that they were hypocrites. Just morons. They were literally too stupid to realize that writing commercials for Axe body spray disqualifies you from displaying, as a badge of revolutionary thought, *Steal This Book*. They didn't realize that it is both impossible and pointless to foment revolution within Unilever. They wore T-shirts to work and thought that made them dangerous. They were rude and thought that made them brave.

Mr. Mattress had been their boss, at $1.2 million per year.

It was midafternoon when Jack noticed a tall young man enter the store. Mr. Mattress had officially been Mr. Mattress at that point not quite five hours, yet he understood already that this fellow was not a typical customer. For starters, he was stag; bed shopping is done by couples. He displayed no apparent interest in the merchandise. Also, he was wearing a silver lamé dinner jacket. This in an ensemble that included a black T-shirt, cobalt-blue nylon track pants, and black loafers.

There was an afternoon lull and only one other customer in the store. Mr. Mattress was thus able to quickly attend to the nonshopper.

"Quite an outfit," Jack said to the visitor, who actually did bear an uncanny resemblance to Robert F. Kennedy, until his mouth opened.

"Thanks. We like to think so."

Jack smiled and pretended to misunderstand the misunderstanding. "Kind of warm to be wearing a suit of armor."

Ah. Casper caught on and chuckled. "Yeah, good one. This is my stage jacket. I'm a performer, and I picked it up from the cleaners and didn't feel like toting it, you know?"

"Cool. What kind of performer?"

"A singer. You know, standards, mostly, and some pop. Casper." Casper extended his hand and Jack shook it.

"Jack Schiavone," said Mr. Mattress. "Bed shopping?"

"Yeah. No, not really. I'm here on a more exploratory basis. See—"

"Gotta tell you, Casper, it's a mattress store. I mean, I'm sure you're great, but I don't really think I'm going to be in the market for live entertainment."

This made Casper laugh very hard. Not the menacing mobster-before-he-pistol-whips-you kind of fake laughter, either. Casper was really cracking up over the snowballing confusion. He wondered if this mattress guy was maybe not so bright.

"No, sir," he choked out. "No, no, see I'm an associate of the Don Donato organization, *in addition* to being a nightclub performer, and I was wanting to introduce myself and let you know how the organization can meet your needs as a businessman in these challenging economic times. We want you to know someone is looking out for your interests and well-being."

"Fantastic!" enthused Mr. Mattress. "Let me ask you a question. How do you sleep at night?"

In an instant, Casper lost his friendly tone of welcome.

"I got nothing to keep me awake. I pay my taxes," he said. Although he had never paid a dime in taxes. Ever.

"No, no, no," Mr. Mattress pressed. "I mean, are you tossing and turning because your back stiffens up? Happens to a lot of guys our size. Happened to me, as a matter of fact. Why? Bad mattress. Actually, a *somewhat* bad mattress and worn-out box spring. Never slept through a night until it dawned on me. Listen to this: I went to Macy's, bought a new bed for twenty-four hundred dollars. Worked like a charm. That was before I opened this store, of course. Now I sell the same bed, with a better warranty, for twenty-one hundred. So how's your box spring?"

Another confusion sorted out! Casper at once unbristled. "Tell you the truth," he admitted, "I don't have one. I just got my mattress on the floor."

"You're kidding me, right?" said the bed salesman. "You make a living on your feet all day—if I understand, never mind performing on stage—and you don't own a box spring? Keep that up, my friend, your next gig is going to be a telethon. Where does it hurt? Lower back, am I right?" Of course, he was right. Everybody's lower back hurts. In Casper's case, though, he was especially right. The singing extortionist had begun seeing a chiropractor.

"Tell you the truth also," said Casper, "it does tighten up mostly at night. A little hard to get up in the morning lots of times."

"No shit," said Mr. Mattress. "This may be your lucky day."

Casper left forty minutes later having neglected to threaten the livelihood and property of a new sucker in town. He did, however, get a $1,600 Slumberpedic double for $1,500, plus a fitted, quilted mattress cover thrown in absolutely free of charge.

CHAPTER 10

I RUSSI

TONY THE TEETH, THE COLD-BLOODED SLOGANEER, WAS A MAN of many contradictions. Strong like a gorilla and smart like an anvil, he was not looked on for anything but intimidation and, failing that, a touch of pitiless retribution. Yet he had a way of getting to the nub of things. He had the gift of the bully savant to ignore obstacles that represented no imminent threat to life and limb. In that respect, he was quite unlike his colleagues. These days, for example, Big Manny was worried about interest rates; he obsessively followed every move of the Fed, every tick in the prime, every monthly inflation report, not to mention the equity, bond, and foreign-exchange markets. He used to sit for hours at the Legal Aid Society, the storefront immediately below the travel agency and the working digs of his goddaughter Angela, watching CNBC—muted—on her office TV. His favorite was *Power Lunch*. "This guy Bill Griffeth," Manny said, "nice suits." Meanwhile, Leonard the Calculator, the bookkeeper of the outfit, was worried about recession. The don, for his part, was worried about the FBI.

Tony the Teeth, who'd gone to the mattresses enough to know a genuine existential threat, scoffed at all of them. He lost no sleep over the discount rate or the NASDAQ or the US Attorney. What bothered him, what made his sphincter spasm, was the Russians.

Friday afternoon, after Casper's rounds but before the *riunione*, the two sat in a back room of the social club playing pinochle and talking about the Ivans.

"In other words, animals," Tony said, baring the dental blizzard that was his trademark. "*I russi*—they got no respect for nobody. They're savages." This from a man who hitched up Joey Sardines like the tin cans on a newlywed car. (You could also ask him about Jumping Lorenzo's heart, the one mailed to the task force cops who turned him, but this was a cute anecdote Tony never discussed. Granted it happened twenty-five years ago, but, as the truism goes, there is no statute of limitations on heart-cutting-out-and-parcel-posting.)

Not necessarily to suggest Tony was a hypocrite, rather that if the Russian mafia was excessively cruel by *his* standards...Well, it stretches the imagination. What most offended Tony's sensibilities was the difference between good, honest vengeance and pure terrorism. No Sicilian don, no matter how ruthless, would permit letting harm come to a man's family. If a guy needed to be whacked, so be it. If he needed to be slightly tortured, this also was sometimes necessary. But no wives, no kids. You don't breach the sanctity of his household. If you've gotta shoot somebody in the eyes, you wait until he gets around the corner from his front door.

The *animali* from Little Odessa lived by no such code. The only code they lived by was "Do what we say or you will wish you were never born." They'd cut up your little girl at her First Holy Communion if it would give them an extra point on their end. Tony the Teeth had heard stories that turned his stomach. Not just revulsion, but also fear. And now they were moving in the Donato crew's direction. The Russians already controlled Brighton Beach and Sheepshead Bay. They had begun moving to Bensonhurst and Crown Heights and were triangulating on the Italians. Their big moneymaker was the gas-tax racket where every filling station on their turf was ringing up not just a federal excise tax, a state tax, and a city sales tax, but a thieving-motherfucking-Ivan tax of four cents a gallon. No station owner was obligated to collect such a tax, of course, just as no Russian or Ukrainian prick was obligated to refrain from firebombing the pumps. So it was voluntary all the way around.

As the racket grew, the Ivans were making millions, which gave them the capital to buy the muscle, and the cops, to expand and consolidate power at the same time. Twenty-five years ago, it would have been suicidal to venture into Bay Ridge and try to poach on the Sicilians, but that was exactly what had begun. Numbers. Loans. The protection racket. Narcotics. Construction. Garbage hauling. Linens. The Luccheses and Gambinos, who once partnered with the Ivans, found themselves little by little squeezed on their end and eventually squeezed out altogether. (We are not speaking here of the Brownies or the PTA or the Little Sisters of the Poor. We are speaking of the fucking Luccheses and Gambinos.) And now word was out that the Russians were here and there in Ebbets Beach, explaining to certain lucky proprietors why the Russian brand of business insurance was superior to the Donato brand. Kind of like, *Fifteen minutes could cost you 15 percent or more in protection payments, but will save your fucking life.*

Casper had heard rumors about the barber. Maybe DiPasquale was filling two bags a week, one for pasta, one for borscht. Maybe this was why he sometimes came up short lately. Casper had gone right to the source a couple of weeks back, but Mr. DiPasquale had denied it up and down, swearing on the soul of his late wife.

"Wait a minute," Casper interrupted. "I thought you hate your wife?"

"It's true," replied the barber, suddenly agitated. "May she only burn in hell forever like the witch she was. But I got nothing against her soul."

Casper was satisfied. He didn't think the Russians had much of a chance in Ebbets Beach. "Yeah, in Hymietown, anyone looks tough. Fuckin' Ivans bully these rabbis till their little pigtails go straight. This is Jew stuff. None of our concern."

Tony the Teeth begged to disagree. "In other words, this ain't no Jew stuff. The Russians ain't no Jews."

"Whaddya mean?" inquired Casper. "They come from Little Odessa, the biggest Hymietown of all, and they pick up where they left off in the old country."

"It's not true," corrected Tony. "What I hear, they're fake Jews. They faked it under the commies to get sprung from the country. They needed visas and so forth, so they faked like they were Jews to get papers or whatever."

Now Casper was truly confused. "Who would wanna fake being a Jew? It's like faking being a nigger. Nothing against niggers or nothing, but who would wanna fake being one, am I right?"

"In other words, you told me what you heard about the barber," Tony said, finally, "and I'm just telling you what I heard about the Russians. You think a Jew could be a butcher like these *animali*?"

Casper mulled this one over for a while. "Teeth, I'm happy to hear you say that. I got nothing against no Jews, although Kornblitt the jeweler gives me a pain in my ass just because he never shuts up, you know what I mean? But Jews I got no problem with. Half my act is Jew songs. Harry Ruby, George Gershwin, Jerome Kern, these here. You talk about brains. You talk about heart." Casper smacked his chest with his fist. "I don't see Jerome Kern blowing up no gas stations."

"Plenty'a good niggers too, Casper."

"No question," Casper said.

CHAPTER 11

RALPH

HENRY COPPEDGE, WHO OWNED HENRY'S BRUSHLESS CAR WASH and Detailing, was exactly the kind of guy Tony and Casper liked. He had twenty employees, mostly Guatemalan illegals whom he treated like family—paid them well, gave them vacations, encouraged tipping, and at the end of a hot day of washing always opened up a couple of cases of Colt 45 and let everybody cool off. You could just sit down with Henry and shoot the shit. You could beat him at cards, and he never walked out in a bad mood. He was a Vietnam vet, and he always had a good story about chasing whores, killing gooks, and fucking with officers. Casper and Tony considered Henry Coppedge a model African American—definitely a hell of a lot better than that Muslim degenerate Obama.

Little Manny had a slightly different take on Coppedge, however. Little Manny despised him.

He despised him because Little Manny was a shylock, and Henry Coppedge always paid on time. For a loan shark, of course, timely repayment is the last thing you want. When the loan is, say, $1,000, with a 10 percent vig per week, and the borrower comes up with the $1,100, you have made two house calls in seven days and have nothing to show for it but a C-note. If, like most mooks, the borrower can't come up with the money for a month, then the juice is $462 plus the original grand.

Little Manny was the son and protégé of Big Manny, who was the consigliere and underboss, and therefore—like some snot-nosed trust-fund brat—the son was both blessed and cursed by nepotism. The curse had to do with the perceptions of one's advantages versus one's actual qualifications, actual contributions, actual worth. Little Manny never saw anybody raise his eyebrows or roll his eyes, but he felt that the rest of the crew harbored doubts. He felt that they couldn't be sure he had earned his way. Ultimately, neither could Little Manny himself, and so he carried a chip on his shoulder. And so he was determined to prove himself to be a model racketeer.

Unfortunately, his racket was in the shitter. The recession had depressed the demand for ready cash and pushed rates down to unsustainably low levels. Never mind a grand at 10 percent a week, Little Manny was doing deals at 9, 8, 6.5. When he got into the crew, the juice was 20 percent a week. So, what, he's supposed to love some goofball who brings him out every month to make him no money? And with all this glad-handing, backslapping, how-you-doin' bullshit? Who the fuck glad-hands a mobster? Could Henry Coppedge show him the courtesy of pissing himself in fear *just once*?

But, no, this guy told jokes. Consequently, at the car wash lately, Little Manny made it his business to behave like a total prick.

"Little Manny, how the hell are you?" Henry Coppedge greeted him, with eleven rolled-up hundreds and a nice friendly slap on the back. "Hey, I saw Manny Senior the other day."

"Who the fuck is Manny Senior?" snapped Little Manny.

"Your dad," said Coppedge.

"My dad ain't no 'senior,'" said Little Manny.

"Well, you're Little Manny and he's Big Manny, so…"

"So the fuck what? His name is Manny and he's big. Who cares?"

Coppedge was still smiling, on the assumption that he was being put on as opposed to being sneered at. And he persisted, "His name is Manny, and your name is Manny—"

"Who says my name is Manny?" asked Little Manny.

"But your name is Manny."

"Fuck it is."

"Come again?" said Henry Coppedge.

"My name ain't Manny," clarified Little Manny.

At this stage, smiling Henry Coppedge had been miraculously transformed—more or less to Little Manny's delight—into annoyed-as-fuck Henry Coppedge.

"Am I in the goddamn *Twilight Zone*? If your name isn't Manny, Manny, what the hell *is* your name?"

"None of your fuckin' business," said Little Manny, who stuffed the cash in his pocket, got back into his T-Bird, and sped off, rather pleased with himself. He had flummoxed Mr. Happy-Go-Lucky-Motherfucker and had told the absolute truth. For Little Manny's name was not Manny. It was Ralph. But, for starters, Ralph is a piss-poor name for a wiseguy. Secondly, when your father is Big Manny—who, in fact, was dubbed Big Manny owing to his girth—your *nomme de mob* is destined not to cleave to your birth certificate. Thirdly, nobody minds being called little when he is big. Little Manny was thick top to bottom, like his father, minus the flab. At Holy Trinity, he was an offensive tackle who might've been all-city if not for too many false starts and car thefts.

Hence, Little Manny concluded, Henry Coppedge could kiss his white Sicilian ass.

CHAPTER 12

AGING

FATHER STEVE DELEWSKI LIKED TO TALK TO PEOPLE ABOUT PABST Blue Ribbon beer. Now he was talking to Mike Franzetti.

"Big seller where I grew up. Chicago. But also everywhere else. I mean, Pabst, who didn't at least sometimes drink Pabst? But, you know, it was mainly for older folks. Older working folks, and they don't drink as much as they used to, and the kids are drinking Sam Adams and so forth. A few years ago, when I got out of seminary, sales of Pabst were so low that they could tell—they could literally tell—when some old mill hunk had died. Because sales on the distributor's truck route went down. A whole brewery knew that Stash had died. I know this because I was in a bar on the North Side and there on the wall was a letter from the CEO of Pabst, expressing condolences on Stash's passing. Very nice logo, by the way. Embossed. Very nice."

"This story got a punch line, Father?" asked Mike as he counted and booked the slender take for Thursday's violent abbreviated bingo. Father Steve was twenty-nine. Mike was fifty-nine, and didn't feel too sonly around this skinny Chicago know-it-all.

"Yep, it has a punch line, Mike. The punch line is this: Our Lady of Grace is Pabst Blue Ribbon. Every time there's a funeral, the echo in the nave gets more hollow. You don't notice much on Sunday, maybe, but during the week, I don't say one mass before more people than I can count on two hands. Not one time. And when we lost Mrs. Camilli, we lost the last parishioner who attended mass every day. Mike, I have been on that altar alone. I have offered the Eucharist to an empty room."

Mike Franzetti shrugged. "I don't like Sam Adams," he said. "Too sweet. Gimme a Miller's any day."

Father Steve shook his head. It wouldn't matter what he said to Mike Franzetti. If Mike were walking under a falling piano and the priest shouted, "Mike, watch out! A piano is about to land on you!" Mike would disagree. They just didn't see things the same way. The way Father Steve saw things was that the parish was in desperate financial straits, that the weekly collection was barely enough to cover the outreach ministry, that the bingo game was bringing in half of what it produced when Father Steve joined Our Lady of Grace just a year earlier, that the school was, thank God, solvent, but he had no access to tuition (that went directly to the diocese), that the church was often literally empty, and that, if circumstances had not made Father Steve available, the Bishop would have shut the church down, and still might.

How Mike saw things was, *I was in this parish before this little shit heel was born. And he wants to tell me how to do my job? Fuck him.* So, yes, slightly different philosophies.

Father Steve did, indeed, want to tell Mike how to do his job. Specifically, he wanted to bring technology to bear on various aspects of church administration more or less under the deacons' control. He wanted to stop spending money printing the church bulletin; this could be done on a blog for free. He wanted a website to create a virtual community for the parish community, which he wanted to call GraceBook. He wanted to use Google search, to serve ads to people searching online for, say, Club Millennium. He wanted the accounting done on QuickBooks. And he wanted online bingo. That was a big priestly thumb in the eye to Franzetti, who had been running the game for twenty years and brought in $3 million doing it. And some knucklehead with an iPod or whatever was going to get into his business? Not likely. "Father," he had said to the young priest, "I'll look after bingo. You look after souls."

The kid just didn't get it. Like the business with the church bulletin. Father didn't understand that the bulletin was more than a weekly newsletter, more than a guide to mass schedules, more than a calendar of events. Baby, it was *evidence*. You got a bulletin on the floor of the car, you've been to mass. Sometimes it was bona fide evidence, to reassure parents or suspicious spouses. Sometimes it was a cold piece—like the unregistered gun placed in the hand of the deceased crack dealer or not crack dealer you and your partner have just shot twenty-four times while he was reaching for his wallet. Hypothetically, you meet up with the assistant manager of a tanning salon or a divorcee in a cop bar, you take her back to her place and fuck her sideways, you swing by the church on the way home, you grab a bulletin…"Where were you, doll?" "Mass, because I, you know, might have to miss Sunday." Naturally, Mike Franzetti did not attempt to explain reality to Father Steve. Instead, whenever the subject of the Internet came up, the deacon stepped outside for a smoke.

Strictly speaking, neither Sergeant Franzetti nor the other deacons owed the priest anything more than respect for his collar. Their duty was to assist him, not to serve him. Their responsibility was to the bishop of Brooklyn directly. On the other hand, some were beginning to see things Father Steve's way. The money situation had gotten truly frightening, and, no offense to Mike, bingo was no longer a reliable cash cow. As Paul Guardini reminded Mike at the most recent parish council, "Yo, Sarge, look at your own mother. I haven't seen her at bingo in a year. How come?" He knew how come. She was at home playing at PokerCapades.com.

CHAPTER 13

BLESS ME, FATHER

IN *THE THORN BIRDS*, FATHER RALPH DE BRICASSART WAS extremely handsome—Richard Chamberlain handsome, as it turned out. He fell into the netherworld between literary archetype and cliché, for the trope of the irresistibly attractive, utterly untouchable man of the cloth goes back at least to Chaucer. The idea itself, so charged with inherent dramatic tension, is irresistible. It's also plainly preposterous, requiring quite an act of literary faith called willing suspension of disbelief. Anybody who buys into the romantic notion of Father Eye Candy need only turn to Google. Search Father Tom, Father Tim, Father Dominic, Father Anthony, Father Patrick, Father Stanley, Father Peter—you name it. The resulting thumbnails are visual saltpeter because the Venn diagram of priests and hotties looks like the number eight. Not to put too fine a point on it, seminary graduation is an ugly parade. This is not likely to be genetic. If anything, celibacy by definition should cull some unsightliness from the gene pool. As to the precise social and spiritual dynamics, there can be but speculation. Are handsome young men too engaged and distracted in the perquisites of good looks to develop their theological identities and cultivate their relationships with God? Or are physically unappealing guys so cut off from the world of sex and romance that they channel their energies into religion? The smart money says c) all of the above.

Father Steve, it happened, was not homely. He was a little scrawny, but another way of looking at that is "lean." He was neither bald nor chinless, and he had piercing blue eyes. They were, perhaps, not large and wide set; they were rather slightly too close together, and his nose was on the piggish side. But he had a silky baritone voice, an adorably curly mop of blond hair, and an easy smile. Neither head turner nor stomach turner, he could have eventually found romance somewhere in the civilian world, but he knew from his teen years that getting laid just didn't mean that much to him. He didn't like men, or boys. He just wanted a higher calling than ass, and his unprepossessing looks were just what the doctor ordered. Here again, if some girl is prepared to give you a hand job, who can concentrate on serving God? Father Steve served God.

He had come east at his own request, after a scandal at his church rattled his faith—not his faith in God the Father, but in his own ability to make a difference. His parish monsignor had been forced into retirement for covering up sexual abuse in Wisconsin decades earlier, and Father Steve was discouraged when he was unable to persuade the shell-shocked congregation that the sins of that particular father did not taint him as well. In all, he felt he lacked the spiritual authority to succeed. "I want a challenge," he told his bishop, "but I do not want Mission: Impossible."

"Hmm," the bishop offered. "Could I talk you into Mission: Improbable?" A year later, with the help of his diocese, Father Steve was appointed to Our Lady of Grace to succeed Monsignor Anthony Paglia, himself a retiree, but an untainted one. Tina fell in lust with the new priest almost immediately. And right now, she wanted him so much her panties were soaked.

There she stood at 5:30 mass, one of three communicants in a church that can hold a thousand. In all, there were Mrs. Melchionni, eighty-eight; Mrs. Grosso, seventy; and Tina, twenty-eight, in a tank top, revealing an impossibly even tan, a patchwork of tattoos, and $19,000 worth of hooters. When the old ladies were finished receiving the Eucharist, Tina stepped forward, her hands behind her back, serving the dual ends of seeming more humble and submissive before God, and thrusting her chest forward, this time with no fear of pizza drippings.

"The body of Christ," whispered the priest as he placed the Host on Tina's tongue, dangling between lips double-coated in Sephora Sweet Dreams gloss, pink-gold with shimmer, matching her heels. Just then, Tina flinched, jerking her head backward.

"Fatha!" she snapped. "You're smudging!"

CHAPTER 14

FLORIDA

DO THE MATH. YOU CUT HAIR FOR A LIVING. YOU GET $16 FROM an adult, $9 for a kid. Every now and then a scalp treatment or a shave walks in, but not very often. On a very good day, you do thirty haircuts. On a bad day, you do none. Average, eighty cuts a week, fifty-five adult and twenty-five kid. With tips, which a lot of people don't pay because you own the shop, that's about $1,200 a week. You own your building outright and get $1,500 a month for renting out the second floor to a tax preparer four months of the year, but your weekly nut of taxes, utilities, supplies, and protection is $400. That means you work fifty-four hours a week for $910, before taxes. The street vendors do better than that. The building is worth three hundred grand, and the chairs alone are probably worth another $5,000. You are almost sixty-five years old, and you'd do just as well by going on Social Security and working part-time packing boxes down at that mail-order fulfillment outfit. Off the books, too.

Why do you stand on your feet all day in a cloud of dandruff and spend your idle moments trying to brainwash a parrot? This is what Casper wanted to know. Tony the Teeth had a theory.

"In other words, Casper, he's lonely since his wife passed away. Whaddya think it's like for him alone in that apartment? I can tell you from experience, you don't wanna sit in your apartment all day alone. You wanna go to the track or something. Cut hair."

"Yeah, but, Tony, you should hear the barber go on about that poor woman. He calls her the devil, no shit. I don't know what she did to that poor son of a bitch, but he hated her."

Tony turned over his hand. "I'm knocking for three."

"Fuck me. I'm sitting here on four waiting for a fuckin' gin. Look at this rock I got," said Casper.

Tony chuckled. "Afraid to knock. Afraid to win."

The two played for a minute in silence until Medium Marco waddled in and sat down with them.

"How y'doin', Marco?" offered Casper.

"Medium," replied Marco. "What are we talking about?"

"Nothin'," said Casper. "Playing gin."

"The barber," said Tony. "Gin."

"What the fuck?" Casper shouted. "I never even fanned my fuckin' cards. Fuck. Ten, twenty, thirty, forty, fifty, and thirty-one is eighty-one over gin. I never got caught with eighty points in my life. Fuckin' A."

"What about the barber?" Marco inquired.

"Marco, we're playing cards here," Casper said.

"In other words, why do he stay in business?" Tony asked. "I think he's lonely."

"He ain't lonely," Casper said. "He got people in there all day long."

"Why do you guys care about some old fuckin' barber?" Marco asked. He sure didn't.

"Just wondering," Tony said. "Me, I'm not gonna be standing there cutting hair. I'm gonna retire, take it easy, go to the track."

Marco was astonished. "You're gonna retire? When?"

"No, no," said Tony. "I'm just saying, I'm the barber, I retire."

"Yeah, when?" Marco repeated.

"Yo, Marco," Casper tried to explain, gently, in consideration of Marco's native medium-wittedness, "Tony's not saying he *is* the barber. He's saying *if* he was the barber, *then* he'd retire."

"Is it because of your stomach?" Marco asked Tony.

"Marco!" Tony barked. "In other words, I'm not goin' nowhere. I'm talking about DiPasquale."

Ah. Now it clicked. To Casper's growing chagrin, however, the sudden clarity only made Marco wish to delve further into this fascinating subject.

"You know," he ventured, "I once saw on TV about some fuckin' guy with the hiccups, some colored guy. He had the hiccups for, like, thirty years. And they were gonna do some operation to cure his hiccups, but he didn't want the operation, because he figured if he lost the hiccups, he wouldn't feel like he was him."

"What's that gotta do with anything?" asked Tony.

"I'm just saying that maybe the barber is afraid to quit cutting hair because then he won't feel like he was him no more." Not a bad insight for a guy who flunked metal shop.

"Get him," Casper said, flicking a thumb in Marco's direction. "Husky-sized fucking head shrinker. Look, the reason the guy ain't retiring is the reason a million stiffs don't retire. If they retire, they die. Get the gold watch, next day keel over on the boulevard. I happen to know this guy, which you two hoodlums do not. He'd rather be broke in his barbershop than dead on the sidewalk. So whaddya think about that?"

"I think I got gin," Tony said. "Spade gin."

"Fuck me up the ass," yelped Casper by way of commentary, not invitation. "You got X-ray vision, or what?"

Casper had exactly as much insight into the lives of his customers that he had in his gin rummy opponents. In actual fact, DiPasquale the barber did not fear idleness and death. Likewise, he was not afraid that shelving his clipper and shears would somehow erase his essential self. As usual, dumb Tony had found the basic truth: the man was lonely. But even that had nothing to do with killing himself trying to sustain a marginal business. He had had every intention of closing the shop and selling the property two years earlier, at age sixty-two and a half. He'd have taken the proceeds to Florida, living comfortably on his nest egg and his Social Security. Then the real-estate bubble burst. *Pfft.* Just like that, his half-million-dollar building was worth two hundred grand less. Now he was just grinding it out, day by day, waiting for the market to bounce back.

He couldn't even be doing that if it weren't for the don. When a water pipe burst under his sidewalk last year, the repair bill was going to be $11,000. He didn't have anything close to that. So he went to the don, who gave the barber eleven dimes right on the spot. And told nobody, not even Big Manny. Definitely not Little Manny, who had wet dreams about the juice on eleven dimes. This was an open-ended loan, from the head of a crime family, with not a single point of vig.

"Don Donato," squeaked his overwhelmed supplicant, "why are you doing this for me?"

The don placed his hand on the shoulder of the barber, who wept in gratitude. "Because, *signore*, we are neighbors."

CHAPTER 15

THE EBBETS BEACH SOCIAL CLUB

EVERY SINGLE THING, BUT ONE, WAS THE SAME. DON DONATO SAT in the corner, the front windows across the dining room to his left, the front door directly ahead at forty paces, tables arrayed four deep between the entrance and the don. Behind him on his left: a mural of Sicily, a cheerfully crude vantage through a Roman arch downhill toward the bluer-than-life Mediterranean, the cobbled street lined by shops with striped awnings and rococo grillework. Behind the don, draped in red, white, and green crepe bunting, hung a portrait of Victor Emmanuel II. This was a concession, from the Sicilian members to the diaspora of the mainland. Or vice versa. The Calabrese, the Umbrians, the Lombardi, the Abruzzi, they outnumbered the Sicilian members one hundred to twelve. Seven of the twelve, by a nutty coincidence, were in *La Famiglia di* Donato. And those wisest of wise, as they did every Friday, began to straggle in beginning at 7:15 p.m. At 7:14, they were still unwelcome.

Don Donato's ritual was to arrive at 7:00, assume his throne, which was the lone banquet chair in a sea of bentwood, and to be served *dua espressi*, each with two lumps of brown sugar, and a tall glass of *Peroni nastro azzurro*. By ritual, the bubbly water was always brought not with the coffee but only after the second espresso was drained. And no matter the convention everywhere else in the world, no lemon rind was permitted on the table. Or in the club. Don Donato hated lemon. As a boy, in Nebrodi, he had harvested them by the bushel, day after sweltering day underneath the scorching coastal sun, standing on a stepladder, his calves and arches aching, his shoulders throbbing with fatigue, from the endless overhead stretch to the orchard's highest branches. For the preadolescent Vitorio Donato was a slight, diminutive boy. Only as an adult had he blossomed into an imposing five feet three inches tall. With skinny legs and a vast barrel chest, he reminded many a casual onlooker of the Tasmanian Devil—of *Looney Tunes* fame. People chuckled about the resemblance—although not, if they were sensible, aloud. In 1971, when Don Donato was merely Vic the Vig, a kneecapper for the late great Don Greco, a young soldier for Joe "Cannonball" Cangelosi's crew cracked up a drunken wedding crowd by remarking to not-yet-Don Donato, "Hey, I seen you in pictures! What's Bugs Bunny really like?" That Joe Cannonball. What a character! Perhaps someday his body will be found.

When Don Donato finished refreshing himself, typically at 7:15 sharp, the rest of the outfit was welcome to join him at the white-linen-covered table. If they were not at their seats by 7:30, they were tardy and at a very high risk of infuriating the don. Be not, however, too quick to stereotype. There were, in fact, only a few things that infuriated the don: tardiness, lemons, Taz, and any talk of the Los Angeles Dodgers. He was patient with his soldiers when they made errors. Casper the Collector once lost his brown bag and its entire contents of $9,000 in protection money. The bag was later returned by a thoughtful merchant who didn't wish to be shot in the face and torso, and all was well. Still, many remarked how generous Don Donato was not to cut off *Casper*'s bag and *its* entire contents.

Yes, Don Donato was a patient man. He was also patient with his daughters when they defied him, which was often. He was preternaturally patient with the Federal Bureau of Investigation, although the bureau had consigned many friends, colleagues, and rivals to long stretches of hard time. "In the immortal words of Meyer Lansky," the don was fond of saying, "this is the business we have chosen." Nobody knew whether Don Donato realized that those were not the words of actual kingpin Meyer Lansky but of his pretend equivalent, Hyman Roth, nor was anyone much inclined to inquire. For all the don's forbearance and preternatural calm, vetting his historical references might have been reckless, much as it was absolutely reckless—verging on masochistic—to mention the Dodgers in the same sentence with "Los Angeles."

To the don, this was blasphemy. This was lemon juice in the eyeball. As far as he was concerned, the Dodgers ceased to exist in 1958, when they moved from Brooklyn to the West Coast. They were traitors, apostates, *puttane*—which means "whores," but sounds worse when said by an angry Sicilian while spitting on the floor, surrounded by armed goons. When the swine Walter O'Malley shamed himself before the whole world, young Vitorio Donato had lived in the United States for only four years, yet more than long enough to fall in love with Duke Snider, Roy Campanella, Gil Hodges, Pee Wee Reese, Johnny Podres, Carl Erskine, and the colored boy, Robinson. ("A credit to his people," the don believed. "Articulate in his words and a hard worker—for a *melanzana*. And I say this with respect.") Furthermore, it was at Ebbets Field where Vic the Vig got his start. At fourteen years old, he stood outside the gates and made loans of seventy-five cents to his school chums so they could buy a grandstand seat. The juice was ten cents a day. His racket was discovered by Joey Gallo's dad—Joey Vaseline, a captain for the late Don Greco—and he was given an option: offer the racket to Don Greco, or run it independently as an orphan. Exactly thirty years later, Vic would succeed the revered don, who slipped quietly into the next world at the ripe age of seventy-nine, after falling off the Verrazano Narrows Bridge while stuffed inside of a fifty-five-gallon drum.

Now the successor was himself seventy-one years old, holding court where he had for decades. Three thousand *espressi* had preceded this Friday *riunione*, and momentarily the bottles of Nero d'Avola would be uncorked and, soon after that, the pasta brought steaming to the table. It was Friday as all Fridays, but for one difference.

It was 7:30. The don was in his place, scanning the room and the front vestibule for outsiders. This was normal. As usual, Marco was the first to arrive, making sure the don was ready to receive him before he took his chair. Don Donato held out his hand toward Marco's place in welcome.

"How are you this evening, Marco?" the don inquired.

"Medium," replied Marco.

"I am pleased to hear this," said the don.

"Thank you for asking, Don Donato," said Medium Marco, who plopped his outsize ass in the chair with an audible thud.

Soon the whole outfit surrounded their boss. Casper, Tony the Teeth, Little Manny, Leonard the Calculator. But for the first time anybody could remember, no Big Manny. Big Manny who came up with the don. Big Manny who did time for the don, or, anyway, the previous don. Big Manny who did all the big thinking for the don. The *uomo migliore* and consigliere. Gone. Nobody spoke of this or dared mention his name. This was a man who was every Sunday morning at Our Lady of Grace for 9:00 a.m. mass and every Friday at the club for the *riunione*—absent for the first time since he was sprung from Allenwood. Before that, never, except maybe once, back in the eighties, when he had shingles. Now his bentwood chair was empty. The don eyeballed the waiter and nodded toward the chair. Paolo scurried to remove it. This made the matter official. Big Manny ceased to exist.

Where the fuck was Big Manny? Little Manny, in a quiet panic, wondered, *Where the fuck is Pop?*

CHAPTER 16

DREAMS

AT 7:30, AS ALWAYS, THE DON STOOD, THOUGH THIS WAS NOT immediately evident. His bandy legs were preposterously short, and he was not much taller upright than seated. Nonetheless, the whole crew was alert as he paused for Paolo to open and pour the wine. Then, per the custom, Don Donato raised his glass in welcome.

"*Salut*, boys. Drink and think."

The don liked to say that. He did not mean it. What he meant was, "Drink and don't think." The don would do all the thinking, the don and, until this night, the absent one who no longer exists. Even Leonard the Calculator—who had studied at the big feet of the master—would have none of the ex-consigliere's authority. He would not be expected to be a visionary. He'd be expected to be the accountant, risk manager, and financier, exactly as he'd been a bookkeeper—not creative, but obedient, divining the wishes of the boss and fulfilling them. The last thing the don needed was a Calculator who could calculate his way into the family's assets. This was professionally frustrating for Leonard, who had a 710 math SAT score (English: 550) and was a man brimming with ideas and observations that nobody but Big Manny wanted to hear. Now whose ear would he have? Nobody's, that's who. This struck him not only as frustrating but, from a business point of view, self-defeating. He loved the guys in the crew, and his respect for the don could not be questioned, but Davos this *riunione* was not. For that very reason, Leonard had been repeatedly counseled by Big Manny to keep his own counsel, so he wouldn't be seen as lording his superior intellect over the rest of the crew, who had, as a group, honed their not-thinking to a fine edge.

Leonard struggled with the self-censorship. On the one hand, he believed his creativity was being stifled. On the other hand, as a Donato crew soldier in good standing, nobody ever tried to kill him, and he got outrageous pussy. Outrageous pussy. On this Friday, however, his mentor was absent, and Leonard could not contain himself. He saw the numbers every day, and every day the numbers got worse. The lending racket was down 90 percent. Not 9 percent. Ninety percent. Not that they hadn't done everything they could think of to keep the racket afloat. The guys at the body shop were into the don for ten dimes when they lost Allstate referrals due to being caught using counterfeit parts. So Little Manny worked out a debt-restructuring program for them and also didn't beat them senseless. When Chase came out with twenty-four-hour approvals on small-business loans, Big Manny gave the go-ahead for twenty-four-second approvals, which Little Manny advertised with fliers designed by Tina and printed by the Handi Copy Center gratis. All to no effect. To Little Manny's excruciating embarrassment, business kept heading south—an obviousness which, for some reason nobody could even begin to grasp, Leonard the Calculator chose to belabor.

"With respect, Don Donato, we are being buttfelped."

That was the other thing about the Calculator. Alone among his colleagues, he did not curse. He lived at home with his folks and his aged *nonna*, who brooked no disrespectful language. *Contadino parlare*, she called it. "Peasant talk." Leonard worshipped his *nonna* and would not defy her, but could not entirely divorce himself from the patterns and rhythms of the street. So he created a whole lexicon of custom euphemisms enabling him to swear like a sailor. A dyslexic sailor. The crew hardly noticed anymore. What they noticed, and cringed over every time, was his occasional nutty outburst of candor. Not because he was showing off so much as because he was at risk of setting off the don, which his perpetually cowed associates regarded as unbelievably felping stupid. This time, so far, Don Donato seemed unagitated. But that meant nothing.

"I am painfully aware of this, Calculator. What advice do you have for me?"

Don't do it, Leonard. That's what everyone was thinking. *Don't presume to counsel the don.* All the boys were on pins and needles. Nobody wished for Leonard to piss off the boss. There was a prolonged silence, a whole dinner table full of palookas praying for Leonard not to say another word—whereupon, of all great sages, Tony the Teeth chimed in.

"In other words, it's the fuckin' subprime," he offered. "Fuggedaboudit."

Leonard understood he had been saved and was visibly relieved. Audibly too. His exhale flickered the votive next to the breadsticks. All eyes were now on Don Donato, who seemed unnerved not one bit by his enforcer's impertinence.

The don merely nodded. "It was never like this when Alan Greenspan was the chairman. This is a man I respect."

"Ben Bernanke," said Tony the Teeth, "What a putz. Fuggedaboudit."

Then they ate. *Linguine vongole* for all. Hardly a word was spoken for a quarter hour, except when Little Manny, in a transparent attempt to camouflage his gathering dread, started to laugh. "Hey," he said to the crew, "remember Eddie No Clams?"

Eddie No Clams was a soldier a few years back, too small potatoes to be included in the *riunione*. He was actually afraid to be invited, because he was deathly allergic to shellfish and terrified that the don—who favored *vongole*—would make him choose between respect and anaphylactic shock. Lucky for Eddie, on the very week of his first *riunione*, he was shot to death in a card game.

Now it was 8:00 p.m. Once again, Don Donato stood, toasting his crew with a grappa. The men knocked their brandies back in unison and came to attention when the don cleared his throat.

Ordinarily, Don Donato was a man of few words. Apart from a few threadbare aphorisms, often enough he was a man of no words. A nod or a hand gesture would express his will, and his will was everyone's command. Indeed, when he did express himself in full sentences, his wishes were sometimes more difficult to divine, as the don was a big fan of extremely ambiguous proverbs.

Such as 1999 and the beer distributor problem.

"Don Donato, we've got a situation," Little Manny had said at the *riunione*. "The Castiglione Brothers are into us for thirty large, and all they do is make excuses. Should I dynamite their warehouse?"

The don let a thin smile cross his lips. "As the Bard tells us, 'All's well that ends well.'"

Little Manny and everybody else waited for the don to elaborate. They leaned forward in their bentwood chairs, to see what wisdom would come next. But no next was forthcoming. The don had evidently said his piece. Little Manny gave a sidelong glance toward his father, Big Manny, but Big Manny offered only a shrug. The don had issued marching orders, and Little Manny had to guess what they were.

Just to be on the safe side, he dynamited the warehouse. The Castigliones then miraculously came up with thirty dimes, and not another word was said on the subject.

Ah, the good old days.

Again, the don cleared his throat. He had something important to say. "My family, I want to ask you a question. What are your aspirations?"

CHAPTER 17

SELF-RELIANCE

ASPIRATIONS? WITH ONE EXCEPTION, EVERY MAN AT THE DINNER table was thinking the same thing: *Don Donato, what the fuck are you talking about?* The aspirations of a made guy are minimal, immutable, and timeless. A wad of cash, a choice of trim, respect on the corner, and not waking up dead in the trunk of a car. Aspirations, like minivans, were for civilians. Of this crew, only one dared to imagine—or imagined to imagine—a life beyond the family. This was Casper, collections man and lounge singer, who, yes, sounded like Bobby Darin, looked like Bobby Kennedy, but unfortunately, had the charisma of Bobby Fischer. Not because he was an asshole, or even because he was a hood, but because he just got so nervous onstage. He had some finger-snapping issues, for example. Casper tried so hard to master the hipster snap— three-finger overhand—but whenever he tried it, he looked like a limp-wristed fairy. Also, he couldn't snap very loudly that way. And then when he went for the thumb-middle-finger underhand, the snap was crisp, but he looked like a dork. More particularly, he looked like Steve Martin in *The Jerk.* So for that alone he was self-conscious. Then there were his stage movements, barely in sync with the beat of the song. He didn't need to look like a Temptation; he didn't have to actually dance. He just wanted to be rhythmic and suave, like Bobby Darin, Frankie Avalon, Fabian, Paul Anka, Dean Martin, Tony Bennett, Mel Torme—hell, Al Martino. No such luck. So, as he was bereft of options, Casper just stood there and sang. Grasping the microphone in two hands, like a teenage Frank Sinatra, minus the hysterical bobbysoxers, he simply crooned. In fact, he crooned his ass off. Close your eyes and he was good. You didn't get the benefit of his sparkling jacket, but you were spared his overpowering awkwardness. With your eyes closed, if you were a woman, his "Mack the Knife" made you want to sleep with him. If you were a man, it made you jealous. Open your eyes and it was Jerry Lewis acting like a retard.

Casper had aspirations. He wanted to sing and snap and move his hips somehow on TV. Then he wanted to marry Angela, for he loved her. He loved her more than beer and hot pastrami. He loved her more than his own life. He loved her more than cigarettes.

Don Donato was just getting started.

"Let me ask you this," the don continued. "Do you have what you want? Do you have what you need?"

Everybody was too confused and too nervous even to exchange glances. Don Donato looked out for his crew, but never before had offered any evidence of agonizing over their deepest desires. Mainly, he just wanted them to bring him bags full of money. Without benefit of exchanging a word, each man came to the same conclusion: *Aha, he was dying.* The old man had outlived the Five Bosses, he'd avoided federal prison, he'd escaped at least one contract on his life, and now he was about to reveal his own tragic mortality. It was the Big C. Everyone knew it. The don was a dead man. Big Manny was out of the picture. And not a single one of the survivors had the slightest chance to run the crew. Who? Tony the

Teeth? He could barely read. The Calculator? Smartass egghead. Little Manny? The worst loan shark ever. They were ruined.

"After all these years, it is time that you all understood that you cannot depend only on me."

Oh shit, here it comes.

"In the words of Henry David Thoreau," said the don, "you must turn to self-reliance."

No shimp! A literary reference from the don! But wasn't it Ralph Waldo Emerson? thought the Calculator, who, unlike his colleagues, had paid attention in high school and whom Big Manny had brought along for exactly that reason—because, as the consigliere had presciently impressed on the don, "Someday I won't be here." But it was for precisely situations like this that Big Manny had also impressed upon the Calculator to keep his big mouth shut. "Nobody likes to be spoke down to," he'd instructed, "especially guys with guns"—which this time, fresh off of a close call, the Calculator remembered to remember.

Thor who? thought everyone else. *Whose crew is he in? Is there a Norwegian mafia?*

"You will always be part of this family, and mark my words, I will brook no disloyalty, but you must also stand on your own feet if you are to achieve your dreams. I must inquire, Casper. You break your back for this here enterprise, am I right?"

"*Si*, Don Donato," Casper replied. "I mean, I ain't complaining."

The don waved off his objection. "And you break it again hollering this jungle music instead of *Quant'e Laria La Me Zita*, which, as I have told you, is never going to go out of fashion like this moptop *rumore*, and what do you got? You earning the kind of scratch you need?"

Casper looked around at his horrified colleagues. "No?" he ventured.

"NO!" the don jumped in. "We are in hard times. Calculator! Would you like to have another nickel, maybe a dime every week? Would you?"

"*Si*, Don Donato."

"Of course you would. Who wouldn't, I ask you. Now let me ask you another question. When you go about your business, how many people do you meet? In a week, let's say. Marco, in a week, do you talk to many people?"

"Eh, medium," said Marco.

"HOW MANY?"

"Sorry, Don. Hundred, hundred fifty people. Medium week."

"One hundred fifty people!" shouted Don Donato. "Do you, Marco, know what that means?"

Marco did not know the right answer. He had no idea what that meant. He knew only that Don Donato was yelling at him, and, historically, such tongue-lashings did not bode well. Joey Sardines got yelled at for ripping off the numbers take, and when the shouting stopped, the don smiled and told him not to worry about it. Don't let these misunderstandings happen again. Then Joey went for the worst ski trip ever.

"Don Donato," said Marco, "I'm sorry. I definitely do not know."

The don smiled. "Don't worry about it, Marco. I don't expect you to know..."

Hail Mary, full of grace...

"You men expect *me* to know, and I do," the don continued, as Medium Marco quietly, politely, attentively feared for his life. "I do know. These people, these one hundred fifty people are customers. They are customers, but they are also partners. Potentially, they are part of our family."

Now everybody was thinking something very different. They no longer believed that the don was delivering his own eulogy. They believed he had gone off his nut. Jayson Reyes, part of the family? Insanity. Mike Franzetti, who runs the bingo game at the church, Sergeant Mike Franzetti, NYPD—*part of the family?* Clearly the boss was losing his grip, which they all bravely acknowledged by staring at him stonefaced as if riveted by his breathtaking vision.

"Marco, I apologize for picking on you, but I am fascinated by this number, one hundred fifty. Suppose each of those one hundred fifty people becomes a customer for what we are selling, never mind what, and suppose each one of them went back to their families and friends and their businesses—do not forget their businesses—and sold the very same product to one hundred fifty others, and for every single one of these sales, we got a taste. Now, suppose each one of *those* one hundred fifty—Calculator, how many are we now talking about?

"Twenty-two thousand, Don…"

"TWENTY-TWO THOUSAND!" shouted the don. "Suppose all twenty-two thousand of them do the very same thing, and we get our end of every sale, and then they fan out and each find one hundred fifty more recruits…Calculator?"

"Three-point-three-seven-five million, Don…"

"AND WE GET A TASTE OF EVERYTHING! And by 'we,' fellows, I mean you. You each get your own end, with me at the top, *naturalmente.*"

At the end of the table, Little Manny fiddled with a package of Sweet'N Low, with a puckish smirk on his face. This insolence did not escape the don's attention.

"Something is funny to you, Little Manny?" he said, in a voice quiet enough to scare the shit out of everyone.

"No, Don Donato," said Little Manny, still pretending not to be scared out of his wits. "I mean, yes. With respect, Don, what you're saying…It sounds like Amway."

So ridiculous and so funny, the bubble of tension was burst. All the guys felt free to chuckle.

Casper was most extravagant with his reaction. He belly laughed and snorted. "Fuckin' Amway! Fuckin' Little Manny… Amway!"

The don did not laugh along. "It's not what you think," he said as a United Way Drive thermometer of red rapidly rose from his neck. "Amway has changed."

CHAPTER 18

MR. MATTRESS

HE KNEW IT WAS LOVE ON A SUNDAY MORNING, ALMOST EXACTLY two years ago, toward the end of a long, hot summer of seashore and sex. They were back from the Vineyard, at his apartment in Chelsea, beginning to be careless about their secret. Amanda, a newly hired producer in the agency's TV department, was several hatched and solid lines below Jack on the table of organization, but he was still technically her superior and therefore obliged to keep his penis a respectful distance from her vagina. She was tall, slender, and athletic, with swimmer's shoulders and a muscled tummy. Her hair was provocatively short and her accent irresistible. Amanda was not from London but some quaint-sounding provincial address Jack could never quite remember. Quisling-on-Shemp, Blistershire, Slurry—or something like that. Didn't matter. She had him at "Ta."

One day, a tall girl from production was hurrying to the elevator, and he, spying her late approach, had displayed the reflexes of a matador to stymie the closing doors with a last-moment thrust of his foot. The doors bounced open and she entered. This Nordic goddess looked upward at him, because at six foot two he still had the advantage, and flashed him the most brilliant and unselfconscious smile he'd ever seen. Whether she was regarding his own ample gorgeousness or his title, he had no way of knowing, but she knew exactly what to say. "Ta." She smiled. That is British for "cheers," which is British for "thanks."

Hmm, thought the pretty-boy creative chief with the chestnut hair so thick and wavy and the eyes so arrestingly blue, *perhaps Anglo-Nordic?* "Not at all," he'd replied flatly, swallowing her glance whole. "Mistook you for a client"—which puckish semi-insult was ad agency for "Please fuck me over and over." She laughed and, without taking her eyes off of him, gave him a more thoughtful, close-mouthed smile—which is universal for "Would right this second be too soon?" Two months later, this delicious woman, whose responsibility was to marshal outside talent and arrange logistics for TV commercial shoots, was in his bed perusing the *Times* travel section. He sat in the living room watching *Meet the Press* and eating cold fried rice from the box. They had not exchanged a word for an hour. He was never happier.

When they talked, they gorged on each other's histories. Conversation was rich with enlightenment, ideas, and hilarity. When they were in bed, everything was right; nothing was perverse, nothing held back. When they occupied separate rooms, absorbed in separate activities, they were separate together—physically apart yet wholly connected. They were symbiotic. The whole was greater than the sum of its parts. They were a couple. As the secretary of the treasury talked about stress tests for the nation's banks, Jack speared a shrimp chunk with his fork and understood. *Aha, love.* Amanda turned the page to learn more about the hidden charms of Malta.

The next morning—Labor Day, in fact—Amanda writhed on the very same Macy's bed, achieving her fifth orgasm and first pregnancy of the long weekend. A month after that, the magical couple sat at the ob-gyn, holding hands and ecstatically imagining a whole new life together, just the three of them. The day after that, agency president and chief creative officer Jack Schiavone was summoned to the CEO's office to discuss an inquiry from the comptroller. A month after that, Jack's career, love affair, and reputation were shattered, with the worst yet to come.

It had to do with false receipts, amounting to about $4,000, but ultimately it was about cocaine. Amanda had a habit, fed at first by powder gratuities from suppliers but in time requiring cash money. This was over with, she tearfully told him, ancient history—and indeed the sketchy receipts flagged by the client were more than a year old. These situations are, of course, precisely why senior management is discouraged from sucking the nipples of junior management; Jack covered for the love of his life. He told the comptroller that Amanda had come to him in tears; she'd left files full of paperwork on the subway and was late for filing her monthly cashflow reports, so he had told her to make a good-faith estimate of actual agency expenses and reproduce them as close to the penny as possible. It was fake, he conceded, but no loss—or gain—to anyone involved. This was, of course, itself an utter fabrication. But it satisfied the finance guys for several days, until $21,000 more in falsified documents—some as recent as three months old—bubbled to the surface. More tears, more confessions, more assurances.

Meeting him had changed everything, Amanda sobbed. For the first time in years, she was clean—clean and in love, with him and their unborn child. He believed her. "This is on me," Jack told the lawyers. "The whole department is unbelievably sloppy, and I let them carry on. I let them believe they could be careless with documents as long as they were clever in cleaning things up. Nothing has been stolen, but if so much as a penny of client funds is unaccounted for, I'll pay out of my own pocket. It's just that these guys are so good I didn't want to have to fire anyone over paperwork. My mistake, and I'll take full responsibility."

He did. By the time the independent audit was completed, more than $260,000 had turned up missing, most of it traced to Jack Schiavone's secret lover, Amanda Waits. *Advertising Age* called the sordid affair "Amandagate." *Adweek* put his picture on the cover beneath the deadline "SchiaPHONY." That was on the occasion of his guilty plea to thirty misdemeanor larceny counts, pled down from felony fraud. Because of his ostensible cooperation—he in fact lied from beginning to end to protect Amanda, and her crimes were never more than supposed—prosecutors agreed to restitution of the $260,000 (not a dollar of which he had ever seen), a fine of $500,000, and a symbolic thirty days in jail, which is symbolic only if you are not the one locked up with depraved criminals behind iron bars. He was, obviously, fired—and sued by his employers, a process that would drain his erstwhile $4 million portfolio of cash and investments. He was also, obviously, unemployable in advertising or any other corporate enterprise. Yet even then he was not ruined. He still had Amanda. Until the day he returned from giving a deposition and found empty drawers where their life had been. She'd left for England with their unborn child. There, she married and disappeared.

On the plus side, nobody had stolen Jack's organs.

CHAPTER 19

DIVERSIFICATION

ALL RIGHT, MAYBE A WISEGUY DOES HAVE DREAMS. CAPTAIN.
Underboss. Don. But not "Diamond Direct." Not hustling soap
and vitamins and water purifiers and setting up easels in hotel
conference rooms. The mob didn't offer dental care or retirement,
but it did confer a semblance of dignity.

Nobody, of course, argued with the don. Rather, they nodded
solemnly at his vision. They didn't know the word *sagacity*, but
they knew how to pretend to have seen it when they believed the
don believed he had offered it to them. So, as they filed out of the
Ebbets Beach Social Club, they now had two matters weighing
heavily on their minds:

1) What happened to Big Manny? Did he squeal to the Feds?
   Did he go over to another crew? Did the boss have him
   whacked?

2) If you are trying to recruit somebody for a multilevel
   marketing opportunity, and you have a 9mm in your
   waistband, does this save you from a lot of embarrassing
   sales tactics? Because, if so, maybe the don wasn't so crazy
   after all. Maybe the second, third, and fourth tiers of their
   downlines wouldn't grow any better than anybody else's,
   but they could sure build up a first tier very, very quickly.

Anyhow, that's what Little Manny was saying at Club Millennium that night. Most of the guys went straight from the social club to the nightclub, to catch Casper's act. They were all pretty impressed with him, especially Marco.

"He sounds like Bobby Darin, if you ask me," Marco said. "The rest…medium."

"Whaddya mean 'medium,' Medium?" asked Little Manny.

"Well, you know that YouTube lady, the homely broad?"

He was speaking of Susan Boyle, the 2009 singing sensation, who flabbergasted the entire world by somehow performing opera arias while ugly. Needless to say, the guys had no idea what he was talking about. Medium kept talking, though.

"Homeliest bitch you ever saw. Voice like a fuckin' angel."

Leonard the Calculator: "Casper isn't ugly. He's a very attractive individual. Not that I'm some felpin' homo, but be serious, this is an attractive individual."

"Yeah," countered Medium Marco, "but he's, like, spastic. When he tries to snap his fingers, he's like one of those special-ed kids."

Who's calling who a sped? the Calculator thought. Marco was as slow upstairs as he was slow climbing up stairs. But what he replied was simply, "I saw him last Friday. He didn't look like a sped."

"Like I said," Marco said, although he hadn't said it at all, "now he just stands still. I could listen all night."

Leonard felt it best to amplify his previous remarks. "What I was saying about Casper. I'm no homo."

Casper's first set went very well. He sang "Volare," "Sweet Embraceable You," "I Got You Under My Skin," "The Way You Look Tonight," "Mack the Knife," "Eleanor Rigby," "Last Train to Clarksville," and "Beyond the Sea." The crowd seemed very pleased, but as he obsessively and awkwardly scanned the audience, Casper was displeased. Angela was not there.

She could not have been had she even wished to, which she had not particularly. As Casper the Collector sang, she sat in her storefront office face-to-face with Big Manny. He had come to the Legal Aid Society not for lawyerly advice but for refuge. He had known Angela since she was a newborn, as would any godfather, lowercase. Manny was desperate to know how her father, the don, might react to his decision to leave the crew. The next morning, he would begin his new life, in an orange smock, at the Home Depot in Bayside. With the outfit's revenues in steep decline, he believed he had no choice but to flee the dark side for the light—specifically, the lighting aisle Tuesday–Saturday, 9:30 am to 3:00 pm. Evenings he'd toil in a boiler room telemarketing collectible American history and *Three's Company* bric-a-brac to morons.

Angela, who as usual was working extremely late—in this case, preparing a habeas corpus writ destined to be dismissed—looked at her father's consigliere in astonishment.

"Uncle Manny," she began, incredulously, "who buys that crap?"

"Your godmother," he replied. "This is where I got the idea." His voiced cracked as he tried to suppress his emotions. "Angelina," he choked out, "I don't know what else to do. I got one kid in college still—you babysat for Maria, but she is now a young woman with big ideas. She's talking about graduate school, God bless her. And God forgive me for saying this about your godmother, but fuckin' Annabella is spending everything I bring home on the 'Washington Crossing the Delaware' dinner plate and this sort of bullshit."

"Oh, Uncle Manny..."

"Yes, and what's left she loses at bingo to the fuckin' cop, the crook. I'm sixty-five years old, and, with respect, we got no 401(k). Angelina, what can I do? A man puts food on the table for his family."

"But why such menial work? What about investments or something?"

"Are you kidding? With my record?"

"Sorry. Stupid me. What did Daddy say?"

"What did he say? I says, 'Don Donato, with respect, I got to make a move. I got this expensive kid, this no-good—God forgive me—wife, and I can't make ends meet. I beg you, Don Donato, I beg you for your blessing.' And what does he do? He says to me nothing. He stands up and walks around the table, and he grabs my face in both hands and kisses me on both cheeks. I nearly died right in my shoes."

"Oh my God," Angela says, more amused than frightened. "Like Michael and Fredo?"

"I'm just sayin'," said Big Manny.

"Uncle Manny, you think you're going to swim with the fishes? Come on, that's Hollywood nonsense."

"Angelina. I'm standing there, you know, trembling, and the don realizes what I'm thinking and he starts to laugh. I never heard him laugh like that. Does your father ever laugh? No, this is a man who never laughs. But he's losing his breath he's laughing so hard. Like your godmother with, whatshisname, Don Rickles. And finally the don says to me, he says, 'Don't worry about it, Manny. I got a plan.' And he starts laughing again, and I back out of the room and go to Our Lady of Grace. I light about sixty candles."

Angela laughed. "But, Uncle Manny, what do you need from me?"

"Angelina, when you talk to your father, would you please remind him not to kill me?"

CHAPTER 20

PROCESS OF ELIMINATION

LITTLE MANNY WAS TOOLING DOWN THE BOULEVARD IN HIS ICE-blue '01 Thunderbird at quite a pace. He ditched the boys after Casper's first set. He had a lot of thinking to do, but at least he'd made an appearance.

Little Manny hung with the crew that night, as he was expected to, not just because it was what they did Friday nights after the *riunione*, but because he had to show solidarity with the family. His own father was missing and unaccounted for, but also obviously one way or another disowned. The old man could be dead, which would be terrible, but not as terrible as if he were holed up in some hotel with the FBI, squealing like a fucking pig. Little Manny could hardly imagine such a thing, but also couldn't quite dislodge that horrendous possibility. And he knew if he could entertain even the slightest possibility of disloyalty, so could—so would—the don. Little Manny had tried to play it so cool at the meeting, feigning indifference to the obvious fact that everybody would be looking at Big Manny's empty place, wondering, and then at Little Manny, wondering some more. The Amway crack was to show how confident and unfazed he was, self-assured enough even to have a little laugh with the don. Who the fuck knew Don

Donato would get caught up in a pyramid racket? Who the fuck was the don's sponsor? Bernie fuckin' Madoff?

In violation of the law and all driving-safety common sense, Little Manny used his cell phone to call Maria but, as he had all night, got nothing but voice mail. Under no circumstances would he call his folks' place; the don would cut his balls off. So he cruised up the boulevard, heading toward the house. If Big Manny was there, that would probably mean he wasn't at the bottom of Plumb Beach Channel.

Glancing off to his right, Little Manny did a double take from the driver's seat. "What the fuck?" he blurted. Smoke was pouring out of a storefront. He began to pull over, and just as he did came the crash and with it a huge roar. The shop's front window had exploded outward. Glass flew everywhere, pelting the T-bird like shrapnel. Flames shot out to the sidewalk. It was DiPasquale's barbershop, completely engulfed in an instant. Manny sped away. He had to find Tony the Teeth. As sirens sounded from the station house two miles down the road, stunned onlookers were kept at a distance by the heat and billows of acrid black smoke. All were equally helpless and equally horrified at the sounds that floated through the smoky cloud, not quite swallowed by the roar of the fire. It was a scratchy, piercing cry: human, but not quite human. "No, no, no," the voice called out. "No, no, no." Then it stopped. Pedestrians gasped, cried out, and also screamed, "No! No!" How could it be? Who was trapped inside? Who was in the barbershop after midnight on Saturday morning?

They didn't know it was a parrot.

Little Manny was driving like a crazy man. In a minute's time he had screeched into the parking lot of Billie's Diner. Tony should be in there handicapping races and wolfing down strawberry pie. Manny tore out of the car, ran to the diner, and rushed inside. The joint was three-quarters empty. A waitress was absently filling ketchup bottles. He looked around frantically. No Tony. *Holy fuckin' fuck*, he thought. *We took out the barber.* God knew where that hairy fuck was now, laying low.

"Can I help youse?" the waitress asked, perfunctorily.

Little Manny waved her off and pulled out his cell phone. This was not something that would have been in the handbook of mob procedure if anyone were stupid enough to put any such thing on paper. Cell phones are practically homing devices for the Feds. The don hated them. Most of the crew didn't even carry one, but Casper did to facilitate his entertainment career and Little Manny did, without the don's knowledge, to have the Internet in his pocket. Little Manny was an eBay addict. At that very moment, he had four bids going, and he had a very good shot at an unrestored 1950 Wurlitzer jukebox, $405 with only seventy hours to go. But he never, ever, ever used the phone for family business. Except that right now he just had to know what was going on.

"Hello?" Little Manny heard.

"Casper, is that you?"

"Little Manny?"

"Yeah, it's me. Hey, Casper, do you know where I can find... our guy?"

"Huh? What guy?"

"You know, the guy...big-boned guy..."

"What the fuck? My next set is in five minutes. What are you talking about?"

"I'm talking about our guy who makes things happen sometimes. Heavyset guy. Jesus Christ, Casper. Hairy. Stomach troubles…"

"You looking for—"

"DON'T SAY IT!"

"Huh?" said Casper, utterly bewildered. "Don't say *what*?"

"Don't say his name. Just tell me if you know where he is."

"Where *who* is? Little Manny, *sei matto*. I gotta go onstage."

"Our guy, Casper. I gotta find him. Do you know where he's at right now?"

"Jesus, Mary, and Joseph, if the guy you mean is the guy I think you mean, bad stomach, hairy back, if it's *that* guy…*I got no idea where the fuck he is*."

Casper hung up. Little Manny stared at his phone in disbelief. Big Manny was God knows where, dead or alive, who knew? The "Cozy Nostra" had apparently gotten a whole shitload less cozy, with God knows what consequences. The Teeth was possibly on the lam but sure as shit not in his usual booth. And Casper was letting show business interfere with family business. Little Manny didn't know his next move, so he was forced to improvise. He let loose a primal, wailing "*Fuccccccccck!*" and pounded the brand-new $4,000 Chicago Gaming digital jukebox over and over and over until Tom Jones shut the fuck up. Heads turned. The waitress went motionless.

Just then, a hairy, big-boned man walked out of the restroom with a *Daily Racing Form* in his meaty paw. He pulled back his lips and unleased a blinding trapezoidal smile.

"Little Manny?" said Tony the Teeth, puzzled. "In other words, what the fuck you doing here?"

Ralph looked puzzled right back. "No, Tony, what the fuck *you* doing here?"

"What the fuck you think? Picking the Trifecta and a slice of pie. What's got your balls in an agitator?"

"I just came from the barbershop."

Now Tony the Teeth was totally and absolutely lost.

"The barbershop?" He looked at his watch. "What fuckin' barbershop?"

Little Manny tried to talk under his breath. "*The* bar-ber-*shop*." He nodded his head in a most theatrical way, which, to Little Manny, indicated to Tony the Teeth that Little Manny knew just who had been taken out and how and why. To Tony the Teeth, however, what it indicated was that Manny was on the verge of a petit mal seizure, like that kid Petey the Fits.

"You drunk?" Tony the Teeth inquired, whereupon it suddenly dawned on Little Manny that Tony had no idea about any barbershop fire of any kind, much less one torched by Tony the Teeth personally. Little Manny put his arm halfway around Tony's massive shoulders and whispered into the enforcer's hairy ear. "DiPasquale's place is burning. Right now." What Little Manny heard in response was a slight rustle and a slight thud as Tony's *Racing Form* fell to the linoleum.

Sweet mother of God. Little Manny now recognized what stupid Tony the Teeth recognized first.

In other words, the Russians.

CHAPTER 21

REVOLT

LABOR DAY WAS IN TWO DAYS. AT 9:00 ON SATURDAY MORNING, the Village merchants sat in card chairs at the Parcel Plus, ostensibly to finalize the promotional plans for Monday's Summer's End Sale-a-Bration, when the doors opened at 10:00 a.m., the hydrants opened at 11:00 a.m., and the free hot dogs and snow cones were served all afternoon. But nobody assembled was interested in talking about snow cones. They were interested in the burned-out ruin of a barbershop, the stench of wet ash, the filthy water pooled in the gutter. They wanted to know what it all meant.

For all anybody could tell, it was an electrical fire in the basement. There were pictures on Channel 11 and Channel 9, but the cause of the fire was said to be "under investigation."

"Maybe the barber torched it," offered Jayson Reyes. "I hear he needed money."

"Like hell he torched it," shot back Sam Calabrese. "Arthur loved that place."

"If Arthur DiPasquale is a criminal, then I'm a criminal," chimed in Tina Donato, an assertion that generated some muffled laughter. Tina, who was no Einstein but also not completely oblivious, narrowed her eyes. "And, PS, I'm not! So fuck youse."

Jean and Larry Rizzo, from J&L, who had lost a ton of business when the pizza slice price war began, had more reason than most to disagree with a Reyes brother, but they didn't think the idea of owner arson was so farfetched.

"Fact is," said Larry, "DiPasquale kept to himself. I mean, Tina, nobody really knew this guy. He was a nice guy and all, but, who knows, it could very well be some kind of terrorism thing. He was probably al-Qaeda or with the Basques. Or the Tamil Tigers. Did anyone ever see his birth certificate? No. We have no idea who he was."

"Christ on a toothpick, Larry, he's not dead," Tina said. "Bad enough you have to disrespect the poor man. Now you're talking about him like he was a suicide bomber." Tina paused. "*Is* a suicide bomber…No, *was*. Whatever."

"Maybe for the insurance," Jayson speculated. "It happens. I mean, where is he, anyway?"

It was a question that, for one brief moment, seemed trenchant. Where was DiPasquale? He'd never missed a Village Association meeting before. Then, just as quickly, Jayson's estranged brother popped the tension like a soap bubble.

"You're so stupid it isn't funny," said Juan, who slouched in his chair like a bored kid in history class. "Your piece-of-shit store burns to the ground, you gonna come to the free hot dog meeting? S'matter with you?"

Jayson dismissed Juan, literally with a wave of the hand, but he—and everybody else but Larry—immediately understood that Juan had a point. Here they were gathered to divvy up final costs and responsibilities—to make sure everyone handed out his fair share of fliers and knew their shifts for manning the food stations—and for DiPasquale all that had become a tragically moot exercise. Anyway, even if the barber had been a bit of a recluse since his wife passed away, he was nobody's idea of a felon. A more solid citizen never honored the boulevard. And he wasn't Sri Lankan.

Meanwhile, in the back of the store, next to the paper cutter, Kim Sung Jim sat with a fierce scowl, his arms crossed militantly on his chest.

"All stupid!" the dry cleaner shouted. Every head naturally turned, startled but not necessarily surprised. The little prick was mad at the world for a change.

"All stupid!" he repeated. "Not matter if barber here. Barber donkey. All of us donkey. We pay good money and still store burn down. We ripped off by crook."

Suddenly, Tina remembered an important appointment. "I'll scoop two shifts if you want," she said on her way out the door. "Sunny'll cover for me." Then, teetering on sandals engineered like sliding boards, she shimmied onto the boulevard, brushing past Jack Schiavone as she did so. Like anyone with a dick would do in his loafers, he took a long careful look as she waggled past him. Arching his eyebrows quickly in commentary, he took a bite of a stale, leftover doughnut and entered Parcel Plus at exactly the moment Juan Reyes responded to Kim.

"Jesus Christ, you nuts?" he shouted. "You got some kind of death wish?"

A fine how-do-you-do. The Snow Cone Society was far more hostile than Jack had expected. He scanned the room to see if he'd blundered into a biker bar, but, nope, there was Larry, dressed like a St. Thomas time-share salesman, and, if he was not mistaken, the guy threatening him had sold him a crappy slice of pizza.

"Sorry," Jack said, "I don't always eat junk food."

"Mr. Mattress!" Rizzo proclaimed. "Welcome, brother. Folks, say hello to Jack Schiavone, who just opened up shop down the road. He has volunteered to help out during the Sale-a-Bration, by way of getting acquainted."

"Actually—" Jack began, but he was immediately cut off by an enraged Korean man shouting from the back of the store.

"Why I be afraid?" Kim hollered, as if the new arrival had not taken place. "We pay. Fire anyway. If Donato do it, we pay for nothing. If someone else do it, we pay for nothing. We donkey. All of us, we pay for nothing. Casper come in my store Friday, I tell him, 'Fuck go yourself.'"

"Go fuck yourself," Jayson Reyes corrected.

"Same to you, 소의 복수형," Kim replied.

Kim then pushed his way through the clot of neighbors and headed for the street, but not before stopping in front of Mr. Mattress, who soared over him. He grabbed Jack's right hand with both of his own and shook energetically, offering a wide smile. "Nice to meet you," he grinned. "No need fuck yourself. Good luck with business. Don't be donkey." Then, resuming his purpose, he stormed out of the meeting.

Well, thought Mr. Mattress, *it takes a village.*

CHAPTER 22

LIGHTING

LITTLE MANNY'S WORLD WAS UNRAVELING BEFORE HIS EYES. HIS crew was in profound jeopardy. His don was flogging a diverse line of household cleaning products, nutritional supplements, gifts, jewelry, and water purifiers, and his father, his mentor, his hero, was standing not ten feet away, at 10:30 on a Saturday morning, helping some schmuck find wall sconces.

"How do I plug them in?" the schmuck asked the gigantic financial-genius ex-con in the orange smock.

"You don't plug them in. You wire them to the junction box," answered Big Manny.

"Do I need an electrician?"

"If you need to fuckin' ask, you need a fuckin' electrician."

Little Manny stared in disbelief as the schmuck stared at Big Manny in disbelief. When the transaction was complete, he approached the lighting consigliere.

"Pop," he said, "what the fuck?"

Big Manny was horrified. He was, however, not going to reveal that to his only son.

"Can I help you, sir?" he said, with a laugh.

"Pop, what the fuck you doing here? What the fuck's going on?"

"Get outta here, Ralph. We'll talk about this later."

"But—"

"Later, Ralph. It's complicated."

Little Manny felt nauseous. Everything was upside down. Last night, he didn't know if his father was alive. Now he saw the man, hale and hearty, yet somehow it was worse. It was a betrayal of everything Little Manny ever wished for and believed. It was a complete surrender to the cowardly universe of the legitimate. Maybe Big Manny was an iconoclast, never quite buying into the family culture of the outfit, but he was never *this*. He was never some clock-punching fool.

Little Manny remembered back to school. The other kids at Holy Trinity were stuck with bulllshit: "My dad's a machinist," "My dad's a plumber," "My dad's an insurance broker," "My dad's a manufacturers' representative." Ralph alone could say, "My dad's 'of counsel.'" Nobody had any idea what that meant, and everybody knew exactly what it meant. It meant, among other things, that nobody—except the nuns, who were afraid of nothing and nobody—fucked with Ralph. So he too was a breed apart, and that defined his self-image. The folks made him study, and Ralph studied well. He wasn't much for reading and essay writing, but, like his father, he was strong in math—strong enough that his aggregate SAT scores would have gotten him into good colleges. Annabella wanted nothing else but for him to get a degree, like Maria, and make something of himself that would not result in having his phones tapped. Big Manny also wanted his son to enjoy the benefits of the life that organized crime had provided—without dirtying the boy's own hands. The life of an actuary may not be exciting, and it might not get you pussy, but for the most part no federal prison terms were involved. Also, rival actuaries did not beat one another to death.

Ralph couldn't have been less interested. He wanted the cheap sex with stupid women. He wanted the money. He wanted the respect. He wanted the fun. He even wanted the danger of mob life. He had made it quite clear to his father that he would do any job, no matter how distasteful, for the family. He would do no job, no matter how respectable, for the man. Big Manny had reluctantly acquiesced, because he would not be responsible for consigning his son to misery, and because he could keep an eye on the boy, and because he could teach him everything he knew about cheating and bullying people out of their money. Now, before Little Manny's unbelieving eyes, his sponsor and tutor was showing some idiot where to find toggle switches.

"Pop," he said to the vast back of the world's only made hardware chaperone, "I'll see y'later."

Big Manny was too far up the aisle to hear him.

CHAPTER 23

LEGAL AID

THERE IS HARDLY A BETTER EDUCATION FOR KEEPING THE INNO-cent out of the clutches of the law than spending the first twenty-two years of your life watching the totally, serially guilty escape the clutches of the law.

Angela Donato had been a bright, pretty, well-rounded little girl and teenager who had somehow managed to forge a life independent of her lineage. She was the elder of the nearly identical-looking fraternal Donato twins, by fourteen minutes, and perhaps therefore the more levelheaded. But for her B's in junior-year French and senior-year physics, she might have been valedictorian at Holy Trinity. She still ranked fifth in the class, the sort of academic achievement that, perversely, can militate against high school social status. Not for Angela. Being a brain didn't stop her from being voted prom queen, a competition in which she had no interest and one she certainly did not enter. Prom monarchs are crowned based on pure popularity; all votes are write-ins. As such, Angela was as surprised as anyone else that she outpolled her wilder and more voluptuous twin sister, who had prevailed upon Daddy to pay for implants just to make her a shoo-in. Don Donato, wholly devoted to his babies, did not flinch. Just as he had bought Angela a fancy microscope and trips to field hockey camp, he provided Tina with the finest tits money can buy. Yet for reasons Daddy and Daddy's littlest girl failed to understand, cool reserve somehow trumped boobage and eyeliner, even among high school kids.

Not that the twins, ordinarily, were rivals. Rather, they lived in entirely different universes, a pattern forged at the age of five, when the nuns insisted they be separated in school and remain so until graduation. The pedagogical theory behind that was to help twins foster self-image and self-worth independent of each other. Worked like a charm. Both girls had happy childhoods and personalities as charming as they were distinct. Tina was outgoing and fun; she squealed with delight under an open fire hydrant when she was six and just as delightedly knocked back shooters last night. Angela was quiet and analytical, eager to try anything and willing to fail. Rather than pouting when she was slow to master the bicycle, she persisted until her legs were covered with scabs. Once she got the hang of it, she was off with the neighborhood boys, exploring.

A few years later, Tina would also go off with the boys, exploring. Not the same thing.

From the time they were second graders, the twins were equally aware of their special circumstances—of the deference accorded them by adults, especially the Village merchants, and playmates alike. In time, they fully comprehended. Whereas Tina exploited every opportunity her royalty conferred, flaunting her mobette status to the max, Angela was embarrassed—and increasingly embittered—by the whole thing. She loved her dad, but grew less and less accepting of his, ahem, life choices. God knows where she picked up this sort of thing, but Angela somehow believed that crime was wrong. At school, she made it her business to cultivate everything in her life that was on the straight and narrow. Behind her back, with admiration not condescension, the other kids called her Marilyn, who was the pretty blonde Munster. Angela was decreasingly Marilyn-like at home. There, she became ever more arrogant and argumentative. That too stood her in perfect stead for a life in the law.

So long as Angela kept her distaste within their four walls, Don Donato and Evangeline did not try very hard to influence her. For an outlaw and a brute, the don was a reasonably progressive parent. He even prevailed on Evangeline to let go. The more they pushed back, he maintained, the more their daughter would be pushed away. His strategy was instead to humor her in her strange predilections. In time, he felt certain, she would grow to understand and embrace the importance of family, of tradition, of suitcases full of money. He had used a lot of that very money to send her for two years to the City University of New York and two more to NYU. Angela's dream was to become a lawyer. Their dream, never spoken within her earshot, was for Angela to be the Donato family's in-house counsel, to use her brains and feisty attitude to keep the don and the rest of the crew out of jail. Why not? She loved her Uncle Manny. Don Donato wanted nothing more than for his eldest, someday, to succeed him as his consigliere. Thus, he picked up the tab for Brooklyn Law School—alma mater of both Martin Light, who defended members of the Colombo family, and Gerry Shargel, who represented John Gotti and other Gambinos. Shamefully, Geraldo Rivera studied there too.

Angela was a star law student. Law review, the whole deal. Upon graduation, she quickly passed the bar and then, in fulfillment of her destiny as a Donato, totally pulled a fast one. She took a job as a public defender, seeking justice for indigent mooks, including—in the words of her adoring father—"every kind of nigger and spic with a crack pipe or a razor." That's how the don put it to Big Manny at the time.

"Fuck me, Manny. I got two kids. One tart and one Mother fuckin' Teresa." "Motherfuckin' Teresa?" Manny had responded, genuinely confused.

The don shook his head. "No, Manny. Mo-ther *fuckin*' Te-re-sa!"

"Ah," Manny said.

As it turned out, for approximately the reason predicted by Don Donato, Angela had hated the public defender's office.

"But why?" her supervisor had asked her. "Angela, it's only been six months."

"I think I've discovered something about myself," Angela replied.

"And what's that?"

"I have discovered that I don't like criminals."

It was a fair point. Every one of her cases was a shitkicker. Every single one of her defendants was guilty as sin, and then some. She spent her days pleading aggravated assault down to disorderly conduct, rape down to lewd conduct, grand theft auto down to trespassing, murder down to manslaughter—all to clear the docket for private attorneys to get better-heeled sociopaths off scot-free or so some wretched crackhead could get thirty years to life for refusing, against penalty of certain assassination, to finger his dealer. The whole process, the whole corrupt system, the whole perversion of justice, nauseated her and made a laughingstock of her ideals. In addition, every assistant DA but the one she liked hit on her every day. And the one she liked was gay.

Had she really alienated her parents and busted her ass through nineteen years of schooling to work for people who make Joey Sardines look like Buzz Lightyear? And so, each day as she dragged herself out of bed she asked herself the same question:

WWLSD?

What would Lisa Scottoline do?

Lisa Scottoline, the legal thrillerista, was Angela's heroine. Ivy League lawyer, best-selling novelist, single mom—through her example, and through the grit of her powerful female characters, she personified the guts and independence, with no sacrifice of femininity, to which Angela so aspired. And, by the way, *Scottoline*. As opposed to, say, Zamostein.

What would Lisa Scottoline do? Well, specifically, what she would do is give up the law to write potboilers. But Angela was no novelist and, in any case, assumed the market for Italian-babe legal-thriller authors was glutted at one. So she left her poorly paying job in the Office of the Public Defender to take an even more poorly paying job as the founder of the Ebbets Beach Legal Aid Society.

There—directly below the offices of Fiesta Tours—she was spending Saturday afternoon trying to help Luz Espinosa, a sixty-year-old domestic who entered the United States illegally in 1971, from being deported. Because obviously, the government assumed, by spending forty years on her hands and knees scrubbing the floors of US citizens, Mrs. Espinosa posed a grave threat to national security and the American way of life.

At 3:00 p.m., a short barrel-chested man entered the storefront carrying a plastic bag full of tomatoes. Walking in from the blazing sun, he was wearing ultra-permanently pressed robin's egg–blue acrylic slacks and a dark-blue windbreaker. On his feet were shiny black oxfords over white crew socks. It was Angela's landlord.

"Daddy!" she blurted out. "Get out of here! You can't be in here."

The don took a seat next to his daughter's desk. "I brung you some tomatoes from Mama's garden. Sweet like apples."

"Daddy, come on. You agreed. You can't be seen in here."

"I know, Angelina, I wouldn't embarrass you, but, sweetheart, I gotta problem."

Angela knew that her father didn't know that she knew about Uncle Manny, so she played dumb. "What kind of problem, Dad?"

"Well, it's not really about Big Manny, which you already know about."

Scary. Angela shut her eyes to gather herself as the don proceeded.

"It has to do with the fire."

"Daddy! The barber! No! Please tell me that wasn't…" She caught herself. The don's name wasn't on the deed, but one of his shell companies was. In any case, she had been well trained since childhood. Everything was bugged until proven otherwise, in which case it was still bugged. Angela took a breath, pointed at her father, arched her eyebrows in question, and shook her head with the answer she wanted to hear—or see. But the don did not play charades.

"You out of your mind?" he hollered. "This is a neighborhood. This is my neighbor you're talking about."

Huh? Neighbor? Angela knew that the family had gotten a bit kinder and gentler in Ebbets Beach. She had been unaware, however, that she was sitting across from Mister Rogers.

"Then…"

"Then nothing, Angela"—here, Don Donato looked all around the room and shouted for the benefit of anybody who might be listening—"I did not torch no barbershop. Understand? I had nothing to do with that outrage. Period."

"So it was an accident, right?"

"Like fun it was a fuckin' accident, excuse my French."

"But then who did it?"

"This, Angelina, is the problem I got. I need a little favor from you."

"What kind of favor, Dad?"

"I need for you to come back to your family."

Angela stood from her desk. She pointed to the door. "I love you, Daddy," she said, "but now you have to leave. Thanks for the tomatoes."

The most feared man in Ebbets Beach, at least as of the day before, rose as instructed and walked to the door. There, he turned to his daughter. "Angelina," he said, "I'll be back." For the time being, he simply walked outside, opened the adjacent door, and trudged upstairs to his travel agency to resume his afternoon of not agenting any travel.

CHAPTER 24

THE GODFATHER

HE WAS TIRED. DON DONATO LABORED TO REACH THE SECOND floor. Lately, his bandy legs had ached, and his breath was short. A cardiologist had put him on some crazy treadmill like a hamster and glued electrodes to his body, alligator clipped to a diagnostic machine, just like his Caddy at the dealership. The diagnosis: strong heart, weak will. The doctor said the patient was exhausted, physically, emotionally, every which way. "Take a vacation" was the advice. "Cut back on the wine. Reduce your stress level."

"How'm I supposed to do that?" the patient had inquired. The doctor had some thoughts on the subject but did not share them.

Don Donato rested on the landing, musing on how it had come to this. Ten years earlier, half of Brooklyn lived in fear of his very name. At any given time, his vault was stuffed with *molti* hundred grand. He ate oysters by the trayful, licked Bosco out of strippers' pussies, and, when he attended the girls' graduation, a sea of Holy Trinity humanity parted to clear a path. He wielded, and exercised, the power of life and death. When did everything go haywire? He supposed it began with the Marco situation.

Marco was the son of Sally and Bernice (née Horowitz) Quattrone. Sally was a sweet guy, a little dim but very kind, who waited tables at the club. He worked nights. Bernice worked part-time days as a receptionist for her brother Jacob, who ran a body shop down the boulevard across from the paper plate factory. She worked Tuesday-Thursday-Saturday. For close to four years, the don fucked her Monday-Wednesday-Friday. On Fridays, he'd leave the *riunione*, slap Sally on the back, and go home and fuck the man's wife in the ass. Nothing personal. He was very fond of Sally and always took care of him—a C-note every Friday no matter even if only three, four other guys were at dinner. The don was fond of Bernice too. Two things: her legs, which had calf muscles like bocce balls, and her sense of humor. She really made him laugh, talking about all the jerks who came into the body shop trying to pull one over on the insurance adjusters and about Sally trying to fix things in the apartment and always fucking up every job. Like when he replaced the fill valve in the toilet, flooded the bathroom, and ruined the ceiling of the apartment directly below. And when he tried to install sconces over the couch and shocked himself so bad he flew backward right over the coffee table. Vic Donato was neither often nor easily amused, but when Bernice described Sally airborne in their apartment wearing nothing but black dress socks and shorts, he cracked up every time. She also liked talking about Sally's dick, which she swore was like a kielbasa. Alas, the poor schnook was embarrassed by sex and just kept his eyes closed till it was over with—which, she complained, seldom lasted more than "a New York—for cryin' out loud—minute." Every time the don looked at Sally, he let his eyes drift to the waiter's crotch to see a sign of the monster. But he never detected anything incriminating. Once the boss stood next to the waiter in the club men's room but couldn't bring himself to take a peek. When Sally shook off the last drop, though, the don said, "Be careful, Sally, somebody's gonna get hurt," and then he nearly pissed himself laughing.

Marco was three years older than Casper and the girls but only one year ahead of them at Holy Trinity. When he was a senior, at the age of twenty, he went on a class field trip overnight to Philadelphia to see Independence National Historical Park and the aquarium across the Ben Franklin Bridge in Camden. It was an unseasonably cold spring weekend. The building had cut off the heat in early April, so Sally bought and installed a portable propane heater. It took the chill off, but the next morning he and Bernice were icicles. Carbon monoxide poisoning. They were there for almost two days before Marco discovered their bloated bodies.

Marco went to live with his Uncle Phil and Aunt Robin Schwartzenberger, who ran a florist shop in Bayside. Marco, traumatized by the tragedy, lost whatever focus and will he had to keep his head above water in school. A month before graduation, with second-semester D's and F's threatening to hold him back for the second time in three years, he dropped out. That's when, at Evangeline's urging, the don took the boy under his wing. Like his dad, Marco was a likeable kid, very respectful and eager to please. He didn't have a lot going for him IQ-wise, but he could read and count just fine, making him more than qualified as a numbers runner. He was a heavyset kid with chubby cheeks and a high-pitched voice—not much of a tough, in other words—and, at first, the other guys thought the don was going soft in the head to bring him in.

More like soft in the heart. The C-note he used to stuff in Sally's palm he began giving to Marco, on top of his weekly take, just for extra walking-around money. Knowing that the kid was born with only one functioning kidney, he sprang for visits to what they both called "the neverologist." He also worked hard to steer business to the Schwartzenbergers' flower shop, by shaking down funeral homes and hotels. Fearing the boy was a virgin, he set him up with a high-class hooker and paid for a room at the Avenue Plaza. The don sat in the bar. After three hours, he went to the room, where he interrupted Marco and Jade playing video games on pay TV. He thought this was the most adorable thing he'd ever seen. Only later did Jade inform him that the kid fucked like a lion and was hung like a mule. "Unstoppable," she said. Go figure.

The other guys, at first, were less generous. Behind Marco's back, they'd call him Pugsley or Flounder, but this lasted only till one day when the don overheard Joey Sardines making a crack. He walked out of his office and, in front of everybody, slapped Joey on the face, right cheek then left, six times. Give the guy credit, he didn't make a peep. Joey also never ridiculed Marco again, nor did anyone else. As it turned out, the very next week, Marco stomped the shit out of a short-bagger, and, with that baptism, they readily accepted him as a brother. There was no denying, however, that the kid didn't exactly inspire awe, let alone terror, among the civilians. As the crew shrank, the net effect was a less intimidating presence around the neighborhood. The don knew his flagging fortunes were largely determined by forces outside of his control, but as he dragged his aging ass up the stairs and heard Marco in the office, in his near falsetto, recounting his prowess in Super Mario, Don Donato wondered to himself, "Is this where I lost my edge?"

CHAPTER 25

RETALIATION

THE RUMOR ABOUT DIPASQUALE PAYING PROTECTION TO THE Russians was wrong. They'd come by inquiring about his security needs, but he had graciously explained that those needs were more than covered. He offered the man a complimentary haircut. The man, whose name was Abram, politely declined.

The next day, Abram had returned to the barbershop with a colleague named Arkady, a husky bald gent who seemed to take great interest in the premises—wandering around the shop, tapping on the bird cage, examining the ceiling, opening the cellar door—while Abram attempted to explain the benefits of engaging a larger, more aggressive security partner. DiPasquale found it curious that Abram employed the word *partner* as a verb, a construction he had never previously encountered. "Ve are vishing to partner vith you for mutual benefit," he said, in an Odessa accent thicker than a slice of black bread.

Still, the barber, pleading financial embarrassment and competing obligations, was in no position to accept. "I appreciate your proposal," he'd lied, "but I know you understand I have commitments." Once again, he offered a counterproposal. "Maybe you gentlemen would like a shave?" he asked.

Nyet, spacebo.

The pair left but did not stray far. Abram leaned against a mailbox on the sidewalk, produced a cigarette, and smoked it as dynamically as DiPasquale had ever seen. Trying not to be observed himself, he pretended to sweep up as he spied the outdoor scene in astonishment. The Russian reduced the cigarette to ash in the space of sixty seconds. Then the two of them moved on. The barber let out an extravagant sigh.

DiPasquale was still more relieved by the third day, when no Russian darkened his door. Over the next two weeks, the anxiety gradually began to subside. Casper had inquired about the Russians, and the barber was relieved to explain, truthfully, that he was filling only the Donatos' bag. Though Abram had demurred on tonsorial services, it appeared nonetheless to have been a close shave.

Then someone firebombed his shop, his building, his livelihood, his nest egg, his parrot, his future. Burnt to cinders. His hundred-dollar-per-week premium to the Cozy Nostra, as it turned out, had bought him nothing.

This was the subject of the evening's *riunione*, for the first time anybody could remember, on a Saturday. The meal was spaghetti and meatballs. Only Tony the Teeth was eating. The don presided and, as always, encouraged his men to discuss the issues as a family. On this night, though, something was different. Perhaps it was the acuteness of the crisis, perhaps it was the absence of Big Manny, but absent too was the usual air of caution—or, put another way, repression. *Riunione* had always been something of a charade; the air was always chilled by the don's intimidating presence. The open discussion was typically narrowed by self-censorship and the certain knowledge that the don welcomed any viewpoint so long as it did not contradict or diminish his own. It was true in Don Greco's day as well: a table full of dangerous men trying to stay in character and retain the respect of their comrades-in-unregistered-arms, while inwardly quaking about committing a fatal indiscretion.

Not Saturday night. Gone even was the don's inscrutable aphorizing. Seldom had he ever been so blunt and clear.

"The Russians are here," he announced. "This is what we have anticipated. There is nothing good that can come of it. As of last night, we are now in a fight for everything we have, everything that we have built, everything that belongs to us. The barbershop, I promise you, is only the beginning. We have no choice here. We got to do something. The question is what. And nobody will leave this room tonight until we have decided. Tony the Teeth, you have been warning us about the Ivans for years. Whaddya got to say?"

"In other words, I got nothing to say, Don. We gotta stop these animals."

A lot of nodding, which the don was having none of.

"What is that? 'We gotta stop them?' I gotta fuck Sophia Loren. Someone tell me how."

At first, nobody volunteered a word. They sat staring at their plates, the whole lot of them, not counting Tony the Teeth, who shoveled in the pasta as if it were his first and last meal. Finally, of all people, Leonard the Calculator chimed in. Fresh off of scandalizing the room twenty-four hours earlier by reminding the don that his pants were being pulled down by the recession, the family bookkeeper opened New Business with a motion as to how to proceed.

"I say we torch Little felpin' Odessa," he volunteered.

It was an interesting plan, lacking—the whole table of lesser intellects understood—only a few details. What would be torched?

Who would do the torching? What would be the next move, after the better populated, better capitalized, better armed, worse dispositioned Russians retaliated with a wholesale killing spree in Ebbets Beach, including, but most likely not limited to, everybody sitting at the table?

But it was a start. Little Manny spoke next.

"Don, you ask me, here are the options. We could take out a store in Brighton Beach like the Calculator says, but that ain't gonna stop nothin'. They'll come back at us bigger. Much bigger. These fuckers is armed to the fucking teeth. They got Tecs like we got breadsticks." Little Manny illustrated his point by gesturing to a vase full of breadsticks, a visual aid that proved helpful to Tony the Teeth, who grabbed a handful and started eating them too. Little Manny continued.

"We could ignore this incident, but then the Russians will really move in fast. There'll be drugs all over the streets, a lot more violence, and we'll start losing—no disrespect, Don—what little we got left."

Don Donato waved his hand, in the spirit of the circumstances, permitting Little Manny's candor.

"We could try to negotiate with them, with this fuck Valentin who supposeably is the boss, and maybe we could draw borderlines and keep the peace. Or we could take out Valentin."

"Whack the boss?" Casper interjected. "Fuck we gonna do that?"

"The don asked for options. Those are the options. I'm just saying what the options are."

"There's options," offered the Calculator, "and there's viable options."

"Suck my dago dick, Leonard," Little Manny replied. "Why don't you fucking come up with a plan? Maybe you could pencil him to death."

"Yeah," Leonard retorted, "well, sluck me right back."

Casper stood up. "Leave him be, Ralph. He didn't say nothin'."

"SIT DOWN!" barked Don Donato, stunning Casper and everybody else. "We don't got enough problems without youse guys mouthing off? Now, Little Manny got it right. Those are the options. Like he says, we let this go, those barbarians'll have bagels in the...the..." Now the don was gesturing toward the few remaining breadsticks. "We'll be tripping over junkies in the street. Now, we don't have the firepower—no disrespect to you Teeth—to be assassinating no bosses. And I don't think taking an eye for an eye...I'm just sayin', I don't think we win. I think we lose another eye and then pretty quick everything else. And a lot of innocent people might get hurt. So this leaves only one option."

"No fuckin' way."

All heads turned toward Tony the Teeth, who was trying to clear his throat and talk at the same time. His empty plate was smeared with red sauce, and a corona of breadstick crumbs encircled it. The Calculator chuckled to himself. The place setting looked like something out of Voyager II. After a spasm of phlegm displacement, the enforcer spoke his mind.

"Don Donato, we can't negotiate with these animals. They're fucking savages. They got no respect for nothing. And I'll tell you what else too. They catch one of their own talking to another crew, like making a deal, they make him wish he was Joey Sardines. They're wolves, I'm telling you. They don't negotiate, and they don't fuckin' share."

"Well," replied the don, "what about this, what the Teeth has to say?"

Meekly, at the far end of the table, Marco raised his hand. "Don?" he said, in his boys'-choir soprano.

"Yeah, Marco, what do you got to say?"

"Don, before, when you said nobody leaves this table…Does that include the restroom?"

CHAPTER 26

A PLAN

FOR TWO MORE HOURS THEY TALKED, UNTIL FINALLY THINGS WERE decided: negotiation it would be. The turning point was a confession from Little Manny, who knew a guy who knew a guy. He'd gotten a phone number in Brighton Beach, supposedly an apartment frequented by Valentin, either as a safe house or a love nest. Little Manny figured he'd call the number and sound bellicose. If the Russians had firebombed the barbershop, they'd know what the call was about and have a seed of doubt planted in their minds before they dared to strike again. If they weren't behind the fire, no harm done. They wouldn't know what the call was about, much less who was calling. This move, Little Manny figured, would demonstrate initiative. It would demonstrate that the apple doesn't fall far from the tree. It would demonstrate that, no matter what had come between Big Manny and the don, Little Manny could be trusted to look out for the interests of the family.

So Saturday afternoon, he'd gone to the pay phone at the Pathmark and dialed the Brighton Beach number.

"*Da*?" answered a deep voice on the other hand of the line.

"You burn down a shop here, I burn down a house there. Get me?"

"Do not again calling this number," the deep voice replied.

"Listen up, moose and sqvirrel. I vill call number venever I fuckin' feel like it, get me?"

"Please not to call again. You now are reported."

"Yeah, Boris, reported to who, you firebug fuck?"

"Government." Click.

Yes, it was true. The fearsome Donato crime family would be placed on the FTC "Do Not Call" registry—the point being not that that meant anything but that the Russians did not take their threats very seriously. This single salient fact informed the remainder of Saturday evening's conversation until at last the decision was made. The Ivans would be approached. A summit would be scheduled. An accommodation, no doubt an expensive one, would be made. As the don had put it, in what was as close to a joke as anyone had heard him make in years, "Half of next to nothing is better than one hundred percent of nothing any day, particularly if you are breathing."

CHAPTER 27

TO WHOM IT MAY CONCERN

THE VILLAGE ASSOCIATION CONFAB HAD NOT ENDED WHEN MR.
Kim stormed out, nor did it end before Mr. Mattress gathered
a great deal more information. First, as a newcomer with only
one inexperienced employee, he was excused from any Labor
Day Sale-a-Bration duties. Tina Donato covered his shaved-ice-
scooping slot. Secondly, he learned that the tanning salon owner
was both the trampy-looking babe who had jostled him on the
way into the meeting *and* daughter of the local mob kingpin, a
pair of facts he didn't quite know what to do with except—out of
vestigial instinct—to make a mental note along the lines of *No
matter how drunk...*

Once upon a time for Mr. Mattress, this would not have
been an idle notation. Women liked him, not merely because
he was charming and handsome, though surely he was that. To
complement his kind aquamarine eyes and swept-back mane
was a dimpled Kirk Douglas chin and a trim, taut physique. He
looked so good in a suit it was easy to contemplate how good he
looked stripped out of one. His appeal, though, far transcended his
looks, just as it transcended his erstwhile money and prominence.
Women were drawn to him because they quickly sensed that he
saw something in them besides their tits and ass. It was true; Jack

liked women for their womanly selves, including their thoughts, their feelings, their quirks, their problems, their conflicts, their sacrifices, their disadvantages, their weakness, their strength. When he looked at a woman, and more importantly, when he listened to one, it was as though no other female inhabited the earth. He was tall. He was fit. His hair was to die for. But his most seductive feature was his eardrums.

He wasn't faking it, either. He was no common seducer, feigning interest with the ulterior motive of pussypalooza. He was genuinely enthralled with the opposite sex, and it was this authenticity that women so greedily fed on. That's one thing. The other thing is that this rare sympathetic male, this extraordinarily kindred soul, this noble among scamps, also had a ball sack. He was a man, and therefore a hound. Until Angela came along, he fucked whosoever would be happily fucked. Oh, he was an unusually sensitive hound; he never proceeded if his partner signaled anything was afoot in her mind but casual, recreational sex. He was also a generous and attentive hound, listening with his body as well as he listened with his ears. And he was a chivalrous hound, never letting anyone feel disposed of or cheap. But he nonetheless embraced his inner hound, because—to paraphrase one of the world's most perfect jokes—he could.

Put another way, long before he was Mr. Mattress, he was Mr. Mattress.

Not lately, however. Along with everything else he had lost in Angelagate was desire. And he wasn't sure why. Was it because he still loved her, in addition to hating her? Was it because he felt betrayed, not just by one woman, but by the world of women in whom he'd placed so much energy and trust? Was it that his fall rendered him, at least in his own eyes, less of a man? Was it that he, so cautious about being a heartless seducer, now felt wary of being seduced himself? Was it his survival instinct, first to create stability, thence to seek comfort? Was it pure despondency? Jack did not know. He still noticed women. He did not lose his easy charm. But after work, all he wished to do was exercise, eat, read, and sleep.

So, of course, naturally, exactly forty-eight hours into his career as a celibate bed salesman, into his store walked Tina Donato, and, somehow in this new context, she struck him as one of the loveliest women he had ever laid eyes on in his entire femmetensive life.

Somehow, too, she had changed her look. A day earlier she was in a tight skirt, T-shirt, and heels; he couldn't be quite sure from their brief encounter, but he could have sworn on her toenails was painted a mural. Now she looked like an ad for Banana Republic or J. Crew, clad in a blousy white cotton safari shirt, sage chinos, and beige flats. Her anthracite hair, yesterday pulled back tight, flopped in a casual pageboy. Also, her fantastically vulgar cleavage had vanished inside the shirt. Altogether, it was a remarkable transformation, and as she was the first visitor of the morning, he crossed the floor, hand extended, to greet her.

"Ms. Donato," he offered, "welcome. Jack Schiavone."

Angela Donato was immediately off her stride. "You know me?" she said.

"Of course. Tanning Depot."

"Expo," she corrected.

"I am so sorry. New kid on the block, but that's obnoxious of me. Of *course*, Tanning Expo."

"Right. That's not me."

"Huh? I'm sorry...you're the daughter of..."

"Oh, yes. Sure am. Fast learner, you are. But look, I'm not..."

Oh, superb. Nicely done. Mental note or not, it had taken him all of thirty seconds to piss off Tina fucking Capone. Whereupon, amid petit panic, he promptly overcompensated. Why? She was not the state attorney; she was a bimbo. He had not been caught breaking into her car; he'd botched the name of her tanning salon. This was scarcely cause for an adrenaline surge, but there it was: racing heart, pins and needles in the face. And so, prompted by some irrational reflex, Mr. Mattress found himself correcting the flub again and again, overtalking her as he did so, as if to somehow lessen the original error. It was a pointless exercise. By its very nature, a blunder cannot be erased, Stalin-like, from history, much less short-term memory. But embarrassment yields strange impulses. Hence the spectacle of a preternaturally confident man, he who once controlled $100-million budgets, transformed into a blathering nitwit.

"Tanning Expo actually caught my eye," he jabbered. "Teal sign, right? Tanning Expo—in the Village, right? Well, yeah, obviously, Tina, or you wouldn't be scooping my snow cones for me, would you?" He so busily tried to dig himself out of the insignificant conversational ditch that he didn't at first register the pretty lady's protest.

"I'm not Tina."

"Thanks for that. I have help, but she's just a kid and...Huh? Not Tina?"

"Twin sister. Angela Donato. Pleased to meet you, Jack."

That shut him up. Yet as his mind raced, as he processed this latest weirdness, all was calm. The panic subsided. This was what geniuses and alcoholics call a moment of clarity, a moment divided in Mr. Mattress's resumed full-wittedness thusly: Appreciating the circumstances, he wondered to himself—neither for the first time nor the last—in what bizarre parallel universe he had alighted. And he internalized in an instant that—having not insulted the floozy, because she was not present—he had insulted nobody at all. It was then for him but to be Jack Schiavone. That quickly he collected himself. The nitwit had left the building.

"I know what you are thinking, Angela," he replied, with a wry grin and a nod of certainty. "You are thinking, 'My, what an impressive man.' I'm sorry. I cannot help it. I was born suave." He picked up a bowl of candy from his desk and offered it to her. "Lollipop?"

A wave of *no thanks* and a hint of a smile in return.

"Wild guess," Jack ventured, "you have no connection whatsoever to the tanning industry."

Another smile from the beauty. She was beginning to get him, which pleased him in a familiar way.

"No, I don't. I'm actually a lawyer, but I'm not here on a legal matter. If you don't mind, I'd like to ask you one or two things about your new business."

In TV commercials, this is where they put the record-screech sound effect. It stands for reality shifting, time stopping, the world on tilt. Not a moment ago, he'd thought he had everything sized up and now—unless he had catastrophically misread the situation yet again—there was only one explanation for this visit: having failed with the shiny lounge singer, the racketeers were following up with mob offspring, in the person of Attorney Helen of Troy. Has a store opening ever been more convoluted? Has a simple hello ever been more disorienting? Has his reasoning ever been less reliable?

Has extortion ever been so exquisite?

"Well, you know...um...Angela, your colleague was in here yesterday, and we sort of went over this stuff."

"My colleague?"

"Casper Benedetto." Because he had indeed catastrophically misread the situation yet again, Mr. Mattress was surprised by what happened next. What happened next was Angela Donato, Esquire, spying the cross section of the Snoo-Z-Lite coil assembly on a display rack and flinging it the length of the store while shouting at the top of her lungs, "GOD DAMN IT! HE'S NOT MY FUCKING COLLEAGUE!"

"Subordinate?"

"HE'S A FUCKING HOODLUM, LIKE MY FUCKING FATHER. THAT DOESN'T MAKE ME A HOODLUM, OK? JESUS FUCKING CHRIST, WHO DO I HAVE TO FUCK TO GET THE PRESUMPTION OF FUCKING INNOCENCE? HUH? WHO?"

All right, now Jack had it figured out. No, really. The outburst sucked the last of the stage smoke from the set piece of the Moliere comedy that had become his life. The twin sister, who was not Tina but Angela, was a lawyer but not a mob lawyer and present on business but not crooked business. He had in the space of four minutes misidentified her, slighted her, insulted her, infuriated her, but also briefly amused her. Now she was in a rage, but most likely not at him so much as the tragicomic circumstances of her life, and, furthermore, she was almost certain to apologize for her outburst, which would confer the advantage on him, in which case no harm done and plenty to talk about from this point forward. Therefore, when she ceased her tantrum, he knew exactly, *exactly* what to say.

"I'm sorry, but...Wouldn't that be *whom*?"

Angela Donato, hysterical nonmob lawyer, glared at him for a long, pregnant moment. Then she commenced to laughing, abundantly, in relief and surprise. Finally, finally, Jack had found equilibrium. The pother ping-pong was over. The cross-purposed were at last uncrossed.

Oh, wait. No, they weren't.

CHAPTER 28

JOB PLACEMENT

"IT'S ABOUT MY UNCLE MANNY," SHE BEGAN.

Proprietor and supplicant were now sitting with coffee at Mr. Mattress's desk. A young couple had entered the store, but Jack was content for them to browse. If he saw some pointed flopping or noticed serious conferring, he'd make his move. Now he was focused on Angela and, of course, intently listening.

"You know," Jack said, "I actually think I know who that is, but just this one time I won't shoot my mouth off."

"Then you've heard of Big Manny."

"Incredibly, I have."

"Well, what do you know about him?"

"Sorry. Not saying a word. Tell me."

Angela offered a crooked smile. "OK, he was in my dad's organization."

"Was?"

"Was," she confirmed, "until the other day, when he retired."

"Interesting," Jack said. "I am, of course, new to this bizarro world, but I wasn't aware that retirement was, you know, an option."

"It's complicated," Angela said. "Things are a little bit out of whack around here. I don't even know where to begin, but the long and short of it is my uncle—actually, he's my godfather...*godfather*

godfather—has left the organization, under reasonably good terms, it seems to me, and is now in an awkward situation."

Jack laughed. "Yeah, because being Big Manny of the mafia is such smooth sailing."

"Because everything's relative," Angela answered, "and because he has a family, a wife, and daughter, who is in college on a very straight path, and he's off the Donato payroll, and because his career as an honest civilian did not last from morning till lunch."

"All right, tell me when I'm being too nosy, but what kind of career was that?"

"He had a job at Home Depot. Electrical supplies or something. Anyway, evidently, he cursed out a customer on his first morning, and the customer complained and that was that. He was let go."

"Myself," said Mr. Mattress, "I might be less strict with an employee named Big Manny. Is he big?"

"A gentle giant, but he's also an ex-convict and apparently lacking in some—oh, I don't know—retail etiquette. Bottom line is he needs a job. I happened to be in Parcel Plus yesterday and happened to be talking to Sam Calabrese, whom I gather you've met, and he happened to mention you are very busy in here with no assistant manager, and I happen to know Uncle Manny is—take my word for it—the Werner von Braun of financial management, plus a very sweet man…"

"As murderers go…"

"No, no, no. Not Uncle Manny. I mean, look, he's one of them, but not like them. He collects stamps, for crying out loud. Daddy found him years and years ago to do the finances. I assure you, my father has plenty of goons to do whatever violent lunacy he does."

"I'm having a little difficulty believing this conversation is even taking place. At least with the two of us in it."

"I have to grant you that the standards of normal around here take some getting used to." She exhaled for what she was about to propose. Angelina spoke directly because coquettishly wasn't in her repertoire. "I guess it would be silly to ask this as a favor."

"Yeah, that would be pretty stupid. Maybe in our *second* fifteen minutes of acquaintance, you could invoke old times, but this is definitely too early. Here's the situation, Angela: It's true the opening has gone well, but I can't project from two days' sales. I haven't budgeted for anything more than Jitnee—she's the kid who helps me—and I was pretty much planning to live in the store for the first year, then reevaluate."

"What if," the lawyer replied, "I make you an offer you can't refuse?"

Now, there's a conversation stopper. And it did. One second… two seconds…three seconds…

"That's a joke, right?" said Mr. Mattress.

Angela nodded. "Joke. I have nothing to offer you. I'd hire him, but I'm eligible for food stamps as it is. It was just a shot in the dark."

The conversation at that point was becalmed. Jack let his gaze fall on the pen he was fidgeting with. Angela smoothed her chinos. Then, just as the silence threatened conversational sustainability, Angela changed the subject.

"So," she said, "beds. This is all new to you, or…"

Jack perked up. "Yeah, all new. My first foray into retail, at least since I was a teenager. Worked in a record store."

"Yeah, I vaguely remember those. Did you have long hair and encyclopedic knowledge of The Ramones?"

Jack smiled. "Bingo."

"Not to stereotype," said Angela.

"Noooo. Not at all. Anyway, my last gig kind of crashed and burned, so I thought I'd try the burgeoning mattress sector."

"Laid off?"

"Not exactly." Jack pivoted to his left as if to address somebody, though nobody was there. "Your Honor, I object on grounds of immateriality. Counsel has established no relevance."

"Ha-ha," Angela said. "All right, I'll back off. Sorry to get into your business."

"No, I'm sorry. Bad experience I don't much like reliving." He could have used that as his chance to dismiss her, but something was stopping him, something—apart from the pure pleasure of looking at her—he couldn't quite put his finger on. Once upon a time, Big Manny himself had sat across the desk from a Donato at a similar crossroads. Jack Schiavone was wholly ignorant of that historic turning point, but he still felt an uncanny tug of destiny presented by Angela's plainly preposterous wishes. So he thought, and in thinking, he latched onto an atom of a molecule of a germ of an idea. He promptly attempted to tease it out as he went along.

"So your uncle is a felon who just got fired for customer abuse, right?"

"I guess, yeah."

"And we're in the depths of a recession, and there are thousands of perfectly qualified, law-abiding people who would love to have an assistant manager job, if there were one to be had, which there is not. Am I making sense so far?"

"You are."

"Uh-huh, so the question is…What possible benefit could I derive by stepping in to rescue your uncle from the vicissitudes of the noncriminal economy? You've mentioned his skills with finances, probably most of which I have no use for because I am myself not a criminal."

Though Mr. Mattress was clearly building up a head of steam, the lawyer just blurted it out, "You're not?"

"Pardon me?"

"A criminal."

Holy fucking fuck. She knew. Jack stared at her, minus any smile, minus any charm, minus any warmth—just the shock of somebody who's been sucker punched.

Angela offered a face-pology, raising her eyebrows and squinching her lips into a sheepish smile. "I Googled you."

Jack nodded. Layers of onion were being peeled back one after another once again, and, lo and behold, he was the onion. Not that he should have expected any less. Changing boroughs does not exactly qualify as an escape into the witness protection program. But hadn't she just asked him if he'd been laid off? Had she been trying to corner him? Catch him in a lie? Just entertain herself? He tried to work this out as he went along too.

"Why'd you ask if you already knew?"

"Jack, I'm sorry, I—"

"And because I have a record therefore I'm running a halfway house for ex-cons? Is that the idea? Nice." Mr. Mattress looked across the store and saw the young shoppers circling a Pillow-Quilt Royale. "You're going to have to excuse me. I see some innocents to prey on."

"Jack—"

"No, it's OK. If they don't buy, I'll just drag them out back and rob them. That's just the way people like me are."

"You're not being fair," Angela protested, and there was something to that. She had hatched her Big Manny scheme before she had any idea that the new store owner was a convicted embezzler. Maybe even credit to her for not dismissing him as a sleazebag unworthy of her convicted tax-cheat uncle. Furthermore, had she not raised the issue of his legal problems more or less as soon as they had begun discussing his background? The layoff question was disingenuous, yes, but hardly felony sandbagging. None of which, naturally, occurred to Mr. Mattress, who—in this crazily fraught pas de deux—now had his opportunity for righteous indignation.

Jack stuck his thumb in his chest. "*I'm* not being fair?" He was sputtering, as will happen when you try to confine your anger to a whisper. But he didn't want to scare away customers. "You know what, Counselor? Seems to me about five minutes ago you were flinging my display materials halfway across my store because I'd supposed—and God knows where I could have gotten this idea—that the mob-daughter lawyer trying to foist a Big Manny on me might just possibly be a mob-lawyer daughter. But you sashay into my business armed with hearsay from, I guess, some clueless fucking trade rags, and you think you have me pegged? Guess what? Google is a search engine, not a lie detector. Who do I have to fuck to be left the fuck alone?" He gestured toward the door with a sweep of the hand. "Thanks for shopping Mr. Mattress. Do visit again."

Stricken and shamed, Angela hurried out. She looked back at Mr. Mattress, but he had already turned toward his customers. As she left, in the fashion of Donato twins everywhere, she jostled two men heading into the store but pushed past them without comment. They filed inside. One milled around the beds, while the other headed directly for Jack's desk and took the seat just vacated by Angela. Jack glanced in his direction and saw a beefy, shaved-headed, altogether disreputable-looking figure. Catching Jack's eye, the creep spoke loudly across the room.

"Mazel tov, Mr. Mattress!" he exclaimed.

Funny. He didn't look Jewish. But the accent was unmistakably Russian.

CHAPTER 29

DIPLOMACY

IT FELL ON LITTLE MANNY, AUTHOR OF THE NEGOTIATION OPTION, to arrange the summit. His earlier freelance efforts had complicated the matter of making contact, but he felt confident he could start over by eschewing the Pathmark for the one phone that still functioned over at Duane Reade. (The ubiquity of cell phones, and the corresponding disappearance of pay stations, was a tremendous nuisance to the criminal class. Untapped, untraceable calls were going the way of running boards and tommy guns.) Anyway, stage one worked like a charm. The Russians answered.

"*Da.*"

"It's me."

"Me who?"

"Ebbets Beach. Listen carefully."

"Vy I should?"

"We need a summit."

"Ha. You vant meet?"

Stupid question, Little Manny thought. "What the fuck I'm gonna do with meat? My uncle's a butcher. I don't need some fuckin' kosher—"

"Shut up, telemarketer. Don't call this number. Ve contact you."

"We choose the place, got it? We choose the place, the time. You show up yourself with one other guy. More than that, it ends badly. You wanna know how badly, ask Joey Sardines, rest in peace, the thieving fuck. You wanna play games, you find out who you're dealing with. You wanna talk like men, we are ready to do the same. Have I made myself clear? Hello? Hello? HELLO?"

Little Manny didn't know exactly when the Russian had hung up, but he figured it was just before "We choose the place." All he could do now was cool his heels, waiting for a contact. And so he did.

The gang was not otherwise idle, however. Don Donato had conceded the wisdom of the silk glove, but he also knew the leverage conferred by the iron fist. They could sue the Ivans for peace, but they had to do so from a position of strength—or at least perceived strength. Little Manny dangled the carrot. Tony the Teeth wielded the stick. His assignment was simple: without actually harming anybody—because a war of attrition would be settled quickly in the favor of the Russians—he would have to scare the shit out of them. Leonard the Calculator was brought into the operation as well, tasked with intelligence. He would find out where in Brighton Beach Valentin laid his head at night and there would take place something memorable, indelible, ominous.

"Can you do this, Calculator?" the don had inquired. "This ain't computer work."

But it was. At 11:00 on Sunday morning, Leonard the Calculator got on the Internet, where it took him about thirty seconds to learn Valentin's last name, which was Smirdov, and the business address of his firm, which was called Astrakhan Fur Storage. The calculator also quickly found several photographs of the feared gangster kingpin who, to Leonard's surprise and substantial delight, looked very familiar. Except for the drooling St. Bernard dog beside him in most of the pictures, the prick was the spitting image of the skinny little Palestinian hot dog vendor at the corner of the Boulevard and 58th Place, the guy whose papier-mâché pretzel sign dislodged in a gust of wind and broke the neck of a sophomore from Moe Howard, whom the family helped out due to the vendor's appalling lack of falling-pretzel insurance. Not too fearsome, that guy.

Having ascertained a business address, then it was just a question of staking out the fur joint to wait for Smirdov to appear, thence to follow him to his residence, where subsequently Tony would sink his dentures.

Because Big Manny had never permitted the Internet to be used for any business but Fiesta Tours, of which business there was very little, the Calculator did his gumshoe work at the library. On Sunday, the Ebbets Beach branch closed at noon. Still, Leonard finished with time to spare. While he was there, he also checked out copies of *The Tipping Point* and *Who Moved My Cheese?*

Medium Marco's assignment was to scout a location for the summit. It had to be a place where the don and his second—in the absence of Big Manny, Marco had no idea who that would be—could be secure, yet where the Ivans also could feel comfortable. This ruled out anything in Ebbets Beach proper, and, of course, Little Odessa was out of the question. It had to be public, but noisy, so that their conversation could be neither overheard nor recorded. And there had to be a nearby police presence, to discourage an ambush. Finally, the place could neither be Russian nor Italian. It had to be neutral—or, as Marco characterized it, medium. The search took him to Brooklyn Heights, well off the beaten track for both gangs and in every respect ideal. On Adams Street, at the base of the Brooklyn Bridge, tucked into the corner of an apartment house, stood Ambrosia, the bustlingest Greek diner in Brooklyn. Though the food was exactly like every other Greek diner in Brooklyn, and the world, the joint was nestled in an apartment cluster, blocks away from the dining cornucopia of Promenade, and thus a convenient option for the apartment dwellers and the strollers hungered by their half-hour trek over the bridge—and therefore perpetually busy. It was brightened by plate-glass windows on both sides of the corner, offering a clear view of approaching threats. And a pair of blue-and-white NYPD cruisers stood hunkered down at the adjacent curb twenty-four hours a day, 365 days per year, to guard the bridge from terrorist airplanes. Marco found a seat at the counter, where he somehow managed to balance the one-hundred-pound sack of flour that was his ass on the swiveling, circular turquoise stool.

"Coffee," he said, in a voice he tried very hard to fashion after young Don Corleone but which more resembled Vanity Smurf.

The waitress ignored him.

"Coffee here," he repeated.

She let out a put-upon sigh, slid a cup and saucer in front of Marco, and poured the coffee without looking at him. Then she slapped two packs of creamer onto the counter and shouted something evidently nasty, in Greek, toward the kitchen. *Perfect*, Marco thought.

Casper was busy too. After the Saturday *riunione*, the don had pulled him aside and whispered instructions.

"Don't mention this to nobody," the don had said. "We need a contingency plan, just in case."

"If you don't mind, Don, what do you have in mind?"

"We need a man who can take care of our problem." Casper looked at the don blankly; the family had so many problems. This tragic fact quickly occurred to Don Donato as well, so he clarified. "Casper, a contract."

Still, Casper was bewildered. "A contract, Don? On the Russian boss?"

The don nodded.

"But, Don Donato, what about the Teeth?"

The don shook his finger. "*Lui non può farlo*. Not Tony. It can't be anyone inside. Too risky."

"So what do you want me to do, Don? Find a hit man?"

The don looked around the totally protected environs of the social club and put his arm around Casper and pulled the Collector's ear toward his lips. "These are words I don't want to hear again, not even here," Don Donato whispered. "Understand, for now we are just window-shopping, but, yes, you find me a guy. By Monday."

"With respect, Don, Monday is Labor Day."

Now it was the don's turn to be at a loss. "So?" he asked.

"Labor Day," whispered Casper, "I think they're closed."

CHAPTER 30

THE CONNECTION

DON DONATO HIMSELF HAD BUSINESS TO CONDUCT. IT WAS 1:00 p.m. on Sunday as he sat in his idling 2004 Cadillac DeVille, air-conditioning pumping at full blast, in the parking lot of Our Lady of Grace. In a minute or two, somebody would walk out of noon mass, as he always did. For his part, the don never attended. He was a believer, and he was technically still welcome, but he didn't care for the attention whenever a homily touched on subjects more or less in indictment of everything in his business and life. He wrote a check here and there; he left the bingo alone. Lately, the family cooperated in community outreach. This did not mean he wanted to sit there, his face burning, listening to some fucking priest tell him not to steal, as if the church weren't the biggest racket in history.

Now he waited. Until recently, this was a job someone else would do, lest the don would dirty his hands, but here was just one more example of how life had changed. The whole thing made him sour in the stomach. Still, the don was not one to surrender—to law enforcement, to the Five Families, to the Russians, nor least of all to the vagaries of fortune. He was no Tasmanian devil; he was a shark, hungry and swimming ever forward for his next taste. Thus he kept his eyes fixed at the church steps, awaiting his target. He was at a ninety-degree angle to the entrance, so it was not easy to recognize the worshippers as they flowed out of Our Lady of Grace. In profile, bleached in the glare of the midday sun, they were a mass of specters, blotches bouncing toward the street. Then among them was a large blotch, a two-hundred-pound blotch. The cop. Franzetti, taking his sweet fucking time. He stood on the top step, shooting the shit with some *idiota* as he folded a church bulletin and stuffed it into the pocket of his yellow golf shirt. At last, Franzetti turned to his left, scanned the parking lot, and spotted Don Donato.

Whereupon he turned on his heels and headed down the church steps in the opposite direction.

Don Donato was prepared for this very avoidance. Leisurely, he put the Caddy in gear and pulled out of his space, weaving his way against the flow of traffic to navigate around to the back of the church. This took several minutes; there is nothing in the universe quite so determined as a departing Catholic. In time, though, the Cadillac made its way to the rear of the church, just in time to intercept Sergeant Franzetti, who stood with his back to the auditorium door puffing on a Pall Mall. He seemed to not even notice the white DeVille inching up to his position and finally coming to rest. Nor did he appear to hear the hum of the electric window as it lowered no more than twenty feet away. Nor was he startled when the don stuck his hand through the opening and called out to him. "*Sergente!*"

Franzetti looked up, sucked a last drag from his smoke, tossed it to the pavement, and stubbed it out with his shoe. Then, slowly, he approached the car, strode to the passenger door, and got inside.

"I'm ready," the don said.

"How many?" asked the cop.

"Five, plus me."

"One thousand fifty dollars," said Franzetti.

"When do I get them?" the don inquired.

"When do you need them?"

"Yesterday."

The policeman flashed a sardonic smile. "Well, Donato, I can't blame you. This is a decision you will not regret." Franzetti checked his watch. "I can drop them by your house at about seven."

"Not my house."

"OK, your travel agency, if you like."

"No," the don insisted. "Bring them to the social club. Meet me in the back room. I'll have the money. And bring the powder."

"That'll be more money. And I'm not sure I can get my hands on—"

"You want the money? Bring the powder."

CHAPTER 31

CONFESSION

"IN THE NAME OF THE FATHER AND OF THE SON AND OF THE HOLY Spirit. Amen."

"May the blessings of the Lord be upon you. As we know from the gospel of John, 'If we confess our sins, he is faithful and just, and will forgive our sins and cleanse us from all unrighteousness.' I am happy to hear your voice."

"Thanks, Father. Me too…I mean, I'm happy to hear your voice too. PS, bless me, Father, for I have sinned."

"Yes. Go on."

"It has been pretty long since my last confession. I don't know exactly. It was with Monsignor. I remember he thought I was my sister, and I let him think I was her for a while, and I think he got pretty mad. Because of the sacrament and all."

"You tricked Monsignor in the confessional?"

"Just for a second, Father. I might have squealed on her a little, but anyway, it wasn't a lie. It was true. She made out with Michael Petrocelli in the middle of *The Mod Squad*, and she let him get to second base, so I confessed for her. It was all true, although I might have kind of exaggerated."

"Explain."

"I might have said third base. I was, like, fifteen. Did you see *Parent Trap*? It was sort of like that."

"Why don't we move on? What are your sins?"

"I gossiped lots of times. I took the Lord's name in vain many times. I charged Mrs. Durante half for a missed appointment even though I had a walk-in that took her slot. Also, if we're going all the way back, I had sexual relations outside of marriage."

"But you're not married."

"Some of the guys were. Also, I used contraceptives."

"When did you last have sexual relations?"

"It's been a while, Father, because I am in love."

"Love! Happy to hear that. He is single, I hope?"

"Oh, yeah, absolutely. He's the singlest. No problem there, Father. But I've had indecent thoughts, mainly about him fucking my tits, but also good ones about cooking for him and having kids."

"No need to be so graphic, I think, Tina."

"But, Father, you don't understand. All I can think of is his cock pressed between my breasts. It's all I think about. And also intercourse too. That and kids, which I want to have a houseful of."

"All right. Enough of the details, please. Have you revealed your inclinations to your fiancé?"

"Oh, he's not my fiancé, Father. He's just a friend at the moment. He doesn't even know I want to have relations with him. I mean, he sort of does, but then again, he doesn't."

"And he has not transgressed with you, correct?"

"Hah. Not even close. He's got, like, a one-track mind, and it ain't me he's thinking about."

"Is the man a homosexual?"

"I don't think so, Father, although I couldn't swear to it. I just want him to love me in every way, but he just looks right through me, which has led me to many indecent thoughts. Titty fucking isn't even the worst."

"Perhaps you should schedule a counseling session with me so we discuss these matters outside the confessional. Please see me or Mrs. Giufrida to make an appointment. Are you ready for your penance?"

"Yes, Father."

"Then…"

"Oh, right. 'Lord Jesus, Son of God, have mercy on me, a sinner.'"

"Say one hundred Hail Marys and one hundred Our Fathers. God, the Father of mercies, through the death and resurrection of his Son, has reconciled the world to himself and sent the Holy Spirit among us for the forgiveness of sins; through the ministry of the Church, may God give you pardon and peace, and I absolve you from your sins in the name of the Father, and of the Son, and of the Holy Spirit."

"Amen."

CHAPTER 32

WATCHDOG

ON SUNDAY AFTERNOON, MR. MATTRESS CLOSED AT 5:00, AT WHICH point the proprietor did something that was—in the modern history of Ebbets Beach commerce—wildly unorthodox. He called the police. In ordinary circumstances, nuisances large and small were dealt with through extralegal means, sometimes through the business association, sometimes through the Donato family. As a newbie, this subtlety was lost on Jack, who was crazy enough to think that his civic duty and personal safety demanded the reporting to authorities of a brazen extortion attempt by toughs obviously connected with the Russian mob.

He'd felt no such civic impulse with Casper, partly because of Larry's bizarre endorsement, partly because Casper was so manifestly benign. This episode, on the contrary, was terrifying. The goonskis had been chillingly polite as they listed all of the hazards facing a small business. They never mentioned the fire at the barbershop up the boulevard, and Mr. Mattress was disinclined to bring it up. He'd been long enough at the Village Association meeting, however, to know that the fire was suspicious. He'd also been long enough in Fantasyland to assume the Donatos had nothing to do with it.

"Let me think this over," he'd told them.

"Of course" was the answer. "Think for one week."

And so he called the cops.

Here's what doesn't happen when you call the police on Labor Day weekend to report a gangland crime in which no explicit threats are made, no money changes hands, no assault takes place, and no property is damaged: a visit by a policeman to investigate the incident. Here's what does happen: a lot of confusion at dispatch about which unit has jurisdiction in matters of cross-cultural exchanges between polite Russians and merchants named after bedding. The NYPD, the district attorney, the FBI, the state police, and the US Attorney are awash in organized-crime task forces and strike forces and flying squads—none of which is on any dispatcher's speed dial. So, the bottom line is, when your life and business have been implicitly threatened by brutal killers, what happens is you are told to call the DA's office on Tuesday.

Unless one of the sociopaths shoplifted, in which case an officer will be sent immediately.

So Jack took a stroll up the boulevard to the Legal Aid Society, against the chance that the feisty, nepotistic nerd vamp would be burning the 6:00 oil. He peered into the storefront window, and, by golly, there she was. Christ, she was beautiful. He knocked on the window. Angela looked up and scowled. Or squinted. Jack couldn't tell. She gestured toward the door, and there they were one more time, face-to-face, with who knows what who's-on-first vaudeville in store.

"Hi," he said.

"Hello."

"I guess I'll get right to the point."

"OK," she replied.

"It's possible, based on certain events of the last eight hours, that our interests have converged."

Angela blinked. She wasn't getting it.

"Big Manny–wise," Jack added.

This news animated the lawyer. "Really?" she smiled. "That's a turnabout."

"All credit to you, for your seductive way of approaching me. Very *Strangers on a Train*."

"All right, all right. I'm sorry. Maybe I shouldn't believe everything I read. And maybe someday you'll enlighten me as to what—"

"What *Advertising Age* and the New York State Supreme Court somehow missed?"

"If that's something you want to do."

"Not necessarily," said Mr. Mattress. "It's not a chapter of my life I like to dwell on. Let's just say, whatever you think you know about me, you know not at all. Now, can we move on? I want talk to you about Big Manny. About your job-placement scheme. Suddenly, it may work for me."

"I'm delighted, of course," said Angela, "but…What happened in the last eight hours to change your mind? Can you tell me?"

Why not? Mr. Mattress briefed the Legal Aid Society about the Russians. He raised the issue of the barbershop. He described his experience with the police. Then he laid out his thinking: Maybe the presence of Big Manny—who did not announce his retirement in *The New York Times*—might discourage the Russians from acting out. And if Manny was as brilliant with the books as Angela represented, this could potentially free Mr. Mattress to attend to sales, marketing, and dinner in a way he hadn't hitherto allocated.

"Dinner?" said Angela.

Mr. Mattress smiled winningly. "Well, isn't that nice? I'd love to."

CHAPTER 33

POWDER

GIVEN THE STATE OF EMERGENCY, THE DON HAD DECLARED EVERY night *riunione* night for the duration. As usual, the boys wandered in to hang out in the back room of the club until they were welcome to join the don at the banquet table. This evening, though, there was unexpected company in the back room: the don himself. One by one, the gang arrived, and one by one, they were startled. It was as if they were cooks at Mickey D's and went through the back door only to find Ronald McDonald sitting on a milk crate stealing a smoke.

Disconcerting, in other words. But also vaguely diminishing of the boss's majesty. The soldiers lounged in the back because they were soldiers. The don sat in the dining room because he was the don. It was hard to know what to do, what to say, where to sit or stand. The reaction as each entered was comical, but each did exactly the same thing. Marco was the first to arrive. He entered the back room, tossed a plastic shopping bag on a card chair, and stopped in his tracks.

"Don Donato," he said. Right first time. Still, he was frozen.

"Relax, Marco," said the don, gesturing for his soldier to take a load off. "Take a load off."

Next came Casper. "Don Donato."

"Relax, Casper."

"Don Donato."

"Relax, Calculator."

"Don Donato."

"Relax, Little Manny."

"Don Donato."

"Relax, Teeth."

Oh, they were *so* relaxed. Relaxed like a charley horse. The nervous silence was ear splitting. Finally, Little Manny broke the tension.

"Ain't seen you back here in a while, Don."

"Necessity is the mother of invention," the don announced, "in the wise words of the famous vocalist Mr. Frank Zappa—who, by the way, Casper, was not afraid to entertain a wedding with *Lu Sciccareddu*, because this man never run from his Sicilian roots."

Huh? thought Little Manny. *Frank Zappa was as Sicilian as a fuckin' chopstick.*

I thought that mother shit come from the guy on the C-note, thought everyone else but Tony the Teeth, because they—unlike the don—had learned something about the Founding Fathers by achieving the ninth grade.

Invention, thought Tony the Teeth. *Fuck's he talking about?*

Fuck he was talking about was this: The situation was dire and moving fast, too fast. On the chronic side, revenues were plummeting. On the acute side, the Russians were making their move in spectacular, pyrotechnical fashion. Some basic facts of Family life—unquestioned and immutable for decades—were suddenly in flux, including strategy, tactics, business model, and even allegiances. Was it possible they would negotiate with the Russians, losing a slice of a shrinking pie? Yes. Everything was on the table.

Everything. All heads turned and jaws dropped when the door creaked open and into the back room barged a familiar figure. The crew tried to be cool, but nobody could believe his eyes. Jesus, Mary, and Joe Friday—it was the cop, Franzetti, out of uniform as usual, the piece of shit. He was carrying a parcel stuffed with what might have been bricks and, resting on it, a briefcase. Incredibly, the don stood in greeting. His soldiers reflexively followed.

"Well, ain't you polite?" Franzetti sneered. "Have a seat, men. We got work to do."

Five heads pivoted toward the don, who had a Tasmanian devilish smile on his face.

"*Famiglia*," he said, with a sweep of the hand arcing from the ragged semicircle of ruffians to the police sergeant, "meet your upline."

The men didn't so much sit in their card chairs as collapse in them, scarcely believing their own jaded eyes. Methodically, Franzetti opened his attaché case and removed a pile of glossy folders, each stuffed with documents of some kind, and distributed them around the room. The soldiers gaped in gathering disbelief at the handouts, on which was imprinted *Amway Opportunity Kit*.

"Congratulations, fellas," said the cop, "you are now independent business owners, with access to the tools to carve your own financial destiny. You report to yourself and yourself alone, but with the support, counsel, and guidance of your upline, who is"—Franzetti nodded toward the don, who raised his hand and waved it slightly, like the vice principal being introduced on back-to-school night—"and immediately upstream of Donato is yours truly. I am very excited to have you dickweeds in my organization."

The soldiers shuffled through their papers, which included application forms, guidelines for distributors, and FAQs about multilevel marketing.

Q: Why do Amway meetings appear to some people like a cult?

A: Amway meetings are full of energy, enthusiasm, and excitement—just like most sales motivation meetings—because this is a proven way to motivate people to sell Amway products and build their businesses by sponsoring others. Some people aren't accustomed to that. Yet, most successful companies know that enthusiastic meetings increase morale and boost results in any sales force. This enthusiasm motivates our distributors to help and support one another, and that builds sales.

As Leonard the Calculator read that one, he started to laugh. He suppressed it at first, but it was no use. He was shaking in his chair, trying to make no noise, but the laughter squeaked out of him. This accomplished the very thing he was trying to avoid: capturing the attention of Don Donato.

"May I ask you, Leonard, what you are finding so fucking funny?"

"Sorry, Don," he squeaked. He didn't much wish to share, since what set him off was imagining Marco at some sales revival meeting, sharing his enthusiasm to lift up himself and his colleagues. (Motivational speaker: "What kind of year are we going to have?" Marco: "Medium!")

"Oh, no, let's hear it. Let's all hear it. What is so funny that you insult our new partner?"

The others looked down at their folders and made a show of looking studious. Casper, for instance, pored over a brochure listing a handful of offerings from the vast array of household cleaning products, cosmetics, small appliances, nutritional supplements, electronics, and furniture the crew would now be offering, and most likely highly recommending, in addition to their standard fare of financial services, security, and abject fear. Leonard, meanwhile, had been sobered by the don's annoyance but still stood mute until the cop, whether out of kindness or impatience, pulled the fat from the fire by simply proceeding with his spiel.

"How it works is, I get a percentage of everything sold by everyone downstream of Donato, which includes you and everyone in the organizations you will build. In turn, you will get a percentage of everything sold by everyone you sign up, and everyone they sign up, and everyone they sign up, so forth and so on till you can walk up to Donato loaded down with bankrolls and tell him to go fuck himself."

Incredibly, Don Donato laughed appreciatively at the affectionate little insult, liberating the soldiers to nervously chuckle themselves. That ended abruptly when the Calculator chose—once again and for what reason nobody could possibly imagine—to blurt out the obvious.

"So it's a pyramid," he said.

He was beginning to become a daredevil. Not one minute earlier, he had irritated the boss and escaped only by the intervention of the cop. This time, he infuriated the cop himself. This gave everyone the opportunity to see what Franzetti looked like three nights earlier when the old lady Troncelitti was kicking him in the balls. His face went crimson, the veins bulging in his neck.

"Look at your FAQs!" he hollered. "This ain't no pyramid scheme, because the buy-in is low and totally refundable. This is multilevel marketing, which Amway has been the leader of for more than fifty years, totally legal and aboveboard right down the line. And you tell that to any prospect who may have gotten bad information from gossip or the media, which I don't have to remind you has a bias against free enterprise."

Just for the record, not one of the assembled independent business owners minded one iota if it was a pyramid scheme. Schemes, they had no problem with. Don Donato sitting there taking attitude from some fucking cop, they did.

Tony the Teeth, looking through his kit, focusing on a flier headlined *Realize Your Dreams!*, inquired, "They give out these boats?"

The cop shook his head. "You build a downline, and they give you a boat to drive to your private island."

Marco had a question too. "What's that package?" he squeaked.

All eyes turned to the parcel of bricks, which Franzetti promptly unwrapped to reveal not bricks but powder. Soap powder. Six boxes of SA8, the laundry detergent.

"This here," Franzetti said, brandishing a box for his new downline, "is what built our company. I got some news for you: it makes Tide look like fucking baby powder. This here, you dipshits, is concentrated."

CHAPTER 34

INSTRUCTIONS

PAOLO, THE WAITER, TIMIDLY ENTERED THE BACK ROOM, ALL BUT backing up as he advanced to the don and whispered in his ear. The don nodded.

"There is a phone call, from a Russian, for 'the telemarketer.' Little Manny, I am thinking that is you."

Franzetti put his hands on his hips. "What's that about, Donato? You expanding your horizons?"

Don Donato ignored the policeman entirely. "I need one hundred seventy-five dollars from every one of you," the don announced, "plus…"

"Twelve bucks," Franzetti said.

"…plus twelve bucks for the powder, total of one hundred eighty-seven. Little Manny, go talk to your friend. I'll get you after."

Little Manny complied, following the waiter into the dining room.

"You men need to fill out these forms and bring them to dinner tomorrow—carbonara, by the way."

The don collected the cash from his soldiers and handed it over to Franzetti, who then explained the mysteries of independent business ownership and sketched the path for a Brooklyn mook to achieve his wildest dreams.

"Everything in the Amway catalog is manufactured according to the strictest standards and can go head-to-head with any name-brand product in the world," he told them. "And the beauty part is, you don't have to go sell none of that shit. All you have to do is build up your own downlines and let them sell to their cousins and neighbors and so forth, and also build their own downlines who do the same thing. You basically fill orders and count the money. Now, let me show you something. This here will get you more business than you can believe. I need a glass of water and a cup of coffee. You, what's your name?" He was speaking to Casper.

"Casper," said Casper.

"Get me a glass of water, a cup of coffee, and a spoon."

Casper looked at the don, who nodded. Meanwhile, at the maître d's podium, Little Manny took the phone.

"Yeah, it's me."

"Mr. Ebbets Beach," said a Russian voice.

"You got it. OK, we got a location. Neutral territory. Adams and Tillary in Brooklyn Heights, northeast corner. It's a diner called Ambrosia. Windows to the street. One entrance you can see from every table. Two radio cars sitting outside to guard the bridge. Sorry, Ivan, no blintzes. We meet tomorrow at noon. You bring yourself and one other guy. We bring the don and me. We see anyone from Little Odessa, the summit is off. You got that?"

"Is varehouse at Milton and Vest. Rear entrance in alley. Locked vith chain. Bring bolt cutter, open door. Big table to right. Be there at six thirty in morning Tuesday. Not six thirty-vun. Brings vun guy, two guy, whole army. Brings guns. Rocket launcher. H-bomb. Doesn't matter. This is matter: every man vear cowboy hat."

Little Manny's mind raced. Cowboy hats? For what? To ID them? To make them better targets? And how would he scout this location in time? It wasn't a Brighton Beach address, sounded like Greenpoint to him, but he had no idea of the layout of the block, much less the warehouse. Should he accept? They still had thirty-six hours to pull out. But, no, the situation was too blind, the meeting point too hidden. Too many concessions, too many unknowns. He would have to refuse. The don would understand. He would have to.

"Sorry, Ivan. No can do. You're gonna have to do better than this. We're not going into some fucking warehouse completely isolated like this. We might bring an army, but we ain't walking our army into no fucking ambush. You don't like Brooklyn Heights? No problem. You give me something just as protected. You call back in one hour. We clear? Hello? Hello? HELLO?"

Little Manny slammed down the phone.

"Fuck me!" he shouted.

Heads turned. The diners saw who was throwing the ram and quickly snapped their heads and gazes on their own veal and linguine. Staring is rude. Staring at angry loan sharks is stupid.

Little Manny stomped back into the back room, arriving just in time to see something unusual. All eyes were on the cop as he removed half a teaspoonful of SA8 and, using the handle of a spoon, stirred it into a glass of water. Then, using the spoon's business end, he stirred two lumps of sugar into a cup of coffee. His pinkie jutted outward as he stirred. Once satisfied, he lifted the cup and took a small sip, pursing his lips and raising his eyebrows in a gesture of further satisfaction. Then he took a step toward Casper, raised the cup to his lips for one more sip, and slurped it into his mouth. Then, suddenly, he tossed the remainder of his coffee onto Casper's white-on-white dress shirt. How more dramatically to demonstrate the amazing stain-removing power of superconcentrated SA8? It was dramatic, all right. In the following five seconds, Casper grabbed Franzetti by the collar, punched him three times in the face, and kneed him in his fragile testicles.

"Yo, dipshit," Casper declared as his colleagues pulled him away, "concentrate that."

Little Manny swiveled his head to see how the don reacted. For the second time that evening—setting a world's record as far as anybody knew—scary, scary, scary Vic the Vig was having himself a very hearty laugh.

CHAPTER 35

ROMANCE

FIRST DATES ARE, OF COURSE, HORRIBLE.

The exchange of autobiographies, the career résumés, the retrospective of failed relationships, the disclosure of family conflicts, the plumbing of the other's tastes and politics, the bookshelves and iPods and filmographies, the precarious business of exporting or importing humor, the feigning of interest and manufacture of charm, the perfunctory declaration of hopes and dreams, the groundwork—exploratory and provisional—for future intimacy. Even very-near-future intimacy. It's so exhausting, and often enough degrading, involving as it does subtle and less-than-subtle dishonesty at almost every stage. "Nice to meet you. I ejaculate prematurely and care only about sports"—a stipulation never in human history so stipulated.

All of this for the longest of longshots, the sucker's bet that anything whatsoever will click. It's a nuisance for most people— i.e., people whose fathers aren't notorious sociopaths. When the family business is a continuing criminal enterprise, it's funny how the exchange of iPod contents never comes up. What comes up is a litany of stupid questions about Family life, or very salient questions you don't wish to answer, or the sudden recollection of an early, early flight, followed by "Check please." This was one reason Angela didn't date much. The other reason is that, in her twenty-eight years, she had seldom been asked out by anyone she could imagine sleeping with, much less marrying, so what's the point? This was because she lived and worked in Ebbets Beach and harbored a deep-seeded prejudice against morons. She'd dated in school and when she worked in the public defender's office, but her luck was poor. Men lusted after her because she was the reincarnation of Natalie Wood. They were also intimidated by her, in part because she was aloof verging on hostile and in part because they did not want to be murdered. This left a pool consisting mainly of narcissists who fancied themselves capable of taming the shrew, sweet imbeciles like Casper who fixated on her from various degrees of afar, and soulless lotharios who coveted a mafia princess to add to the trophy case.

Yet here she was, on the cozy patio of a little northern Italian *osteria*, owned by a cheerful Croat named Igor, tucked onto far East 88th Street by Gracie Mansion, with a man who called himself Mattress. Unlike most of her previous first-date experiences, this one was charged with possibilities. There had already been so much conflict, heated and passionate, wholly out of proportion to the slight acquaintanceship. There was the strange magnetism of their shared impurity, hers for living unestranged from her criminal family, his for whatever culpability in whatever crime he was a refugee from. Also, both of them were superfuckable. *Super*fuckable.

Jack stood when Angela arrived. They'd taken separate taxis so that he could drop in on an old friend. He didn't get to Manhattan much these days, but he did wish—for reasons of vanity or full disclosure, he wasn't sure—to show Angela where he came from. He moved around the small table to pull out her chair and said, "With this gesture, I apologize for everything so far, with no warranty expressed or implied on anything hereafter."

"Fine," she said, with as bright a smile as she'd given him so far, "me too."

"Good, now let me get some things out of the way. Favorite book, *Anna Karenina*. Favorite group, weirdly, Louie Prima and Keely Smith. Favorite movie, a tie between *The Sweet Smell of Success* and—sorry about this—*Goodfellas*. I hate walking on the fucking beach. The sand always winds up in my shorts. Never been married. Sign, diplodocus, the plant eater. Now, give it to me, baby."

"Book, *A Civil Action*. Group, weirdly, Guns N' Roses. Movie, *Casablanca*, duh. Sign, diphtheria, the infection, on the cusp with Porcelana, the medicated fade cream. Never been married, never been kissed."

"Never been kissed?" Jack inquired.

"Well," Natalie Wood replied, looking down as she arranged her napkin on her lap, "not today."

All right, that was settled. When this meal was all over with, they would sleep together. Now they could relax and talk, about Big Manny, about the comic-book otherworldliness of Ebbets Beach, about Bush and Obama, about public-interest law, about Paris and Rome, about the Vatican, about pornography, about artichokes, about Chris Rock, about *Mad Men*. Jack had the good grace not to bother her just yet about the family dynamics of murder and mayhem. Angela, in turn, did not inquire about his unsavory or ununsavory past.

Angela dined on mixed salad and braised veal. Mr. Mattress had black risotto and grilled calamari. They shared a bottle and a half of a light, fruity Swiss merlot. In the taxicab to Brooklyn, they kissed and pawed like teenagers. They slept on the mattress of Mr. Mattress, but not much.

CHAPTER 36
SHOPPING

"COWBOY HATS? NO FUCKING WAY."

Little Manny shrugged. "No, Casper, the don says we gotta do it."

"We'll be sitting-fucking-ducks."

"Don says not to worry. He and Teeth have it covered. It'll just be him and Tony and me. You, Marco, and Calculator will be staked out outside. Any problems in the warehouse, we pick off the Russians when they walk to their cars—kaboom. Which he says the Russians know, so they won't make no stupid move, he says."

"Oh yeah?" said Casper. "So you got a cowboy hat? Tony the Teeth has a cowboy hat?"

"Course not. The don neither. Big deal. Tomorrow, we get a few."

"Really? Tomorrow?"

"Yeah, tomorrow."

"So where do you get a cowboy hat on a holiday weekend?"

"Simple. A hat store."

"Ralph, ain't no hat store gonna be open tomorrow."

"Tough shit. I got a key."

"You got a key to a hat store? What the fuck you talking about?"

"Casper, a cinder block key."

"Oh. OK. Got it."

"Yeah, and you're not gonna believe this. They give me orders. Tony the Teeth wants a hat like Clint Eastwood."

Casper, ordinarily as generous of spirit as any mob gorilla, doubled over laughing. Tony the Teeth was Clint Eastwood the way Little Manny was Audrey Hepburn. He laughed himself to tears, in a squeaky falsetto that sounded nothing like Bobby Darin. "And what," he quavered, "about the don?"

Now Little Manny laughed. "You ready for this?"

Casper was still roaring, even more in anticipation of whatever Little Manny would tell him. He could barely catch his breath he was laughing so hard. "Yeah…ready…tell me."

"You sure?" Now Little Manny was coming unglued. The two of them had lost control of their motor functions. They looked as if they had twin cases of Saint Vitus Dance. Little Manny couldn't speak. He held his index finger up, indicating, *Wait till I catch my breath*, which he was having trouble doing. The laughter was shaking him. His shoulders seemed to be bouncing independently of the rest of his body.

"Come on! Tell me!" Casper begged.

"OK, Casper…ha ha ha ha…Don Donato wants one like…ha ha ha ha ha ha ha ha." Little Manny fell to the floor, rolling, laughing, gasping, snotting himself till he all but retched.

"Who?" Casper screamed, as best he could through his own convulsions. "Who?"

"Ha…huhh…huhhh…huhhhh…"

"*Who?*"

"Hooo…hahh…huhhh…h…h…h…*HOSS!*"

Cartwright. Now both soldiers were on the floor, flailing and hooting. Yet, through the hilarity, the hyenas somehow managed to hum in hysterical unison.

"*Dumdiddy dumdiddy dumdiddy dumdiddy DUMMM-DUMMMMM. Dumdiddy dumdiddy dumdiddy dumdiddy dumdiddy dum-dum DUMMMM.*"

They rolled on the floor in euphoric agony, hugging their own midsections, keening like hired Sicilian mourners. Hoss! It was a bonanza.

CHAPTER 37

LABOR DAY

AT 9:00 A.M. IT WAS NINETY DEGREES. ALL ALONG THE BOULEVARD, the merchants dreaded the day ahead. They'd be standing on the sidewalk for hours, in the scorching sun, handing out refrigerator magnets and hot dogs and snow cones and beer cozies, all on the theory that the freebies would attract Ebbets Beachians to the Village for the best deals of the summer. That was the *Sale* part of the Sale-a-Bration. In these temperatures, the level of *Bration* was anybody's guess. Why leave your air-conditioned home for a dollar's worth of shaved ice or eighty-seven cents' worth of practically cheeseless pizza? It was all particularly problematic for Larry, the Parrothead sandwich slinger, who depended on the recipients of free food to venture into his place to pay for food. In previous years, remarkably, J&L's did enjoy an uptick of traffic and sales on Labor Day, but not at a level to justify sweltering on a sidewalk over a helium tank blowing up balloons for brats. Yet he, uniquely among his retail neighbors, looked forward to the annual event. Indeed, he was the chief organizer, not out of direct self-interest at the cash register, but in the name of building excitement and familiarity for the Village as a whole.

And why? So one day the DINKS would move in, and the gays, and the single professionals, and the other urban pioneers, and turn

Ebbets Beach into the next Williamsburg. Because Larry, unlike almost all the other merchants save the poor barber, owned his own building with nine apartments above the store and also the one that housed the Parcel Plus, and he had been waiting twenty years for prices to elevate enough—his target was $1.6 million—so that he and the better half could get out of this hellhole and move to the Virgin Islands where they belonged. All they wanted from life was to waste away in Margaritaville, not this stinking sauna. Until that day arrived, no sacrifice—not even Labor Day heatstroke—was too great if it served the greater good of property values. This was why he so accepted the Donato crew. The way Larry saw things, they were on the same page.

When 10:00 came, sweat was already pouring off of Larry in sheets. The temperature had climbed to ninety-four. Yet, amazingly, there they were, clotting on the pavement for nearly worthless handouts. He was happy. Larry looked down the sidewalk and laughed to himself. Tina Donato was filling snow cones—and the eyeballs of passing males. She was stuffed into microscopic white-duck cutoffs, cork-heeled canvas sandals inclined like twin sliding boards, and the world's last remaining tube top. Light blue and bulging. The immediate consequence was a cluster of teenage boys forcing their way past little kids to get second and third snow cones.

Right next to her, in front of the agency, Casper manned a skirted card table next to a mammoth West Indian registered nurse named Lolita on one side and a movie-poster-sized tent card on the other. FREE BLOOD PRESSURE SCREENING. COURTESY OF YOUR COZY NOSTRA. With Big Manny's previous permission, which Casper had not troubled himself to reconfirm with the Don, he also had a big stack of CDs, self-produced, *Casper Sings Cole*, fifteen dollars a pop. By noon, he'd sold six of them, given one away to a babe he'd fucked on the Fourth of July, and given a five-dollar discount to some old lady whose pressure was 175/141 and he figured wouldn't live to hear "Too Darn Hot."

At 12:15 p.m., along came Angela Donato. She had slept late at Jack's place, waking long after he had left to man the store. And, in a way that she hadn't since…forever, she felt euphoric. Who knew if this was the beginning of something important, but it had been profound unto itself. This man had touched her, in many ways. He had made her laugh. He had made her feel important. He had made her feel tender. He had made her come. He had made her a pot of coffee and a frittata, with simple instructions for microwave heating (in the blocky, stylized hand of an architect, or, as it happened, art director). He had made her want to inhabit his apartment, and at least the next week of his life.

As she pivoted toward the office, she did not even notice the man sitting next to the overstuffed nurse.

"Hello, Angela."

"Casper! How…um…How are you?"

"Good. Missed you Friday."

"Yeah, Friday. Sorry. I had a brief to file and a client came in very late. I'd really love to see you sing sometime."

"I'd like to see you sometime, singing or not, Angela."

Oh shit. How, after all these years, could this man possibly imagine she was interested? Doesn't an entire decade of avoidance send any sort of message? Anything at all? But, suddenly, Angela realized she had an opportunity. She had never been able to lie to Casper, and she had never been able to tell him the truth, but now she could say something that once and for all would put this sad nonaffair to rest. And she could say this thing because—it thrilled and terrified her to realize—the words might be entirely accurate.

"Oh, Casper, I don't think my boyfriend would be very happy about that."

Then, for precisely the second time—the first being at the prom ten years earlier—she leaned down to peck the king on the cheek and made her way briskly past him into the Legal Aid Society of Ebbets Beach. This way she didn't have to see the pain on his face, the crushing, humiliating, infuriating, and, most of all, jealous pain. Casper's face darkened, and so did the sky.

A cold front was moving rapidly into the city and was about to broadside a tanker truck full of hot, humid air. The clouds became engorged, first as if with ash, then bile. They cast a heavy shadow over the city and by the time the thunder rumbled had achieved a sickly green. The rumble gave way to a huge distant explosion and a blinding instant of acetylene-white light. Then came the rain, pouring sideways as if dumped from a million heavenly trash cans in the path of God's blow-dryer, flooding the boulevard to the curb as trees bent limbo-style and lightning flashed viciously ever closer. Merchants and shoppers alike scurried into whatever shop was nearest. Little Manny, dry in his T-Bird but unable to see the street six feet in front of him, cursed God.

"Jesus fuck!" he screamed. "I got shopping to do!"

Tomorrow would require an early start, and anyway, *riunione* was at 7:00, so he'd contrived to head for Brooklyn Heights by day to outfit the summit. With rain gushing out of storm sewers and streets pooling like black lagoons, it took him two hours to make the fifteen-minute drive to the East River. He arrived in ill humor at one of the two hat stores he had identified in Brooklyn. In his trunk, he had two cinder blocks and a crowbar, to make quick work of his window-shopping. He threaded his way through the overflowing streets, crawling through Carroll Gardens on Court Street, detouring past the Long Island College Hospital, finally locating the corner of Henry and Montague. There, halfway down Montague, was Huggins & Huggins Hats. He took the turn and, to his horror, was instantly jettisoned from rainstorm to shitstorm. The front window of Huggins & Huggins featured plenty of cowboy hats but was protected by a locked accordion gate. The window was unsmashable. Little Manny said more bad words. It was nearly 2:30 as he pulled away, headed for Williamsburg.

Labor Day traffic is notoriously heavy, but Ralph was not on the New Jersey Turnpike. Nor even the parking lot that was the BQE under the best of circumstances. He was on Flushing Avenue. No matter. The flooding had created gridlock throughout the borough, which was looking more like Venice than Brooklyn. Little Manny spent a half hour going one block from Montrose to Meserole, pounding on his horn and cursing, as if the schmuck in front of him were any less stymied. By the time he pulled up to The Hat Rack on Devoe Street, just past Graham, it was 4:09. Little Manny took one look and screamed to heaven and hell.

Accordion gate. Every store on the block, in fact, was protected by an accordion gate—every shop but one, two doors down. Fogelman's Costumes. *Why couldn't the fucking Ivans ask for Dracula capes?* Little Manny thought as he angrily eyed all the perfectly accessible merchandise that was no use to him whatsoever. But then he saw them, obscured in the back of the window display by a fairy godmother: four western hats. Two red ones for little cowboys, two pink ones for little cowgirls.

"Fuck it," he grunted. Little Manny ducked out of the car into a drenching rain, liberated a cinder block from his trunk, and hurled it at the plate glass. The shattering of the window, as luck would have it, was completely drowned out by a thunderclap that made Little Manny jump half out of his sneakers. Covering his face with his hand to shield himself from jagged glass and security cameras, he grabbed all the headgear a junior cowhand could ever wish for, got back into the T-Bird, and took the fuck off.

CHAPTER 38

SPAGHETTI CARBONARA

THE *RIUNIONE* WAS JOVIAL, SEEMINGLY ALL OUT OF PROPORTION to the circumstances.

Marco was supposed to have scouted a secure venue for the summit, and returned with what he claimed was an ideal spot. But the Russians evidently weren't impressed. It had been a fool's errand. The don, however, seemed satisfied. He was certain there would be no violence, and he rather liked the idea of talking business within a vast industrial space, versus some crowded restaurant where some nosy civilian or even cop could eavesdrop. Casper, on a hush-hush assignment for the boss, had also come up empty-handed so far—but he had, after all, warned Don Donato that there were no Assassin-a-Brations. The soldiers, upon filing in at 7:15, were a bit stunned to see Casper already at the table; nobody ever intruded on the don while he enjoyed his two espressos. They could only guess Casper enjoyed early arrival privileges by special invitation, but as to why, they could not know. They also were unaware Casper's heart had a few hours earlier been torn out of his chest by the don's elder daughter, but were pleased that no such evisceration seemed to be in progress at the table. Marco was the only one to hear a fragment of the conversation, which was the don saying—in

Marco's estimation "medium cheerful"—something about wishing for "better fucking Yellow Pages."

Little Manny had nominally succeeded in his errand but was keeping mum on the particulars. The boss simply asked him if the goods were obtained, and he simply replied, "*Si*, Don Donato." The don's plans were coalescing quite well, so, on the whole, spirits were high. And why not a moment of optimism? The departure of Big Manny had created a void and cast a pall, but hadn't the Calculator performed spectacularly in a task that otherwise would never have fallen to him? In the space of twenty-four hours, Leonard had not only obtained a thorough dossier on Smirdov, but actually staked him out and followed him to his residence, which was not in Little Odessa at all, but in fancy-schmancy Park Slope. The tracking was facilitated by an unwitting accomplice: Smirdov's gigantic, hairy, slobbering dog, who walked with him like a Budweiser Clydesdale to his S-series Mercedes and sat panting in the rear seat for Leonard to follow the entire jagged route to the Russian's house. The dragon's lair turned out to be a handsome, nineteenth-century brownstone, with white impatiens spilling over from window boxes and a pink-and-purple bicycle tilted against the railing of the front stoop. Tony the Teeth already had plans for the address.

"Tonight?" inquired the don.

"Late," said Teeth, or gurgled it. He was swilling from a bottle of Mylanta, prophylactically. It was carbonara night. His stomach couldn't handle the stuff, but his mouth couldn't leave it alone. That was the second elevator of the Family's mood. Everyone in the crew loved carbonara night, and because daily *riunione* had accelerated the menu cycle, this was the second one in a month. Membership has its privileges, and upheaval has its rewards. Ambrosia, thy name is not Bolognese, nor linguine *vongole*, nor fettuccine Alfredo, nor lasagna, nor penne with pesto. Ambrosia, thy name is carbonara. For it is better than sex, and no hugging afterward.

"Louie knows the secret of this dish," said the don, referring to the social club chef, as he usually did on carbonara night. "The secret is the bacon. The secret is not too much bacon. Everybody, even my wife, uses too much bacon. It has to be crispy like a *grissini*, but you should barely see it. You should feel it, taste a shadow of it, and the crunch when it happens should be a gift, a surprise. And the eggs. Men, do you see any eggs? Is this an omelet? No, the eggs and the garlic and the parmesan have to melt into a cream— not a soup, not a gravy, just a film of cream. And when you toss the pasta in the pan, you don't fry it. You just seal the sauce to the *spaghet. Capische?*"

Yeah, they understood. This was from the liturgy. They knew it like the Creed. And to a man they could not reply, because they were wolfing down their spaghetti, because it was so phenomenally delicious, because Louie, the chef, had solved the mystery of the bacon, because on carbonara night the boss always picked up the check. They nodded and grunted and ate as if there would be no tomorrow—which might have been just as well.

CHAPTER 39

THE WAREHOUSE

"WE WILL TALK LATER."

"But, Don Donato—" Little Manny protested.

"We will talk later. And we will talk seriously."

So unfair, Little Manny thought. He'd made a heroic effort under horrendous conditions to fulfill a nearly impossible request. To his way of thinking, he deserved an attaboy, not the opprobrium of the boss. On the other hand, it was not lost on him that there was also the matter of dignity to consider. And simple anatomy. What he, Tony the Teeth, and the don had in common—apart from zero-balance Social Security accounts—was the size of their heads. Stupendously big, all three. Little Manny was little in no dimension. He was within two inches in height of Big Manny and weighed in at upward of 235 pounds. He didn't have his father's brains, but he certainly had his outsize cranium. And of the three of them, he was the delicate one. They didn't used to call Vic Donato "Taz" for no reason. His huge upper body was a mismatch for his skinny, short bowlegs, and his head was a mismatch for his body—like a snowman assembled upside down. A snowman with stubbornly black hair swept straight back and a bushy unibrow cantilevered over deep-set green eyes, vulture beak, and square jaw draped with stubbled jowls. Then there was Teeth. In the admittedly unlikely event his image were ever to be carved into Mount Rushmore, it could be done actual size. If he had a neck, nobody had seen it lately. He was a boulder in a half-sleeve shirt.

All of which is to say, at 6:28 on Tuesday morning, as the sun rose on Greenpoint—after squandering ten nerve-racking minutes in search of a Vest Street that turned out to be West Street—each one of these fearsome desperadoes looked extremely, extremely stupid in his tiny little cowboy hat. Out of a sense of responsibility and self-preservation, Little Manny made sure to grab a pink one. The older guys donned the marginally less humiliating reds. The hats were so small they rested atop the men's heads without cradling them, like organ-grinder monkeys of the Wild West. The chin cords were too short to be very useful, although the don briefly cinched it around his nose. The men kept their heads down, hands securing their chapeaus, as they hustled around to the side entrance, making sure they were in view of Casper, Marco, and Leonard—who were parked in three locations.

With Casper on West, Marco in the alley, and Leonard on Milton, they triangulated the warehouse. Sure enough, the fire doors facing the alley were secured by a steel chain. Little Manny used bolt cutters to make quick work of it, just as the Russian had dictated. Tony used a crowbar to finish the job, easily peeling back the right-hand door to reveal the interior of the dark warehouse. Dusty shafts of morning light filtered through filthy industrial windows, half illuminating a long, crude worktable ringed by metal folding chairs. It was 6:30 on the dot when the men took their seats.

The don let a thin smile cross his face. The Russians had managed to stage this little drama thinking they held an advantage. They thought that jerking around the family would leave the

Italians rattled and off balance. What the don knew—and what he was quite certain the Ivans did not—was that the advantage resided with him. By following the dictates of Smirdov, or whoever it was Ralph had been talking to, he permitted the smartasses to get comfortable. Recklessly comfortable. Meantime, what he also knew was that they had vastly overplayed their hand and were smack in the crosshairs of the cops. A faithful friend at NYPD had encountered a phone inquiry from an Ebbets Beach merchant— some new joint called Mattress City, or some such—complaining about threats from the Russian mob. The message had yet to wend its way through channels to the appropriate investigative unit, but already the don knew the Ivans' mistake: they had hinted to the mattress guy that the barbershop fire was their doing. This was priceless leverage. When the Ivans sat down to squeeze him out of some or all of his turf, he could say, "Be my guest. Every step you let fall in Ebbets Beach is one step closer to the penitentiary." Furthermore, as of a couple of hours ago, thanks to Tony the Teeth, the fear factor, too, favored the Cozy Nostra. Smirdov, devoted St. Bernard owner, had awakened to a grisly surprise.

Yet Tony the Teeth, stolid as ever, sat now with his massive arms on the table, his sausage hands clasped like the Catholic schoolboy he once was—as if nothing untoward, let alone bloodcurdling, had taken place. Little Manny fidgeted with the coins in his pocket and rocked back and forth, using the flimsy rear legs of his chair as a fulcrum. The don whistled a tune neither Tony nor Ralph could identify. Neither could have Patti Page, although the song the don was thinking of was "How Much is that Doggie in the Window?"

At five minutes before 7:00, the Russians had yet to show up, but this pleased the don even more. They would arrive arrogant and overconfident. This was hubris, and it would be their undoing. Then, at 7:00 sharp, all at once, the fluorescent lights flickered on, and moments later a loud whirring sound commenced. Yet still no company at the table. Perhaps a minute passed before the source of the whirring zipped past them. It was a forklift truck, on a path to a large pallet of cartons. The men looked all around them. Workers were arriving, and other forklifts were humming to and fro. A man in a hard hat and carrying a press-to-talk phone hurried toward them.

"Yo, buckaroos," he barked, "what do you think you're doing here?"

He was not Smirdov. He was a supervisor. This was not an abandoned warehouse; it was a working warehouse. The Russians were not present nor would they be. They were otherwise occupied, in Ebbets Beach, firebombing Coppedge's car wash.

The buckaroos did not know that. All they knew was that they had been made fools of. They threw their cowboys hats to the floor and stalked out of the building. Little Manny waved off the other soldiers standing by in their cars, signaling them to go home. Once the summiteers were in the don's Cadillac, with Little Manny at the wheel and Tony riding shotgun, the don questioned his goon.

"Teeth," he said to his goon, just to re-reassure himself, "you took care of that thing?"

"*Si*, Don Donato."

"You put it in his bed."

"Yeah, in his bed."

"Dead."

"Naturally, dead."

"How did you get into the house?"

"The usual. In other words, it's like riding a bike, Don. After all these years, I could still pick anything as easy as picking my nose."

"And how, may I ask, did you get the dead dog in his bed?"

Tony shrugged. "Yeah, Don, that I couldn't do, on account of my allergies, but no problem. I took care of things."

The don, already beside himself with humiliation, sprang forward in the backseat and slapped the back of Tony's head. "What the fuck are you telling me? You didn't kill his dog? What the fuck did you kill?"

"Me? Nothing."

"NOTHING? You just told me—"

"It was predead."

"Huh? Teeth, what are you saying? What the fuck was predead?"

"The lox."

"What fucking *lox*? Teeth. *WHAT FUCKING LOX?*"

"That I put in the Russian's bed to scare him. It's a Jew thing."

Tony the Teeth was being modest. It was not just any lox. It was hand-sliced nova. Two pounds!

On the floor at the boss's feet sat a lone kid's cowboy hat, pink, unneeded in the historic mob conference that had not just taken place. Don Donato snatched it from its resting place on the luxurious Cadillac deep-pile beige carpeting and used it—again and again and again and again—to swat his enforcer's *gigantesco cranio idiota*.

CHAPTER 40

LOVESICK

"NO YOU DID NOT!"

"Yeah-huh," Tina insisted.

"How can you even tell me this stuff?" the incredulous Sunny wanted to know. They were opening the shop Tuesday morning. "Isn't that shit secret? Isn't there some *Da Vinci Code* or something?"

"Not for me. For him, yeah. Not for me. What can I tell you, Sun? I just love him to death."

"But you said all that? About"—Sunny lowered her voice—"titty-fucking? What did he do? Did he, like, kick you out? He didn't come on to you, did he? Tell me he didn't. I couldn't handle that. Seriously."

"I don't know. He's behind a screen. He told me to get counseling."

"Maybe he was in there choking the chicken," Sunny ventured.

"Sunny! Gross!" Then Tina started to laugh. "I didn't hear no grunting."

There was almost nothing Tina couldn't tell Sunny. Her encounter with Father Steve was her first Catholic confession as an adult but not her first act of confidence. With Sunny, she shared every infatuation, every hookup, every dream, every embarrassment, every insult, every disappointment, every nugget of juicy gossip, every aspect of her life but what went on in her parents' home, where she still lived. Anything remotely touching on her father or his Family was strictly off limits, which Sunny well understood. And appreciated. Sure, she was curious, but there was some knowledge that was best not to have. This was one of the reasons the two bonded so well. Sunny showed respect. She didn't pal around with Tina because Tina was some sort of freak. She wasn't a hanger-on. She was a true friend.

"You are such a cunt!" the true friend squealed.

In a moment or two, though, the naughty hilarity subsided.

"Aw, Sunny, I know you think it's sicko, but you have to meet Father. He is so gentle, but also at the same time very manly. He's like…You know how all guys are just trying to impress you all the time like they're God's gift to women? Father, he's just himself. And he *is* God's gift."

"I hear you, Teen. But are you absolutely sure it's not some sort of, like, married-man thing? You only want what's not available? You know what I mean? Maybe he's just, like, forbidden fruit."

Tina thought that over. Then she shook her head. "I don't think he's a fruit."

More laughter. Then more quiet. Both women understood that beneath the superficial perversity of the situation was hidden a solemn dilemma. Tina had pushed it out of her mind. Sunny spoke it aloud.

"Teen, let's just say your priest was maybe interested. I mean, face it. I never met the man who didn't want to at least fuck you. So let's just say. But if you really love him—and, look, I don't know anything about your religion—but if you really love him and this isn't some sort of stupid crush like you always have, is it right to ask him to break his vows of chastity? You know what I'm saying?"

"Celibacy," Tina corrected.

"Yeah, that's what I mean. Celibacy. Wouldn't it be, like, cheating?"

Tina closed her eyes and pinched her lips together against the gathering emotion. She shook her head rapidly from side to side as her mouth twisted into a tortured grimace of a smile. She wasn't saying no. She was saying she didn't know.

Casper knew. He was in the midst of a very busy morning. But as he ducked out of the travel agency for an important meeting, he knew he was going to find the fuck who was banging Angela and do some banging himself.

CHAPTER 41

VALENTIN

THE RUSSIAN WASN'T.

Valentin Smirdov, thirty-eight, was from Moldova, a wretched sliver of Eastern Europe sandwiched between Romania and Ukraine. He was probably, but not certainly, a majority ethnic Russian in a country with large Ukrainian and Romanian and, until recently, Jewish minorities. He hailed from Tiraspol, Moldova's second-largest city and capital of the breakaway Pridnestrovian Moldavian Republic—aka, Transnistria—dominated by ethnic Russians. From 1990 to mid-1992, Smirdov fought with the separatists against the mainly Romanian-speaking Moldovan army and enhanced—although did not originate—his reputation for cruelty that he had long since acquired at the State Orphanage #3, where he had been warehoused from the age of four and reared in a laboratory of Darwinian struggle.

He was not a large boy to begin with, and as he reached adolescence his taller and bulkier comrades increasingly dwarfed him. Slight stature is a natural disadvantage in a survival-of-the-fittest environment, so he compensated by making himself very strong and extremely frightening. At the age of eleven, he gouged the eye out of a fifteen-year-old who was attempting to strong-arm the weekly slab of fatty meat from Smirdov's dinner plate. This earned him perfunctory thrashing from the indifferent adult staff and immediate respect from the minor population. Quickly, he learned the more boys he beat and humiliated, the more powerful he would be. By the time he was fourteen, he was the most feared boy in the facility—lean but muscular, vicious but canny. He was a teenage black marketeer, dominating a small but powerful orphanage trade in alcohol, soap, cigarettes, candy, pornography, dried beef, and, eventually, heroin. The latter he did not touch personally. Even at his tender age, he knew it was a tool for enslavement, and he used that tool well.

At the age of eighteen, he was discharged from the orphanage with the clothes on his back, nine hundred rubles, and one item of inestimable value. This was his Soviet passport, identifying him as Jewish.

It was possible that Smirdov was actually a Jew, in whole or in part. Until mass emigration in the 1980s, Jews had represented a large, oft-persecuted ethnic minority in Tiraspol. Under Gorbachev-era Glasnost and Perestroika, however, liberalized visa policies led to a latter-day exodus—and young Valentin was determined to be part of it, whatever and whoever his parents might actually have been. By the time of his mandatory expulsion at the age of eighteen, orphanage records from previous decades were missing, destroyed, or simply too hidden within the labyrinths of Soviet bureaucracy to bother looking for, and Smirdov was permitted to be Jewish by merely so declaring. All he needed to do was raise a stake to pay his way out of the USSR.

Luckily for him, the society he was disgorged into was in chaos. The Soviet Union was in midcollapse, leading to the declaration of an independent Moldova. But in Tiraspol the Russians and Ukrainians wanted no part of the new Romanian-dominated republic, so they took up arms. Soon, the menacing young Valentin Smirdov was in the fold. He was not a guerilla warrior in the purest sense; he harbored no ideology or political sympathies. It just so happened that the separatists gave him food, shelter, and all he could steal if only he would kill Romanians. When he desecrated corpses too, terrorizing the enemy, the rewards were even greater. By late 1992, he had parlayed his stature as a sociopath into control of a key smuggling route for arms, heroin, and the impoverished young women who rapidly were overtaking grain, furniture, and wine to become Moldova's leading export. By eluding Moldovan and Ukrainian authorities along the Transnistrian strip, smugglers were able to traffic girls to Turkey, Cyprus, and the Gulf States, where they were highly prized for their long legs, white skin, and abject desperation. They were the pale beyond the pale.

Young Valentin's lifelong goal was to immigrate to the States, to lead the life of an *Easy Rider* on the back of a Harley, leisurely smuggling dope from Mexico and fucking hippie girls along the way. Soon enough, though, his success made such a mom-and-pop enterprise seem ridiculously unambitious, on the verge of being quaint. He had become a heroin and flesh supplier for another fast-rising boss, Lev Krensky, a onetime driver for Brighton Beach kingpin Evsei Agron. After Agron's assassination in 1985, Krensky shared power with the fearsome Marat Balagula until Balagula was imprisoned for gasoline smuggling. Krensky's ascension corresponded with Smirdov's, and—sight unseen—the boss helped grease the skids for his new protégé's American Dream. In 1993, at the age of twenty-one, Valentin Smirdov landed at Newark International Airport on a rainy March evening. It was a Friday.

First thing Monday morning, another Krensky soldier drove him to Staten Island. The driver filled up his Chrysler Imperial while the new guy stabbed the gas station owner in the heart. For the next six months, Krensky unleashed Smirdov's savagery from Coney Island to Connecticut until history repeated itself; soon the slender brute was the most feared man in Brooklyn, even among the men he nominally served.

Those were different days. Despite his youth and inexperience, Smirdov was shocked at Krensky's association with the Gambino crime family, a relationship that had been forged by Agron and later Balagula to gain a foothold in Brighton Beach. As the business grew from local rackets to international heroin smuggling, and as the Russian mob's power increased, Krensky expanded his partnership with La Cosa Nostra. To Smirdov, this strategy made no sense. He implored the boss to squeeze the Italians out, which gradually they did in Brooklyn and the other four boroughs. Funnily enough, the key point of persuasion was Smirdov murdering three Gambinos and a Lucchese, all with Molotov cocktails. Not only was this guy a strategic thinker beyond his tender years, he was not afraid to roll up his sleeves to get things done. His can-do attitude and unflagging work ethic went unnoticed by nobody, and he rapidly gained favor with and influence over Boss Lev. But on one point Krensky was stubborn. The international drug trade was so obscenely lucrative he refused to sever his alliance with the Italians—an intransigence with catastrophic results. In January 1994, thanks to Gambino informants trying to exact vengeance and win a get-out-of-jail-free card for themselves, Krensky was arrested and charged with laundering tens of millions of dollars in drug money. This was both financially and organizationally devastating for the enterprise, creating the third Little Odessa power vacuum in nine years.

But not for long. The vacuum was quickly filled when Krensky's underboss was found decapitated on the steps of the Theodore Roosevelt Federal Courthouse. The head was found in a waste can above the Borough Hall subway station for the 2 and 3 trains. This mishap was also unnoticed by nobody. With very little internal resistance, twenty-two-year-old Valentin Smirdov assumed the throne of blood. He was just like Robert Morse in *How to Succeed in Business Without Really Trying*, minus the adorable gap-toothed grin and any shred of human feeling. Over the next nearly two decades, he further consolidated power, along the way to making the Brighton Beach mob a $130 million annual cash cow, a formidable army, and the most homicidal criminal organization north of the Rio Grande. And he was determined for his mob to remain so. This meant repeating none of the mistakes of his predecessors. In order to go unassassinated, he was protected twenty-four hours a day by a minimum of three soldiers, all of whom with families, all of which families would be annihilated if Smirdov were to come to harm. In order to not be arrested, he signed nothing, wrote nothing, and said nothing aloud that would implicate him in the vast portfolio of wrongdoing his people undertook every day. And to keep his organization safe from interlopers—police and criminal both—he enforced a rule about fraternization. If a Brighton Beach boy were caught talking to a cop, a Fed, an Italian wiseguy, a Crip, an MS-13 gangbanger, or the meter maid, the traitor would get to watch his wife, mother, and/or kids be shotgunned in the face. Then he would be buried alive. Just to make sure this was not perceived as an idle threat, when one of his soldiers got pulled in for DUI and did an overnight in a Queens lockup six months into the Smirdov dynasty, Smirdov personally shot the poor wretch's Down-syndrome son in front of the pleading father and everyone else, then locked the careless drinker in a refrigerated fur vault. He didn't pull out the corpse for ten days, although the shrieking and sobbing subsided after three.

CHAPTER 42

POWERLESSNESS

SATISFIED THAT, IF PUSH CAME TO SHOVE, BIG MANNY AND JITNEE could handle a transaction between them, Mr. Mattress headed up the boulevard toward Billie's. Manny's parting words were of some concern—"Nobody can prove no arson"—but Jack was pleased law enforcement was at least on the case. The latest fire had evidently gotten the cops' attention; it had certainly gotten Larry's. Jack and Angela were awakened by the sandwich man's hysterical screaming—which, incidentally, hadn't been entirely easy to decipher. If you wish to puzzle someone more than alarm him, phone him at 7:00 a.m. shrieking, "CAR WASH! CAR WASH!"

Now Jack was on his way to Billie's to meet Larry, the barber, the owner of the car wash, the cops, and one special guest star. Even at high noon, the walk was pleasant. Wet tree twigs and litter still clogged the sidewalk grates and sewer openings, remnants of a storm that had blown away several awnings and all of the heat and humidity. The temperature was in the midseventies and the air almost crisp. Autumn, along with ratcheting terror, had arrived overnight.

Jack was the first to arrive at the diner, where he took a booth in the far corner. The next was Henry Coppedge, whom Jack greeted with a hug of condolence and solidarity, though they'd never met.

Coppedge had spent the last five hours with police and fire investigators at his burned-out business and he stank like soot. Then came Larry, dressed as usual for a Jimmy Buffet concert. Then the barber, who struck Jack as looking sleepless and frail. Then came the cops, Detective Sergeant Peter Vukovich from something called the CCE Task Force and Special Agent Henry McWiggin from the federal Bureau of Alcohol, Tobacco, and Firearms. The bomb police. The cops were just squeezing into the booth when the final participant arrived.

Vukovich flinched. "What's that bozo doing here?" he snarled. The bozo was Casper, who apparently was violating the unwritten convention about no extortionists being present during a police investigation into extortion.

"Interested party," Mr. Mattress replied. Casper raised one hand, as if roll were being taken at Holy Trinity.

"Present," he volunteered.

"And I promise you," Jack added, "not your man." This seemed to satisfy the cops, at least for the moment. Thereupon Jack laid out the history of events as he knew them, leaving out Casper's aborted shakedown attempt for the sake of focusing attention on the brazen activities of the Russians. DiPasquale told them about the Russians' visits to his barbershop, and Coppedge offered a similar tale. Larry demanded that something be done "before these assholes torch the whole neighborhood." The ATF guy was sympathetic but unencouraging.

"The thing about arson, Mr...."

"Rizzo."

"Rizzo. Easy to identify, nearly impossible to prosecute."

Turns out that motive, means, opportunity, physical evidence—all the things that can convict a thief or a murderer—are insufficient in proving arson. What you need is a witness, or a videotape, or even a cell-phone-call trail that can place the suspect at the scene at the time the fire was started.

"And nobody," added Vukovich, "is that clumsy."

"So what are you saying?" asked Coppedge, who had remained silent, if a bit glassy-eyed, so far. "You saying there ain't nothing we can do? These guys threatened my business; then they burned down my business. What do you need? A notarized confession?"

McWiggin glanced at Vukovich. "Yes, sir," he said, "that's basically what we need."

Coppedge, now quite agitated, stood up. He was stuck in the middle of the booth, the table of which leaned too far out over the vinyl-upholstered benches, so that he couldn't even stand erect, much less squeeze by the others. So he fell back down into his seat and spoke not excitedly but in an eerie monotone. Glancing around the table at the other Ebbets Beachians, he whispered, "Well, maybe this is something we can handle ourselves."

"No, sir!" insisted Vukovich. "No, sir. I'm not saying we aren't following these creeps. We are, and we will eventually shut them down. There is nothing you can do yourselves without exposing yourself and others to great danger. I know you're angry, but don't make matters worse. The agent and I and many others are on the case. We just have to ask you for your patience." Then he turned to Casper. "And you"—he pointed—"you morons stay the hell out of this."

McWiggin, staring directly as Casper, had something to add, as well: "Anybody ever tell you you look like Robert Kennedy Jr.?"

Casper did not reply to either good cop or bad. He was in an end seat and merely stood to allow the others to go about their business. Also, he had to run back to the travel agency to discuss with the don exactly how to murder Smirdov.

CHAPTER 43

CONTRACTORS

GOOD. THE DON WASN'T BACK. AFTER THE STRESSFUL MORNING, he'd driven home for a nap, leaving Casper to do his due diligence in the matter of Assassinations While-U-Wait.

Don Donato had made things quite clear: Events had gotten ahead of them. They needed to find someone good, someone available, someone trustworthy, someone fast. In his zeal to do things the new Ebbets Beach way, he admitted, the Family had made a mistake. Protect what you have, he said, lest it be forsaken. Albeit not exactly in those words. The exact words were, "Give these *bastardi* an inch, they'll take a piss," which, as Casper interpreted the philosopher don, meant he was out of time to locate an individual with the job description Casper was not permitted to actually say.

Alas, as the boss had also intimated, the unmentionable vacancy was not the sort of thing you can fill via craigslist. It's all about knowing someone who knows someone, a networking challenge made all the more difficult by the demands of absolute secrecy and the insanely short turnaround. Still, Casper had not returned to the travel agency empty-handed. He told the boss about an Irishman named Moriarity, whom Casper was able to locate through a cousin with Genovese connections. An hour earlier, Casper had used the Duane Reade pay phone to reach the you-know-what at a pay phone somewhere else, he knew not where. The connection, however, looked promising. Come up with the money and Moriarity—or the guy answering the phone "Moriarity"—was ready to move. The money was $100,000. Casper was enthused. So pleased with himself was the Collector, in fact, that he treated himself to a roll of Necco wafers at Duane Reade. A half roll remained when he held it out to the Don by way of polite offer. The gray Necco was on top.

"YOU *STUPID*, CASPER?"

"With respect, Don, it's not lemon. It's licorice. Like anisette."

"AM I SURROUNDED BY STUPES? WHERE IN THE HOLY NAME OF CHRIST DO I GET ONE HUNDRED DIMES?" Don Donato caught himself shouting, which displeased him too, for he prided himself on being an even-keeled despot. For a man to shout, to lose his temper, to appear out of control, this was not regal. The don lowered his voice. "I'm thinkin' twelve, fifteen grand tops," he said, in a measured tone. "Where does this clown come off asking for one hundred thousand dollars?"

"Everything's high these days," Casper replied, pocketing the Neccos unshared.

"SHUT UP! YOU THINK I'M TALKING ABOUT A PORK ROAST HERE? HUH? YOU THINK I'M TALKING ABOUT A POUND OF APPLES? 'EVERYTHING'S HIGH.' DON'T TELL ME EVERYTHING'S HIGH, CASPER. IF I WANT YOUR FUCKING OPINION ON HOW HIGH EVERYTHING IS, I'LL ASK FOR IT!" Sometimes, despite his enlightened forbearance, the boss's ire simply got the best of him, and then, just like that, quiet flowed the don. "You think he'll settle for less?"

Casper said nothing. Also a mistake.

"I ASKED YOU A QUESTION!"

"Don Donato, it's the Russians. Nobody wants to—"

"ENOUGH!"

Casper was in an unenviable position, because so was the don. The day had begun in disgrace and then gone downhill. The future of the Family—and maybe the entire community, not to mention possibly all of their lives—hinged on this contract. Perhaps, he thought to himself, he'd underestimated the severity of the Family's financial position. Perhaps the buttfelping was even worse than Leonard the Calculator had understood. The upshot was, now, far from being congratulated for his speedy resourcefulness, he was taking the full brunt of the don's frustrations. And he hadn't even gotten to the two other options, which Don Donato was not asking for, and which Casper therefore was loathe—no, make that terrified—to bring it up. He could not remember the boss ever being so pissed off, at least not since poor Paolo, the waiter, gave him an expensive Dodgers jersey for his birthday. No regal equanimity that evening, Casper had never seen such carrying on. Even way back, when Joey Sardines went for his ride, the don was soft-spoken about the whole thing. Now he was pacing back and forth, muttering to himself like the homeless guy in front of Original Reyes, that guy who wrote numbers down in a notebook all day long and raved about the gold standard, whatever the fuck that was. Still, you don't get to be a mob soldier being a pussy, so Casper gathered his courage and laid his cards on the table.

"With you permission, Don Donato," he began, "can I ask you something?"

The boss had his back to Casper. He was leaning with both hands on his desk, head bowed, exactly like JFK during the Cuban Missile Crisis—assuming JFK mumbled to himself in Sicilian.

"Don Donato?" RFK repeated to JFK.

"Ask," the don whispered.

"Could we do this, you know, in-house? I know you said it's risky, but if we don't have the dough, maybe the Teeth—"

The don shook his head and, still in a whisper, shot his soldier down.

"I told you. Not Teeth. Too easy for it to lead back to us. Plus, he's on light duty. With his diverticulitis."

"But, Don—"

"He has a doctor's note."

That settled it. Desperate situations call for desperate measures. Casper wasn't going to play this hand to gin, so, down to one card in the draw deck, he knocked for ten. "Well, then, Don," he offered, "there is this one other guy."

Don Donato, at this sentence, lifted his head. Like Nipper cocked toward his master's voice—no, not quite. But at least in response to his goon's news, yes, so it appeared. And so Casper the Contractor sucked in a deep breath and told Don Donato about the Chiropractor.

What Casper had to say made no sense to the boss whatsoever. The scenario laid out by his loyal but erratic soldier sounded like nothing he had ever encountered in fifty-plus years. "This here what you've told me is strange," he said, although he notably was not shouting or muttering any longer. You couldn't say the don was intrigued. You could say he was resigned. To Casper's enormous relief, he agreed at least to meet the pro whom the boss had never in his long, violent life heard spoken of. Casper got busy. While the don ducked out to run an errand, he ran to

Duane Reade to reestablish contact with his long shot. And he succeeded.

"Yo, Don," he said excitedly a half hour later when the boss returned from his errand. "It's set for five fifteen. Bring your sweet tooth."

CHAPTER 44

THE CHIROPRACTOR

THE RENDEZVOUS TOOK PLACE AT AN ICE CREAM PARLOR IN, OF all places, Brighton Beach. ("Near our gentleman's office," Casper had explained, citing the location as a major advantage in executing the execution.) The interior walls were broadly striped in yellow, white, and pale green; it was like walking into a very cheerful abscess. To seem inconspicuous—or as inconspicuous as two plundering reprobates can look in a sweet shop—Casper ordered a pistachio cone, the don a cup of fudge ripple.

"I enjoy a taste of ice cream now and then," the don commented.

"Who don't?" replied Casper, a careless lapse in the protocol of hyperrespect and unwavering formality that neither he nor the don noticed. Their minds were elsewhere. This was Tuesday afternoon. The way the don figured it, Smirdov had to be out of the way by the end of the week, Friday at the latest, before the Russians could make the big move the don believed was imminent. They sat at a tiny table, a glass circle no bigger than a large pizza pan, framed in white-enameled wrought iron.

"Your friend can get that son of a bitch to Jew heaven?" the don whispered.

"Tony says they ain't Jewish."

"Is that so? Little Odessa. To me, he smells of Jew."

Casper stuffed the dripping remainder of his cone into his mouth and swallowed hard. "Don Donato, with respect, Don, you might want to go easy on the Jew talk." Wiping his mouth with the back of his hand, the soldier gestured with his head vaguely in reference to their environs. "Around here, they're everywhere."

The don, once again, chose not to take offense. "You know what, Casper? You are exactly right. I am ashamed. I don't need to come into someone's neighborhood and badmouth them and show disrespect. You are very right about that. Anyway, Jews, I got no issues with. They are very smart and shrewd people." He leaned forward and whispered into Casper's ear. "But when they start butchering people, I don't want no part of them. This is not how Jews should be. They should be doctors and comics, not killers. OK, maybe some embezzling."

"What you're saying, what comes natural to them."

"Correct, Casper. This is what I'm saying. A Jew is your scientist, your violin player, your tax cheat—"

The door to the parlor opened. In from the street walked a nondescript man of middle age and medium height. His curly brown hair was thinning on the top and graying at the temples. He had a close-cropped beard, also graying, trimmed right up to his jawline, such that it was. He wore black dress slacks, a loosely fitting black knit cotton shirt (apparently to minimize the bulging of his spare tire), and a pair of gold-rimmed readers on a chain dangling over his chest. "The Chiropractor" didn't look like a hit man; he looked like a chiropractor. The banality of evil. Adolf Eichmann was a sales clerk. The Boston Strangler was a plumber. Walter O'Malley was a bankruptcy lawyer. Verily, you can't tell a mook by his cover. *This character looks*, thought the don, *like he*

*couldn't rub out a...a...whaddyacallit what Angela had years ago...
the toy, the magic slate, she shook it and the picture disappeared...
fuck do they call that thing...with knobs...like a little red TV...*

"Etcha Spex!" the don blurted out, and pounded the table with
his fist, rattling the glass top and at least two grown men. Casper
had risen to greet the Chiropractor and was reaching out to shake
hands when Don Donato shouted so emphatically and inscruta-
bly. The Collector, of course, knew from grim experience never to
betray his consternation over any given Don Donato non sequitur.
The Chiropractor had no such habit of caution. In his business, he'd
learned to size up a situation immediately and—before the subject
could get cold feet—commence cracking bones. That very trait is
what found him in this place at this moment. Thus, he fingered
his reading glasses and replied.

"No, sir," he offered. "Just supermarket magnifiers."

"Supermarket?" the don responded. "Casper, fuck is this guy
talking about?"

"The specs, sir," the Chiropractor further explained. "Nothing
fancy. The better to spy you with, m'dear!" The last quip was delivered with a chuckle.

The don, however, was chuckleless. Spy? My *dear*? Casper
could only imagine where this could go, so he decided to change
the subject before the don went all lemons on them.

"Doc," Casper said, "meet my boss. Don, this is—"

The chiropractor raised his hand. "Wait!" he snapped. "No
names! 'Doc' will do fine for me. And you, sir"—he reached for the
don's hand—"you are the representative of Patient B." Some might
say the man in black was laying it on a little too thick, like some nitwit who had seen too many mob movies, but operational security

being as critical as it was, this wasn't an entirely harebrained way to commence the relationship.

Casper handed the farsighted assassin a manila envelope, from which the Chiropractor—still standing—slid printouts of the photos Leonard had harvested from Google Images. He donned his readers so that they were perched halfway up his nose.

"Interesting," the Chiropractor mumbled as he scrutinized his target. "Lumbar and sacrum subluxation."

"Wait," the don jumped in. "Lumbago? You sayin' the Jewish Johnny Cash over here is a real chiropractor?"

Casper and the hit man exchanged a smile. "Doc," Casper prompted, "siddown and tell...the representative of Patient B... about your thing, your system."

The Chiropractor nodded, grabbed a tiny chair from one of the other tiny tables, and huddled with his prospects. "Very simple," he whispered. "I have what you might call a special technique. By applying firm pressure to the baroreceptors of the carotid sinus at the base of the neck, I can trigger what we call the 'baroreceptor reflex,' which almost instantly and very dramatically slows the heart rate—we call this bradycardia—until the subject loses consciousness."

"Like Mr. Spock," Casper offered, adding, for the benefit of the Don, "who happens to be also Hebrew, by the way."

"Then," the Chiropractor continued, "once the subject is neutralized..."

No need to finish that sentence. There were uncertainties to deal with, such as how in the world an extremely careful and probably paranoid professional killer like Smirdov would allow himself to be close enough to a total stranger to render himself susceptible to the ninja death grip or whatever the fuck the Jew was talking about. The question did not go unanticipated.

"You know where this individual lives?" the Chiropractor asked.

"Yeah, we know," Casper said, looking not at his healer but at the don for his reaction.

"Well, then..."

The don was skeptical; knowing someone's address no more facilitates an execution than knowing where your dick is facilitates seduction. You still have to get in, take care of business, and get the hell away in one piece. But the don was also out of options. He leaned toward the Chiropractor. "What is the fee for your service?"

"My nonnegotiable fee is seventy-five thousand dollars," replied the Bradycardiac Kid.

"No," said the don.

"Seventy thousand," countered the Chiropractor.

The don stood up. "Forget it. It's too cold in this joint. Come on, Casper. Let's go."

"Sixty-seven thousand five hundred, and I'm afraid that's the best I can do. I gather we're speaking of a"—he whispered in the direction of Don Donato—"high-value target."

"That's correct, Doc," said the don, who sensed weakness—and he hoped not too much of it. "But high value to me. Not to you. You'll take what I offer."

True, that. Bold and confident as he tried to appear, the Chiropractor was not in an especially strong bargaining position. For one thing, he had no idea what the rate card was for eliminating a kingpin. Nor did he know what the client could afford. Indeed, the don at the moment had but $16,000 cash on hand. In addition, and more problematically, the Chiropractor's murder résumé was a bit thin. Smirdov would be Patient B. Patient A—one Anat Wieselberg—had been a year earlier. And she was pro bono.

It was while adjusting C2 and C3 for cervicocranial syndrome in Mrs. Wieselberg the previous fall that the Chiropractor discovered that he was capable not only of channeling the body's spinal energy to heal but also the opposite; the poor woman died on his ErgoBasic adjustment table. The cost of fighting the lawsuit was devastating, not even taking into account the effect on patient morale when elderly patients are removed from the office by EMTs hoisting a cadaver pouch. So—for the sake of his own survival— he'd recently decided to make lemonade out of lemons and offer his services as an occiputal euthanasiast. Casper, a satisfied patient of two years standing, had actually planted the idea that one man's malpractice is another man's business model. In point of fact, he'd planted the idea within the previous six hours. "Play your cards right, Doc," he'd told the chiropractor late that morning, "and you can make a lot of dough."

The hint hadn't been dropped recklessly. It was perfectly obvious to the doctor, as it was obvious to everybody else, that Casper—he of the odd hours, fat bankroll, and wiseguy swagger—was not sustaining himself at Waldo's crooning to barflies. The Chiropractor was naturally fascinated and had, over two years, increasingly drawn Casper out on the nature of his day job. At no point had he expressed revulsion, nor even objection. As far as Casper could tell, the guy was jealous. The doc couldn't get enough of the sordid details of the life—which sordid details Casper dispensed semicautiously, minus names, dates, and anything else patently incriminating. The guy just ate it all up. So, this morning, under dire circumstances, the singer/hood/spinal patient made his move. Now, in an ice cream parlor air-conditioned far too low for the unseasonably pleasant late-summer's day, this doctor/groupie/ prospective assassin steeled himself for the challenge of filling the role suddenly thrust upon him.

In the end, they agreed on a figure: $40,000, sixteen large upfront, to purchase one guaranteed homicide and three free adjustments for the whole crew. The Chiropractor had found the supplemental income he so desperately required and the Family had found just what it needed: an off-price hit man. As the conspirators shook hands on the deal, the Chiropractor looked Don Donato up and down, frowning as he did so. *Terrible lordosis*, he was thinking. He was just about to comment on it when Don Donato abruptly stood and headed for the door.

"So long, representative of Patient B," the Chiropractor said.

"*Buona sera*, Seth," said the don. The chiropractor froze. What was going on here? Had Casper blown his cover? Already? Were they police? Undercover? What?

"H…how…"

The don pointed at the Chiropractor's shirt.

Puzzled, the man who would be called "Doc" glanced downward and sighed in disgust. *Glick-Mermelstein Wellness Center* was embroidered over one pec and *Seth* over the other.

This struck the hitman as an opportune moment to make his departure. He sauntered out of the ice cream parlor, affecting as casual a mien as he could summon considering his heart was doing somersaults in his ribcage. In fact, the man damn near sashayed, with his wide, flat ass swiveling to and fro as he made for the door. He was overdoing the insouciance, but that was just the Chiropractor's way - whether with a business arrangement or a cervical spine. The don nudged Casper and rolled his eyes. Fortunately, he did not pay as close attention to Seth's butt as he had to his shirt. Sticking out of the chiropractor's hip pocket were two tickets for the night's baseball game between the Mets and the Los Angeles Dodgers, Seth's favorite team.

CHAPTER 45

GOING TO THE MATTRESSES

ON HIS FIRST DAY, AS FAR AS THE OWNER COULD TELL, BIG MANNY had not cussed out any bed shoppers. So far, so good. Jack had guessed correctly that traffic would be slow. It was also the first day back to school in Brooklyn, a good retail day for stationery, a black hole for the sleep trade. The new assistant manager had spent most of the afternoon on the Internet, mainly perusing info on a 1925-issue Tanganyika ten-cent stamp—with a heavy cancellation mark, unfortunately—featuring an adorable giraffe engraved in black, framed by tropical flora etched in greenback green.

But that's not all.

Mr. Mattress returned at about 5:00. For his part, and to his substantial amazement, he'd spent most of his afternoon with Larry Rizzo trying to learn the history of mob influence on Ebbets Beach, and particularly to understand what the new threat was all about. Larry was a pest and a bit of a loon, but not a complete nincompoop; he had a pretty good fix not only on the significance of the week's events—ominous, or worse, he concluded, and probably *much* worse—but also the fragile ecosystem of local commerce and criminality. "Think of it this way," he'd told Mr. Mattress. "It's global warming, so warm things are catching fire." Jack could find no fault with the analogy.

Big Manny stood as his boss entered the store. "Don Schiavone," he said.

Mr. Mattress winced. "Yeah, don't call me that. Seriously."

"A sign of respect, is all," Manny replied. "You definitely saved my fat ass."

"That's true, Manny. I definitely did. But only with the hope that your fat ass would protect my skinny one. Any surly Russians come in this afternoon?"

"No, no Russians. A couple of Puerto Ricans. They came in for the apple cider. I sold them a bed."

"No shit? See what I mean? *Free* is the most provocative word in the English language. Any trouble writing it up?"

"No, me and Jitnee figured it out. She left after. I told her to. Quiet day."

"Fine," Jack said. "In fact, I'm going to close the store early tonight anyway. There won't be any traffic, and we have to get ready."

"Ready for what?"

"Inventory liquidation. The biggest sale in our history."

Manny didn't understand. The store had only been open for four and a half days. He said nothing; he was not consigliere of this outfit. The puzzlement, however, was written all over his face.

"Manny," Jack explained, "at Mr. Mattress, every weekend will be the biggest sale in our history. Every single one. We'll take down the *Grand Opening* banner Thursday and replace it with *Inventory Liquidation*. Then *Fall Festival. Oktoberfest. Columbus's Birthday. Presidents' Day Clearance.* I've got more banners than I've got beds."

This information amused and impressed the assistant manager. It also emboldened him.

"So you was in advertising, right?" he asked.

"Wow," Jack replied. "That's the worst-kept secret in town."

"Yeah, my goddaughter mighta mentioned it. So today I was what they call surfing on the Internet, and, I was wondering, you ever heard of search?"

"Search as in Google search? Search advertising?"

"Yeah, that," said Manny. "You familiar with this thing?"

Oh, he was familiar, all right. Search, along with the rest of the Internet revolution, was having its way with the ad business. If Jack hadn't been shamed off of Madison Avenue, he'd eventually have been priced out of it. His former agency was in a precipitous slide, along with most of the competition. For some reason, though, none of this financial devastation broke his heart.

"Sure," he answered. "Of course. Why?"

"Well, like I said, I was just screwing around on your computer, and I kind of got wondering, if you bought search advertising, only for people in Brooklyn searching on the Internet for beds or mattresses and what have you, you could get some good leads, couldn't you? See what I'm saying? It's targeted. And as I understand it, you don't pay for the leads unless someone clicks on your ad. So it seems like it could be a pretty good deal. Five-buck lead, thousand-dollar bed. You sell to one in fifty of the leads, you still come out ahead, right? But you're the ad guy. I don't know nothing about this shit."

Jack was flabbergasted—not so much at Big Manny's ability to discover, grasp, and mentally spreadsheet the arcane economics of online advertising, but that it had never occurred to Jack for a second to buy search ads for his store. He'd used direct mail and space ads in the *Ebbets Beach Pennysaver*, but online had never crossed his mind. Oh, and it was exactly the right thing to do.

"Holy Christ, Manny. What are you gonna come up with on your second day at work?"

Manny shrugged. "Just doing my job, ma'am. Just doing my job."

The phone rang.

Manny answered. "Mr. Mattress. Can I help you?...How ya doin', sweetheart?"

Sweetheart? Jack jerked around to look at Manny on phone. Was another Home Depot moment going to take place? Was he going to offend another customer?

"Nah, just sitting here mostly...Nah, none of that nonsense... Yeah, you wanna talk with him?...Boss, it's Angela."

Mr. Mattress took the phone. Angela was inviting him on a date. At Waldo's, 9:00 p.m.

"Casper's performing," she said. "I've never seen him sing, so..."

"Is there a punch line to this?"

"No, I'm dead serious. I kind of upset him...Well, I can explain that later. But, anyway, it won't just be us."

"Oh? That's cool. Who's joining us?"

"Actually, it's my parents."

That was not what Jack was expecting to hear. If she'd said the First Family, he wouldn't have been as stunned. If she'd said the von Trapp family, he wouldn't have been as stunned. If she'd said the Manson family, he wouldn't have been as stunned.

"OK," he said, in as tentative a voice of agreement as he'd ever marshaled, "I can do that."

"My dad wants to meet you. He came in here this afternoon. He said he wanted to speak with you."

"With *me*? What about?"

"He didn't really say. Maybe something about your Russians."

"Holy shit. All right. Meet you there?"

"Yes," she said. "Too busy for dinner tonight. Will grab something. Meet there."

"Angela? I thought you were careful about being in public with your father. This is pretty public."

"I know, Jack. But I've never seen him like this. He looked so worried. He looked so...sad."

The Saddest Don. Hmm, Jack thought, *not a bad title for a children's book.* Knock *Old Yeller* right out of the juvenile canon. *Little Women* too. Anyway, it promised to be a memorable evening. The vocal stylings of a mob bagman and Bud Light pitchers with a melancholy sociopath. What a great opportunity to be back on the front pages, photographed in a pool of his own blood.

"OK, Manny," he said, after smooching the phone in good-bye to Angela, "you asked me. Now let me ask you about something *you* used to do for a living."

Jack pulled up a chair next to Manny and began laying out the recent events as he and Larry had discussed them, including the fires, threatening visits, declining fortunes of the Donato family, and future dangers posed by the Russians to all involved. He told him what the police had to say. He told him about Coppedge's rage, about the loss of livelihoods for twenty-some young men, about the barber's abject ruin.

"Manny, I know you're not a violent man. I know you weren't just the brains but also the moral compass of the Family. So if you were still working for Donato and you faced this Smirdov and his organization, what would you advise?"

Somehow Big Manny had produced a toothpick, which he now rolled in his mouth, obscuring all but a centimeter of the wood. Jack looked away. The sight made him want to gag.

"You're saying, what would I tell the don?" Manny asked.

Jack nodded, still turning away from his assistant manager.

"Simple."

Jack turned back, because this answer, too, stunned him. There seemed to be nothing simple about this situation. On the contrary, it seemed convoluted and dangerous and maybe even hopeless.

"Simple? Simple how?"

"Simple. You just get face-to-face with this here Russian…"

Ah, face-to-face. Once again, so far, so good. Angela was right. Her godfather was *not* one of them.

"Yeah, you just get face-to-face with this guy. Then you kill him."

CHAPTER 46

REDEMPTION

TRAFFIC WAS HEAVY, SO THE DON INSTRUCTED CASPER TO DRIVE straight to the club.

"Can I ask you something, Don?" said Casper the Chauffeur to his backseat passenger.

"Ask."

"Maybe tonight, just *antipasti. Insalata.* All this pasta…" He patted his expanding belly with his right hand. "Plus I ain't shit a decent loaf in three days."

The don did not immediately respond. The question did seem to weigh on him, like carbonara in Casper's colon, for he wore a frown and stared out of the Cadillac's tinted window.

"Casper, can I ask you something?" It was question time in Ebbets Beach. Why, just *everybody* was doing it.

"Of course, Don Donato. Always."

"Where am I gonna find twenty, thirty dimes to pay Dr. Spock in two days?"

The Chauffeur had no ready answer, so he chose to keep his trap shut. They arrived at half past 6:00 and walked in through the dining room entrance. The table was set for the crew, standing starched and empty in the far corner. Other tables were already filled with diners reading menus and chewing on breadsticks. At first, the mafiosi, didn't notice the bald human floral centerpiece sitting in the vestibule, literally hat in hand.

"Hello, Casper," the voice said. "Hello, sir. Don Donato, sir."

It was Larry Rizzo of J&L's. He was bowing on one knee. It looked like next he would genuflect, but he quickly stood up. "Can I have a word with you about something super important? I won't keep you long, I swear."

The don looked at Casper. Casper shrugged.

"Don Donato," whispered the sandwich man, "it concerns the Russian mafia."

The don glanced at Casper, who was already scrutinizing his boss's face for signs of whatever the lately unpredictable dictator might be thinking. In this particular instance, Don Donato's eyes widened in their vast dark sockets. Trouble was, Casper did not know how to interpret what he saw. Was the boss offended? Angry? *Very* angry? Or was he simply registering surprise? Casper had not a clue—until Don Donato closed those very widened eyes into an expression of pure solemnity and nodded.

"Yes, of course. Bring the gentleman to the back room," which Casper naturally did.

"Right this way, Larry," he said, arm around Larry's shoulder. "Good to see you."

Casper would have glad-handed Larry even if in the back room the guy were to be beaten with a pipe. Still, he intuited that the boss was for whatever reason pleased, and he could hardly wait to find out why. The hosts got Larry comfortable, offering him a glass of wine, an appetizer, anything. He declined.

"Truth is," he confessed, "I'm a little nervous…Maybe a glass of water, brother, if it isn't too much trouble." No trouble. Casper was out of the room in an instant to fetch a cold pitcher and a glass. The don pulled up a chair next to Larry, tugged his trousers at the crease to create some slack for his thighs, sat down, and patted the supplicant on the leg.

"OK, Mr. Ricci..."

"Rizzo, sir."

"I apologize, Mr. Rizzo. What is it that brings you here this evening?"

"Sir, basically what it is, I got a mutiny on my hands. Understand, I'm not talking about me. I been—my wife and I, we run J&L, you know—we've been loyal to Casper straight through. You can ask him. We have always been very happy to, you know, work with your Family, and we never felt for one moment like we had any reason to gripe."

"Thank you, Mr. Ricci."

"Yeah, and we plan to keep on keepin' on, if you know what I mean. But, Don Donato—"

Larry jumped half out of his seat. Casper had walked in with the water and let the door slam behind him, startling the pudgy riot of tropical color who was rambling on to the don. When Larry realized the noise was only Casper, he blinked his eyes, sucked in a breath, and continued babbling. "See, what it is, I got a mutiny on my hands. I mean, basically, you got a mutiny on your hands."

"What kind of mutiny, Mr. Ricci?" As he spoke, the don squinted downward toward his shiny black loafers. There was a wide scuff on the left shoe that seemed to command his attention even as he conversed with the idiot sandwich slinger.

"Rizzo, sir. See, the thing is, certain members of the Village Association who I will not name believe that the payments they've made—"

"I scuffed my shoe," the don said. "These are brand new."

Larry did not know what to say, not that that had ever stopped him before. He glanced toward the don's feet. He couldn't see anything amiss there, and mistaking the boss's observation for conversation, he was moved to offer his thoughts. "A little polish," he ventured. Then Larry wiggled his hand, like Al Jolson or a gypsy shaking a tambourine.

"What's this here?" the don inquired. He too wiggled his hand, his face darkening and a scowl forming around his cavernous eyes. Then he repeated the gesture. "What's this? You got something you wanna say to me? In Palermo, you know what I do when somebody gives me the *dimenare*…the whaddyacallit…wiggle-waggle? Casper, is this how a man behaves?"

Casper didn't know what to say, for though he was more than fluent in Italian hand-gesture vulgarity, he was fairly certain there was nothing offensive about tambourineless tambourining in Palermo or anywhere else. Was this Etcha Spex all over again? "Unfuckingbelievable, Don," he said, covering every base, he figured.

"Mr. Ricci, you're not going to tell me you don't know what this is, *il dimenare*. I am not a fool."

Larry kept staring at the don because he could not actually reply; his larynx was paralyzed. Where the words were supposed to be he could form only muted quacking noises, as if he were choking on a slice of genoa salami. Casper offered him the water glass, which Larry half spilled grabbing for. His head bobbed up and down as he gulped, gasped, and generally struggled to regain his voice and equilibrium. He was so anxious to clear up whatever insult he'd inadvertently committed, though, that he gulped from the glass with his left hand while he continued wiggling with his right—repeating and repeating the very gesture that had instigated the tension.

"Casper, look at Donald Duck here, still with the insult. Maybe you better explain to him what he is saying."

"Explain to him…?"

"Yeah, explain to him what he is telling me, *con questo gesto vulgare mano*."

"You want me to tell him what the wiggle-waggle is, Don?"

"Tell him."

"Tell him the insult, Don Donato?"

The don nodded.

Larry's anus spasmed.

And Casper's stomach flipped. He by now had more or less concluded that Don Donato was trying to intimidate Larry, which struck him as gilding the lily livered; Larry had entered the club preintimidated for everyone's convenience. But now it fell to Casper to characterize the blasphemy. How the fuck was he going to invent an offense without offending the don himself? How could this not end badly? But he was stuck. Maybe he'd open the door with the tiger. Maybe he'd open the door with the lady.

"Yeah, OK, Larry, it's like this. When you wiggle your hand like this"—he repeated it as best he could considering his limited manual dexterity—"what you're saying is…what you're saying about the don is that he's a…sort of a…what you call a *donnicciola…*"

"*Donnicciola!*" the don jumped in. "A sissy. Is that what you're saying, Casper?"

"Yeah. No," Casper elaborated. "I mean, not me, Don. The wiggle. I heard it's like…sissy."

"Sissy," the don repeated. "Is that right?"

"No, not, like, faggot sissy cocksucker. Kind of a little pussy." Casper tried not to make eye contact with the don. "I don't mean little, like, short or nothin'. More like scaredy cat kind of pussy, but not necessarily short, not saying that anyone's short. Just, when you wiggle like…" Casper demonstrated once again, and soon he would be quaking in fear himself had not Larry finally rediscovered the capacity for speech, as a single word lurched from his throat.

"BUFFING!" Larry croaked, then frantically spewed the rest of his explanation. "Polishing. Buffing. The shoe, with polish, is all. That's all. Buffing your shoe is all I was saying, I swear to Jesus and Mary, mother of God. Buffing."

"Buffing," the don said, glaring at Larry. Then he looked up at Casper who hoped his trembling was not visible as he drank directly from Larry's water pitcher. Mercifully, what the don did not do was bark, *Casper! Who you calling a midget coward?* What the don did, simply, was to once again reenact the wiggle and inquire, "How is this buffing? Casper, is this buffing?" Casper was draining the pitcher, his mouth bejeweled by half-melted ice cubes, as he vigorously shook his head no.

"Casper!" squeaked Larry. "How can you say that? You know me for years already."

"What do I know?" Casper squeaked right back, wiping his mouth with the back of his sleeve. "Keep your fuckin' hands to yourself."

But then, that quickly, the don brought the subject—and the sphincternastics—to an end.

"Let's be clear about this, Mr. Ricci," he offered. "Assuming you didn't come here looking for trouble, although I promise you we carry that kind of merchandise, and assuming you're not trying to imbue my good name by suggesting I wear sissy shoes, which I again say I do not because I happen to know Tony Bennett and Mayor Bloomberg wear the very same style, let's just agree that you don't know shit from Shinola, buffing-wise. Let's leave it at that, OK?"

"Thank you, Don Donato," Larry said. He was relieved, and so was Casper. The don seemed satisfied to have scared the crap out of the visitor and not all that put out by Casper's improvised slanders, even if they did cut a little close to the bone. Now the don had his good-cop thing going full bore.

"Because we got other worms to conquer, such as your so-called mutiny. Am I correct?"

"Yes, Your Honor. Like I was saying, we pay…they pay every week for years…"

"Mr. Ricci, let me understand you. You are speaking of the voluntary contributions to the Family's community efforts in our community?"

"Yes, sir, Don Donato. Those."

"Excuse me for this," the don said, and then gestured to Casper with a wave of the finger pointing back to Larry. Casper nodded, took Larry's water glass away, gestured for him to stand, and commenced to patting the visitor down.

"Oh my God. Casper, now you think I'm wired for sound? Brother, how long we worked together? Don Donato, I am here to help you."

"Better safe than sane, Mr. Ricci. I apologize to you. Of course, you know that we can't be too careful these days. So you come here looking to redeem your coupons, that it?"

Casper finished feeling up his customer and gave his boss the high sign.

Larry sat down, reached for his water glass, and sipped again. "Bottom line, Don Donato, they don't want to pay. These fires, they all think they're next, and they think they're getting no protection, so why fill Casper's sack?" Larry now finished draining the glass with a huge, sloppy gulp. He had never intended to be so blunt. And now here he was in the back room of a noisy restaurant with two dangerous men he'd just announced were about to be defied. Stiffed. Disrespected. He wondered if anybody in the dining room would hear his gasps or screams. His face had reddened, and it seemed as if his Hawaiian shirt were changing color too. It was the sweat seeping all the way down to his belt, some beading on the fabric and dripping down his belly, some leeching into the side of the shirt.

Casper, whose immediate responsibilities were at stake here, responded first. "Excuse me, Larry. You telling me you got a problem with how I do my job?"

Larry stood up abruptly. "No, Casper. No! I'm just saying—"

"SIT DOWN," requested the don, a suggestion Larry felt to be helpful and with which he immediately complied. "I'm very sorry, Mr. Ricci. I hear what you are telling me. You are absolutely right."

Huh? He was? Casper didn't blink, but he certainly couldn't imagine what the boss was thinking. For his part, Larry simply assumed the politeness was Evil Mastermind protocol, that the racketeer's next words would qualify the initial agreeableness in a way that would be genuinely terrible for Larry. His life did not pass before his eyes, but he did feel like he would puke. Sure enough, the don did proceed to amplify his remarks. Oh, Christ...

"You and many others in this community have been donating to our fund with the expectation that it would help provide for the health of our community, let's say. Now we have two tragic events at businesses in Ebbets Beach, and all of us are wondering what the fuck is going on. You want this *follia* to stop and so do we. Why should you pay your hard-earned dollars if some lunatic is gonna firebomb your store, God forbid? Is this your point, Mr. Ricci?"

Wait. That wasn't too bad. "Yes, sir. It's Rizzo, actually, sir. But, yes. Not me, but some other merchant—"

"Fine. That's what it shall be. On Friday, Casper will not come around."

"At all?" Casper blurted out, at exactly the same time Larry said, "At all?"

"At all," said the don. "Tell you the truth, what's Casper gonna bring back anymore? Two, three dimes? Half of that for the fuckin' raffle? I ask you, Ricci, what's that gonna buy? That's not gonna buy shit. So you save your money. Let the Russians go crazy. Me, I got a nice place in Egg Harbor. I don't mind spending a little time staring at the ocean, playing with the grandkids."

Now Larry was more terrified than before, when he was merely on the verge of being shot or suffocated. What Donato was talking about here was surrender. Retirement. Letting the Russians do to Ebbets Beach what they'd done to Eastern Europe. Violence. Terror. Destruction. Pollution. Slavery. Ugly buildings. Casper was less terrified. Sure, he was a little obtuse, but not an imbecile. He knew the boss had neither a beach house nor a single grandchild. What the boss had was more stage presence than Casper commanded on his best night.

"So, you're saying…" For all the water, Larry's mouth was cotton dry. When he tried to speak, his tongue stuck to his palate like batter on a waffle iron. "Um…What *are* you saying?"

"I'm saying good luck to you, Mr. Ricci. I am proud to have done business with you."

"We're on our own?"

"Ain't that what you come in here asking for?"

"But—"

"But nothin'. You wanted off the hook, now you're off. You want the Russians off your back, that's another discussion."

That discussion began immediately. When the discussion was over, Larry, on behalf of the entire Village Association, had pledged $25,000 within forty-eight hours to the cause of eradicating the Russian threat in Ebbets Beach. The means were not mentioned, but Larry was no dope, either. As he hurried back to his store, where he would phone every merchant he could think of, he was sure of two things. One was that the unused food and novelties from the rained-out Sale-a-Bration would be recycled Wednesday and Thursday for an impromptu Back-to-School Daze, where donations would be solicited from shoppers and freeloaders for the Ebbets Beach Neighborhood Watch. The second thing he knew was there was and never would be an Ebbets Beach Neighborhood Watch; that was the Cozy Nostra's job. The entire proceeds would underwrite a contract killer. And this time his hyperactive imagination wasn't running away with him.

"It's like *The Magnificent Seven*," he would explain to all of them—except for Mr. Kim, whom he'd tell, because obviously Korea is exactly the same country as Japan, "It's like *The Seven Samurai*."

When he left the social club, he was as exactly as energized as he'd been petrified coming in. Not only that, he carried with him a second insurance policy against financial ruin, this one for only $175. It was his Amway Opportunity Kit.

CHAPTER 47

NEED TO KNOW

"FIRST ORDER OF BUSINESS," BEGAN THE DON, SPEAKING QUIETLY and deliberately, whether out of exhaustion or caution his audience could not tell, "per Casper's request, no pasta tonight. Paolo will bring us some beautiful Jersey tomatoes and mozzarella and some mixed green salads, if you want. This is for your own good. Also, we been up since early, and I caught forty winks, but maybe you didn't, so you need to get some sleep tonight. This is going to be a busy couple three days. Second order of business, on Friday, we whack the Russian. Third order of business, I want a report on your downlines. You had two days already—how many partners you guys signed up?"

The soldiers tried to look invisible. As the don had just said, they had been up since dawn on the summit fiasco, and Monday had been the monsoon. Furthermore, they'd all dutifully completed their own application materials but had nothing yet from Franzetti to give to prospects, so the boss couldn't possibly expect them to be out tossing coffee on other suckers yet.

"Nine. I got nine." All heads turned but Marco's, because he was speaking. "I got my aunt. I got my cousin Richie and my other cousin Nadine. I got two kids at Moe Howard. I got some girl bartender at Waldo's. I got some trucker who was trying to hit on the girl bartender. I got a guy on the loading dock at Pathmark. And I got Tina."

Ten wide eyes gaped at Marco, two of them slightly wider than the others. They belonged to Don Donato.

"Tina who?" he inquired softly.

"Oh, your daughter Tina, Don."

The boss was rendered mute by this news—not because Medium fucking Marco had poached on the don's familial downline, but because Tina, when the don himself approached her, had scoffed. ("Is this Amway?" she'd asked. Then she'd started snorting. "I'm busy, Dad. I'll talk to you later.") Nobody could believe what he was hearing, least of all the boss. A silence would have enshrouded the table, but Marco wasn't finished.

"Yeah, and I got a call today. Three of my distributors signed people up today. So now I got, like, sixteen folks in my downline."

"You got sixteen people in your downline?" Little Manny sputtered. "*Sixteen*?"

"So far," confirmed Marco. "You know, medium."

Leonard the Calculator was even more astonished. Staggered would be a better word. He sat there with his hand up in the air, like he was back in twelfth grade biology with Sister Mary Aloysius. At first nobody noticed, but then he steadied his contracted bicep with his left hand as he waved the right. Marco noticed him before the boss did.

"Don Donato, I think the Calculator has something to say," said Marco, and then all heads turned to Leonard.

"Excuse me, Don," he offered, haltingly. "Could I ask you to remind me, what was the second order of business?"

Oh. That.

Taking care not to be overheard by the civilians clustered in the center of the dining room, the don patiently explained to the family that the time had come to make a move on Smirdov before Smirdov could make his next move on them. On the second pass, the news prompted no more vocal reaction than it had the first. The men just looked at him—except for Casper, who was feeling full of himself for being the plenipotentiary in the thick of the most important mobstering the outfit had planned in years. He sat picking a cuticle—or seemed to be. Actually, he was practicing his overhand hipster snap for the night's gig at Waldo's. Little Manny, fresh off of the ballbusting at the OK Corral, was feeling not so sanguine. On the contrary, he felt pretty sure this ambitious foray back into the world of capital murder was far beyond this crew's current abilities, especially without the guiding hand of his father. Somebody was going to die, he was quite certain, but not Smirdov. Tony the Teeth felt strongly as well. He felt strongly that, as soon as they were dismissed, he would head for J&L's to get a cheesesteak, then maybe to Billie's for a slice of pie.

Finally, Marco's right hand shot up again. "Don Donato, how are we gonna—"

The boss stopped Marco with a traffic cop's open palm. "The precise plan of action," he explained, "will be divulged on a need-to-know basis."

It was a prudent way for the don to handle the question, mainly because he still needed to know how the fuck they were going to pull this off.

CHAPTER 48

COUNSELING

FATHER STEVE HAD AN INTERESTING TUESDAY. AT 8:00 IN THE morning, he'd met with the parish council. There, for the first time, he'd prevailed on a majority of the deacons to back his modernization plans for Our Lady of Grace. There was only one vote against him—Mike Franzetti, who stalked out of the meeting threatening to take the matter up with the bishop. The priest found it difficult to savor his political victory, however, because it had antagonized the man who was far and away the most energetic parish volunteer and rainmaker. The bingo rake was dwindling, but it still topped collection proceeds by plenty.

At 9:30, the bishop phoned. "Don't sweat it, Steve," His Excellency assured him. "Your deacon is the least of your problems. Do what you think is best, but know that it's an uphill battle. Our Lady of Grace is on the list." By which the bishop meant *the* list. For closure.

Father Steve was both unsurprised and heartbroken by this revelation. "What will it take to get off of the list?" he'd asked the bishop.

"A miracle" was the reply.

At 11:00, Father Steve stood in the narthex in preparation for mass. As far as he could tell, he was the only one in the church.

He was wrong about that. Mrs. T, the organist, was present, but not playing the organ. What was the point? The priest conducted the processional solo and a cappella. He said mass to himself, his deep voice echoing in the empty sanctuary.

At 11:45, having prepared the Holy Eucharist and served communion to exactly no one, he was accosted by Mrs. T, who had heard a rumor that the bingo game was being discontinued. The priest tried to assure her that the rumor was false, that the game would continue, that in time it would be taken online, but she was in a rage. The five-foot-tall elderly organist began to punch the pastor in his midsection as he tried to hold her off with his hands. Then she died.

In a proverbial heartbeat—or more correctly, no heartbeat—she was gone, not so much slumping to the floor as imploding, like a building razed by dynamite. One moment upright, the next a fallen heap. This was shocking in so many ways. There was, of course, the perversity of the circumstances. A parishioner had died while playing Rock 'Em Sock 'Em Robots with the pastor, bringing grief and remorse to the priest for whatever role he may have had in the tragedy. There was also the suddenness. One moment Mrs. T was feisty and passionate and ever so much alive. The next moment, gone. Most troubling of all for Father Steve, though, was the horrifying deadness of death. He had held many a hand in many a nursing home, many a hospital bed, many a hospice in the final moments. He had seen death creep up and take over. Even then, he struggled; a dead body was nothing like a living one, so still and flaccid and hauntingly unhuman. But here he had witnessed the embodiment of vital energy just turn off before his eyes, slumping to the floor as the embodiment of nothingness. Sudden death was creepy in a way that challenged his physical and emotional even keels—and more than that, his spiritual one.

Mrs. Troncelliti's expiration, naturally, caused some commotion. Paramedics arrived quickly, detected no vital signs, and hung around waiting for the cops. Police visited the parish for the second time in five days, listened incredulously to the priest's recounting of events, jotted notes for their reports, and laughed their asses off the moment they got back into their squad cars. The priest notified Mrs. T's children and offered his condolences. He also told them the story, leaving out nothing, including his manhandling of their diminutive mother in the instant that her heart exploded. This appalling turn of events left neither child hostile nor bitter, nor even much taken aback. They'd figured it would all end approximately like this. They apologized to Father Steve for their dead mom.

At 6:00 p.m., after mass, he kept his counseling appointment with Tina Donato, slutty daughter of the local mafia kingpin, at which session the first thing she did was profess her undying love for him and desire to, in her words, "feel your fatherhood on my tits, Father."

That was a first for Steve Delewski, in his collar or out of it. He didn't know whether he should feel flattered or insulted, sympathetic or disgusted. Mainly, as he had been doing all day, he tried to keep his composure. It had never occurred to him that the object of the sinful desires she so graphically described in confessional was himself truly. Now, on top of everything else, he had to remember what he'd been taught in seminary about transference. He knew it was not uncommon for a counseling subject to mistake unresolved emotions of another sort with love for or erotic fixation on the counselor. But it seemed to him that this typically occurred with lonely married women and widows—not the curviest young tart in the parish. Not that her curves and brazen sexuality should have factored into his thinking. He was still a man, and he did not doubt that the act she described would feel just absolutely wonderful, but his "fatherhood" belonged to Christ. Period. And therefore what he said to Tina was this:

"Oh my."

Which is a euphemistic truncation of "Oh my God."

Tina seemed unabashed. "Look, Father, I know you think I'm a head case"—*ha-ha snort-snort-snort*—"no pun intended, but it ain't like that. I been in love with you since I first ever saw you. You're not like other men. You care about me as a person. I can tell that. Other guys just want to stare at my tits, but you see my soul. And my soul belongs to you."

"No, Tina. Your soul belongs to God. And so does mine. The things you are saying are simply…improper. They are disrespectful of me and of the church. And I also think they are disrespectful of yourself. You are a strong woman and a fine person, I am sure. But I believe you are confusing things. I am happy to try to help you, but you must understand I can never reciprocate in the way you have said. This house is full of Christ's love. I hope you can feel that. But especially in this day and age, there can be no more talk of sexual fantasies with…a member of the priesthood."

"No pun intended?"

"Tina. Stop it."

The dirty joking was bravura. Tina was shattered, and she began to cry, tears that quickly became heaving sobs of disappointment, embarrassment, pain. "But, Father, it's not a fantasy. And it's not just sexual."

"I'm sorry. But our relationship is pastoral only, and that's that. Understood?"

She was a tough girl and regained her composure enough for more truth telling. "Father, I know it isn't right. But it's how I feel. Please don't be angry with me. I couldn't stand that."

"I'm not angry, Tina. As they say, this isn't about me. It's about—"

"Because, I have to admit, I was gonna...when I came in here today...I was gonna try to get on your good side, sort of, because I can help you with something, and I wanted you to think..." Again, she fell into convulsive sobs, hyperventilating as she tried to catch her breath.

Father Steve took her hand in his. "Tell me. Help me how?"

"Because I know the church is doing bad, and I was going to...not blackmail...but get you to take me seriously by helping you with that."

"Tina, how in the world could you possibly help Our Lady of Grace?"

Tina removed her hand from Father Steve's grasp and opened her purse for tissues. She blew her nose, took some deep breaths, and regaining her composure, looked the priest square in the eye.

"Through my dad."

CHAPTER 49

WALDO'S

THERE WAS NO WALDO.

Once upon a time, there had been a Walt and Dorothy Jankowski, who had joined their first names to formulate their bar's. They divorced, however, in the early nineties, selling Waldo's to the current owner, Randy Black, who was both. The perpendicular neon sign fastened to the exterior faux brick and the gold-on-black matchbooks were the only remainders of the Jankowskis' union. Except for Stan Jankowski, their only child, a laid-off supermarket butcher who lived in Red Hook and came by every so often for old times' sake, trying to cadge drinks and bar snacks off of Randy.

Yet there *was* a Waldo. He was the God of Cocktail Lounges, the supernatural force that darkens the interior to obscure the filth in the carpet and the crow's-feet on the divorcées. It is He who installs the casters on the heavy oak-and-Naugahyde chairs to save wear and tear on the gold-on-black nylon Stainmaster fleur-de-lis. It is He who makes the laminated cocktail tables sticky no matter how many times they are wiped with a bar rag. It is He who orders the peppermint schnapps, peach brandy triple sec, and other Hiram Walker–flavored ipecacs. It is He who adds Wheat Chex to the party mix. It is He who programs the tent-card menu of fried mozzarella sticks, nachos, onion rings, and other cardiovascular time bombs, catering to the I-surrender demographic. It is He who quilts the vinyl in the booths so as to retain evaporated beer and other grime permanently in the seams. It is He who books the talent. Tonight: Casper the Crooner.

Jack arrived before Angela, and before the entertainment began. Scanning the room, he saw an older couple in a rear booth. The woman had dyed-black hair in a style he hadn't seen in many years, if ever. Her coif was sculpted with sweeping curves and sharp edges, the Sydney Opera house of hairdos. She was a tiny woman who, at about sixty, had kept her good figure. But her face was leathery, and her eyes too heavily lined, even before the false eyelashes. She was going for Liz Taylor but had arrived at Jerry Mahoney. Next to her was a man of indeterminate height and a vast barrel chest. He too had unusually dark hair for a man his age, but with streaks of gray, his was surely real. His eyes were dramatic too, deeply set beneath an overhanging brow, but sparkling like green aggies nestled in velvet pouches. Mr. Mattress, unless he was wildly mistaken, had located his hosts. He sucked in a breath and made his move to the booth.

"Mr. Donato?" he inquired, bending at the waist to equalize their height.

"You the bed guy?"

"Yes, sir. Jack Schiavone." He turned to Jerry Mahoney and extended his hand. "Jack Schiavone. How do you do?"

"Nice to meet you, Jack Schiavone. Evangeline Donato. Vic, scoot over. Let the man sit down, for crying out loud." The don did and, as Jack took a seat, was kind enough to break the conversational ice.

"So you're the guy shacked up with Angela, huh?"

239

"Victor!" Evangeline snapped. "What's the matter with you? Get the man a drink and watch your mouth!" She leaned over the table to pat Jack's hand. "Don't mind Victor. You know, an old-fashioned dad, always worrying about his little girls."

"Mr. Donato, I don't know what—"

"You think I don't know who's tapping my kid? In my business, you'd better know what's going on, or, believe you me, you're a dead man."

Jack made a show of looking for a waitress. Didn't help. Angela's father was wound up. "People need a bed, you sell a bed. I don't mean to offend you, but there ain't nothing to that. Me, I gotta hustle every second, be on my toes every second. What you call an occupational hazard."

"He's in the travel business," Evangeline explained. "Very, very tough."

Really? The travel business? Did she not know? Did she pretend not to know? Did she know and think Jack didn't know? Did the green-eyed monster think Jack didn't know? What could he possibly say in response? *I'm sorry, but I think maybe this isn't the best way to get acquainted. Please apologize to Angela for me. Pleasure to meet you. Good night.* Yeah, not that.

What he said was, "I'll bet." He did try to make it sound sympathetic, versus sarcastic. He might not have succeeded.

"You bet you'll bet," Angela's father said. "Evangeline, do me a favor. Get me a pack of cigarettes?"

"Huh? They don't sell cigarettes in bars no more."

"Evangeline, cigarettes. Take your time."

"Christ, Victor, you don't even smoke. For crying out loud, you gonna talk business, why do you even bring me? I'm coming back when Casper starts, you like it or not."

As Evangeline excused herself, still leggy in a pair of chalk-white pumps, it was easy to see where the twins had gotten their looks. It sure as hell wasn't from Dad, who, to Jack, looked a little bit like that Bugs Bunny character…What was his name? Something "Devil"? Strange-looking guy. But ever so gracious. The charm offensive was the gift that kept on giving.

"How's Manny, who you poached?"

Jack fiddled with the Yuengling coaster, which awaited the drink he seemed destined never to be offered, never mind served. No employee had yet approached, and time stood still. He hadn't agreed to this double date in order to be browbeaten by some hoodlum, and he certainly hadn't done it to play mind games. Then he decided, oh, what the hell. The guy wanted to talk about Manny? They'd talk about Manny.

"Doing very well, thanks, considering how different a mattress discounter is from a travel agency." Common sense tells us that nothing good can come of smart-mouthing a man who orders murders, yet doing so made Jack feel strangely serene. It is the same sensation reported by many survivors of near-death experiences. The rude host, however, took the delicate little slap rather well.

"OK, kid, sorry if I come on a little strong. So I guess you're on your toes a little too."

Jack shrugged. "Well, I know pretty much everything about you—and not from Angela, either. We've only been seeing each other for a few days, and believe it or not, we've barely discussed her family."

"No, I don't believe that."

"Well, it happens to be true. The thing is, Mr. Donato, even if your underboss weren't now my underboss, you don't keep a very low profile in this town. *Everybody* knows everything about you. The baggers at Pathmark know everything about you, and they're developmentally disabled."

"Yeah, I think we do something for the retards. Some sort of sports thing we sponsor."

Jack ignored that. He had more to say, and he was beginning to feel his oats. He lowered his voice and spoke to the don's shoulder. "And I know what you're up to—with the Russians."

Now, there was a conversation stopper. Mobs benefitted from being connected with rubouts after the fact; it made them more feared. But best practices in the business of premeditated murder demand secrecy going in, lest certain parties get wind of the scheme, such as the police or the target. Don Donato did not at first betray the anger that was rising, like pump water, from the artesian well of his vascular system to his enormous head. So Jack finished his thought.

"The contract. I know about it. By now, I'm sure half the town knows."

The don balled his right hand into a fist and pounded the table. "It's that fuckin' Ricci!" he spat.

"Who?" Jack wondered.

CHAPTER 50

THE PITCH

JACK HAD KNOWN AT LEAST THE OUTLINES OF THE PLAN BEFORE the sandwich man even got back to J&L. Larry had used his mobile to alert everybody in the association to the need for rapid deployment—Sale-a-Bration redux Wednesday and Thursday—in order to underwrite Trotsky redux. There'd been a tremor in his voice, one that struck Jack as evidence more of thrill than of anxiety. What Jack did not hear was any evidence of Larry's understanding that he had become a criminal conspirator and possible accessory before the fact to felony murder—although, apparently for fear of being eavesdropped on by the authorities, the Man in the Aloha Shirt had contrived a foolproof code: "We need to raise *oney-may* to *iquidate-lay* the *ussians-Ray*."

Try to crack *that* cipher.

Evangeline had gone to the bodega, not for the MacGuffin cigarettes, but just to cool her heels while Lucky Luciano finished with his business. Angela—on purpose or not, Jack didn't know—was so far a no-show. And Casper hadn't started performing yet. A keyboard player was busy on the modest carpet-squared stage trying to find the setting for snare drum brushes. The sound kept coming out maracas. This was Jack's opportunity, and he grabbed it.

"Listen, Mr. Donato, I don't know you, and no matter how much you've been snooping, you don't know me. But I've been paying attention this past unbelievable week, and I have a pretty big stake in what's going down. I'm sure you know that two Russian assholes came to my store trying to shake me down, and they weren't terribly delicate about it. I don't particularly want to be the next car wash or barbershop."

"Don't worry, son. This situation is under control," the mobster said, himself now trying to make eye contact with a waitress. "In a few days, it will be water under the dam."

"I don't know how a man of your experience could possibly think that. I've been reading about these Russian guys. They have an army over there. Whatever you manage to do to them, they will come back and blow up this whole neighborhood."

The don pretended not to hear that. "Girlie! We need some service over here!"

Janelle, the waitress, nodded and walked in the opposite direction to the service bar. She was the only server working.

"Son, I don't need your advice on taking care of my business. You wanna sell beds to Puerto Ricans, God bless you. You wanna play hide the pepperoni with Angela, be my guest. She's a grown woman. But don't interfere in my business. You got that clear?"

Jack had that clear. But he kept talking, for he was not your typical mattress retailer/pepperoniast. He was the Master of the Pitch. He'd spent his career dealing with clients and prospects who had all the money, all the leverage, all the power to hire and fire, yet he was preternaturally gifted in the art of persuasion. Not the actual advertising his agency produced—that was mediocre or worse and persuaded barely a soul. But in the conference room,

Jack Schiavone was a cold-blooded killer. He could look even hostile clients in the eye the same way he looked at a woman and seduce them, bedazzle them, bend them to his will. He hadn't become his agency's president by creating ad masterpieces. He was a modestly talented art director. His skill was creating and cultivating relationships. It was his singular genius.

"You know what?" he told the big boss in feigned surrender. "Do what you want. Go crazy. Get yourself killed. Get your family killed. Get me killed. Just understand…What you're really killing is Ebbets Beach."

"I'm killing Ebbets Beach? This is my town, son. You know that? This is my town. Don't tell me I'm killing my town."

"No? Didn't you just get done telling me you support Special Olympics?"

"Who? What?"

"Special Olympics. For the mentally challenged folks. Didn't you say you support that?"

"So what? We support a lot of things."

"Exactly," Mr. Mattress said. "I don't know how the mafia is supposed to run, but all I see is free blood pressure readings and raffles and—excuse me—the Legal Aid Society. Seems to me the Donato family is a shitload less like organized crime than the Gambinos or whatever and a whole lot more like a shadow government. This neighborhood doesn't function without you, am I not right?"

"Like the man says, our thing is to care."

"Yes!" replied Jack, slapping his hand on the table. "Yes! Yes! Yes! So please tell me why, in the name of Christ, you would go back to your old ways, back to that nasty Sicilian shit."

At those words—"nasty Sicilian shit"—the don's expression changed. He was no longer looking at Jack but somewhere over the mattress peddler's shoulder. Without warning, he leaned forward, balancing himself to stand, simultaneously revealing his massive chest and what must have been weirdly short legs, for he wasn't much taller on his feet than he'd been an instant earlier in his seat.

"Angelina," he said.

Jack swiveled around, saw his date, and jumped up, off balance every which way. Her arrival had startled him, and he stumbled as he rose to his feet. He fell sideways toward Little Caesar, who reflexively used his enormous upper-body strength to keep Jack from toppling altogether. There was a secondarily disconcerting aspect of Angela's appearance: it was spectacular. Gone were the chinos and oxford cloth. She was still J. Crew, but now in a peach-colored silk and linen bustier dress and heels. He had seen her naked, but he had never seen her turned out, and she was a vision. Even lipstick and a touch of eye shadow. The woman was just jaw-dropping. Regaining his balance, Jack gave Angela a kiss on the cheek and helped her into the booth.

"Just talking to your bigmouth boyfriend here," the don told his daughter. "I was gonna warn him to treat you right, but I oughta warn you. The boy's a fool."

CHAPTER 51

RUBBING HIM THE WRONG WAY

MARCO, LEONARD, LITTLE MANNY, AND TONY THE TEETH WERE defying the don. He had told them to get some rest, but it was too early. So instead, they sat in Tony's regular booth at Billie's enjoying a slice of pie and exchanging thoughts on how, exactly, their anonymous and unseen temp employee could get close enough to Smirdov to take the man's life.

"Teeth broke in just like that to plant those lox," Marco volunteered, but Tony waved a thick finger no, no, no. His mouth was full of piecrust, so Leonard the Calculator stepped in to explain.

"It's not 'those lox.' It's 'that lox.' One lox, two loxes."

"That don't make no sense," Marco argued. "Then it would be, like, one guns, two gunses. One horses, two horseses."

"No," Little Manny clarified, "Leonard is right. Lox is singular. Like 'meat.' You don't say, 'Gimme some of those meat,' do you?"

Now Tony the Teeth was shaking both his fat finger and his head, strenuously, as crumbs of pie spilled out of his mouth. It was his turn to clarify, and what began as grunts of objection began to form into words: "No, no. The lock. *The lock.*"

Little Manny threw up his hands. "You're wrong, Teeth. It's like Leonard says. Not one lock, two lox. It's just lox. It's that orange shit. Lox. The Jews love it. They put it on their bagels."

Tony the Teeth took his sledgehammer of a fist and pounded the table, rattling his Mylanta bottle, the ketchup bottle, the aluminum-domed sugar dispenser, the oil and vinegar cruets, and every plate on the pale-blue Formica. "NO!" he bellowed.

"'Fraid so," said Little Manny.

"No, you ain't listening. The *lock*. The lock *on the door*. In other words, I picked it easy, but no way the Russian hasn't deadbolted everything now. Nobody's gonna walk into that place now. I don't care what kind of hotshot he is."

Ah. The orange salmon was a red herring. Tony was talking actual logistics.

"Maybe," offered Leonard, "maybe the guy gets the Russian walking his dog."

"Fuggedaboudit," Tony objected. "Same thing. After today, the Russians will be in lockdown. One of his guys will walk the mutt, I guarantee it."

"Maybe we can lure him into the open," Marco countered, his pink apple cheeks looking even more sweetly out of place than usual, what with the assassination talk and everything. Anyway, his suggestion just made Little Manny laugh.

"Sure, Marco, 'cause we been so good at being one step ahead of this guy."

It was a dispiriting conversation. Unspoken, but on everybody's mind, was the likelihood of yet another debacle, this one ending in not mere embarrassment for the Family but bloody eradication. Then, in the spirit of the black comedy, Leonard the Calculator had a laugh too.

"You know what we should do?" he grinned. "We should hit that pretzel guy on the corner of Fifty-Eighth Place."

"What?" said Little Manny.

"Yeah. Guy's a total body double for the Russian. Same hooked nose, same crew cut. We shoot him. Then we take a picture, show it to the don. Boom. Boom. No more stale pretzels, no war."

Leonard was quite amused with himself. He laughed and laughed and laughed. It wasn't that it was a stupid idea; it was that it was no idea at all—just a funny notion based on a weird coincidence. He was so taken by his absurd suggestion he didn't look around the booth. Had he done so, he would have seen Tony the Teeth, Marco, and Little Manny all very much not laughing.

CHAPTER 52

FAMILY

"JESUS, DADDY, WHAT IS THE MATTER WITH YOU? WHY ARE YOU being such a prick?"

That struck Daddy as amusing. "That's what your mother wants to know."

Angela looked around. "Yeah, where is she, anyway?"

"Getting cigarettes," Jack said.

That made no sense to her. "Mom doesn't smoke."

Jack shook his head and pointed to the old man. "They're for him."

"Huh? He doesn't smoke, either. Would someone please tell me what's going on here?"

Jack couldn't. The reason for this hazing was a mystery to him. Not that he was shocked, especially. For the past few days, most everything had been, in varying degrees, a mystery to him. Beyond that, he came from advertising. He was often summoned to client dinners for the sole purpose of being demeaned and degraded by some asshole chief marketing officer just to remind the agency pipers who called the tune. For whatever reason, it seemed, Daddy Short Legs felt the need to assert himself, but why the new boyfriend should be the assertee the new boyfriend couldn't quite fathom. As it happened, clever as he was, Jack was fathoming out of his depth. Angela's father requested his presence with a specific thought in mind. He was simply working up to it.

"Maybe," the don said, "I want to find out if the Mattress King here is good enough for our family."

This was just too surreal. One second, this bully was talking crudely about hiding pepperoni; the next, he's usurping his adult daughter's right to navigate her own romances. Can you really be a doting father and vulgar barbarian at the same time? It dawned on Jack that his significant other's father was something significantly other than a mob don. He was also a douchebag.

"First of all," Jack said, "this is, what, Tuesday night? I had my first dinner with Angela on Sunday. So, with all due respect to your daughter, of whom I am very fond, I think family talk is a little premature. And a lot presumptuous. Secondly, before you go any further with your character tests, let me respectfully remind you that I'm not the criminal here."

"That's not what I hear, sonny. I ain't never been convicted of nothin'. You, on the other hand, are a real-life ex-con."

Oh, Holy Mother of God.

Again with the dark chapter of his life. The Donatos might be an unusual clan, but their due diligence skills were top drawer. Just like his teachers had always warned him, his one scrape with authority lingered on his permanent record. Jack had no quibble with that. What's done is done, and what he did he accepted responsibility for. Still, it's one thing to have skeletons in your closet, and another for everyone you meet to go skeleton hunting. Deflated, Jack closed his eyes, took in a breath, exhaled it in a sardonic half chuckle, and shook his head slightly in a kind of amused resignation. "Google?" he inquired.

"Google," the gangster confirmed. "Angelina, were you aware of this?"

"Of course, Daddy, I know what he did."

Also the wrong answer.

Abruptly, the Grand Inquisitor sharpened his tone. "Wrong!" he snapped. "He did nothing!"

Angela turned to Jack, who held his hands up and shook his head, this time to convey, *Beats the shit out of me.* Because it beat the shit out of him. As had become typical of his encounters with the Donato family, he knew not where this was headed. Ever since he came to this neighborhood, he'd found it difficult to predict what was coming next. That's because he'd been repeatedly confounded by whatever had just happened. Hell, most of the time he was stymied just getting a fix on the here and now.

"Your sweetheart didn't embezzle nothing," the don went on. "*Il pazzo*, he took the fall for some broad. I read every article. You gotta be stupid not to see what went on. I told you he was a fool and he is, giving up his career for some cokehead trim. Tell me, Mr. Schiavone, you fall in love with every piece of ass you sample?"

"Jack, is that true?" Angela demanded, in as soft and guilty a way as a woman can demand. If what her father said was correct, then Jack had stolen nothing; he was merely chivalrous. Maybe even heroic. And, yes, a total fool.

Jack stared down at his coaster. "Mr. Donato, that is none of your business."

"Oh, it's my business, all right."

"Yeah, and how is that? You're not *my* father."

Victor Donato mugged for his daughter, screwing up his face into a look of cartoonish bewilderment. "See, honey, like I said, a fool. He don't know what I'm talking about."

"Daddy," replied Angela, "I also have no idea what you're talking about. I've been lost since I came in here. Jack's great, but he's not a member of our family."

"Maybe not yet," her father retorted, "but anybody can see he will be. Anyway, you two dopes, that's not the family I'm talking about." Because while Don Donato did not necessarily have an absolute command of, say, Bartlett's *Familiar Quotations*, he was nonetheless an extraordinarily astute judge of talent, opportunity, and—excluding certain niceties, such as the criminal code—character. In this case, he recognized two things at once: one being that these smart alecks were made for each other, the other being not to let this guy slip through his fingers. More than at any time since he met a travel agent named Manny thirty-plus years ago, Vic Donato realized that he was kissing distance from a character that could take his organization to the next level.

None of which either Jack or Angela quite understood. Independently, they had more or less gathered that they'd been bestowed with the old man's blessing for a marriage neither had thought of, or thought of thinking of for weeks or months or years to come. Interestingly enough, neither was much offended by the oracle's absurd relationship forecast. They were more perplexed by the other thing, which they hadn't fully decoded. They looked at each other from opposite sides of the booth, thinking the same thing. Had the old man just recruited Jack into the Cozy Nostra? Impossible. Simply impossible—unless the pressure had gotten to him, and he had gone completely off his nut. They gaped at each other amid mental commotion—immediately complicated by physical commotion. Suddenly, the three of them were the five of them. From one side, Evangeline had returned.

She threw a carton of Virginia Slims at Victor, hitting him right in the head with it. "There you go, wiseguy," she snarled, "You owe me a hundred and ten dollars." Then she turned to Angelina. "Hello, sweetheart girl! Give Mama a kissy kiss."

Simultaneously Janelle the waitress had finally made her way back to the table. "Sorry, folks. Busy in here. What can I get youse?"

"Champagne," said the little big boss. "Bring me your best champagne."

"We got Korbel."

"Bring that," he agreed.

"Special occasion?" inquired Janelle, perfunctorily, as she scribbled the order on a guest check.

"Yes, it is," the boss went on, pointing out Jack to the waitress. "See this good-looking young man? His life is about to change."

CHAPTER 53

MIRTH

WHEN THE WAITRESS WALKED AWAY, THE SUDDENLY LIGHT-hearted paterfamilias turned to Angela.

"Sweetheart, don't you need to go to the ladies to freshen up?"

"No," she replied.

"Evangeline, you girls go do whatever you do in the powder room."

"Fuck you, Victor. You wanna talk privately, get your own ass to the men's room. I'm finished with goose chases tonight, thank you very much."

"I'm staying right here, Dad."

Oh well, thought Jack, *since it seems to be disrespecting time, might as well pile on.* "There's no reason to talk to me alone, anyway," he said. "The answer is no."

Again, Dad addressed his daughter. "He ain't even heard what I have to say."

"I've heard enough," Jack snapped. "Forget about it. I've got a business. A legitimate one."

Donato to his daughter: "What'd he say?"

Evangeline to her hubby: "You deaf now? He said he's got a legitimate one."

And at that, the boss of Ebbets Beach bosses lost it. He began with a sniff, then a snigger, then a giggle, and soon a resounding, booming, quaking peal of guffaws. Because he had suddenly realized something. Addressing Angela and pointing to Jack, he choked out a question. "Did he…hee hee hee…he think I was asking him to…to…to…ha ha ha…to join Fiesta Tours? Are you kidding me? Ha ha ha ha ha ha ha ha ha." He wasn't faking, either. This wasn't stage laughter. It was a rare, spontaneous outbreak of donly mirth. The great stone face, in the past few days, had suddenly turned into Ed Wynn.

Angela had never seen her father in such a fit of hilarity. She also didn't get it. It sure seemed to her the old man had been asking Jack to join Fiesta Tours, which meant the gang. What else could he possibly have been hinting at?

Whatever it was, Evangeline certainly didn't want to hear it. To protect herself and her husband, she assiduously avoided all business matters. She'd tried to put Victor in his place and didn't wish to give in, but—pride or no pride, laughter or no laughter—she more didn't wish to be a witness to any incriminating declarations. "I'm gonna powder my nose," Mrs. Donato said, and made haste to the bathroom. Through all, her husband roared.

"Someone care to tell me what's so goddamned funny?" Jack demanded.

The formerly stone-faced don nodded his head vigorously but couldn't quite summon speech. Little did he know that only two days earlier his own soldiers were in similar hysterics about his own preferences in headgear. Nor did he realize that Mr. Mattress had been a serial victim of ludicrous misunderstandings and was finding the surrounding comedy decreasingly comical. All that the world's most dangerous travel agent knew was that this particular mixup was hysterical. Thus he was forced to hold his hand up to the poor bed salesman until, eventually, he could catch his breath.

"Son," he began, trying to stifle the laughter, "I like you, I really do. I can tell you and Angela are halfway to Our Lady of Grace. You look like a fine couple. But when I say I want you to join the family, Jack, for crying out loud already, I'm talking about the Amway family."

"Amway?" Jack parroted.

"Amway," replied Marco's upline.

"You're in *Amway*?" asked Angela, incredulously.

"Independent distributor of four hundred eighty fine products, delivered directly to your home."

There was a long moment of nothing said as the laughing don's giggles wound down. Jack and Angela exchanged baffled glances, then looked back at the Amway missionary and back at each other—whereupon they too dissolved into laughter—though the merry don believed they were laughing at Jack's folly, not his own.

"You're part of a global family, yet you're your own boss," he observed.

"I think I peed myself," Angela said, still giggling. "Excuse me." She followed in her mother's trail. This left Jack alone again with his reputed future father-in-law. Equal parts embarrassed and amused, he had no idea what to say. In the wake of the previous outbursts, neither man immediately had anything useful to add. The offer was on the table. Victor Donato, unlike his dinner guest, was not the sort of man to sell.

"Nice place," his own boss offered.

"Yeah," said Jack, glancing around and thinking pretty much the opposite. "Classy joint."

Providentially, Janelle arrived with the champagne, popped the plastic cork, and filled four cheap flutes for the two guests still seated there. Becalmed, the men hoisted and toasted.

"*Alla salute!*" said the don.

"Family," said Jack.

"*L'chaim!*" said someone else. Jack looked up and saw a tall, doughy middle-aged man with a creepy, too narrow, too closely trimmed beard. Donato did a double take, requiring two looks to make the connection. Jesus, Mary, and Joseph—what the fuck was he doing there?

"I came to see my pal Casper perform. Mind if I join you?" He didn't wait for a response before he took Angela's seat and held out his hand toward Jack. "How ya doin'? I'm Doc."

"Jack Schiavone."

"My chiropractor," explained the sponsor of Patient B, looking extremely uneasy.

"Schiavone, eh?" the Chiropractor greeted Jack. "So, you're in the...family?" This elicited a big grin from the prospective Amway recruit.

"So this man tells me," he smiled.

Seth Glick-Mermelstein leaned forward and whispered to the side-by-side family members. "Good. So we can talk about the Russian job."

The don's eyes widened. "NO, WE CAN'T."

"All I gotta do is get him on my drop table. Then...ker-*RAACK*!"

The don rose, slightly, to his feet. "Doc! Shut the fuck up! SHUT THE FUCK UP!"

Too late. For once, for *once*, to Jack the nonrecruit of Fiesta Tours, all was extremely, perfectly, totally, horribly, criminally clear.

CHAPTER 54

KICK IN THE HEAD

FOR REASONS ALSO PERFECTLY CLEAR TO MR. MATTRESS, MR. Amway quickly ushered Mr. Blabbermouth out of Waldo's. Jack was, of course, appalled to get confirmation that a murder plot was absolutely in motion. Yet he was shocked and in a way embarrassed to see who was contracted for the job. This was a hit man? Let's just say the man called Doc didn't quite conform to the stereotype of contract killer. He conformed more to the stereotype of *Star Trek* nerd. A chiropractor. What kind of sorry-ass gang brings in a semidoctor to do its dirty work? Who tossed their firebombs? A podiatrist? It was strange, pitiful, and frightening, all at once.

And there was one other thing that Mr. Mattress puzzled over: if the plot was as Doc incautiously described, how in the world would the gang that couldn't hire straight get the Russian menace on a chiropractor's table?

"Hey! Look what the cat drug in! It's Mr. Mattress!" It was Casper, resplendent in gold lamé. "Glad you come. I'm kinda surprised to see you!"

Not as surprised as he was to see Don Donato approach and take a seat next to Jack.

"Hello, Casper. When you sing? I don't got all night."

"Looking forward to it," said Jack. "Break a leg." Ha. To this, considering the cast of characters, he felt the need to add, "Your own."

Don Donato and Mr. Mattress, together. This was a hard circle for Casper to square. So he offered a feeble wave and withdrew to the service bar as a dinky spotlight was illuminated above the dinky stage. It was just before 9:30. The keyboard guy—in a lime-green dress shirt, black slacks, patent leather dress shoes, and slicked-back, lye-relaxed hair—ambled to the stage microphone. "All right, y'all. I'm Calvin McCoy. Waldo's welcomes you to the evening's entertainment. Y'all give it up for my man, Mr. Casper Benedetto!" Calvin resumed his spot behind the keyboard, playing the introductory bars of "Mack the Knife" as Casper took the stage. The entrance was really something. Casper walked up to the mic as if he were walking up to the counter of the Department of Motor Vehicles. The gold lamé was shimmering; he was not. He looked like Bobby Kennedy at a costume party, dressed as the lunar lander. He wasn't even smiling—just doing something strange with his right hand, like a pantomime of flicking a yo-yo. It took a second to figure out he was snapping his fingers, almost but not quite to the beat of the fake snare drum. Then, with his left hand, Casper grabbed the mic stand, closed his eyes, and sang.

> *Oh, the shark, babe, has such teeth, dear,*
> *And it shows them pearly white.*
> *Just a jackknife has old MacHeath, babe,*
> *And he keeps it, ah, out of sight.*

Angela and Jack exchanged looks of astonishment. Yeah, he was awkward, nearly to the point of palsy, but if you only closed your eyes like he did, Bobby Kennedy disappeared, replaced by Bobby Darin himself! Casper's voice and phrasing were cool, sexy, tender, catchy—all at the same time. In short, fantastic. He was a revelation. Jack watched the people at the other tables. The further into the song Casper got, the more they turned to see the performer.

Ya know when that shark bites with his teeth, babe,
Scarlet billows start to spread.
Fancy gloves, oh, wears old MacHeath, babe,
So there's never, never a trace of red.

But soon they turned their heads back to their friends, averting their eyes from Casper as if he were a homeless panhandler. It was so much better to just listen, and not worry that the poor guy would have a nervous breakdown or simply fall and hurt himself.

I said Jenny Diver, whoa, Sukey Tawdry,
Look out to Miss Lotte Lenya and old Lucy Brown.
Yes, that line forms on the right, babe,
Now that Macky's back in town...

Look out, old Macky's back!

Any lounge singer can tell you that audience response is the exception, not the rule. The performer is meant to be background music more than entertainment, a purveyor not of excitement but of mood. As a general rule, if there is a cover charge, management wants you to come for the show. If there is no cover charge, management wants you to come for the ambience. The more you pay attention to the act, the less you pay to your friends; the less attention you pay to your friends, the less booze you buy.

Casper was somewhere in between. He had a following in Ebbets Beach. Some were younger women, who thought he was adorable. Most were older women, who also thought he was adorable, but connected emotionally to his oldies and American songbook repertoire. Long story short, when he finished his opening number, he received generous applause, which he acknowledged by bowing stiffly at the waist like a feudal Japanese serf to the shogun. He got an especially wild burst of applause from the don's table, where Angela and Evangeline had returned and actually rose to their feet with genuine enthusiasm. Evangeline whistled like an ironworker. Angela said, and this is a quote, "Woooooo. WOOOOOO!" Only the don was unimpressed. He didn't understand what the fuss was about. If Casper wanted women to swoon, there was nothing the matter with *La Storia Di Cicciu Ulivieri*.

Casper, now smiling, glanced over to acknowledge his people. What he saw was the boss sipping champagne; Mrs. Donato with her thumb and index finger jammed between her pursed lips and making the shrillest sound he'd ever heard from a woman not in the throes of anger or ecstasy; his bedding salesman and potential new account on his feet with a wide smile and clapping like crazy; and, finally, the love of his life grinning madly and hugging Mr. Mattress. The smile disappeared from his face.

Casper's impulse was to jump from the stage-ette and beat Jack unconscious. But there sat the don. And the audience. So for one of the very few times in his life, Casper exhibited impulse control. Calvin was playing the introductory bars of the next song. Casper sucked it up, stepped back behind the mic stand, and channeled Dino.

How lucky can one guy be;
I kissed her and she kissed me.
Like the fella once said,
Ain't that a kick in the head?

He glared at Jack and Angela, but they had no idea he was expressing hostility, versus his default onstage demeanor. They therefore failed to detect the searing irony of the selection. Casper, who'd programmed the set with no advance knowledge of cruel betrayal, felt the irony like electroshock. But all he would do for now was sing. He'd been up since 5:00 a.m. being made a jackass of by Russians. He was exhausted from playing the fool.

No problem. He'd kill Mr. Mattress later.

CHAPTER 55

PILLOW TALK

"SO WHEN ARE WE GETTING MARRIED?" JACK ASKED. THEY HAD just spent a half hour grunting, so now he had an urge to form words.

"I'd marry you," Angela replied from the bathroom. This caused Jack to sit bolt upright in bed.

"Get outta here! You hardly know me."

"I've got the picture pretty much."

"How do you know I'm not a pedophile? How do you know I don't fart at the dinner table? Maybe I chew my toenails. Maybe I watch *The Bachelorette*."

"Do you? Watch *The Bachelorette*?"

"Fuck no."

"Good. That would be a deal breaker. Otherwise, you're acceptable."

"Well, darling, you are just a romantic fool."

"The 'Mr. Mattress' thing would take some getting used to," Angela added, "but I supposed I'd survive. Obviously, dignity has never really been a big part of my life experience. Christ, I've been Miss Donato all my life. I guess I can handle Mrs. Mattress."

Jack felt the need to clarify. "Just to remind you, strictly speaking, I did not propose to you. Your father proposed me to you, and that doesn't count. I generally don't commit my life to someone before at least the week is out."

"Really?" Angela said as she lay down next to Jack and stroked his chest. "My dad seems to think you are less discriminating. Anyway, whatever, I'll give you three more days. I can't squander my entire September waiting for you to commit. The clock is ticking over here."

"Now we're having kids?"

"A houseful."

"Oh, for God's sake," Jack replied, tossing a pillow off the bed, then a second one. Then he slid his hand under the small of Angela's back and pulled her toward him, whispering, "Come on, we'd better get started."

Afterward, as midnight struck, they were both wide-awake, Angela lying on her side, curled into the contours of Jack's embrace. He caressed her neck, letting the silky black hair sift through his fingers.

"Look," he said, "there's something I've gotta tell you."

"OK," she said. "Tell me."

"It's about your father."

"Probably not much you can tell me about him."

"He's gonna kill some Russian. Or try."

Angela wasn't buying it. "Come on, Jack. You're paranoid."

"Angela, I'm not paranoid. They're planning a hit. And tonight I met the hit man."

That was breaking news. She sat up, tucked her knees under her chin, with the light Indian-print cotton bedcover clamped between them as Jack told his story: Manny's verdict; Larry's excited call;

and, finally, the clumsy beans-spilling by the loose-lipped chiropractor. Angela began to quietly cry.

"I let myself think this bullshit was over," she whispered. "Sometimes I feel like I'm cursed."

And with that, she fell into Jack's arms. He held her closely while she wept, pondering how unfair her fate had been. He also pondered one other thing: wasn't there some other way to scare off the Russians?

CHAPTER 56

DEJA VU

SAM CALABRESE WAS ALSO PLOTTING A MURDER. IN HIS FANTASIES, at least, he was plotting the murder of Larry Rizzo.

Larry had phoned him six times in the space of fourteen hours to remind him about Back-to-School Daze and about what was at stake. One of those calls woke Sam and June at 3:15 a.m. It concerned pickles, he seemed to recall, but what about pickles he couldn't remember. It was especially irritating to Sam, who had never gotten quite such attention from his landlord in the winter of 2006, when the furnace died in the midst of a cold snap, or last year when the city padlocked him for unpaid taxes—unpaid, that is, by Larry. But about the neighborhood watch Larry was unbearably vigilant.

But what was Sam going to do to get on the bandwagon? Parcel dispatch was not exactly an impulse purchase. If people needed to send a package, they sent a package. If they had no package to send, all the balloons and colored pennants weren't going to put them in a parcel frame of mind. Sam also strongly suspected that Larry was a paranoid schizophrenic who was losing his touch with reality. Sam's uncle Lance had lived in the same building with David Berkowitz, aka the .44 caliber killer, aka Son of Sam. Berkowitz thought his dog ordered him to kill. Larry believed the neighborhood watch money was going to underwrite a gangland slaying. What a crackpot.

At 9:20 a.m. on Wednesday, when he arrived at his store, resting by his front door was an empty jar. Ah. A big-ass pickle jar, with a slot carved into the lid. Now he got it. What he didn't get was how to fill it up. As he bent down to retrieve the cucumber depository, he noticed Casper the Collector coming out of the door leading upstairs to Fiesta Tours. Was there a celebrity ball game of some sort today as part of the festivities?

It was 9:31 when Casper, huffing and puffing a bit from the brisk walk up the boulevard, strode into Mr. Mattress. Looking neither left nor right in the store, he made a beeline for the sales desk, where Jack sat at the computer composing a Google AdWords buy. He glanced up just in time to see Casper raise a baseball bat, two-handed, above his head. Jack flinched and instinctively pushed back from the desk in his roller chair, but the bat still smashed down in front of him with a tremendous crash, jostling everything on the surface and splintering the bat in two. The handle, sharp as a stake, remained in Casper's grip. The barrel flew sideways and landed at the foot of a Snoo-Z-Lite Pro.

"Casper! What the fuck? *You out of your mind? What are you doing?*"

Jack was terrified and unbelieving. He couldn't believe somebody was coming after him with a baseball bat. He couldn't believe the Donato mob would be intimidating the Villagers and almost-Villagers while simultaneously trying rally them to the cause. He couldn't believe the Donato gang would be coming after their new son-in-law or whatever the fuck the old man called him. And he couldn't believe Casper, the laid-back bagman, would suddenly get so violent.

"Yeah? Well, fuck you, Mattress. *Stay away from my lady!*"

"*Jesus Christ, are you nuts? What lady? Get the fuck out of here. Manny sees you with that—*"

"*Just stay the fuck away from Angela!*"

Casper flung the bat handle at the front window, where it hit broken edge first and caused no further damage. He then stalked out of the store.

Jack gulped. That quickly, he thought, he could have been dead.

At 11:44 a.m., a Mr. Victor Donato of Fiesta Tours walked into Mr. Mattress and made a beeline for the sales desk. He was brandishing no sporting equipment, just a bottle of grappa, which he placed on the desk in the midst of the sensation of déjà vu. Across from him sat Emanuel Aiala, assistant manager.

"Hello, Manny," said Don Donato.

"Hello, Vic," said Manny.

"How things with you?"

"Fair to middling," said Manny. "Learning about beds."

Manny's former boss and mentor surveyed the store. "Yeah, nice place. How's the young genius treating you?"

"Good. He's a good guy. He's at the post office."

"You know he's shacked up with your goddaughter?"

"Yeah."

"You keep an eye on him."

"Nah. I don't need to do that. He's good people."

"He called me, said Casper come in here with a baseball bat."

"Un-fucking-believable," said Manny. "The goof's sweet on Angela. Who knew?"

"Has she ever resuscitated this affection to your knowledge?"

"She never said nothing to me. I think Casper was, like, stalking her, maybe."

The don then did something that everybody in the movies does but you hardly ever see in real life. He screwed up his face and pinched the bridge of his nose. Fatigue, physical and nervous, was taking its toll.

"Look here, Manny, when your boss gets in, tell him I come by. Give him this brandy. Tell him I'll take care of Casper. I offer my apology. I will make this up to him, this I promise you."

The saddest don got up to withdraw, but Manny had more to talk about.

"So, Vic, you gonna whack the Russian?"

Now he sat right back down. "What, did you read that in the *PennySaver*?"

"You went outside? A fucking chiropractor?"

"Manny, you're outta line. You ain't in the Family no more."

"I got my kid to think about. Anyway, why ain't I heard of this guy?"

Donato sighed. "You ain't heard of him because money is tight and I had to lower my specs a little bit."

"You got a *discount* triggerman?"

"Value priced, let's say. But that's good. Nobody knows nothing about him, makes the contract harder to trace back to us. To me."

"He's got a bead on the Russian?"

"He's seen pictures."

"So what did he say?"

"He says the Russian's got a lumbago subway station, or something like that."

"A what?"

"Some kinda cockamamie backache. Tell you the truth, Manny, we don't know how he's gonna do it. I mean, we know how he's gonna *do it*, but not how he's gonna get close. But that's his fuckin' problem."

Manny looked at his former don. Donato looked at his former protégé. Both men knew very well this was absolutely the Donatos' problem. Last thing they needed was a botched hit and an amateur in the hands of the cops, or, worse yet, the Russians. The situation was untenable, on the way to unsurvivable. And Donato, exhausted in body, mind, and spirit, was feeling frightfully cornered.

"Maybe you should ask your new boss the criminal mastermind what he would do, he's so fucking smart."

Manny looked down at the crease in his dress pants. He hated to hear the don talk like that. No point in taking his frustrations out on Jack. Anyway, Jack was pretty sharp for a Manhattanite. Probably, he'd...wait. Manny's head popped up like a jack-in-the-box.

"You know what?" Manny said, a sliver of a smile crossing his lips, just as it did once upon a time in the matter of first-class air tickets. "Funny you should mention that."

Donato remained sour. "What? Embezzling Jack's gonna help me? I'm going to the mattresses. He gonna sell them to me?"

"No, but it just kinda hit me, something my boss says to me."

Something his *boss* says to him. That stung the mobster. "Vic" stung the mobster. Being the supplicant stung the mobster. For the lonely, consigliereless don, this was a moment of truth. He could stand on protocol, and pride, and take his leave. Or he could do what he did thirty-five years ago in a nearly identical scenario and listen carefully to an underemployed fellow Sicilian capable of seeing the unseen.

"I'm listening."

"Your chiropractor's gotta get close to your Russian, right?"

Donato nodded.

"And your Russian has lumbago, right?"

"Yes."

"So what Jack always says is, 'Everyone's back hurts.' That's how he sells beds."

"So? What's that got to do with the price of fish?"

"Fuckin' A, Vic. It's also how chiropractors get patients."

Once again, the don was surveying the store, his glance alighting on a small table backing up to a pillar on which rested a bowl of treats. He turned to Manny. "Are those Milk Duds?" he asked.

Manny waved. "Help yourself."

CHAPTER 57

BACK-TO-SCHOOL DAZE

EVEN IN THE MORNING, WHEN THE IMPROMPTU BACK-TO-SCHOOL Daze event was handicapped by the fact of school-age customers being back in school, traffic was quite good. The weather was so cool and dry nobody really missed the snow cone booth, which had been blown over and damaged in the Labor Day storm. So far nobody had been sickened by reheated free hot dogs, and all the merchants had managed to find a bunch of crap to display in sidewalk bins at a discount, the entire proceeds of which would go to Neighborhood Watch Plus. Everybody also displayed big pickle jars, courtesy of Larry Rizzo, soliciting cash donations for the cause. Those were quickly stuffed with coins and small bills, even a twenty or two.

Particularly enthusiastic was none other than Mr. Kim, who finally saw tangible benefit from associating with the Italians. To lure folks into his store, he offered two-for-one on shirts. Then he offered zipper repair for half off and put the proceeds in his jar. A twenty-nine- to sixty-nine-dollar item. And on top of that he encouraged every customer to donate his or her change. Ostensibly, the money would pay for radios and security cameras, as opposed to health-care-professional executioners.

"Bad fire two times," he told Jeanine Petro, shaking his jar in front of her. "Need to stop. Neighborhood watch."

He wasn't alone. Original Reyes offered one free slice with every slice purchased. Across the boulevard, Famous Reyes had a chalkboard outside announcing FREE BABYSITTING. Turned out to be a deft move. The place was jammed with runny-nosed little three- and four-year-olds, nominally supervised by Juan's girlfriend, Betty. But every mom bought a slice or two. This was land-office business for a store that usually sat abandoned till 11:00 a.m. Juan too was able to prevail on grateful moms to feed the jar. Coiffe Medicine Unisex Styling Salon put all wash-and-sets in the jar, and the cutters unselfishly added their tip money. At the bodega near the corner of 57th Place, Kim Gun-woo (no relation to the dry cleaner) sold neighborhood watch roses for three dollars a stem. He kept one dollar and put the other two in the jar. Not to be outdone, Aaron Kornblitt, the jeweler, offered neighborhood watch gold chains—10 percent off on anything in his inventory with another 10 percent donated to the cause. He sold eighteen chains, compared to most days when he sold one or two. Korny was an outgoing, talkative guy, always ready to regale you with a funny story in his coarse-sandpaper voice. In chatting up his Back-to-School Daze customers, though, he didn't mention that 25 percent was his everyday discount from the inflated "list" price, so his chain customers were actually paying a premium. At Parcel Plus, Sam Calabrese offered free foam packing peanuts. His jar was empty.

Larry wandered from place to place egging on both merchants and shoppers. By noon he had counted almost $3,600 in proceeds. An impressive sum by any measure—except for the measure that mattered. Multiply that take times four, assuming similar good luck in the afternoon and the next day, and he'd wind up $10,600 short of the sum he'd pledged to the underworld. It was easy for him to imagine having not one but two crime bosses on a rampage.

It was a nervous and increasingly pessimistic conspirator who arrived at Tanning Expo, which happened to be the bustlingest establishment of all. There the first-annual Bikini Day was being staged. Every woman who showed up in a bikini got a free tan. Sunny and Tina wore thongs. But all men paid the fifteen-dollar admission to sit there and watch the exposition. Even Tina was surprised by how many men who are at loose ends during business hours have the fifteen dollars to stand around watching mainly ordinary-looking women climb into tanning beds—although, to reiterate, Tina wore a thong.

So distracted was Larry Rizzo that, unlike the other males present, he neglected to gawk lasciviously at Tina's breasts. When she jiggled toward him, swinging her hips on the path, he was counting the money in the neighborhood watch jar. A whopping $360, leaving him still, at the current pace, almost nine grand short. This presented some concerns, *Magnificent Seven*–wise.

"Pretty good, huh, Larry?" Tina said with a big smile.

That's when he noticed her spillage. Even then, he by no means leered at her. Not Larry's style. He was an analytical guy, and he simply did what came naturally to him. He analyzed.

"Those are big bongos, sister," he observed.

"Don't be fresh, Larry."

"Not being fresh. I'm a happily married man, as you well know. Also, too, with the Zoloft, frankly, I'm not really in the game, so to speak. It's just that you look like a Hawaiian Tropic calendar, only in three-D." That's when he thought of a hilarious witticism. "Or thirty-four-D, heh heh heh heh."

"Thanks for the compliment," Tina replied. "Enough, OK?"

"Sure…But can I ask you something? Are they real? You're such a tiny girl, and the bazooms are frankly enormous. These are implants, correct?"

"Christ, Larry, shut up before I smack you."

"I'm not saying they look fake. They are very nice and bulbous, if that's the right word. They got a nice shape to them. A nice, large shape. You know that tranny hooker who used to loiter by the bodega? Better than hers—his."

Tina slapped Larry on his face so hard his eyes watered.

"Ow," he said.

"Are you finished yet?" she asked, with less anger in her voice than you might expect. Fortunately for her, Larry was right on the verge of getting the message that Tina wanted to stop hearing about her tits.

"If they aren't real, that's OK," Larry assured her. "I'll still respect you as a person and a businesswoman. I'm just saying, I'm not sure. Sister, take that as flattery."

Tina only had to hit him one more time before he changed the subject to the tragic shortfall shaping up for the merchants' premeditated-murder fund. At that point, Sunny Kaplan stood by, shaking her head. The night before, she had argued with Tina about the whole idea, on the grounds of illegality, immorality, recklessness, and likelihood of failure—to which Tina thoughtfully answered, "Those aren't arguments." Turned out the mafia princess liked the idea of doffing the tiara and rolling up her sleeves. Today, she'd rolled her sleeves up so far her ass cheeks were visible from outer space. Unlike Sunny, she had not considered the possibility of failure. If Larry was right, circumstances called for something drastic. And she had the best idea ever.

CHAPTER 58

ADVERTISING

MR. MATTRESS WASN'T AT THE POST OFFICE. HE WAS ON THE WAY to the Handi Copy Center to print up fliers advertising a new service, delivered right to your home. He'd gotten his brainstorm at Angela's and mocked it up on his Mac as soon as he got home to shower and change. First stop, though, the Ebbets Beach Legal Aid Society. He took a seat at Angela's desk at precisely the same time her father was taking a seat at Jack's.

"Hello, handsome," said the legal aide. "Can't get enough of me, huh?"

"Never ever. I've gotta talk to you."

"Oh, Jack, I'm up to my ears in landlord-tenant stuff. Can this keep till after work?"

"No, it can't. Two things. First of all, your friend Casper just came after me with a baseball bat warning me to stay away from his girl."

"What? He came after you with a baseball bat?"

Jack demonstrated, in pantomime.

Angela gasped. "But he's not…I've never…Jack, that is crazy. I've never…I've been blowing him off since high school."

Jack arched an eyebrow.

"You're disgusting. You know exactly what I mean."

"Someone ought to inform Casper. He seems to think you are his sweetheart. I called your father. I don't want the idiot coming after you next. I want you to be extremely cautious, all right?"

"Sure, but—"

"I'm actually not all that concerned. If he were going to hurt somebody, he would've smashed my skull, not my desk."

"Oh, Jack, I am so sorry. You do know I never led him on. The opposite, I swear to you."

"I know, I know. I just want you to be careful. Promise me."

"Of course…Jesus, baseball bat…What could possibly be the other thing?"

"Yeah, here's what I wanted to ask you: You mentioned landlord-tenant. By any chance have you ever heard of the Brighton Beach Community Council?"

"No," she replied. "I mean, maybe. I guess they do landlord-tenant relations too. And maybe immigrant work."

"Yes, immigrant work," Jack confirmed. "And social services assistance. Just like…"

"I give up."

"Come on, Counselor. Just like…"

"Jack, for fuck's sake, just come out with it…"

"*You*. They do what you do. I've been reading up on Brighton Beach—for I suppose obvious reasons—and I ran across them. They're doing God's work there."

"Yeah, so?"

"So they also do some things you don't do, specifically. They provide some low-level social services. They coordinate some charity work and help nonprofits apply for grants. They string up the holiday lights and put up the giant menorah. They offer debt counseling and some emergency low-interest loans. See what I'm getting at?"

"Excellent question, Jack. No, I have no idea what you're getting at."

"Angela, darling, who pays your rent?"

"Come on, Jack..."

"The Donato gang. Who strings the Christmas lights? Who provides emergency low-interest loans? Who provides security to the neighborhood? Who sponsors the antidrug campaign? Who sponsors the Little League? Who runs charity drives?"

"Who," added Angela, who was catching on, "paid the medical bills for the pretzel kid?"

"Huh?" Jack asked.

"Never mind. You're saying that the Cozy Nostra is looking like a beneficial organization."

"Looking *a lot* like a beneficial organization. Your father told me, just by the way, that they sponsor the Special Olympics. The Special-fucking-Olympics!"

"Yeah, I don't think they do, actually. Some other sports thing for special-needs kids, but I see what you're saying." She paused, thinking about Jack's pitch. Like many of her attorney colleagues, he had fashioned an impressive-sounding argument by conveniently disregarding a number of salient facts. "Look, far be it from me to find fault with your premise, or with the sainted Donato family, but didn't you tell me last night they're about to murder someone? I'll bet the Brighton Beach Community Council turns to murder only as an absolute last resort."

Jack smiled. "I know, I know. But what I'm saying is, if we were able to persuade your father that he's already half-legitimate and that turning back to the old ways spells only ruin, maybe…I don't know…I don't even know *maybe* what. But maybe something better than organized crime and killing."

Angela took the measure of the man across from her, then chose her words very carefully. "Jack, that is obviously the dumbest idea anybody has ever thought of," she said. Jack lowered his head, not knowing whether to be more disappointed or embarrassed. Angela, who'd suffered the collateral damage of Donato perfidy her entire life, had not merely thrown cold water on his silly idea, she'd firehosed it like a riot policeman on a drunken looter. And now, as he stood there wallowing in his own foolishness and deflation, she started right back in on him. "I mean, come on, Jack, you sound completely delusional." Then she reached out to touch his shoulder. "But, hell," she added, "what do we have to lose?"

What Angela did not realize is that she could not have been more wrong. The dumbest idea anybody had ever thought of was the one that Jack withheld, the one that had kept him up half the night. After kissing her good-bye in a most unprofessional manner, he headed off to complete his errands. First, he went to Verizon, where in less than one hour he walked out with a new phone number and a cheap new camera phone. Then he headed to Handi Copy, where he printed five hundred beautiful copies of the following flier:

THURSDAY THURSDAY THURSDAY!
Chiro-PRACTICAL!
Back Relief and Other Spinal Therapy Right in Your Home!
FREE TRIAL! ONE DAY ONLY!
Call the Back Doctors…

And after the word *doctors* was Jack's brand-new phone number. He'd considered adding an amusing visual homage—images of Snap, Crackle, and Pop—but he discarded the joke as unserious. He was trying to get a customer, not a laugh. That wasn't all he didn't include. He did not make the ad mainly an image combined with a headline making some visual pun. He did not using a shocking photo or graphic sexual imagery to get the reader's attention. He did not employ Photoshop or other digital effects to miraculously skew reality (although God knows he had in his career overseen such trickery a thousand times, making cars, glasses of beer, and vacuous fashion models look positively unworldly). He did not use a celebrity, anthropomorphic Rice Krispies, or otherwise. What he did was state the precise offer, the benefit of the offer, and the means for further investigation—information, in other words. In still other words, exactly the kind of ad that would be sniffed at by every one of his former employees as well as every employee of every other agency creative department in the world for the crime of being so vulgar as to communicate a sales message to the audience.

But, of course, Jack wasn't doing this on some client's dime to burnish his portfolio to get the next job. He was doing it at his own expense to ensnare a maniac. And he was fairly confident. He knew that the real smoke and mirrors of advertising was performed in conference rooms where new accounts were won. Every agency screened its most energetic and entertaining ads, along with trumped-up data such as "share of mind," to prove that it, and only it, had cracked the code of consumer desire. What nobody ever told a prospective client was that, apart from a Marlboro cowboy, Nike swoosh, or "A Diamond is Forever" here and there, they were all selling a commodity. The central truth was this, and only this: advertising works.

Because he had left his store shortly before Donato entered it, he could not realize that the essence of his diabolical plan had just been divulged, innocently, by Big Manny. Therefore, he did not know that, very soon, he and the mob would be on parallel tracks that, in defiance of geometry, were destined to cross. He did know, however, that he would need help.

Next stop: Tanning Expo.

CHAPTER 59

NOON

DON DONATO, WHO HAD BEEN KNOWN TO DRESS UP LIKE A JUNIOR cowpoke, drew the line at a bikini. He walked in street clothes into Tanning Expo and an unexpectedly big crowd. Tina had only three beds and two booths, but the place was, as it were, mobbed. It was like an OTB parlor for the Belmont. He didn't get past the door before Tina came running up to him and put both of her delicate, bronzed, exquisitely manicured hands on his massive chest. Elbows locked, she backed up a step and pushed against him to halt his advance.

"Sorry, mister. That'll be fifteen bucks. In the jar." She nodded toward a Sharpie-lettered sign in the window advertising the cover charge. Her father read the mirror image of the bled-through ink, made a face, and fished into his pocket for his Armour-Vienna-sausage-can-sized bankroll.

"You got change for a fifty?" he asked. Tina shook her head no, peeled a fifty-dollar bill off her father's wad, and stuffed it into the pickle jar.

"Thanks, Daddy."

"Excuse me. Excuse me." Someone was pushing his way through the crowd to reach the door, ducking his head so that the crown of his panama hat was all Tina and her dad could see of him as he skulked out.

"Bye, Larry," Tina said, to which he responded with a timorous left-handed wave as he pushed the door open and achieved the sidewalk alive.

"What's with him?" Don Donato wanted to know.

Tina whispered. "Whaddya think? He's scared shitless of you. He says we're gonna come up short for"—she made air apostrophes—"'neighborhood watch.'"

"That's why you called me? Your mother was also scared shitless. Marco said she said you was yelling into the phone."

"Sorry, Daddy. It's so noisy in here. I called Fiesta, but Marco said he didn't know where you were."

"Marco knew where I was. He just didn't tell you where I was. He run halfway down the boulevard to get me, poor kid. It was like a hippo escaped from the zoo. Anyway, I come to rescue you, and here I walk into a fuckin' orgy. Casper ain't been in here, has he?"

"Casper? No. Why?"

"Never mind. So what's so important you gotta terrify your mother and bother me when I got bigger fish to fry?"

And so Tina took her father into the storage room, leaving Sunny alone to handle the teeming tanners and the swarm of hooting onlookers. There, she told him about her idea. Her really, really, really big idea. Like the author of mankind's other great epiphanies—Isaac Newton, Archimedes, Hugh Hefner—she'd been applying eye shadow when, *boom*, it just hit her, the perfect solution: what if her father got Our Lady of Grace to hand over Thursday's bingo proceeds to take the fundraising drive over the top?

Tina Donato, like her big sister, was accustomed to being stared at. Men had been gaping at her since she was thirteen years old.

This did not trouble her at all. She fed off of the attention. Some women found the lewd gazes degrading; Tina found them empowering. Now, huddled in a closet, wearing the skimpiest of bathing suits, she found her own father staring at her as if she were not a complete person. He was gaping at her, though, not as an object of fantasy. He was gaping at her as an object of pity, or worse—and she knew it. Tina did not feel empowered.

"Are you a moron?" he asked. "A handout from the church for...the neighborhood watch?"

"Daddy—"

"You think Our Lady of Grace is gonna give money to me? Why the fuck would they do that?"

Tina raised her voice. "Because you're gonna save the church!"

"I'm gonna save the church? How'm I gonna do that?"

"Because, Daddy, when you whack the Russians and save Ebbets Beach, and people want to thank you, you're gonna say, 'Go to fuckin' church and write a check when you get there.' I thought this through, Dad. It's gonna work."

Dad was thinking it through too. The conclusion he was coming to was that the silicone, or whatever the fuck it was, had seeped into his kid's head. She was totally fucking *folle*. Crazy like a wall. Her father's stubborn negativity left Tina crestfallen. Still, she was glad she hadn't revealed the plan she had immediately before this plan—the one she had when she didn't know her father was broke, the one where the mob boss would swoop in to save the church so that she could more easily romance the priest, her one true love. Because, as it was, Daddy was looking at her and not seeing Archimedes.

"Tina, sweetheart, think about what you're saying. I go see the priest—and I am a notorious individual to these civilians—and

I tell him to bet on the come with the church's money. Let's say he's the one person in the tristate area who don't know about the Chiropractor. He's still not going to embezzle no bingo money."

"What's the Chiropractor?"

Merda. All this craziness and stupidity, maybe it was catching.

"Never mind that, neither. No priest is gonna run no Ponzi scheme for souls."

"But I think he will, Daddy. I already softened him up."

"You what?"

"I softened him up. I talked to him. He is the loveliest and sweetest man in the world. You got no idea how tender and strong he is, and spiritual and kind."

Tender and strong? Lovely and sweet? Some faggot in a robe? Now, what the fuck was she talking about? "Tina, you got the hots for some priest? You're...*intimate* with the parish priest?"

"No! I mean, no, I'm not intimate with him, but I love him, if you must know."

Don Donato shook his head. It was getting hot and stuffy in this closet. Also, suddenly, both his daughters were gravitating away from him—even further away from him, that is. Also, he had a Jew chiropractor for a hit man, a weirdo in a Hawaiian shirt for a bagman, and now, who the fuck knows, maybe Father Son-in-law. Everything was topsy-turvy. Whatever happened to the good old days, when you just brokered predatory loans and hit guys with lengths of pipe?

"Just talk to Father Steve," Tina pleaded. "He's got big troubles. The church is, like, always empty. I told him you could help the parish."

"Yeah, and what did he say?"

Tina fanned herself, ineffectually, with her slender hand. "Well," she replied, "he didn't say no."

Father and daughter walked out of the storeroom, moist with perspiration. This caught the attention of one of the paying customers, a big young guido with cannonball shoulders squeezing out of his wifebeater like the finials bracketing Evangeline's drapes.

"Yo!" he shouted. "Nooner!"

As the goombah yucked it up with his mouth-breathing friends, Tina's retirement-age dad made his way across the salon, looked up at the kid who towered over him, and said, quietly, "*Perdonatemi*?"

The guido replied, "Way to go, Pops!" and tried to fist-bump the underworld kingpin. Pops was not familiar with fist-bump protocol. He bumped his fist into the young man's mouth, leaving behind a gush of blood and four loosened teeth.

CHAPTER 60

A MODEST PROPOSAL

SEPTEMBER 7TH WAS THE MOST BEAUTIFUL DAY OF THE YEAR.

Jack stepped outside of Handi Copy and sucked in the lovely chill. How can the simple act of respiration be so bracing and delicious? This was on a Brooklyn sidewalk, after all, not some grandiose mountaintop. Yet, as he stood on the pavement, steeping in the cool bath of autumnal air and basking in the deepwater richness of the sky, he felt a twinge of panic. This day was not just stirringly gorgeous; it was September 11th gorgeous, a saturated cerulean sea of bad karma. Obviously, calamity awaited.

Jack was not, by nature, superstitious. He didn't believe in luck, or palm reading, or any brand of destiny. He never so much as glanced at his horoscope, except for the ones in Chinese restaurants, because these are the only places in the dining world where you are volunteered a drawing of a rat, and he respected that. But his Eastern mysticism went no further. No I Ching. No chakra quackera. Likewise, no psychics, no ladder avoidance, and no houses of worship. Not that he was some sort of militant atheist trying to deny you your faith. He figured that's your call. "Maybe there's a God," he liked to say, "but I don't wanna bother him when he's busy." There are too many children to sicken, too many destitute Sri Lankans to drown. With all that mayhem on the divine platter, plus all the prayer spam, to Jack it hardly seemed sensible to try vying for His attention. So, no, usually he wasn't the sort of man to divine the future from the weather report.

Still, who doesn't get an ominous vibe every now and then, and who doesn't know what that sky means? It means someone will fly airplanes into buildings, in order to be holy. It means a dandelion puff of flame and debris in stereopticon relief against the impossible blueness—scarring cerulean, and a city, forever. It means beauty is tricking us again. God is up to something, the fucker.

Maybe not 9/11 redux, but something crazy awful. Shifting his weight atop the feet of his own crisp, diagonal shadow, Jack actually felt his blood run cold—in exactly the way the expression means to describe. In that chilling instant, it occurred to him that maybe Mark Twain was correct: he who hesitates is sometimes saved. Tempting fate is one thing; taunting it is quite another. Why blunder into the teeth of doom, when he could simply walk back to his store and sell a whole mess of mattresses?

Here's why: for some reason he couldn't quite explain, he felt responsible.

He crossed the boulevard midblock, dodging cars as he headed for the Tanning Expo. And who should be walking out just as Jack approached but his future father-in-law? Dad did not see Jack because he was examining the back of his right hand. There was some blood there, where somehow the travel agent had barked his knuckles.

"Mr. Donato!" Jack hollered.

Angela's father glanced upward.

"I need to speak with you today. Would that be possible?"

"I just been to your place. I left some nice Italian grappa, as a token of apology for my man. Don't worry. That situation will be dealt with real fast."

"Yeah, thanks. I appreciate that. I was just worried, you know, about Angela."

"The boy is emotional. He don't got no death wish, however. Leave this to me."

"So can I drop by your place? It's almost twelve now. About one, one fifteen?"

"Suit yourself. I'll be there till maybe three. Then I gotta go up to the church."

The church? For what, an exorcism?

"Have you given any thought to my proposition?" the travel agent inquired.

Jack did not know how to respond. He fully intended to make a proposition to Donato, but he couldn't remember being asked to participate in any part of the crisis. He quickly scanned his hard drive, but nothing came to mind. Unless…

"You mean," he tried, "marriage?"

The father of the bride laughed. "You kidding me? That's none of my business. I figure you two geniuses will do that when your fuckin' computers tell you to. I'm talking about my *proposition* proposition."

Proposition proposition. *Proposition* proposition. *Proposition* proposition. What in the world was he talking about?

"Son, you got Oldtimer's disease? *Amway*. I'm talking about Amway."

Jesus Christ, he was actually serious. Again, the hard drive whirred. How to respond? How to respond?

"Oh, yeah. Of course. I've been thinking about that. It's one of the things I want to discuss this afternoon."

Brooklyn's most fearsome detergent salesman seemed satisfied by that answer and, without further comment, headed back toward his office. After walking a few paces, though, he did something that struck Jack as very strange. Don Donato turned on his heels. Looking back at Jack, in relief against the low Ebbets Beach skyline and the cloudless blue sky, he grinned to expose his espresso-stained choppers. Then, with his bloodied right hand, he waved.

CHAPTER 61

YES AND NO

JACK HAD NEVER QUITE MET TINA DONATO. SHE HAD BRUSHED against him briefly on her way out of the Village Association meeting, which introduced him to her body but not to her actual self. Now he intended to get acquainted so that he could exploit her for his nefarious scheme.

From Larry Rizzo, he already knew that Tina was a gung-ho participant in *The Magnificent Seven* operation, maybe even the gungest of hos. So he felt certain she'd be a willing volunteer. The trick was to get her signed on without revealing the endgame. A wallflower she obviously was not, but that didn't mean she would accept any risk. A tanning salon owner she was, but that didn't mean she'd expose her own skin.

He stood outside Tanning Expo, amazed at the scene within. There was Tina, standing at the front window, exposing her own skin. There was more fabric in his necktie than she had in her entire bathing suit. Naturally, she looked very much like Angela: the facial features beneath the makeup, the slender waist, the rounded hips, the smooth olive skin. But her boobs were what the ad trade calls a differentiating benefit. The girl was, as his dear mother used to say, a real doozy. And just what the doctor ordered.

He entered the salon, worked his way through the crowd, and tapped her on the shoulder. She turned around and looked up at him.

"You paid?" she demanded. Jack looked at her quizzically. "Fifteen bucks, please. In the jar."

"I need a word with you. I'm Jack Schiavone."

He'd assumed that those words were *Open Sesame*, that she would, of course, be delighted at long last to meet her colleague and future brother-in-law of whom she had no doubt heard so much. So he was a little taken aback when her response was to point to the check-in counter and repeat, "Fifteen dollars, in the jar, or scram."

She had no idea who he was.

That made some sense. Jack didn't imagine that Angela and Tina would lay prone on their respective beds, turning the pages of *Brides* magazine, and flip-flopping their fluffy pink slippers against their heels during endless phone conversations about their love lives. Still, he'd become so rapidly woven into the fabric of the family it hadn't really occurred to him that he'd be approaching her as an unrecognizable stranger. So he put fifteen dollars in the pickle jar and tried again.

"I've come about the Chiropractor," he said.

Jack didn't know that Tina didn't know the identity, or even the medical specialty, of the remorseless killer who would be emptying her pickle jar. By the same token, he didn't know that, minutes earlier, a feared mafia don and signatory of an inviolable *omerta* had inadvertently blabbed the secret to his daughter, as if he were discussing how to flour the *vitella* for the *scallopini*. The bottom line was that this second mention of that mysterious character piqued Tina's attention and aroused her sense of underworld intrigue.

She pulled Jack into the storeroom. No problem, the goombahs had followed her father out the door. When he headed left, they headed right.

Only after Tina closed the door behind them did she notice how totally cute the stranger was. To her credit, she was more absorbed in the thrilling mystery than in anything that would make her innocently guilty of incest-in-law. When Jack finally introduced himself more fully, Tina squealed in delight about Angela's good catch and then was rapt in hearing him out. After learning that Jack came from the world of advertising, she blathered for a while about her dream of dreams—producing and starring in a cable reality show called *The Guidettes*—but the whole riff more or less whooshed past him, as if he were a dog hanging its head out of a car window. In the heat of the stifling closet, there were only three Tina Donato words he paid attention to: "Yes. I'm in."

"It could be dangerous," he warned.

"Yeah, I told you, I'm in."

"And potentially pretty embarrassing."

"What, are you deaf or something? Sign me up. I'm *in*."

Sunny was not stupid. She was not blind. She was not murderous. And she was not idle. After the cute mattress guy left the store, she pulled Tina aside. "Teen, I gotta get a slice. Fifteen minutes, OK?" The place was still jammed, but Tina could never say no to her best friend. So her best friend threw on a sweatsuit and rushed to Original Reyes to rat her out. Mike, in uniform, was waiting for her at one of the five skinny little tables that lined the wall behind the Pepsi cooler. There were paper plates at both places: two slices on Sunny's, nothing but grease drippings on Mike's. He had taken his lunch into his own hands.

"You gotta do something," Sunny insisted of her lover. "They're gonna kill this Russian guy."

Franzetti was stuffing his face with his paid slice and his free slice sandwiched together, cheese on cheese, forming a makeshift calzone. "So what?" he replied through the mush of mostly dough.

Sunny leaned forward across the table and whispered, "They hired a hit man. This 'neighborhood watch'—it's like a front. They're using the money to pay a contract killer."

Franzetti laughed. "Pretty good idea, if you ask me. Good riddance to bad rubbish. Anyway, it's not my table."

"What's that supposed to mean?"

"Honey, you know this ain't my precinct. They kill him under the Manhattan Bridge, gimme a shout. If I'm not too busy cuffing a drunk investment banker at one of them DUMBO wine bars, I'll race to the scene and commence an investigation." Franzetti must have amused himself with this remark, for he laughed a cheese chunk onto Sunny's acrylic zipper top.

"But it's murder!" she insisted, ignoring her fuck buddy's detritus.

The police sergeant, who was too concentrated on his lunch to notice either Sunny's genuine distress or the pizza booger on her right breast, simply shrugged. "It's murder if killing rats and bugs is murder. These Russians are fucking vermin. Who you think's been blowing up buildings around here—the fucking Girl Scouts? Hey, aren't you gonna eat nothing?"

Sunny rolled her eyes. "I can't believe you have an appetite, with all this. They can't even afford to pay the hit man 'cause the pickle jars aren't full enough. I think they're gonna try to get money from the church."

The cop had grabbed Sunny's untouched slice and started working on it, but he raised his head from his paper plate at the news.

"From the church?" he asked.

"Yeah, I think so," Sunny replied. "Tina said her father's gonna talk to the priest."

Franzetti chuckled. "Maybe for his downline. Donato shouldn't bother. I tried that. Faggot don't care about the free enterprise system."

"Come on, Mikey, this is serious."

"Sunny, baby, listen to me. You know the expression, 'You can't get blood from a stone'? Our Lady of Grace is a fucking sand quarry."

"Yeah, I know. That's why they're gonna take it from the bingo."

Franzetti's head snapped up. The muscles in his jaw suddenly were tight, his face suddenly flushed.

"They're gonna *what*?"

There was one travel poster at Fiesta Tours. It said COSTA RICA! Otherwise, there was nothing about the shabby office that shouted "travel agency." It was a three-room office that apparently had not changed when the previous tenant, a CPA, moved out and the Cozy Nostra moved in. In each room, there was an old Steelcase double-pedestal desk finished in vivacious battleship gray. In the back offices, there were matching steel filing cabinets, dusty and moldering from disuse. In the main office, a nine-year-old cathode-ray video monitor rested on the desk, plugged into God knows what underneath. One hundred percent of the remaining furniture consisted of a dozen white molded-plastic lawn chairs, scattered throughout the suite.

In one of those chairs, as Jack entered, lounged Little Manny. In another was Casper the Slugger. He jumped to his feet when he saw Jack.

"Yo, Mr. Mattress, I come to apologize."

Little Manny laughed. "What the fuck you talking about, Casper? He come here."

"That's what I mean," Casper corrected. "I'm very sorry for losing my temper. I was totally out of line. And I will pay for any damage out of my own pocket. And if there is anything you need from me, like the song, I'll be there, twenty-four hours a day."

"And…" This voice came from the back office.

"And," Casper concluded, his eyes downcast, "you have all of my blessings."

Jack nodded and slapped Casper on the shoulder. "Forget about it," he said.

Little Manny found that funny as well. "Yeah," he laughed. "Fuggegaboudit." In either pronunciation, Casper certainly would not.

"Back here," shouted the voice from the back room. It was the boss. Jack wandered into the room, pushed the frosted-glass-windowed door behind him, and took a seat in a picnic chair.

"Welcome to Fiesta Tours," said the host. "Where you traveling to?"

That was an excellent question. Jack had been wondering himself. But, as they say, in for a dime, in for an incomprehensibly reckless association with perpetrators of unspeakable crimes.

"So, this time," Jack began, "we've got a proposition for you."

"Is that right? I see you. Who's 'we'?"

"'We' is me." There in the doorway stood Angela, escorted by Casper—almost as he'd always wished, but surely not to deliver her to the company of another man. She took a seat. Burning with the ongoing humiliation, Casper withdrew. Whereupon, without hesitation, Jack laid out his thinking, point by point, sparing no exaggeration, no rationalization, no opportunity for flattery. Angela, like a jazz sideman, picked up on every line and riffed in perfect synchrony. The way they pitched it, Don Donato combined the best qualities of Robin Hood and the Red Cross—without all the politics, the bureaucracy, and the annoying municipal, state, and federal law.

"Like Manny says," the don humbly agreed, "we're like the Halvah."

Neither Angela nor Jack knew where that had come from. Or cared. This was no time to be distracted by a malapropism, no matter how Vic-elicious.

"Daddy, you can actually make history."

Jack could see that the notion appealed to the little big man. And so he was ready to close. "Look, Mr. Donato, I've been thinking a lot about this. I met your chiropractor. Maybe this is beyond my skill set, but he doesn't inspire a lot of confidence, frankly. Maybe he can *ker-RAAACK*, as he claims, but I don't see how he gets himself in a position to *ker-RAAACK* the Russian. But I've solved that problem."

"You've solved that problem?"

"Yep. Sure have."

"You wanna tell me how, Frank Nitti?"

"Nope."

The don sat up straight. "Whaddya mean 'nope'? Don't fuck with me."

"I said we have a proposition. First, you've got to hear me out."

The don was not amused by this gambit. It was, first of all, impertinent. It was, secondly, an insult. It was, thirdly, emasculating for a bona fide kingpin to be entertaining crime hints from any one called Mr. Mattress or anything else in the home furnishings category. Still, the boss of the Ebbets Beach Boys had already pegged this guy as the second coming of Big Manny. And hadn't he himself pleaded with Angela to come into the Family? Now was the time for a canny despot to sit back and listen.

"Talk," the don commanded.

"Simple," Jack says. "We put your Russian in your man's hands. Only, one condition."

There were, in fact, two conditions. In the interest of not being laughed out of the office, and in the same way that he had told Tina about only half of his scheme—and in the grand tradition of bait-and-switch advertising the world over—for the moment, Jack floated only one of them.

"As of the end of this week, the Cozy Nostra stops being a criminal gang and publicly rebrands itself as a community organization."

"No more protection racket," Angela amplified. "No more numbers. No more loan-sharking. You go one-hundred-percent legit."

Don Donato, his back against the wall as it had never been before, glowered as he peered across his massive desk to take the measure of this brilliant and daring man. He rubbed his sore right hand with his left. He scratched at his three o'clock shadow. He reset himself in his plastic chair. He smiled at his daughter. He glowered at her boyfriend. Then, at last, he spoke.

"No," he said.

CHAPTER 62

OUR LADY OF DISGRACE

FATHER STEVE DID NOT RECOGNIZE THE VOICE BEHIND THE screen.

"It's been fifty, sixty years since my last confession."

"That's a long time."

"Yeah, about that, Father. I been kinda tied up at work. If it ain't one thing, it's another."

"OK, please go on."

"I took the Lord's name in vain probably maybe a million times. I coveted my neighbor's wife and banged her a half dozen times. I had sexual relations outside of my marriage many times, but that was years ago, Father. Last ten, fifteen years, I enjoy home cooking. I took the life of another individual once, but he was a prick. And I ordered two killings—also, I had no choice on them. Another guy died after I worked him over, but he don't count because they made a mistake in the hospital and put his feeding tube into his vein instead of his stomach. I have not received Holy Communion since Nixon. I also have told lies and stolen money. I try not to lie because my people need to trust me. Mostly they're ugly-baby lies. Someone has an ugly baby, you don't say, 'That's an ugly baby.' One time, I called Evangeline a cunt, which she was being, but I felt terrible about it and bought her a diamond you wouldn't fucking believe."

"Language."

"Sorry, Father. That's the other thing. A lot of times I'm rude."

The priest had a pretty good idea now who was confessing. He took a deep breath and began.

"Do you understand that you are engaged in a Holy Sacrament?"

"Yes, Father."

"This isn't about unburdening yourself so you feel better about yourself. The Sacrament of Reconciliation requires contrition. Do you know what I mean by contrition?"

"Yes, Father."

"You have confessed to the gravest sins of God and man. Mortal sins. Absolution from a mortal sin does not come lightly. Do you understand that?"

"Yes, Father. I'm not getting outta here with some Hail Marys." Silence.

"Sorry, Father. Don't mean to be fasciitis. I understand what you're telling me, I swear to God."

"There are conditions for absolution. Very serious conditions. We discussed contrition. Tell me what that means to you."

"Apologizing, like, to God."

"And?" prompted the confessor.

The follow-up stumped the penitent. "The widow?"

"Listen carefully, please. Penitence means righting a wrong in your heart, in the eyes of God, in the eyes of society. You cannot come into this church and clear the slate without the intention of true reparations. If you have murdered, you must confess to the police. Then, and only then, can the Church bestow absolution. Do you understand?"

"Yes, Father."

"You will turn yourself in for your crimes?"

Now the silence shrieked, boomed, deafened from the penitent's side of the screen.

"Father, can you gimme two, three days to think about this?"

"That isn't my decision. It's yours. What hangs in the balance is your immortal soul."

"You talkin' hell?"

"I am talking about eternity without God."

The don thought about what he had heard. "Tell you the truth, Father, I didn't come in here thinking I had to cop a plea, but I hear what you're saying. I've gotta think about this. A lot of people depend on me. I go to prison, I'm not the only one who pays, see what I mean?"

"I'm not here to bargain, either. You know what God asks of you. The rest is in your hands."

"OK, Father. I need to ask you about one other thing."

"Go on."

"It's about Our Lady of Grace. I hear you got some financial problems. Tell you the truth, so do I. But I got an idea, we could kill two birds with one stone."

Goodness gracious, the young pastor thought. *Nymphomaniacs. Mobsters. This was one hell of a family in the parish family.* He could not begin to imagine what this killer would say that would not be corrupt, immoral, sinful, illegal, and, for all he knew, violent. Not to mention letting business, however malign or innocent, intrude on the sanctity of the confessional. But whatever it was this child of Christ had in mind, the priest totally had to hear it for himself.

"When you leave the confessional," Father Steve instructed, "go into the rectory office. Tell Mrs. Giufrida I asked you to wait for me. All right?"

"Yes, Father."

"Give thanks to the Lord for He is good."

"For His mercy endures forever."

"Amen."

The confession, and the subsequent crossing through the cavernous church—where every creak and footfall echoed, and where a mere man was diminished amid all the stern gothic majesty—had not left the penitent unmoved. He had unburdened himself of sins never hitherto spoken of and been confronted with a choice that had never so much as crossed his mind. As he had said to Big Manny so many times, he wasn't going to live forever. Maybe all of his immediate crises were just God's way of telling him the jig was up. Maybe they weren't crises at all, but opportunities. Maybe the time had come for him to get out, clean up some messes, make some amends, stay the fuck out of hell. Sicily was too hot for him; what would hell be like? He imagined himself on a ladder in a blast furnace, flames licking at his feet, perpetually reaching over his head to pick lemons from a tree infinitely replenishing itself with yellow fruit. The thought made him shudder. But having envisioned the wages of sin, he quickly calculated the wages of surrender. First, it was surrender, which was not his way. Secondly, that meant prison. Probably dying in prison.

Fuck that. He made his way to the rectory to deal.

It was an interesting meeting. With the advance knowledge that the priest had been softened up, the petitioner parishioner saw no need to try to dazzle the wimp the way Jack Schiavone might. He just got right to the point.

"Father, our interests are aligned. I can use all of my powers and all of my influence to get people back in your pews, and not freeloaders, either. This is how I make a living. I know how to do this. All I'm asking you for is a small loan. You give me your bingo rake tomorrow night, and on Sunday, you're turning 'em away at the doors. And every Sunday after."

Young Father Steve Deleweski, his back against the wall as it had never been before, glowered as he peered across his desk to take the measure of this preposterous and dangerous man. He removed his clerical collar. He rubbed his Adam's apple where the collar had chafed. He leaned back in his magnificent antique mahogany-and-leather swivel chair. Then, at last, he spoke.

"No," he said.

The meeting was interesting, and the meeting was brief. The thwarted petitioner didn't even bother with the formalities of a good-bye. He rose from his chair and walked out, dispirited, exhausted, and humiliated. Yesterday made a monkey of by the Russians, today by this twerp priest. As he traipsed to his Cadillac, though, he was bothered by a nagging thought: what if he'd made a mistake? There was so much shit piled on top of him now, how much worse could prison be? Could he really erase a lifetime of sin? That was a theological mystery he was in no position to answer. But as he unlocked the DeVille and climbed in, he surely knew this:

There is no carbonara in hell.

CHAPTER 63

ADJUSTMENT

IN A SECOND-FLOOR WALKUP ON AVENUE X JUST OFF OF CONEY Island Avenue, above Brighton Beach Gymboree, Tony the Teeth stood helpless. He was heavily strapped to an upright steel contraption at his chest and at his hips, with his tree-trunk arms constricted and immobile under the straps. Trigger-hooked to the chest strap after passing through a dangling pulley was a bungee cable feeding from a manual ratcheting winch. As the man in black cranked the winch, the cable tightened, its force multiplied through the block-and-tackle leverage. This action wrenched Tony's upper body forward, forward to ever more grotesque extremes. For the first time in his life, the enforcer could enforce nothing. He was in bondage.

"In other words, stop," he grunted, his dentures clenched not in his typical semigrimace but the full-blown Lon Chaney Sr. "Don't go no farther. Please. I'm begging you."

The man in black laughed. "So, tough guy," he sneered, "you don't like the rack?"

"It hurts," replied Tony with a grimace.

"You can handle it," said Dr. Glick-Mermelstein. "It's just biophysics. The sagittal traction unit is correcting both lumbar and cervical subluxations, which are affecting your entire sympathetic chain. Not just your anterior head syndrome, which is the cause of your headaches, but the whole bioenergetic structure. Your chronic fatigue is a function of cervical misalignment. I believe your allergies will respond to this therapy too. You're drinking antacids like it was Yoo-hoo, your pal Casper tells me. We'll see if you still are six months from now."

"Six months?" Tony said. "I thought I'm only good for three sessions."

"I guess that depends on whether you want a little relief or holistic wellness. We're talking about an investment in yourself."

"Lemme ask this, Doc. Once this sympathetic chain is all greased up, will I be able to stuff a deadweight in a trunk again?"

"From your lips to God's ears," replied the Chiropractor.

The soldiers were there at the insistence of the don, but they did not know why. Seth had been warned to keep his trap shut. Unless Casper told him differently, as far as the guys were concerned, this was just part of the outfit's preventative-care program. The other part of the preventative-care program was free bullets.

Leonard was sitting there waiting his turn. His problem was eczema. This gave him a flaking irritation on his elbows, knees, and eyebrows, plus a monster case of dandruff. Seth prescribed spinal adjustment. Marco was due too. He had no health problems he knew about, not counting morbid obesity, but had reported to the chiropractor through Casper that he was born with one kidney and enjoyed, as the don put it, "no margin for air." The chiropractor contemplated a precautionary treatment: preventative spinal adjustment. When Marco arrived, though, he looked as plump, pink, and healthy as a prize sow—and also quite pleased with himself. In he sauntered, fresh off of some gumshoe work, tailing Aziz, the pretzel vendor.

"Piece of cake," he whispered to Leonard. "Guy leaves his house at six thirty, drives his wagon to a commissary in Brooklyn Heights, loads up, tows it back to the boulevard, unhitches, and he's selling coffee and Danish at eight fifteen. We could hit him in the car. Piece of cake."

Leonard shook his head. "It's stupid, Marco. Who says the don will fall for this? He reads the papers. News'll say a pretzel guy got killed, not a Russian. It's stupid."

"Your idea."

"Gyro Cripes, Marco, I was joking. It was a felpin' joke."

Oh, a joke. "This might be a problem," Marco confessed.

"What kind of problem?"

"Medium problem."

"How 'medium'?"

"I already talked to Little Manny. He's nervous we're running out of time."

"So?"

"So I think maybe he's gonna do it in the morning."

Leonard then made a statement that applied to the particulars of the situation, and so much of the human comedy. "Felp me," he mused. "This is felpin' felped."

It was almost 5:00 p.m. *Riunione* was at 7:00, and they were going to fight traffic as it was, but they cooled their heels. Seth promised he'd be quick.

"Just don't put me on that felper," Leonard requested. "You want me to talk, just ask."

"He'll squeal you look at him cross-eyed," Marco joked.

"I'll squeal just for fun," the Calculator said.

A buzzer sounded, triggered by the doormat on the landing. Marco and Leonard were facing in the direction of the door when it swung open, revealing the ample figures of Casper and Little Manny framed in the doorway. Talk about two guys in need of a tune-up. Both were drained of color and breathing heavily from just two flights of stairs.

"Yo, Joe DiMaggio, how you doin'?" laughed Marco, delighted just this once to be the needler and not the needlee.

No reaction from the desk-smashing interpreter of d'lovely Cole. He just stood there panting. Leonard the Calculator read the body language and knew at once that something very serious was afoot. Heedful of the chiropractor's presence, he employed the universal sign language of mayhem, crossing his fingers along the throat and nodding a question mark. Little Manny, eyes shut, nodded back.

"Aziz?" whispered Marco, medium too loud.

Huh? Little Manny's face was suddenly twisted in contempt, incredulousness, anger, grief, and fear. "They got the don," Little Manny said.

Leonard and Marco jumped to their feet. The chiropractor's head turned on a swivel. Only the Teeth—restrained by leather and steel—remained motionless. And only the bulging of his eyes as he strained to see the soldiers in the doorway revealed the profundity of his fright.

"Don Donato," said Casper, "he's dead."

CHAPTER 64

THE GOSPEL OF MATTHEW

IT HAPPENED IN THE CHURCH PARKING LOT. IN THE DEVILLE. HE'D sat in the driver's seat for a moment before switching on the ignition, pondering his life. *All that, for* this? he'd thought. And then he'd wished to himself that there were, in fact, that little place waiting for him in Egg Harbor, where he could go and seal ships in a bottle, or whatever the fuck they do when they don't have to salvage their life's work without the help of Big Manny or even that senile *bastardi* Don Greco, may he rest in peace. The thought of the old man made Don Donato chuckle to himself. As bad as things were, at least he wasn't being drummed out of the corps, as it were. Then he turned the key.

The Cadillac was not brand new. Still, the engine never coughed or spat. Turn the ignition and *hummm*. He remembered so many cars from the old days, when you sometimes had to crank and crank just to get the damn thing to turn over. The reassuring modern hum, powering such a big boat, always gave him satisfaction. A sense of security. A sense of trust that he lacked for the human beings in his sphere. With the climate control and seat warmers, being in the Caddy was like being back in the womb, only much faster at zero to sixty. Don Donato wore the faintest hint of a smile as he put the car in gear and headed for the exit. Then someone made a phone call to the mobile wired to the explosives in the undercarriage, and the DeVille disintegrated in an explosion that rattled windows in a three-block radius. Turns out the don had been right all along: those cell phones were nothing but trouble.

The stained glass at Our Lady of Grace remained intact. Only two ground-level windows shattered, and also the glass encasing the scripture quote on the marquee sign facing the boulevard. This left the white plastic press-in lettering exposed to the elements— such as they were on this crisp, cloudless, exquisite day. The verse was Matthew 43:

Ye have heard that it have been said, Thou shalt love thy neighbor, and hate thine enemy.

One of the first on the scene was Father Steve Delewski, who had been rocked half out of his chair by the blast. He and Mrs. Giufrida came running, along with passersby, but they could not get near the car. What was left of it was on fire. They knew, though, who—or what was left of him—had perished inside. Father Steve prayed that Mr. Donato had resolved in the previous three minutes to make amends. Father Steve prayed, as well, for himself, for his faith, for his vows, for his sanity. Death and despair were getting to him.

Firefighters and police soon arrived, pouring water on the car and trying to keep onlookers away. Within thirty minutes, the media began to converge as well. The cops soon put them in a separate pen, enclosed by sawhorse barricades, with a clear camera angle to the smoldering wreckage. Helicopters circled overhead, not police aircraft; they belonged to WPIX and Fox 5. What a fantastically lucky break! A gangland bombing, just in time for the six o'clock news.

The press beat the feds to Ebbets Beach. Soon enough, though, the ATF and FBI were there in force. The first thing they found was disappointment—not that they had given short shrift to the merchants who only thirty hours earlier had solicited their help, but that neither the church nor neighboring businesses had surveillance video of the parking lot or its entrances. No Times Square moron, this perpetrator. They knew who was responsible, but despite assurances for the media, they also knew the chance of assembling a chain of evidence to the Russians was practically zilch.

So they did what cops always do when they are bereft of promising investigative options. They rounded up the victim's family members to drag them further into the depths of hell. On Wednesday evening, Evangeline, Tina, and Angela experienced the fulfillment of the deceased's worst nightmare: police and federal agents milling around in his living room, bothering his family and getting into his business. Tina didn't much enjoy the process, either. Not any part of it. But especially she hated the patronizing tone of their voices, as if they cared one bit for her dad, as if they weren't just fucking delighted that another menace to society had been eliminated via the Darwinian natural order of things.

"Miss Donato," began Agent Vukovich, sounding more like a nursery school teacher than a cop, "to your knowledge, did your father have any enemies?"

Through her tears, her face contorted into a grimace that was also a sardonic grin. "No, asshole." With a wad of tissues bunched in her hand, Tina extended her arms and shook her head—as in, *What planet did this moron just beam down from?*

The caustic sarcasm was not lost on Vukovich, who was just doing things the way things are done.

"Do you know who these people are?" he asked.

But Tina didn't have the stomach for the exercise. "Maybe a rival travel agency. Hey, brainiac, why don't you leave us the fuck alone?"

Tina had been sobbing heavily through most of the two hours since she'd heard the explosion and, quickly thereafter, the grotesque news. There was so much to grieve for. For her daddy. For the family. For the terrible things he had done. For the man he was. For the man he could have been. For the joy he had brought into her life. Even for the mortal embarrassment he had caused her; it was a part of her life with him, part of the texture of growing up, and she cherished even that.

Evangeline and Angela were mostly quiet; they seemed to accept the inevitable—or were simply more in control of their emotions. Angela had always harbored so much anger toward her father and resentment over how his criminal choices had scarred her and her sister. In recent years, some of that bitterness had subsided. This had partly to do with evolution of the kinder, gentler Donato criminal conspiracy, but mostly to do with Angela's own evolution. She'd decided that she was no more in control of her upbringing than anyone else. She could have been a crack baby. She could have been the fifteenth son of a subsistence farmer on an arid dirt patch in Sierra Leone. She could have been royalty, enslaved for life in a gilded European cage. She could have been an Olsen twin. But she was not. She had to deal with the randomness of the universe no more or less than any other offspring on the face of the earth. Once she accepted the vagaries of chance, she was able to take responsibility for her own life. And once she did that, she was able to reconcile her feelings of anger at Victor Donato, thug, with those of affection for Daddy—Daddy who'd played hide-and-seek with her, pretended to gobble up her piggies like gumdrops, read Dr. Seuss to her, and, finally, held his tongue while she pointedly and sometimes even cruelly put as much distance between herself and the hallowed family as she possibly could. Don Donato easily could have been possessive and irate about that, even monstrous, yet he was not. For this fact alone, Angela felt gratitude. And now an aching loss.

Evangeline, for her part, was living the moment she had always dreaded and had always known would come. Thirty years ago she had made a deal with the devil, fully cognizant of the risks. Every waking moment of the subsequent three decades—and many a sleeping one—she had waited in dread for this day to arrive. That is why she was calm. But she loved her Victor. That is why she, in every way but bodily, had died with him.

CHAPTER 65

STAY PUT

THE FIRST THING THEY DECIDED WAS TO HUNKER DOWN, AT LEAST temporarily, right where they were. The cops and Feds were crawling all over the neighborhood. TV trucks and reporters too. Better to get mobilized—or organized, or whatever—there in Little fuckin' Odessa, the last place any cop would look for an Ebbets Beach boy.

But what to do? What? The soldiers looked at one another and didn't even know who among them should do the thinking out loud. Marco? The pipsqueak Calculator? Please. Tony the Teeth, special-needs enforcer? No. Little Manny? Hadn't his "negotiations" gotten them right where they were now? This left Casper the Collector, the crooner, the sultan of swat, the part-time bagman with the lamé jackets, and, lately, short fuse. But wasn't he the one the don entrusted with the whack? In the gaping absence of Big Manny, didn't that make him the de facto underboss? Those were all questions, ones on the mind of the whole crew—what was left of it. No answers were forthcoming because, for the moment, they all were silenced by the unimaginable enormity of what had befallen them. For "What now?" was not even the foremost question on their minds. The foremost question on their minds was "Who's next?" But then, finally, it was indeed Casper who spoke up.

"All right, listen up," he began, having stepped from the doorway to the Zenith Cox 95 Flexion/Thoracic Drop table, against which he leaned at exactly the jaunty angle he had never once been able to approximate onstage. "First thing is, now there's only the six of us."

"Five of us," Leonard corrected.

"Six of us," Casper repeated. This time he was pointing to the sagittal traction unit, where the Chiropractor was busy liberating Tony the Teeth.

"And Teeth makes five," Leonard insisted. "Casper, what the felp?"

"And the Doc makes six," Casper explained. "Fellas, meet our guy."

Seth, having released Tony from bondage, held his hand up and wiggled his fingers. Needless to say, this cleared up nothing. So Casper continued.

"The Doc is the man the don and I brung in for the job. The Russian job. He's our guy."

Synchronized double takes. The way the soldiers looked around at the Chiropractor and back at Casper could have been choreographed for *Bye Bye Birdie*. That was the contract killer? *Him?* Little Manny spoke for the whole crew when he eloquently expressed his puzzlement and panic, using the same delicate phrasing that, a few days earlier, he'd summoned to characterize the barbershop fire and its ramifications. And then some.

"Holy fuckin' fuck," he observed. "You fuckin' gotta be fuckin' kidding."

Casper shut his eyes and put up a hand, traffic cop style.

"Hold on, hold on," he said. "The don told youse he'd give you details on a need-to-know basis, so I guess now youse need to know." He paused. "It's kinda complicated. Long story short, the Doc here has a technique that can put Ivan—whose name is Valentin, by the way—out like a fuckin' light. Then we throw him down the steps till he's dead as a doorstop. That's the plan, OK?"

"No offense, Casper, that's no plan." It was Leonard the Calculator, who had calculated Casper's scheme and reckoned that some significant elements were missing. He gestured toward the hired killer/healer. "Like, how you gonna get this guy close enough to the Russian to put him out?"

Little Manny, shook up when he arrived at the Glick-Mermelstein Wellness Center, was now highly agitated. He began to shout. "WHAT THE FUCK YOU GUYS TALKING ABOUT? WE'RE NOT WHACKING NOBODY. JESUS FUCKING CHRIST. THEY KILLED THE DON. WE DON'T HAVE NO ARMY. FUCK, WE DON'T EVEN HAVE A FUCKIN' POKER GAME. *FIVE GUYS AND A FUCKIN' CHIROPRACTOR? YOU FUCKIN' SHITTING ME?*"

Casper's instinct was to assert his newfound possible authority by cutting Little Manny off. Unfortunately, he could not think of one single thing to refute his pal's key points. So, like so many managers before him—interim and otherwise—he immediately shifted the responsibility elsewhere.

"Yeah, so in regards to logistics and so forth, this is the Doc's area. Doc, you wanna explain how you plan on getting within striking distance?"

Seth remained standing by the rack, hands on hips, gym teacher style. His lips were clamped together, and he was nodding furiously, much as he'd been doing since he was introduced to the crew. He took this opportunity to step from the back of the office to the drop table and stand shoulder to shoulder with Casper.

"OK," he began, "the situation on the ground is this. Casper is, of course, correct. I was engaged by...your late...Boss Donato... to eliminate a certain subject using what"—he nodded indicating Casper—"my friend has accurately described as a special chiropractic technique. Now, as this gentleman"—he indicated Little Manny—"has pointed out, fulfilling this contract will require me to be face-to-face with the subject. Now here I suppose I must defer to Casper—and, Casper, please correct me if I am wrong—but it was my assumption that you gentlemen would arrange to put me in the position to execute my responsibilities. So—"

Little Manny: "DID WE PAY THIS MOOK? TELL ME WE DIDN'T GIVE MONEY TO THIS FUCKIN' NUMBSKULL."

He might have continued carrying on, but something occurred that shut him up instantaneously. His cell phone was ringing—or more precisely, playing an instrumental of "Beat It." His contraband cell phone, the one nobody knew the number to because he never, ever used it for Family business. Who the fuck had tracked this number down? The Russians? The cops? Who? He dug frantically into his pocket to produce his mobile. The display read, MR. MATTRESS. Little Manny answered. "Hello?"

"Where you at?" asked a voice.

"Brighton Beach," Little Manny replied.

"Where?"

"Chiropractor's office. Avenue X off of Coney Island."

"I'll be there in an hour. Stay put."

Little Manny replaced the phone in his pocket.

"Yo, Ralph," snapped Casper, "who the fuck you giving this address to?"

"Shut the fuck up, Casper," replied Little Manny. "Who died and made you boss?"

The voice on the phone had been Big Manny.

CHAPTER 66

BOSS OF BOSSES

UPPER MANAGEMENT AT MR. MATTRESS WAS DISTRAUGHT.

Jack had been face-to-face with the deceased only two hours before the bombing. He had seen a man struggling with his circumstances, his pride, his own disordered sense of self. Maybe it was Jack's imagination, but as he left Fiesta Tours that afternoon—however dejected, rejected, and repudiated—believing that the don had so quickly answered no because further contemplation would have surely led to yes. Jack felt like he'd reenacted George W. Bush peering into Vladimir Putin's eyes and seeing a soul. The don's soul wanted salvation, Jack was sure, even though the don's mouth told him to go fuck himself. Now Jack suffered for the man's torment. And he suffered for Angela, whom he could not even try to comfort; she'd immediately been pulled in by the cops. And he suffered for himself. The horrifying episode carried him back to his own grim teenage experience when his own mercurial father, an IBM salesman, had died suddenly in a boating accident in Montauk. Jack had just seen his dad too. Before heading to the wharf, Mr. Phillip Schiavone had pleaded with his son to join him. "No," Jack had said.

Manny had spent more than thirty years side by side with Vic the Vig in a relationship filled with complexity, brotherly affection, and a peculiar, symbiotic sense of inferiority. Just as Big Manny had been intimidated by Don Donato's anger, cynicism, and brutality, the don shrank in dread of the consigliere's judgment. Shrewd as he was, the don felt very much in Manny's intellectual shadow, and his emotional shadow as well. The boss was by nature hotheaded; Big Manny, deliberate. The boss learned from Manny's caution and, over the years, was able to suppress his Sicilian impulses, such as pointless vendettas and reflexive violence—not so much because he felt moderation to be more prudent, but because he knew Big Manny would think less of him. Equally, in matters of business vision, Manny regarded himself very much a second banana. Sure, the consigliere was a clever money manager and prudent steward of the mob's assets, but when it came to how to steal and bully money from others, he could not hold a candle to the boss.

He was actually in the car on the day in 1980 when Vic the Vig—spying an Allied Van Lines truck—conceived of the moving van hijacking racket. It was so memorable because it was the birth of two profit centers back to back. One second, the boss was wondering why anybody would burglarize household goods if somebody else already took the trouble to pack and transport them, and then—just like that!—he realized that the time for house burglaries was immediately *after* the moving vans pulled out. The gang made more money stealing copper pipe that year than they made running numbers. Alas, the rise of PVC plumbing materials soon ruined that revenue stream, but that was no reflection on the Donato genius.

The proudest day in Manny's life was the one he stood on the altar of Our Lady of Grace, renouncing Satan on behalf of infant Angela. In one glorious moment, he was fulfilling roles in the

Donato family, in the Donato Family, and in the church family. This was his trinity, trumping even his own children's baptisms, to which he was merely an interested witness. Big Manny never really liked Don Donato; he merely worshipped him. And now, finally, Big Manny was the angry one.

"What happens now?" Jack asked Manny.

Uncharacteristically, Big Manny was pacing and literally wringing his hands.

"What happens? What happens is the Russians move into Ebbets Beach, blow up a store or two. Our boys either disappear or the Russians disappear them. That includes Ralph. Little Manny. Ralph, my son. The cops put on a big production, like they're right on top of this. But they know it'll be years, if ever, till they can make a case. They need a Russian to squeal, and that's not gonna happen. They'll pick somebody up—probably some soldier they think they can turn—but they'll spring him right away, because they got nothing. And whoever they pick up, the Russians'll probably whack the poor fucker. They have what you call a zero-tolerance policy toward their people in cahoots with anyone else. Some guys they buried alive, I hear."

"That is too sick," Jack said, an observation that Manny was in no position to embrace, what with Don Greco and Joey Sardines. Jack was having difficulty fathoming the depravity. "What can we do?" he asked.

"We can't do nothin'. The don needed to hit the Russian. That's that."

"I went to see Donato today, just before…"

Manny turned away from the Pillow Quilt Royale and toward his boss. "I didn't know that. Why?"

Jack shrugged. "Well, I had an idea, sort of a plan. It had to do with this chiropractor lunacy. Thing is, I had an idea to get their hit man alone with the Russian boss. But your don didn't bite."

Manny's eyebrows arched. "Respectfully, Boss, how the fuck you were gonna do that?"

"I wasn't sure I could. I figured it was, at best, maybe a one-in-four shot. Maybe worse, maybe two percent, but possible."

"And this is what you told the don?"

"Yeah," Jack replied. "But I didn't tell him everything, and, even then, he wanted no part of it."

"You know why not?" Big Manny asked.

"Yeah, I know." And Jack proceeded to explain his plan.

Big Manny, as Big Manny always did, listened very carefully to what Jack laid out and came—uncharacteristically—to three quick conclusions:

1) What Jack had promised the don was a promise he could not keep. Manny had also pondered the advertising gimmick, but getting the discount hit man in the killing zone was a trifecta longshot even Tony the Teeth wouldn't bet on, and Teeth was every bit as bad a horse picker as he was a prodigy in gin rummy.

2) The part of the plan Jack had been afraid to mention to the don—the part about raising suspicions about Smirdov within his own gang—wasn't a plan at all. It was just a plan to have a plan. And the plan it planned to have, even to Manny's racketeer sensibilities, was absolutely repulsive.

3) If they dropped everything, right this minute, and tried to pull the whole massively half-assed thing off, and the

Russian didn't bite, the crew and Ebbets Beach would be no worse off than where they were at this moment—i.e., a desperate place to be. In that sense, he and his goddaughter thought exactly alike. Nothing ventured, nothing gained.

So Big Manny walked over to the sales desk and picked up the phone.

"Hello?" answered a voice on the other end.

"Where you at?" asked Big Manny.

"Brighton Beach," the voice replied.

"Where?"

"Chiropractor's office. Avenue X off of Coney Island."

"I'll be there in an hour. Stay put." Big Manny replaced the receiver in its cradle.

"Where you going?" inquired Jack.

"You mean, where *we* going?" Big Manny answered. "As soon as Jitnee gets here."

The voice on the phone had been Ralph.

CHAPTER 67

PHILATELY

WHAT DO YOU DO DURING THE LONGEST FIFTY MINUTES IN THE history of time? One option is to learn the relationship between neuroskeletal misalignment and ADHD, migraine, menstrual cramps, high blood pressure, bedwetting, asthma, deep-vein thrombosis, and bipolar disorder. Even under such grave and harrowing circumstances, Seth Glick-Mermelstein, DC, fairly well held the attention of the jittery savages with his explanation of "nerve interference."

"Think of your body like the electrical grid of New York City. There are high-tension lines, power substations, transformers, generators, and big power plants, like Indian Point. Let's say Indian Point is your brain. The energy flows from there through the whole system. But what if some kid thinks it's funny to shoot a twenty-two at a transformer and make it blow up? Well, whatever homes and businesses are served by the wires coming out of that station lose power. Fellas, your organs are those homes and businesses. Your friend Lawrence here—"

"Leonard," corrected Leonard.

"Leonard here has a case of eczema. My guess is he's been going to dermatologists and other medical doctors for this condition for years. Am I right?"

Leonard nodded.

"And they're giving him ointments and pills and salves and God knows what kind of treatments—am I right?—and still his skin is flaking off like an Earl Scheib paint job. Leonard, am I right?"

Again, he nodded in agreement.

"This is because the so-called medical profession can't see past symptoms to the underlying origins of disease. Leonard's problem isn't in his skin. It's in his spine. It's what we call a subluxation. The nerve pathways that control the glands that deliver hormones to the skin are short-circuited, because some kid shot a twenty-two at his transformer, which happened to be right here." He strode to Leonard and pointed to the base of the Calculator's calculator. "C-one governs the thyroid. If I'm correct—and I admit sometimes things are more complicated by how we all abuse our spines our whole lives—but if I'm correct, we put this character on the drop table for C-one adjustments twice a week, three months later, good-bye flaking. You wanna see what that looks like?"

"Sure. Why not?"

Leonard clambered atop the table, facedown into the crotch of the headrest, which was swaddled in Tidi Chiropractic headrest paper unwound from a roll affixed just below. Seth used his knee to elevate the headrest an inch or two above the bed. He then placed the heel of his right hand on the back of Leonard's skull and, suddenly, smashed it downward. With a loud thump, the headrest fell the entire distance to bed level. It was like a prone hanging.

"Hey!" Leonard yelped.

The Chiropractor laughed and repeated the action three more times.

"That what you're gonna do to the Russian?" inquired Tony the Teeth.

"Well," replied the Doc, "let's see. Leonard, are you conscious?"

"Yeah," said Leonard, in a muffled voice, for his face was still buried in the headrest.

"In that case," said the Chiropractor to Tony, "no."

The Doc went on to crack Leonard's back and did the same for Marco. Then he turned to Little Manny and inquired after his symptomology.

"None of your fucking beeswax," Little Manny replied. "I don't need no witch-doctoring."

Casper sprang to the Doc's defense. "It's not witch-doctoring, Ralph. Seth worked wonders for me."

"Oh, yeah? Wonders? Two years getting cracked by this quack...Don't your back still hurt?"

"Sometimes, but—"

"Plus you're still a retard. No, thanks."

Just then, the buzzer sounded. Big Manny had arrived, and with him, to everyone else's surprise and consternation, was some other guy, turned out like some hotshot in a fancy suit and tie. Little Manny recognized him. The Chiropractor recognized him. Casper especially recognized him, the way a cleanup hitter recognizes a hanging slider. Now that the don was dead, Casper could see no reason for biting his tongue and losing face and generally kissing the ass of this pretty-boy interloper. Mr. fuckin' Mattress. Fuck him.

Except that Mr. fuckin' Mattress had entered with Big Manny, who was *Big Manny*. So Casper kept his mouth shut.

"Come on," announced Big Manny, "we gotta get busy."

The first order of business was to ascertain the details of the plot that the crew was engaged in, just to make sure Big Manny knew what was what. In fact, what the Chiropractor and Casper described was exactly what Jack had understood. Little Manny, as he listened to this nonsense once again, sat shaking his head at the stupidity of it all.

"Sorry, Pop, these guys are fuckin' mooks."

Casper, who was growing tired of being made a fool of, could contain himself no longer. He got right into Little Manny's face, shouting angrily. "YOU KNOW WHAT, RALPH? FUCK YOU! THIS WAS THE DON'S DECISION, SO, FIRST OFF, WHO THE FUCK ARE YOU TO QUESTION THE DON? YOU CALLIN' ME A MOOK? YOU, WHO WANTED TO WHACK LEONARD'S FUCKIN' PRETZEL GUY? *FUCK YOU AND FUCK YOU AGAIN!*"

Marco and Leonard had to pull Casper away from Little Manny, who stayed right where he was during the whole confrontation with a smarmy, superior smile plastered on his face. When Casper was dragged away, he merely looked toward his dad and gestured, as in, *See what crazy bullshit I gotta put up with?*

Big Manny, however, was not prepared to take sides. He had one thought, and one thought only: survival.

"What pretzel guy?" he asked, quietly.

Little Manny just looked down at his shoes.

"What pretzel guy, Calculator?" the big man persisted. "The one we took care of?"

Leonard, kneading his neck to relieve the spasm that had followed his miracle eczema cure, tried to explain. "Yeah, this Arab kid we took care of."

Big Manny nodded.

"Yeah, so I'm at the library on the computer looking up this Russian a-hole, Smirdov, and I see his pictures, and he looks just like the little pretzel guy. Jews, Arabs, you know, they sometimes look the same. And these felpers are like twins. No felpin' shimp. So I'm kidding around and say, felp, the pretzel guy owes us. Here's his chance to pay us back plus the vig. And the vig is we kill him. We whack the pretzel guy and make the don think we whacked the Russian and everything would calm down."

Now Big Manny was shaking his head, because this plot—one apparently embraced by his own flesh and blood—was obviously ridiculous. It was so ridiculous Mr. Mattress couldn't understand what he was hearing.

"Wait," he asked, "you were going to murder an innocent guy to trick your boss?"

Leonard turned to Big Manny. "Felp's this guy?" he asked.

"This is our friend Jack," Big Manny replied. "Answer his question."

Leonard shrugged. "It was, like, a joke. I was just felping around."

"Ralph wasn't fucking around," Casper jumped in. "Him and Teeth was serious. Marco too. They wanted to hit the pretzel guy."

Jack still couldn't quite follow. He turned to Little Manny. "To trick your boss into *not* hitting the Russian?" Jack asked.

"To stop a war from happening," Little Manny answered, satisfied the ends justified the gigantically illogical means.

The retailer of beds and mattresses, inexperienced as he was in the logistics of homicide, was fairly well acquainted with the behavior of news media. He immediately seized on the very flaw that, an hour earlier, Leonard had explained to Marco. The gang might have been able to momentarily deceive the don into thinking that a Russian, not an Arab, had been cut down, but they couldn't deceive the police, the family of the victim, and every news organization in the city of New York. The ruse made no sense. "Can you see why that makes no sense?" Jack asked Little Manny.

"I'm not saying we were gonna definitely do it. I'm just saying if we had to. "

It was all so monumentally half-witted, but there was one detail of this confederacy of dunces that did intrigue the mattress salesman. He turned to Marco. "This pretzel guy who looks like the Russian, you say he owes you?"

"Big time," replied Marco, who proceeded to recount the story of the windstorm, the accident that hurt the high school kid and the Cozy Nostra's intervention to subsidize the victim's medical care. The story actually rang a bell with Jack; Angela had made some reference to it that afternoon. And with that recollection was something of a brainstorm—a way to pull this off without exposing Tina to immediate danger.

What a gift from God. Ebbets Beach was awash in doppelgängers, a whole neighborhood full of Doublemint twins. Mob princesses, Bobby Kennedy in lamé, and now a halal version of the pest of honor. If this were in a pulp thriller manuscript, the rejection slip would say, *Too contrived*. On the other hand, if Jack had learned anything in advertising, it was that serendipity beats creativity every time. He shot a glance at Big Manny, hoping to see that the scales had fallen similarly from the ex-consigliere's experienced eyes. On the ride over, they'd discussed whether, in fact, they could get the Chiropractor face-to-face with the Russian and what they could do if they could. They'd discussed Jack's Tina scenario, which they agreed could very well eliminate Ebbets Beach's threat from Brighton Beach for all of eternity. But they'd also agreed that it was all just too fucking dangerous, especially for Tina, to be within murdering distance of the Russian. Yet this look-alike vendor suggested a fascinating and altogether less hazardous possibility. Jack couldn't be sure the lightning bolt had struck his new partner-in-crime, but what he could absolutely see was that Big Manny could absolutely see that Jack somehow had absolutely seen something. This recognition emboldened Jack to step a few paces toward the sagittal traction unit, address the assembly of obtuse hardened criminals, and make the following announcement:

"All right. It's on."

The soldiers, two of whom still had no idea who this guy was, naturally turned to Big Manny for direction. Big Manny, who in fact had not caught up with Jack's thinking, nonetheless said not a word. He simply pointed at Jack, pointed to his ear, and nodded. The message was, *Pay attention to this guy.* Thence, the man called Mattress began dispensing orders, beginning with Little Manny.

"Ralph, any chance you can get this pretzel guy to the travel agency tonight at ten?" Little Manny looked at Marco, who made a face but nodded yes. "Good. Do that, and you guys be there with him, OK?"

Again, the soldiers looked at Big Manny, who again nodded in assent.

"Yeah, whatever," Little Manny said, whereupon Jack turned his attention to Tony.

"You, sir. You know Tina Donato, right?"

"Yeah, I know her," Tony replied, flashing a bleached-skull smile so blindingly, inhumanly white that Jack actually flinched.

"Please collect her at her mom's place and get her there at ten too, all right? My friend Casper can go with."

"Can I ask for what?" the Collector inquired.

"No," Jack said. "But if the police are still there, wait for them to leave and keep us posted at the agency about any delay. Try not to say anything incriminating. You have a cell phone?"

"Uh-huh."

"You *do*?" blurted out a surprised Big Manny, who was already disgusted by his son's stupid, freakin', Feds' wet dream homing device.

"For show business only," Casper assured the former consigliere, who shook his head incredulously.

At that point, Jack turned toward the Chiropractor, tossing him a set of car keys.

"Sir, in my blue Saab nine-three parked right in front of your store are a few hundred fliers. You will go out immediately and stuff them everywhere in Little Odessa you think this Russian gang hangs out. They run a fur company, right?"

"Astrakhan Fur Storage," Leonard volunteered.

"OK, Doctor, blanket the place. Then do the same for his house. You also know where he lives, right?"

"Park Slope," said Leonard.

"Doctor, every place in Park Slope where he or his people might go, you put a flier. Especially his mailbox and under his door. It's gotta be you, because they might recognize these men." He swept his hand, signifying the Donato gang. He then consulted his wristwatch. "It's seven thirty, sir. You need to start right now."

The Chiropractor showed no signs of leaping into action. "I'm sorry," he apologized to the motley congregation of conspirators, "but at this point, I have to point out something important: I have forty thousand dollars coming to me, in advance. I understand the predicament you fellas are in, but I'm the one risking my hide."

All eyes turned to Big Manny, and Big Manny spoke.

"It's like this here, Doc. We give you sixteen grand in advance tomorrow afternoon. Then when the job is done, you get the rest."

The Chiropractor shook his head. "I'm sorry. No dice. As Casper can attest, I made a deal. Very clear. Cash up-front. Period. There is no way I put my life on the line for sixteen grand." He turned toward Casper. "You remember that I lowered my fee in deference to your financial limitations. I've already sacrificed a lot. Isn't that right, Casper?"

"He wanted seventy-five large," Casper confirmed.

At that point, Big Manny, the gentle giant, walked over to the Doc with a pleasant smile and enveloped the Chiropractor's shoulders with his massive right arm. Pulling the hit man aside, he quietly posed a question. "What do you suppose the Russians will do when they find out about this contract?"

"Huh?" Seth responded. "How would they find out?"

Now Big Manny turned to Little Manny. "Ralph, you still got the Russian's number?"

"Yeah," Little Manny said, producing his phone. "Gimme a sec…"

Seth rushed to Little Manny and closed up the soldier's phone. "All right, *all right!*" the Chiropractor squealed.

"And one more thing," Jack added, "you have a camera on your phone?"

"Yes," said the Chiropractor.

"When you get to Park Slope, take a picture in front of a store. Diner, bodega, whatever. No people in it. Just the background. Got it?"

"Sure."

"OK," said Jack, "it's late. Get going."

Within three minutes, with Leonard as his driver and babysitter, the Doc began canvassing two neighborhoods. Little Manny and Marco were dispatched to locate the pretzel guy, whom Jack had realized on the spot indeed had to be shot. Casper and Manny were on their way to the late don's home to escort Tina to the mattress store the moment the cops cleared out of the don's place. Big Manny and Mr. Mattress climbed into Little Manny's T-Bird and made their way back to Ebbets Beach.

Jack, who was squeezed uncomfortably into the pitiful excuse for a backseat, had a question for his assistant manager.

"So where does the money come from? Larry says he's only going to get halfway."

Big Manny nodded. "I got that covered."

"I don't understand," Jack said. "How? You don't have any cash. You told me you can't even pay Maria's tuition."

"I got it covered," Manny repeated. "There's sixteen grand in the Fiesta safe. And I got my stamp collection. It's worth fifty, sixty grand. I figure I can turn it around quick for twenty. At least ten."

Ralph jerked his head toward the passenger seat, his face twisted in horror. "Dad!" he cried. "No! You can't do that! You spent years putting that together."

Big Manny stuck his hand out the window to feel the wind rush into his outstretched palm. He loved that feeling. He imagined he was sailing. He had to imagine it. He'd lived his entire life within four miles of the water and never in his life set foot on a boat. "Ralph," he said, "just fuckin' drive."

CHAPTER 68

MONEY TALKS

AT 10:30 P.M., FIESTA TOURS WAS BUSY. IN THE BOSS'S OLD OFFICE, Big Manny sat in the don's former throne, with Ralph posed at his right shoulder seated in a plastic Kmart patio chair. Opposite the desk from these giants sat a slightly built, bald young gentleman who appeared to be counting many thousands of dollars of cash money. Oddly, the smaller man was not keeping track; he was just repeatedly thumbing through the six banded stacks of twenty-five C-notes and two stacks of twenty-five twenties. This he did again and again, as Jack Schiavone stood just on the other side of the doorway snapping pictures. Periodically, Mr. Mattress checked his watch. So far, no Casper, no hairy round guy with the exceptionally creepy smile, and, most of all, no Tina. Marco sat by the front desk thumbing through an old issue of *Barely Legal.* The phone had not rung.

Then some heavy breathing was heard on the steps and the door flung open. It was Tony the Teeth, minus the usual grin, looking like none too keen a messenger. The enforcer knew he had bad news to deliver. But he didn't know why it was so bad. So he just stood there, silent and massive, like a hairy Stonehenge, before Jack noticed him loitering by the door.

"Where's Tina?" he asked.

"In other words," said the Man from Polident, "Tina unfortunately cannot be with youse guys tonight."

"WHAT?" Jack shrieked. This wasn't bad news. It was catastrophic news. Tina with cold feet froze them out.

Teeth glanced at Jack, but now saw Big Manny rushing from the don's office.

"What's going on, Teeth?" he calmly inquired.

"So the cops are there three, four hours, interrogating and what have you."

"And?" said Big Manny.

"And one of the cops asks her a question she don't like, like where was she when the bomb went off? Which she didn't like the tone of, I guess. I guess she's upset about the don. Irritable. Like women get."

Yes, like women get when their fathers are blown to bits at church, those frail creatures. Those delicate flowers who, in their shock and grief, are given the third degree by a team of flatfoots utterly incapable of protecting her and her family and her business for even a mere twenty-four hours before she plans to stand face-to-face, utterly defenseless, with maybe the most dangerous man in the United States, and then on top of that bullshit, they want a fucking alibi. Women, so fragile and unstable, the little sparrows.

Now Big Manny was impatient. "Teeth! *What*?"

"Yeah, so she coldcocks the guy. The polack."

"What polack?" Jack asked.

"Vukowski or whatever."

"Fuck. Vukovich," Jack told Big Manny, then added for Tony, "it's Serbian or Croatian."

"Yeah? She Serbo-Croatians him right in the fuckin' schnoz, I hear. With the heel of her hand. Broke his nose. Blood everywhere."

"And he hit her back?"

"No, not that. The guy goes flying backward, outta the picture. But Tina's in these fuckin' mules or whatnot, and she loses her balance too, and slams into the coffee table. Breaks her spatula in two places. She's in the hospital right now. They have to operate, but she's a little on the drunk side, so they'll do it tomorrow. I just took Evangeline and Angela over there."

"She arrested?" Jack asked.

"Nah. In other words, not yet."

Big Manny kicked the air, soccer style. Jack slumped back in his chair. So much for that mobster elimination. A nearly perfect plot—except for a vast majority of its assumptions—foiled just like that by a piece of living room decor. What a mundane end to some genuinely exotic and imaginative pro-am conspiring. Manny then took to reflecting too. What he reflected on was that Ebbets Beach sure was becoming a dangerous place for cops to piss off itsy-bitsy little dames.

CHAPTER 69

BACK, GOT YOUR

THURSDAY WAS A TWIN OF WEDNESDAY. THE EVER-SO-SLIGHT breeze made the ever-so-slight chill a soothing sponge bath to the senses. On the boulevard, shoppers enjoyed the remnants of summer and the foreshadowing of fall as they took in the second bargain-filled half of Back-to-School Daze. Larry Rizzo, soothed not at all, visited the merchants one by one to tally the proceeds. The noontime totals gave him all the information he required. By the end of shopping hours, the alleged neighborhood watch would be endowed in the vicinity of $13,000 or $14,000, tops. The shocking news of Don Donato's murder weighed heavily on Larry, but he did not know whether to feel relief or panic. Relief because it was Donato's order for him to raise $25,000, so now at least he would not have to report his failure to the fearsome kingpin. Panic because the violence had already exploded, quite literally, out of control. Without the don alive, who would go forward with *The Magnificent Seven*? Who would protect Ebbets Beach? Who?

This was the dilemma he took to Mr. Mattress, whom Larry now understood had forged a fast and intimate relationship with the Donato family, lowercase. For that reason alone, Larry was unnerved by his reception. You don't live your entire life as Larry Rizzo without noticing that people avert eye contact when they see you on the street, or that they mysteriously lose their cellular connection when you have them on the phone, or that they develop a taste for nearly cheeseless pizza so they don't have to walk into your shop. Still, that's different from walking into a mattress discounter, seeing the owner look up at you, and then immediately bury his face in his hands, as if you were the Grim f'in Reaper. But you also don't live your life as Larry Rizzo if you don't ignore all such body language and barge right in.

"Good day, brother! 'Inventory Liquidation'?" This was Larry's opening salvo as he entered the store just past 1:30 in the afternoon. "You've only been open for a week."

"Larry," replied Jack, in a tone exactly synthesizing fatigue, contempt, irritation, and pity, "what is it?"

It wasn't that Jack hated Larry. It was that he couldn't stand him, which is not the same thing, and that he had no time for him. He was, indeed, occupied preparing for the biggest sale in Mr. Mattress history—that, and one other task of commandeering a crew of armed professional brutes to eliminate the threat of a much bigger and more professional crew of armed brutes, drawing on his applicable experience as an advertising executive, plus one week of bed retailing. He was therefore justifiably weary. He'd been up till the early hours, sorting the output of the underpopulated modeling session and going back and forth with Big Manny on what, if anything, could be salvaged without Tina. It was mainly a question now of whether they could somehow in the next few hours reschedule and record the assignation on the off chance the target sociopath should call for a free back rub. While Big Manny snoozed fully clothed on the Snoo-Z-Lite, Jack manned the sales desk trying to work out the ever-diminishing odds of success. Resting on the desk in front of Jack was his new mobile phone. Larry, who was fifty-six years old going on six months, saw the shiny object and immediately reached for it with his nearly thumbless right hand.

"DON'T TOUCH THAT!" Jack barked.

To Jack, that phone may as well have been the *Dr. Strangelove* CRM 114; everything depended on it. Since about 9:00 on Wednesday night, it had rung eight times with inquiries about the Chiro-PRACTICAL free trial. None of them was from a Russian gangster or his proxy. A moment after Jack snatched the phone from Larry, it rang again. Jack gestured for Larry not to speak as he answered the call.

"Hello, this is the Back Doctors. How can we help you?" He made a sour face. "Oh, ma'am, I'm so sorry. That promotion has been going on for almost a week and, as you can imagine, has been very popular. I'm afraid all the doctors are all fully scheduled for today. Can I try to book you for an appointment with one of the doctors for November?…OK, once again, our apologies. Thanks for calling the Back Doctors."

Larry Rizzo didn't understand. "I don't understand," he said.

"Oh well," said Jack. "Tell me what's going on with the money."

"So…Are you a doctor too? I can't say as I'm surprised."

"LARRY! The money. Tell me."

Taken aback by Jack's display of short temper, Larry—in a most un-Larry-like way—temporarily let go of the question he had in his mind and gave Jack the unfortunate accounting he'd requested. "Maybe fourteen thousand dollars, maybe less. But I don't even know what to do with it. Because of—"

Jack cut him off. "Bring it here at six."

"Bring it here? Why would I—"

"No need to be paranoid, brother. Just giving you the lay of the land. Bring the money here at six. I won't be here. The sleeping giant over here will be. Give him every penny from the pickle jars."

"Some of the stores won't close till nine thirty."

"Larry, can't you just listen for a change? At six o'clock, bring every penny that is collected as of six o'clock and give it to your close personal friend Big Manny. Do you think you can handle that?"

"So we're going ahead with the"—he lowered his voice—"*h-i-t*?"

"I don't know what you're talking about, Larry."

Larry leaned forward and spoke in a whisper. "The *h-i-t*. The *hit*. We still in business?"

Jack wearily lowered his own head and shook it from side to side, like a horse trying to dislodge his bit. "Jesus Christ, Larry. First of all, there is no 'we.' I don't know what crazy ideas you have in your head, but the only thing 'we' about you and me is the Village—and, come to think of it, I'm not in the Village, so 'we' don't exist, OK? There is no 'we.' *Orget-fay e-way, et it-gay?* Second of all, I personally am not *h-i-t*-ing anybody."

Larry stood upright again, wearing a sly smile. "Perhaps I should have said, 'Terminate with extreme prejudice.'"

Jack looked up at the nincompoop in bedraggled amazement. "Prejudice? What?"

Larry nodded and replied, again, *sotto voce*. "I know how it is with you guys in the company. You think I don't know what 'inventory liquidation' is?"

Jack didn't even have it in him to laugh. His lips formed a cockeyed grimace of a sardonic smile, and he puffed some air from his nostrils as he shut his eyes. "Now I'm with the CIA? Really, Larry? The *CIA*?"

Larry Rizzo, meatball sub preparer and covert intelligence expert, pinched his semithumb and forefinger together and drew the fingers across his lips. The secret was safe with him.

"Larry, I don't know how to break this to you, but I am not with the CIA—which, by the way, does whatever it does overseas, not domestically. I'm not CIA. I'm not any kind of spook."

"Yeah, you are," Larry replied, grinning.

"No, Larry."

"Yeah-huh...Mr. *Chiropractor!*"

Jack nearly swallowed his tongue. He jumped up, came around the desk, and dragged Larry to the back of the store. "What do you know about the Chiropractor?" he demanded.

Larry just grinned. "Don't worry, I'm a little chiropractorish myself."

"Huh? What?"

Larry leaned forward and whispered. "I've got your back."

"I'm gonna fuckin' punch your front," Jack said, forming a fist and cocking his arm in a way he hadn't done since a flying-elbow incident in a three-on-three hoops game when he was sixteen. "Who told you about the Chiropractor?"

"Who do you think? *Ina*-tay."

"Tina *Donato*?"

"Ten-four," Larry replied, still smirking about his success in sussing out the government hit, the secret code name, and Mr. Mattress's true identity. "Everybody knows about the...operation... but I'm the only one who's got the whole thing figured out. Your cover and whatnot. Do you use a silencer?"

342

"Oh, for fuck's sake, are you nuts? Listen to me: There is no silencer. There is no gun. No C-I-A. Just the neighborhood W-A-T-C-H. Larry, please pay attention: just bring me the money, and just maybe the problem will take care of itself. Understand?"

Larry nodded his head. "Yep, brother, I understand…It's polonium, isn't it? You have a polonium isotope you're gonna slip into his samovar. Am I right?"

It's not that Jack was out of patience. Where Larry was concerned, he'd begun with no patience and commenced deficit spending. But now he was also out of time to be going back and forth with this delusional lamebrain. And now that the word about the Chiropractor was out, Jack had to quickly shut the dunce up before he blabbed his way into everyone's undoing. But how? He couldn't tell the truth; that would be like skywriting the scheme above the entire borough. And he didn't wish to lie. There remained but one choice: he had to take Larry Rizzo into his confidence. Jack put his arm around the sandwich man's shoulder and walked him slowly to the farthest corner of the store.

"OK, Lar, it's like this," he whispered. "I'm not with the company." Then he winked. This made Larry smile.

"And I'm not code name Chiropractor." Wink. Smile. "And none of this cash is being used to finance a TWEP."

"Twep?" Larry said.

"Termination with et cetera et cetera," Jack whispered.

"Roger that," said Larry, winking.

"But here's the thing, Larry, and this is strictly on the downlow: the nonoperation is currently nonoperational." If you parsed that convoluted statement, Jack felt confident, it was not, strictly speaking, untrue. "Orders," he added.

"From Langley?" Larry whispered.

"No," Jack replied. Wink.

"But what about the Russians?"

"There's going to be a 'transaction.'"

"You're gonna buy them off?"

"Absolutely not." Wink.

Larry nodded, trying to make sense of the remarkable secrets with which he had been entrusted. "So what should I do?" he asked.

"Just bring the money at six and sit tight for further instructions," Jack whispered. "We cool now?"

Larry glanced furtively around the store to make sure they weren't being observed. "Affirmative," he replied. Then he too flashed a wink—or some approximation of one. His upper lip curled up and both eyes closed, his left slightly more than his right. This exposed Larry's protruding canine, which was as gray as cigarette ash.

Jack managed a weak smile of acknowledgment. "Good. You saved me a phone call by coming here, and I appreciate that, but now you have to let me get to some—"

"Tradecraft," Larry offered.

"Yes, tradecraft. Absolutely. Now, remember, six sharp, OK?"

Larry gave him a thumbs-up, at which point Jack noticed something peculiar. He squinted quizzically. "Is that the same shirt you were wearing yesterday?"

"No," replied Larry on his way out the door. "I have twenty-three of them."

CHAPTER 70

BACK, SORE

WITH THE TROPICAL PARASITE GONE, JACK WAS FREED TO FURTHER contemplate the chances of this quixotic scheme actually working as planned—changes hinging entirely on Valentin Smirdov behaving like a garden-variety consumer, not cloistered in his gangland hideaway out of the view of law enforcement. If Manny was right, maybe for the very reason that the Russians *were* in lockdown, Smirdov would be just bored enough to attend to his nagging backache.

Supposing, that is, the oddball chiropractor had guessed right and the target happened to have one. Notwithstanding Mr. Mattress's glib shoptalk, not everybody suffers from them. Only 62 percent of adults, and only 40 percent more than once. Furthermore, although Jack liked to say that advertising works, it doesn't work on everybody all the time. Advertising works because it reliably influences a minority of the population an unknown percentage of the time. All in all, the odds truly sucked. Jack was less optimistic than he was when his agency launched GermMane, the world's first oat-bran shampoo—and that was a $190 million flop.

The phone. It was ringing with caller number ten. Would this be the winner of the free chiropractic adjustment?

"Hello, this is the Back Doctors. How can we help you?"

Jack's eyes widened. On the other end of the phone was a man with a Russian accent. He scooted across the sales floor, jostled Manny awake, and gestured toward the cell phone.

"Yes, sir. And where are you calling from please?…Brighton Beach. Uh-huh. And you'd like to see one of our doctors at your office, your home…uh-huh…uh-huh."

Jack was jumping up and down, like he'd just peeled off the liner from a Mountain Dew bottle cap and won a radio-controlled airplane.

"I see. And your home is located where?"

He stopped jumping, his enthusiasm spontaneously drained.

"Coney Island. I see." So much for that. As he'd been doing since last night, he very politely got the false-alarm caller off the phone. He also became successively more aware of time. With each useless response to the flier, and with each passing minute, failure loomed larger. In point of fact, failure was looming its ass off.

Jack sighed. "Face it, Manny. It's over."

"No, it ain't. Lemme ask you something. That Google ad you took. When did that go up? Yesterday?"

"Yeah."

"You seen our website today?"

"No."

"Yeah, well, twenty people downloaded coupons. Just from that ad. While you were fucking around with that banner this morning, I already sold a bed from the coupons. Jitnee sold two last night."

"So?"

"So you make a good offer and you get it in the right people's hands, they will respond, which is what you told me. The flier ain't even been on the streets for twenty-four hours. In this business, you gotta be patient."

This business? Which business? Mattress discounting. Human life? The fact that Jack didn't know the answer struck him as disturbing and very, very weird.

He sighed. "Anyway, Manny, without Tina, we've got nada."

Big Manny disagreed. "I don't know why you say that, neither. Yesterday, you didn't have the pretzel guy, just Tina. Now you got the pretzel guy and no Tina. Same difference. Get your appointment with the Ivans and we're in business."

"Look, Manny, I appreciate the pep talk, but listen to what you're saying. This whole thing is built around the appointment. The whole thing. The Mr. Spock thing. Moving the Russian's body. Everything. The pretzel guy…I mean, that's a lucky break, sure; the shots with the money are good. But it's not *the* money shot. We need Tina doing what Tina said she'd do. Without her, the Chiropractor is useless. Anyway, who's kidding who? We don't have a fucking appointment in the first place. The guy hasn't called, and, the more I think about it, he isn't ever going to call. He's got money. Why would he be inviting strangers to his fucking armed fortress for two hundred bucks' worth of spine cracking?"

"That's not what you told me before."

"What's not what I told you?"

"Since I come here, you got me putting out Milk Duds and coffee and apple cider and all this crap."

"For the customers, yeah."

"Yeah, like you keep telling me, 'The most powerful word is *free.*'"

Big Manny had a point. He had accurately reiterated the article of advertising faith often cited by Mr. Mattress. Alas, it was just a saying, and the saying wasn't true. Furthermore, he was gradually realizing that the notion *anything* he'd ever done in his life prepared him for the job at hand was plainly fatuous. Jack made a mental note not to try to make a living as an underworld kingpin. It was hard.

Manny walked over to the area behind the sales desk, where there was a marbled cardboard storage box, which he bent down to lift and placed on the counter. Jack watched as Manny removed the lid and pulled out a cloth-covered binder. Upon further scrutiny, Jack realized this was an album—one of Manny's stamp albums. He wanted to philatelize one more time before selling the collection. His last acquisition had been a 1943 one-centime stamp, uncancelled, from French Indochina—*Indochine*—featuring a profile of a mutton-chopped military officer and Mekong River explorer named Francis Garnier. He loved the specimen because the sepia portrait of Garnier was superimposed on a stylized wake of disturbed river water, splitting the difference between a Japanese woodcut and the back of a 1963 baseball card.

"Manny, you can put that away. You're not selling your stamps."

"I already did," Manny replied. "Guy's coming by tonight. He's gonna give me fifteen dimes, cash, if he likes what he sees."

"But it's worth four times that, you said."

"It's like anything else," replied Mr. Mattress's resident expert in markets. "It's worth what I can get for it."

Jack shook his head. "No fuckin' way. I'll figure something out. I'm not going to let you do that."

That was a good one, and the assistant manager chuckled. "Oh," said Big Manny, "*you* aren't gonna let *me* do that? Ha ha ha ha ha."

Jack's cell phone started to ring again—or play, actually. His ringtone was the "Great Gate of Kiev"—it just seemed appropriate for the task. Not only was the music Russian, but Jack figured he and the composer had a lot in common: big, sweeping ideas threatened by a complete inability to orchestrate. So now, in the midst of a lull in the borough-wide excitement surrounding the biggest sale in Mr. Mattress history, Mussorgsky was once again filling the empty store. It was, if nothing else, a nice sound track for his soap opera, and now for the latest useless inquiry from the latest Coney Island cripple. The phone display read, UNKNOWN CALLER.

"Hello, this is the Back Doctors. How can we help you?... Uh-huh. This evening. Home or office, may I ask?...I see. And the residence is located where?...Can you give me that address in Park Slope?"

Handsome Jack was white in the face, his eyes shut tight as he went through his patter. On the other end of the line, unless he was vastly mistaken, was the Russian.

CHAPTER 71

KING, QUEEN, FULL, AND

ESPECIALLY TWIN

CERTAINLY, HE HAD PLOTTED AND ANGLED AND PAPERED TWO neighborhoods to achieve this little miracle, but he never really imagined the Russian would take the bait. "Well, I'll be goldarned," he announced aloud to nobody. "Advertising seems to fuckin' work." The appointment with Valentin Smirdov was set for 8:00 p.m. Jack had gently tried to persuade the caller to take the "last remaining slot" at 6:00, but the Russian insisted on not interrupting his dinner hour. Jack made a "special exception." This gave them six hours to get Tina out of a hospital bed to violate the laws of God and man. It also gave the Russian six hours to change his mind.

Meanwhile, Jack needed to pay his respects to Evangeline and to see Angela. He'd spoken to her for only a few seconds yesterday, seconds dominated by her whispered plea, "Not now, Jack. Maybe tomorrow. Not now." Three and a half days into their love affair, he had no standing to insist otherwise. But this was now tomorrow. At least he could kill two birds with one stone. He also desperately needed to speak with Tina in the hospital, which is exactly where Angela and Evangeline were to be found. So with Big Manny minding the store, he headed for Maimonides Medical Center in

Borough Park. This would have to be quick. In a couple of hours, Mr. Mattress needed to be back at Mr. Mattress, where he would try to twist the long arm of the law.

At Maimonides, Evangeline and Angela sat on a waiting room window seat on square cushions of taupe-and-beige vinyl, each in her way looking enervated and beautiful.

First, Jack embraced Evangeline. "I am so sorry," he whispered. "Truly sorry." Evangeline was not fully present. She thanked him as she would any kind stranger and resumed her vinyl vigil.

Now Jack and Angela were hugging, wordlessly. Wordless is good. Death is usually a poor occasion for conversation. To the raw nerves of the mourner, so much can be the wrong thing to say. Earnest condolences can sound trite and perfunctory. Reassurance can sound presumptuous. Gallows humor can be cathartic but easily taken as insult. Genuine warmth can be mistaken for unctuousness. Even the purest expression of empathy—the innocent "I know, I know"—is skating on thin ice because, of course, you do not know. You do not know shimp.

Angela helped Jack by speaking first. "I didn't expect that this would be so hard," she said, to which Jack gently kissed the top of her head.

"Tell me about Tina," he said.

"She'll be OK. She'll be out in an hour, I think."

"Out of the hospital?" Jack said, with a flash of more than welcome surprise. "Fantastic. I thought her leg was broken."

"It *is* broken, Jack. In two places. They need to put pins in. She'll be out of surgery in an hour. She's on the operating table now."

"The operating table…" Jack tried not to reveal how crestfallen he was. Luckily, his sudden overwhelming sense of failure and disappointment looked exactly like his expression of somber concern.

"Yeah," Angela laughed, "when they wheeled her in, it was cold as hell in the corridor and her nipples were popping up like crocuses. I'm sure the doctor has a total boner."

Yes, cathartic gallows humor can touch tender nerves, but Jack had no standing to be sensitive to a real mourner's catharting, so he tried to further disguise his overwhelming despair by chuckling at Angela's bawdy little joke. "And you say *I'm* disgusting," he offered, none too convincingly.

Angela took him by the hand and led him through the swinging doors to the corridor. "Speaking of which, Tina tells me she missed a chance to make pornography history."

Yikes. Jack hadn't anticipated that Tina would share that unsavory secret, even with her sister. He intentionally hadn't mentioned Tina's involvement to Angela, mainly to spare Tina embarrassment and partly to preclude well-intentioned sisterly intervention over Tina exposing herself, in several ways, to genuine peril. He'd assumed Tina would, for her own sake, keep her role to herself, but this was what he got for underestimating the guidette's sense of pride and overestimating her sense of shame. As far as Jack knew, when he arrived at the hospital, Angela would think her father's murder had rendered their neutralization scheme moot. He'd entertained no thought, in the midst of her distress, to tell her otherwise. Now Tina's surgery ruled out any photogenic acts of sodomy, thus finally consigning Operation Vulcan Nerve Pinch to the fifty-five-gallon drum of history.

But now Angela wanted to know everything, so he filled her in. He told her about the Russian taking the ad bait, he told her about Tina's original role in the plan (discarded quickly on danger grounds), he told her about the gang's unbelievably stupid notion of foisting a dead pretzel vendor off on the don as a dead Russian, and he told her about the same vendor's *deux et machina* role in adding verisimilitude to the fraud.

"Wait," Angela interjected. "I agree that Daddy's cretins are cretins. But now I'm not so sure about you. If Tina was going to catch this Russian piece of shit with his pants down, why bother with the look-alike? It's like something from those cheesy paperbacks, the ones in the supermarket aisle, with the embossed covers. Does he have amnesia too?"

"For the same reason that Edmund Hillary climbed Everest," Jack replied.

"Because Mount Everest looked like a Russian murderer?"

"Because it was there. The pretzel guy fell into our lap. He made it possible for us to keep Tina away from the hit itself. Why wouldn't we take advantage? Your uncle even thinks Aziz all by himself would represent the Russian's death warrant. But we'll never know."

"Why is that?"

Jack looked down at the incredibly shiny linoleum beneath his merely impressively shiny shoes. He could see their reflections, distorted by the fluorescent oscillation and film of floor wax. Everything else he saw clearly, which is why he'd come to a decision. "I'm calling it off."

"Calling it off?" Angela blurted out so loudly that a passing orderly snapped his head around. She saw this and began to whisper. "*Calling it off? You can't do that.*"

"I have to," Jack said. "The Chiropractor's a total klutz. He's going to get killed."

Angela shook her head. "Isn't that the risk a hit man takes? He's a professional. He's going to walk away with a lot of money. Isn't the danger kind of his problem?"

Jack didn't want to upset Angela at so painful a moment. So he didn't point at her when he laughed in her face. Instead, he extended his hands and gently grasped her shoulders. "Angela, darling," he said. "First of all, this guy is no professional. He's a novice. But, besides that, are you listening to yourself? We're talking about someone getting killed here. The hot Tina action could have reduced the risk about a thousand percent. Without her, it's over. We tried, but it's game over."

"You can't reduce something by a thousand percent," Angela absently observed as she eyed orderlies down the hall wheeling a gurney at none too brisk a pace toward the elevator. She was trying to see the face of the patient. Squinting, she still couldn't make out whether the rider was female or male, living or dead. Then she turned back to Jack. "The most you can reduce anything is by its entirety. One hundred percent."

"OK," Jack said. "Then let's say ninety-five percent. Tina was the only way this thing could come off without this numbskull chiropractor winding up in cold storage, probably in small pieces."

"I'll do it," Angela said.

"Huh?" said Jack. "You'll do what?"

"Whatever Tina was going to do. I'll do it."

"Angela, what are you talking about? We're trapping him with Victor Donato's slutty daughter. His slutty daughter is in surgery."

Angela, who was exactly as tiny as her sister, had to stand on her tiptoes to reach Jack's face with her fist, which she used to play knock-knock on his forehead.

"Hel-*looo*? Duh, we're twins. You wanna play *The Prisoner of Zenda*? Fine. Double the pleasure, double the fun."

Jack looked straight down at her, trying to process what his girlfriend had just volunteered for and what she had just said. His hard drive whirred. Yes, twins. But, no. He couldn't possibly allow her to so debase herself. Wouldn't that be unforgiveable? But then he thought, *Wait, if I couldn't do that, how could I possibly have allowed Tina to debase herself? And, anyway, was their decision any of my business in the first place? Was Donato not their father and Ebbets Beach their neighborhood? Did they not have their own volition? If I tried to stop Angela, would she just tell me to stick my permission up my ass?* These were hard questions, so he answered a different one.

"Twins?" he finally replied. "Yes and no." And he was not merely changing the subject. For one thing, Angela's hair was much shorter. Secondly, they projected entirely different images. Surely the Russians would have no trouble distinguishing the demure from the debauched. More troublesome was that, from his angle, he could see a third major flaw in her assertion; that is, he could *not* see what the flaw was in her assertion—namely, gigantic breast implants. Angela followed his eyes to her own lovely but unenhanced chest. Then she swatted him.

"You know what, smartass? I'll stuff 'em."

All right, maybe she could. So much for the bongo deficit. But Jack continued to stare at her, saying nothing.

"Jack, did you hear me?" Angela asked. Of course, he'd heard her. But his mind was still racing. "Now, hold on," he said. "The plan was to shoot her butt naked on film. Nothing left to the imagination at all. Even assuming we can locate the guy and get him to cooperate again today, do you really want to be captured in compromising positions with Aziz the pretzel vendor?"

Angela looked up at him blankly. "Absolutely not," she said.

"I didn't think so. It's disgusting."

"I'll do it live."

"Live?"

"With the Russian."

"No fucking way," Jack snapped. "The Chiro is planning to put this guy out of commission. I wouldn't let Tina be there in the flesh, and I'm not letting you."

"Fuck you, Jack! Who the fuck are you to *let* me do anything?"

Well, he had the volition issue sized up just about right. "Funny," he replied, "that's just what Manny said."

"Huh?"

"Nothing. Never mind."

"So tell me," Angela insisted, "what do I need to do? Jack? Jack? Fuckin' answer me, Jack."

Jack thought very, very hard before, finally, he did answer her. "Go stand against that wall," he said.

"Huh?"

"Please. Go stand against that wall."

Angela did as he'd asked, backing herself up to the industrial-green corridor wall, during which time Jack produced his new phone. "Look at the birdy," he said, holding the phone up to capture her image in the camera. "Now, don't smile." Don't smile?

He snapped the picture, checked it, folded the phone, kissed his girlfriend, and headed for the elevator. Then he stopped and turned to her. "Two things: One, be at the chiropractor's place at six thirty. No later. It's in Brighton Beach. Big Manny will give you the details. Number two, I love you." On cue, the elevator doors opened, and Jack ducked inside.

All of a sudden, things were coming together in such a way that abject calamity was now merely probable. But he had to find Tony the Teeth and get back to Ebbets Beach. He had some computer work to take care of pronto, and at 4:00 the Feds would be coming to the store. If by some miracle they were prepared to make a move on the Russians, all of this craziness and risk would be unnecessary. And if they weren't prepared to make a move on the Russians, they had to be safely out of the way. The very last thing he needed in his attempt to neutralize murderous racketeers was to be arrested for murderous racketeering. So, of course, as he hurried to influence law enforcement, he ran smack into law enforcement. At the hospital's front door, a patrol officer and a uniformed sergeant stood in his path.

"Jack Schiavone?" the sergeant asked.

It was another one of those moments. Adrenaline and cortisol surged through his body. Paresthesia, those creepy pins and needles, stung his face. Exactly as he'd experienced in his first anxious moments with Angela a week ago, the fight-or-flight response was lighting his body up like a pinball machine. There was nothing, not one blessed thing, that a policeman could do but make his day worse. The possibilities ranged from informing him his store was ablaze to arresting him on the spot for criminal conspiracy.

"Yeah," he said, "that's right."

"We don't want to detain you," said the cop, "if you're in a hurry. Like if you're going to meet someone. Someone Russian."

Oh, no, no, no, no, no.

The sergeant started to laugh. "This is Officer Glover," he said. "I'm Mike Franzetti."

I'm Calabash McWaggledaggle. I'm Slurrel Bermp. I'm Tarvicious Lefevre. It was all the same to Jack. Who in God's name was Mike Franzetti? Jack didn't think it was entirely prudent to inquire, so he simply shook the cops' hands and tried to act like somebody not in the midst of gangland warfare.

"Nice to meet you. Was there something…Is there something I can help you with?"

"Hah!" Franzetti laughed. "I was thinking maybe there was something we could help you with."

Jack tried not to betray his utter failure to understand who these officers were, why they knew him, why they were laughing about Russians, and why they had tailed him to a hospital in Borough Park. For all the good that did. He looked like a cat being teased with a rubber mouse on a string. Franzetti held the string.

"I mean," the cop continued, "it's sort of come to my attention that you are in arrears on a certain contractual matter…"

That did it. The police did know. He was totally and thoroughly fucked; that was obvious. What was less than obvious was why the cops were being so goofy and coy. It was like dialogue from some crappy buddy flick. So Jack felt no choice but to engage.

"Look, what is it you officers want, exactly?"

Franzetti looked at Glover. Glover looked at Franzetti. And both dissolved into laughter. Franzetti slapped Jack on the back. "Relax, pal," he said. "I'm a friend of Tina's. We just come to see how she's doing. Curtis here"—Franzetti lowered his voice—"he knows you're taking out the Russian. So don't worry about that."

Nooooo. Why would he worry about that?

"No skin off my nose, that's for sure," the patrolman chimed in. "Thing is, if you are running into some financial issues, I think we—Mike and I, both—might have a long-term solution. Nothing we have to discuss right now, but I'd love the opportunity to sit down with you at your convenience." Then he cracked up again. "Maybe after you're finished killing the Russian."

To say Jack was flustered does a disservice to the chaos being visited upon his nervous system. His heart was pounding, his throat constricted, his palate sawdust dry. But then something dawned on him, something ludicrous and hilarious and, on many levels, horrifying.

"Wait a second," he squeaked. "Is this Amway?"

Franzetti thumbed in the direction of Glover. "He's my upline. You should see his fuckin' boat."

CHAPTER 72

INVESTIGATORS

YOU HAD TO HAND IT TO THE DULY APPOINTED CIVILIAN AUTHORI-
ties. They certainly did know how to proceed with procedures. They
knew how to isolate crime scenes, to sift for evidence, to interview
witnesses, to send charred materials to labs for molecular signa-
tures of explosives and propellants, to canvas for more witnesses,
to establish a commanding presence with dozens of uniformed
personnel milling around up and down the boulevard, to wiretap
phones and subpoena cell phone records, to stake out addresses,
and to harass suspects. This was not so much law enforcement as
theater, making a good show of looking diligent and police-ish.
Not that solving the crimes was all that challenging. The what,
where, when, why, how, and approximately who behind all three
acts should have been apparent to everyone. No sifting through
smoldering crime scenes was required to deduce that deduction.
The entire point of all three outrages was for the victims and the
entire community to know who was responsible. The two-pronged
problem for law enforcement was, one, being able to charge anybody with a crime and, two, to do so before anything or anyone
else was harmed.

Jack understood the problem. At the diner, the city and federal task force members had been depressingly candid about the

onerous burden of evidence they required to prosecute an arson or bombing case. They needed an eyewitness, fingerprints, surveillance images, DNA, or a dropped business card to place a suspect at the scene. So Jack was guardedly pessimistic when the investigators asked to pay a visit; he seriously doubted any of the Russians would be so careless as to help the cops make a case. Still, although elements of his almost plan were beginning to fall almost into place, he'd have been happier if the authorities had found a way to take the motherfuckers down without the help of a housing lawyer, bed salesman, bone cruncher, stamp collector, and gangland krew of Keystone Kops. When he got back to the store, he therefore had two surprises waiting.

The first was the, ahem, mob scene at Mr. Mattress. There must have been twenty-five people in the store, being served by only Jitnee and Manny, who by all immediate appearances were redeeming coupons and selling beds one after another after another. Jack, whose inventory was set up to handle twenty-five to thirty-five beds per week, wasn't sure he could fill all the orders. This nonetheless amounted to a pleasant surprise. Perhaps Manny was right, and they had cracked the code for accelerating the mattress-sale ecosystem. If so, the business model—as the MBA dickwads phrased it—would "scale," and a bedding empire could reasonably flow from it. He'd expand rapidly, use Google AdWords and couponing to squeeze a zillion quick sales at other locations, and flip the business at an unheard of multiple reflecting the industry-leading sales velocity. By the time the new owners realized he had sped up the demand cycle and depressed future transactions, he'd be in Tahiti sipping tropical drinks.

It was just a fleeting thought, but it amused him. What did not amuse him was the second surprise, decidedly unpleasant and idiotic and infuriating. So unexpected was this development that it took a while for him to catch on. Jack had begun to pitch in at the sales desk when the entourage of flatfoots walked in. It was the ATF guy, McWiggin; the city cop, Vukovich; and a third guy—right on time for their confab. Jack saw them enter, motioned for them to cool their heels a sec, passed the paperwork for a Pillow Quilt full over to Jitnee, and crossed the store to greet them. McWiggin was bouncing on the edge of a Snoo-Z-Lite.

"Hello, gentlemen," Jack said, "how can I help you?"

"Nice bed, Schiavone," McWiggin said. "Expensive?"

"A good value," Jack replied. "This whole place is about value. Highest quality at prices the department stores can't touch. That's a continuous-coil innerspring, you know. Like a Serta, at about half the price. And that's fourteen-gauge tempered steel."

"Yeah, like that matters." This skeptical remark came from the third visitor.

"Have we met?" said Mr. Mattress, extending his hand. "I'm Jack Schiavone."

"Jeff Blatt," said Deputy US Attorney Jeffrey Blatt, "Justice Department." Blatt was about forty and the skinniest adult male Jack had ever seen. The guy's gray JoS. A. Bank suit hung on him like a drop cloth draped on a floor lamp.

"Nice to meet you. Fact is, though, if the coils aren't tempered steel, they get misshapen and squeaky very fast. Might as well use rotini."

"You claim this bed is as good as a Serta?" Blatt persisted.

"Nope," Jack said. "Better. A lot better. More support. More durable. Highest-quality fabric. Less edge breakdown."

"Never mind that," interrupted Detective Sergeant Vukovich of NYPD. "We have other business to conduct."

"All right," Jack agreed, but then suddenly focused on the lengths of adhesive tape strapped across the detective's nose and the purple coronas under his eyes. "Hey, what happened to your face?"

"Never mind that, either," Vukovich snapped. "The reason we wanted to see you is certain developments related to our investigation."

"Well, thank God for that," Jack replied.

"Not necessarily," countered Blatt.

"Huh?" said Jack. "What's that mean?"

"That means we have some questions," said Blatt. "A number of them, as a matter of fact."

"Such as?" inquired Mr. Mattress.

"Such as we see your new girlfriend is a Donato," said Vukovich. "Such as this character over here"—he gestured toward Big Manny—"is an interesting choice of employee. Such as you meeting Victor Donato at a nightclub. Such as you paying a call to Victor Donato's front business."

"You cannot be serious."

"You shouldn't think we aren't," Vukovich shot back. "Look, you open a store on Ebbets Beach Boulevard, and the next day a store burns on Ebbets Beach Boulevard. You immediately hire a career criminal from the Donato mob, you start banging Donato's daughter—"

"Watch it!" Jack barked. "Why don't you just get the fuck out of—"

"Quiet. I'm talking here," Vukovich interrupted. "You're paying visits to his other daughter. You call on Donato two hours before he's killed. We got pictures. We also have pictures of you afterwards with members of the gang in Brighton Beach. And, whaddya know, you're a convicted embezzler."

"You've been tailing *me*?"

"Duh," Blatt said.

"Yeah...*duh.* What a pack of idiots. The Russians are burning down Brooklyn and you're chasing me. How fucking stupid can you get?"

"Relax, Schiavone," said McWiggin, "these are just questions."

Jack let his head fall to his chest. "OK," he sighed, "what can I tell you? You guys are too smart for me. I may as well confess."

"Really?" McWiggin said.

"What's this guy up to?" posed Vukovich. "Schiavone, I don't need you jerking me around."

"Read him his rights," Blatt said.

"Not necessary," Jack demurred. "I waive my right to remain silent. I waive my right to an attorney. I just want to get this off my chest."

"Is this kosher?" Vukovich asked Blatt.

"You are waiving your Miranda rights?" Blatt asked Jack.

"Of course I am. Why wouldn't I? You have me cold."

"Take notes," Blatt told the cops.

CHAPTER 73

QUESTIONS

WHO AM I?

This was one of two big questions, among many smaller ones, that Angela asked of herself while sequestered in Examining Room A of the Glick-Mermelstein Wellness Center in the beating heart of Brighton Beach. Jack wasn't there yet. It was 5:20 p.m. She'd arrived early, to be on the safe side.

Ha. The "safe side." On the other side of the door, in the treatment area, a chiropractor was awaiting instructions for insinuating himself into the kill zone. With her as his sidekick.

Contracts. Torts. Criminal procedure. Civil procedure. Wills and trusts. Evidence. Constitutional principles. Taxation. Mergers and acquisitions. These subjects she was trained for in law school. "Filial vengeance" was not among them. How does the prom queen wind up entwined with this goof in the next room, a schleppy spine adjuster on whose dubious gifts she was risking life and limb? How does a daughter who spent her life ashamed of her father's transgressive life conspire to transgress herself in search of closure? How in the world does a believer in the principle of justice through law—and only law—find herself in cahoots with hardened criminals to exact revenge from a gang of even more hardened criminals?

Angela's world, not to put too fine a point on it, was in flux. First, she was in love. This man, this beautiful and charming man, had arrived from nowhere to fill a void too overflowing. And not just in a dirty way. Although that too. Her Daddy, this larger-than-life figure whose extreme paternalism had informed her own character, was taken away from her too soon. But not in the way of the cliché. "Too soon" in the sense of maybe a few days or hours. She'd sensed that Victor Donato was seeking escape from the prison he had built for himself, even as he avoided the one society had awaiting him. When she and Jack offered the fearsome Don Donato a way out, bizarre as the proposal must have seemed to him, she believed they had gotten through. Maybe he'd dismissed them so instantaneously because he knew that a moment's serious reflection would tempt him to turn his back on, and thus to acknowledge, a lifetime of wrong.

And now this. This quixotic, demented conspiracy so ungodly dangerous that she could not think about its actual possibilities without trembling. Her legendary sangfroid she had left behind. Maybe it was in Jack's car, in the trunk, rolled up like a mob victim in a banner for the Oktoberfest Sale. She sure as Christ didn't have it with her. Even now, one hundred minutes before zero hour, she felt like any second she would heave.

Yet here she was, thinking not for one instant of backing out. Angela had no doubt that, in time, the Russians would be ensnared by the law, in just the way the Gambinos and Luccheses had been. Or perhaps wiped off the face of the earth by the Vietnamese or MS-13. But not soon. There would be years of intimidation, years of cruelty, years of theft and blackmail and terror before they got what they deserved. If tonight went as planned—or more like as dreamed, because the plan was tethered to reality by spider silk—genuine justice would be served in a way that the US Department of Justice could not itself dream of.

If she did not live through the night, though, then what? Would she be a victim of the Russians, or just the latest victim of Don Donato's Cozy Nostra? And if, in the end, it all came to a tabloid headline, "Marilyn Munster in Gangland Slaying," what had her adult life been all about, the one she defined by being the anti-Donato? What of that? Who the fuck *was* she?

That was one big question. The other one was this:

"Where are the Nerf balls?"

CHAPTER 74

ANOTHER CONFESSION

HIS TIME WAS RUNNING OUT. THE COCONSPIRATORS WOULD already be gathering. Law enforcement was ready to listen, so Jack took a deep breath and began.

"It all started a week ago when I was looking to get back into the world of work. I was looking for business opportunities and saw an ad in the *Times*. It said, 'Wanted: experienced art director to terrorize Brooklyn neighborhood. Arson background helpful.' And I thought, 'Sounds perfect.' It was just a lucky coincidence that I'd spent a year investigating the bed market, negotiating a franchise, hunting for a property, contracting the build-out, acquiring inventory and licenses and insurance and utilities in the very same neighborhood—so I could get busy right away setting fires to other small businesses in case somebody asked me to. Truthfully, I thought I'd gotten away with it. But you guys are just too good."

"All right," Blatt said, "that's enough."

"Don't you want to hear the part about how I tricked my employer's daughter into falling for me and plotted with her to kill her father so she could give up her life's work of seeking social justice to move into his failing numbers-and-protection rackets? It's the best part. That woman is evil. She just gets up in the morning wanting to kill. I think her mom is next. Then schoolchildren. Vukovich, do you need for me to go slower?"

"Fuck you, Schiavone," the cop snapped as he stuffed his note-book back in his pocket. "We're just following every lead."

"Uh-huh. So then how many guys do you have following Smirdov? I mean, I know he couldn't be a suspect, because all he has is a long history of moving in on other mobs' territories, and I'm sure the fact that he threatened all of us before he firebombed us is immaterial."

McWiggin stood up from the edge of the Snoo-Z-Lite. "What do you know about Smirdov?"

"Oh, for God's sake, the whole city knows about him."

"Is that who you were seeing in Brighton Beach?" Vukovich asked.

"No. I have never in my life met that prick and hope never to cross his path. If you must know, I was in Brighton Beach seeing a chiropractor."

"You got a bad back?" McWiggin inquired.

"Who doesn't?" Jack replied. The more precise answer might have been no, but he also didn't say yes. Let them infer what they wished.

"Listen, Mr. Schiavone," said Blatt. "We know you didn't bomb anything or anyone. That's not why we're here. We're here because, in the course of this investigation, we have realized that you are up to your neck in connections with a crime family, and we don't appreciate it. These are not white-collar criminals. These are not embezzlers. They are hardened criminals whom we've devoted our careers to bringing to justice—not 'social' justice, *justice*

justice—and, lo and behold, every time we turn around in our murder and extortion and arson investigations, there's Mr. fuckin' Mattress."

"Well, you do have me there, but I promise you it's nothing like you think."

"We don't think," said Blatt. "We know. We know you are in deep—maybe innocently, but still dangerously deep. You may even be violating your plea agreement. There's usually boilerplate in there about not associating with felons, and, Christ, it looks like you've joined the New York Felon Association. It is time to back the fuck off."

Jack's first impulse was to give them exactly the same advice. The only problem was they were right. Pissed off as he was to be answering questions of the sort being posed, he had to concede they had reason to be suspicious about him. Verily, circumstances had led him to insinuate himself into the very inner machinery of a mafia gang. From disgraced ad exec to wiseguy life coach in the space of six days. Even *his* head was spinning. At this rate, by February he'd be in a Tony Montana white suit and neck jewelry machine-gunning feds from his marble balcony. Or in a cave with Mullah Omar. Or, God forbid, Wall Street. He was just grateful the investigators didn't ask him if he was in the process of masterminding a gangland rubout. He hated to lie.

"McWiggin, what in the world are you doing?" This was Blatt, who had just noticed the ATF agent lying supine on the Snoo-Z-Lite full, then flipping over to prone, back and forth.

"I'm just loving this bed," McWiggin said.

"On sale beginning tomorrow and even cheaper with a coupon," Jack said. "Inventory clearance."

"Wow, that's kind of a lucky break. My wife has been complaining about our bed sagging. Do you deliver?"

"Free in the five boroughs."

Vukovich was incredulous. "McWiggin! What the fuck is the matter with you?"

"Give it a rest, Pete," McWiggin said, now curled on his side. "Our business with this guy is over. Yo, Schiavone, where do I get a coupon?"

Jack did his best to keep a straight face. "It's online. Look, I don't want to be offering anything, you know, special..." He said this more to Blatt than to McWiggin. "For the sake of propriety, I'm not getting in the middle of it, but I'm fairly certain if you want that bed, Jitnee over there will give you the coupon price tonight. You'll have the bed tomorrow, Saturday latest."

"This is nuts, but I really dig this bed," McWiggin said.

"Your federal tax dollars at work," said Vukovich, now laughing at his colleague. "McWiggin, you never cease to amaze me."

"That right, Pete?" McWiggin retorted. "You wanna discuss Red Hook?"

"Shut up, Henry," Vukovich said.

"Red Hook?" said Blatt.

"Never mind," said Vukovich. "Go crazy. What the fuck do I care?"

"You take away the old bed?" the federal agent inquired of the person of interest.

"Yes, we do," said Mr. Mattress. "It's fifty bucks. If you look pathetic enough, Jitnee will throw it in. That's between you and her. I'm staying out of it."

"Hey, Blatt," said McWiggin, "we cool?"

The prosecutor shrugged. "Yeah, I guess. If he doesn't give you anything another customer wouldn't get, it's no matter to me."

"But you're still an embarrassment," said Vukovich.

"Blow me," said McWiggin.

"OK, but not on duty," said Vukovich.

"Fuck you," said McWiggin. "Red Hook."

"Fuck you," said Vukovich. "I didn't know she was connected, and you know it."

"Red Hook?" said Blatt.

"Forget about it," said Vukovich.

"Nothing," said McWiggin. "Just ragging his ass. Schiavone, what's the warranty?"

Jack could handle that one. "See that sign next to you that says *twenty-year warranty*?" McWiggin turned to look at the poster.

"The warranty, Poirot, is twenty years. Look, this is making me uncomfortable. I'd love for you to get your bed. Get two. Get a dozen. But can I recuse myself now? See that young woman over there? That's Jitnee. She'd be happy to take care of you."

McWiggin climbed off of the Snoo-Z-Lite, looking less sheepish than you might expect.

"What the fuck," he said. "Opportunity knocks." A few minutes later, Jitnee had written up her ninth sale of the afternoon. While they waited, Jack took the opportunity to interrogate them.

"Off the record," he began. "No bullshit. Do you have any chance of nailing the Russians?"

Vukovich made a face—a face that expressed skepticism—but Blatt was having none of that. "Sure, there's a chance," he said. "But it won't come from this investigation. It'll come from one of their soldiers making a mistake down the road, facing hard time and getting squeezed. That's really the only way we ever close these things. It can take years. It can take twenty years. But look at the Five Families. In time, we got almost the whole lot of them."

"So I guess I shouldn't expect much in five and three-quarter days," Jack offered.

Vukovich laughed. "No, Mr. Schiavone. We're just the police. Only you can get that deep into the mob in five and three-quarter days. We can barely get a search warrant in that time. A wiretap? Fugeddaboudit."

"No arrests tonight, then?"

"No, you were our best shot for an arrest. We're still thinking of charging you with being a doofus. On the other hand, I've seen your girlfriends. Pretty impressive. Maybe I'd consort too."

"What are you talking about…girl*friends*? Angela is my girl-friend. Nobody else."

Vukovich, again with the raised eyebrow and the contorted sea clam lips of dubiousness. "I got a photo album of you entering a closet with the sister. In a bikini. Hooters to die for. What were you doing in there—inventorying the suntan oil?"

Once again, Jack's first instinct was to defend his honor, and Tina's, and Angela's, for that matter. Instead, though, he decided to let the cop think what he wanted. It seemed to impress him, the pig. "Like I said, Sergeant," he replied with a mischievous grin, "you're one step ahead of me at all times."

Vukovich, who was himself good-looking in a high-school-jock, protruding-brow sort of way when not swollen and bruised from ass whippings inflicted by petite professional tanners, was indeed impressed with the supposed sister act. He turned to Blatt. "Whaddya think of this guy, huh? Quite the Italian stallion."

Blatt was barely paying attention. He was bouncing on the Snoo-Z-Lite and checking it for firmness.

"Fuckin' A," said Vukovich, "not you too."

The lawyer looked up at Jack. "Hey, Mr. Mattress, you carry this in a queen?"

Absolutely, he did. So Blatt bought a bed too. It was almost 5:00 before the three left the store, but not before Jack asked for a favor.

"We can agree that this interlude has been surreal, can we not?" he ventured. Displaying varying degrees of amusement at the question, the cop, the agent, and the prosecutor all nodded. "Alrighty then, let's capture this for posterity." Jack abruptly held up his camera phone and snapped the cops in front of the door.

"What the fuck!" yelped Vukovich, who was in no mood to be posterity-ized.

McWiggin thought it was hilarious. "Yo, Schiavone, send me a wallet-size!" Chuckling about the whole strange episode, he led his colleagues out to the street.

Jack waved. Then he checked the image on the little screen. The investigators all looked unposed and unhappy.

Perfect.

The moment they hit the pavement, he hurried to the computer.

CHAPTER 75

HOUSE CALL

NOBODY FROM THE CREW WAS VISIBLE. EVERYONE WAS NEARBY.

Not that there would have been anything they could accomplish were things to go haywire. They had no eyes or ears in the house. Even Jack couldn't hang on the block; two of the Russians had visited his store and might recognize him. Their presence, scattered around the neighborhood, was more like a gesture for Angela's sake, and, eventually, God willing, a livery service. About the Chiropractor's personal safety, only Casper among them could have cared less. Angela had a cell phone—Jack's new one. This was her lifeline.

Endless discussion at the Doc's office had centered on when the pair should arrive. Five minutes before the hour, to be safe? Five minutes after the hour, so as not to appear too eager? Tony the Teeth had won the day with the crazy notion that they show up at 8:00 sharp. Which they did. Seth pulled up to the 5th Street address in his 2004 Hyundai XL360 dead on the hour. He pulled his ChiroPort collapsible adjustment table from the trunk and, with the aid of his chiropractic assistant, ascended the eight limestone steps. They made sure not to exchange significant looks, in case they were being monitored by video cameras, which, in fact, they were. The door opened before they rang the bell. A not especially terrifying young man in an oxford shirt and khakis saw them in. He looked like a publishing house intern from the University of Virginia—except for his voice, which was right out of *Alexander Nevsky*.

"главный!" he hollered up the stairs. "Доктор здесь." *Boss, the doctor is here.*

"OK!" was the reply. "Чтобы найти их, а затем отправить их." *Search them and send them up.*

The preppiest *soldat* gave them a perfunctory once-over. Apart from the table, they had not much with them. Angela, wearing white nylon warm-up pants, a plain white T-shirt, and lab coat, carried only a clipboard, a digital camera, and a handbag containing her wallet, cell phone, keys, some hairdo combs and elastic bands, and ordinary cosmetics. Seth carried only keys, reading glasses, and in a shoulder bag, his Thumper Maxi Pro handheld massager. He was asked to lift his shirt to expose any recording device any cops might have placed on him.

"Lift my shirt?" Seth argued, feigning surprise so as not to tip off their lack of innocence. "What for?"

"For to stay, not to being keeked out" was the reply.

"Is this guy some sort of big-shot celebrity?" Seth persisted. He was finding this role-playing to be just about the funnest thing *ever*, while Angela prayed for him to cut it out. With every bit of chiro-method-acting came a chance for a slipup, and for blown covers, and then maybe for blown-off heads. For instance, Angela's lab coat was brand new, purchased and personalized on a rush basis that very afternoon, reading *The Back Doctors* over one breast pocket and *Rachel* over the other. The Back Doctor himself was wearing one of his knit shirts on which was embroidered *Glick-Mermelstein*

Wellness Center and *Seth*. She noticed it now and had to suppress a gasp. What a fucking nitwit.

Seth Glick-Mermelstein—secret code name Seth Glick-Mermelstein—obliged the Russian. "You're looking for a wire, aren't you?" he asked, revealing his pallid belly and sparsely forested chest.

Shut up, Angela thought.

"Shut up," the Russian said. Angela didn't have to lift her shirt. Her T-shirt hugged her. The only thing she had underneath was one of Tina's bras, strapped tightly against her chest. The effect of the baggy pants and loose-fitting coat was to make her seem vaguely mannish, bordering on butch. For the same reason, she wore no makeup, not even lipstick. She had her pageboy combed on a bias so that the bangs hung down like a teenage boy's. Angela could not be ugly, nor even plain. She had, however, achieved unravishingness. As expected, the Russian did not ask her to remove her ugly black athletic shoes, so he never saw the Nerf balls flattened beneath her feet.

"Thees vay, Rah-chel," the Russian said, trying to lead them to the stairs.

"What?" she said. This being one of her first tries at undercover tyrant-elimination, she was a little bit nervous. Seth's shirt had all but paralyzed her, and now she'd forgotten her *nom de guerre*. The chiropractor, on the other hand, was thoroughly enjoying his adventure. With every passing second, he warmed further to his role. Shirt or no shirt, of the two of them, he was, so far, the more poised.

"Come on, *Rache*," he prompted. "We're gonna run behind in our appointments."

He also had the presence of mind to scope out the lower floor. The house was rich in the day's last sunlight, glinting, as dusk settled, off of the highly polished blond-oak floors. Here and there were scattered some antique Persian throw rugs. The furniture was sparse and contemporary, including what Seth took to be an Antonio Citterio sofa in beige leather. That struck him as kind of funny; Mrs. Glick-Mermelstein had furnished their apartment in Italian contemporary including a knockoff of the same sofa, only in black. And this one had a St. Bernard dog curled up on it, slobbering on a rawhide chew toy the size of a child's arm. As for other gangsters, he could see none, but he heard two or three voices from what he presumed to be the kitchen. He also noticed the TV was on in the living room, tuned to *The Vampire Diaries*. How pleased he was to have so risen to this occasion. If the kids at Massapequa High School Theater Arts Club could see him now.

Halfway up the steps, they saw a door open on the second floor and from it emerge a beefy bald guy whose beef was squeezed into a purple wifebeater. He was on his way downstairs and, as he edged his way past them, briefly made eye contact with not-really Rachel. This triggered an instant glimmer of semirecognition; she'd seen that dull expression somewhere before, and no more than a second elapsed before she made the connection. It was Uncle Fester—whose real name was Arkady—the goon she'd hollered at a week ago for pounding on the jeweler's display window. So he was a mobster, after all. Jesus Christ. If she recognized him, would he also recognize her? Yes, she was in something of a half-assed disguise, but the way he'd stared at her that day—it could have cut through a bank vault door. If he remembered, she and Seth wouldn't live to see the landing. Angela did not dare turn her head to see the soldier's reaction. She simply kept climbing as her heart pounded three times for every step achieved.

Ten, nine, eight, seven, six, five, four, three, two, one. They got there. Fester, she could hear, had reached the foyer and beyond. Maybe, just maybe, Nurse Rachel had uglied up just enough. *Next time*, she thought, *false nose.*

Upstairs, they were led past walls lined with lithographs by Dali, Erte, Chagall, Miro, and Warhol. These looked like authentic signed and numbered prints, although they were almost certainly fakes. Seth was impressed by the collection. Angela noticed them too. She wondered whether the Russian had been duped or if this was actually one of his rackets. She also wondered if she would be able to keep it together for the duration. At the threshold to the master bedroom, they met the fearsome Smirdov. He was wearing a gold silk robe and Nike shower shoes, exposing tufts of hair on the knuckles of his toes. The thinning black hair on his head was cropped short, his nose hooked long. He was like a Little Odessa Minotaur—half Shylock, half Barney Fife.

"Thenk you for coming," he said. "Thenk you for verking around my schedule."

"No, problem, Misterrrrr"—Laurence Olivier was consulting the clipboard—"Smirdov. Where can we have a look at you? Oh, I'm sorry. This is my assistant, Rachel. She'll be taking some pictures, recording some measurements and so forth."

The Russian received this information without comment. He merely led them into the bedroom, where Seth uncollapsed the table and set it up by the foot of the king-size bed. The bed-chamber was also handsomely turned out in a way the interiors-interested chiropractor at first couldn't place. Damask drapes.

High-thread-count Egyptian cotton sheets. Interesting but unrecognizable abstract prints in spare, gilded frames. Ah, but of course.
It was like the Ramada Renaissance minisuite he'd stayed in at the
Biomechanics Convention in Orlando. The Russian sat on the bed
then lay back supine.

"Why are we here this evening, Mr. Smirdov? Pain issues?"

"Steef back. Een morning, I am having deeficulty to valk down
stairce. And headache, right here"—he pointed to the base of his
skull—"sometimes they are lasting vun day."

"Mmm-hmm," responded the Chiropractor.

He removed the massager from his bag, located a socket to plug
it in, and asked the Russian to remove his robe and lie prone on the
table. Patient B complied. The hit man and hit woman were surprised
to see the body beneath the robe. He was wearing a plain white
undershirt and silk boxers, revealing a body more slim than skinny.
His fine and shallow musculature was hard and lean, contouring his
shirt—as Clive James once put it—like a walnut in a condom.

"Now, Mr. Smirdov, ordinarily we would take a full set of films,
frontal and ninety degree, which we would process through special
software that pinpoints vertebra by vertebra the curvature of your
spine. For the purposes of this consultation, we'll have to make
do with still photos, which Rachel will take very shortly. First, I'm
going to loosen some tight muscles." Thereupon he switched on
the Thumper and commenced to loosening.

"So, tell me, Mr. Smirdov, how do you make your living?"

Ironworkers and roofers must be comfortable at great heights,
lest they get nervous and lose their balance. Equally, those workers
must not be too comfortable at great heights, lest they get careless
and lose their balance. Seth was too comfortable.

SHUTUPSHUTUPSHUTUPSHUTUPSHUTUP, Angela demanded with her mind.

"Ferris," came the bored reply.

"Ferrous metals?" Seth asked, because how often does a chiropractor ever really get to do a Night at the Improv? He had been in *Once Upon a Mattress* in high school, but that was kids' stuff. This performance was playing for keeps.

"Ferris," repeated the Russian. "Mink ferris. Fox ferris. Chinchilla ferris. Storage company."

"Fascinating," Seth said. "My aunt Ida had a mink coat. My uncle Morris used to complain about paying for storage. He used to say, 'I gotta pay for an icebox? Next anniversary, I buy you a salami.'"

"Not get joke," said Smirdov. "Uncle I think eembecile."

"A very bright man. Shoe repair. Twelve shops in Brooklyn, ten in Queens, six on the Island."

Angela's telepathic screams continued. *SHUTTHEFUCK UPSHUTTHEFUCKUPSHUTHEFUCKUPSHUTTHEFUCKUP.*

"I think stupid man. Please, 'salami.' Animal skeens dry in heat."

"You, of course, did not know Uncle Morris. He had all the Great Books, leather bound. Let me ask you this: landsman?"

"Vat?"

"Landsman. You a fellow member of the tribe? I'm guessing yes, but there's no mezuzah by the front door, so—"

"You are asking me, am I Jew?"

Angela's brain was boiling with fear and fury. This jabbering asshole would talk his way into a shallow grave. It was as if he wanted to be murdered. Strangely, the Russian—positioned back up—did not get his back up. He displayed preternatural calm in conveying to the Chiropractor that his religion was none of Seth's business, that his occupation was none of his business, that the efficacy of fur storage was none of his business. He did this by not replying. Seth, of course, interpreted that as a request for a follow-up.

"Near my office, we have a Judaica district. Five different places to get a quality mezuzah. Hey, did you know they don't come loaded? You buy the mezuzah, you still have to buy the scroll. That's nuts. Like ordering a Reuben and having to buy the pastrami separately, am I right?"

Angela prayed to Jesus for intervention. Jesus did not step in, however, perhaps because He couldn't fucking believe what a fucking moron this fucking chiropractor was and just wanted to see how it all played out. The only miracle was that the Russian did not freak out. *Maybe*, Angela thought, *that's how you get to be a kingpin: the rare combination of brutality and composure. Come to think of it, just like Daddy.*

Meanwhile, Seth refused to take no answer for an answer. He was obviously determined to keep running his mouth until the Russian finally decided to strangle him in situ with his bare hands. "Feeling a little better now that I'm working you over? We want those core muscles strong, but also supple. Drink much water?"

"*Nyet.*"

"You need to be drinking two quarts of water a day."

"Don't like. Drink tea."

"Nope. Pure water. Very important for lubricating the soft tissue, the joints, basic cellular activity. You should be drinking eight full glasses every day. That's not negotiable."

That did it. Patient B snapped his head around to glare at Seth. Many a man bristles at being dictated to, among those least willing to endure being issued orders: dictators. If Angela had been blessed with supernatural powers, her thoughts would have Seth struck mute. As it was, it was all she could do not to grab the Thumper from his hands and thump him unconscious. Her hatred was being transferred from the man who had murdered her father in cold blood to the man who just wouldn't keep his stupid piehole shut.

"Dr. Seth," she offered, desperately, "don't forget our seminar."

"Huh?" the Chiropractor said.

"The *seminar*," she repeated. "The posture seminar, at the office. Nine o'clock."

"Oh, right, the seminar. Thanks, Rachel. I cancelled that. I had Lance call the folks this morning. Can't believe I didn't tell you that."

Cancelled? Lance? LANCE? Lance did not exist. What was the matter with this asshole? Did he want to get them both killed? The liquidation target was getting a little impatient too.

"Enough veeth voder and pose-ture. Feex back and neck."

"All right, sir. Let's get those photos taken."

"No photos. You chiropractor, yes?"

"Of course I am, but I don't just—"

"Feex back like chiropractor."

Angela could not believe what she was witnessing. This whack job was hired to perform a whack job? He was actually talking his way out of being in a position to take the Russian down. She knew it was dangerous—maybe even reckless—but if Jesus Christ would not intervene, she would have to.

"Mr. Smirdov," she ventured, "what happens next is Dr. Seth will manipulate your spine. Your pain is caused because poor alignment is triggering spasms in your muscles. Doc, wanna demonstrate?"

Smirdov was now facedown in the crotch of the headrest, so he didn't see Angela's furiously widened eyes and frantic gestures, accomplished entirely with her head, urging the Chiropractor to clam the fuck up and begin chiropracticing. Seth finally began to register her annoyance, yet was still mired down either in role-playing or medical professionalism, Nurse Rachel couldn't tell. Incredibly, when he did start in on the Russian, he began with the lumbar spine. Now she knew that the only truly reckless thing was for her not to completely commandeer the consultation.

"Dr. SETH," she said. "This patient mentioned headaches. Let's begin with the cranial-neckular despasmitization."

The what? The Chiropractor knew very well that what she'd just said was nonsense. Why would she do something so stupid? Even the rankest amateur would recognize her double talk. He shot Angela a scolding glare and was jarred to receive a scalding one in return. Clearly, she was furious—and, at last, Seth understood. In his virtuosic display of sangfroid, he had possibly strayed from the purpose of their nefarious errand. He hadn't been engaged to propel this man on a journey toward holistic wellness or to undertake a *bravisimo* masquerade; he'd been engaged to turn the fucker's lights out. The Chiropractor decided to move things along toward that goal, even if conventional chiropractic protocols had to be discarded.

"Sir," he said, "I think Rachel is right. In consideration of your cerviocranial syndrome manifesting an acute subluxation of C-one and C-two, we'll begin with an adjustment to vertebrae adjacent to the spastic muscle tissue." In pure chiropractic nomenclature, what he said didn't mean much, either. Now that he had regathered some of his wits about him, he was cunningly trying to introduce some of the terminology invented on the spot by Angela, rendering her patter somewhat less ridiculous. Luckily, against all odds, the Russian seemed satisfied.

Angela stood by almost breathless as the Back Doctor placed his fingers on the Russian's neck, near where it was surrounded by the halo of his collarbone.

"You'll feel some pressure here," Seth told Patient B. "Don't be alarmed if you begin to feel a little light-headed." With that, Seth jammed his thumbs on the spot below which, he hoped, lay the baroreceptors of the Russian's carotid sinus. It was a remarkable scene to witness. Angela watched as the Russian shuddered and tried to lift his head and speak, but then suddenly seemed to relax. It had taken only five seconds for his heartbeat to slow, his blood pressure to plummet, and the "that's all folks" aperture of presyncope to shrink all light into dark and all consciousness into dreamless sleep. He had fallen into the waiting arms of Morpheus. Next stop, according to the chiropractor's terms of engagement, Hades.

CHAPTER 76

DEDICATION

BEFORE THE FIRST NUMBER WAS CALLED, FATHER STEVE DELEWSKI stood before the bingo-goers for a benediction, in memory of one of the two parishioners who had in the last two days passed away.

"My friends," he began, "this week we lost a blessed member of the parish community, one known to you all for her energy, her enthusiasm, her selfless contributions to Our Lady of Grace, and, of course, for her fierce dedication to our bingo. Please join me in remembering our beloved sister and organist, Mary Troncellitti."

God our Father,
Your power brings us to birth,
Your providence guides our lives,
and by Your command we return to dust.

Lord, those who die still live in Your presence,
their lives change but do not end.
I pray in hope for my family,
relatives and friends,
and for all the dead known to You alone.

In company with Christ,

Who died and now lives,
may they rejoice in Your kingdom,
where all our tears are wiped away.
Unite us together again in one family,
to sing Your praise forever and ever.

Amen.

The elephant in the room was the ghost of Don Donato, who was maybe not the teacher's pet, but nonetheless the most well known Ebbets Beachian and the only one ever to be blown to smithereens in the church's own parking lot. Father Steve felt it inappropriate to dishonor Mrs. T by lumping her passing in with that of a violent man who had died by violent means. He also deemed this prayer venue-specific. The deceased was known by many as an organist; she was legendary as a bingo player. And had she not been legendary as of a week earlier, her full-frontal ninja attack on Mike Franzetti sealed her legacy. Yes, it had been an eventful week at Our Lady of Grace, so eventful that Father was giving serious consideration to the family business, which was HVAC contracting.

Funny thing about this Thursday evening, though. It was a full house. Franzetti and his volunteers needed to set up extra tables and chairs, not having a clue as to why the crowd had doubled. Maybe it was the end of summer, maybe the knowledge that the late harridan Mrs. Troncellitti could not make a spectacle of herself and ruin the game anymore, maybe the widespread assumption that the Donatos had been rigging, or at least skimming, the game. This they had not, which was why the priest—in

Franzetti's view—should have offered a prayer in the late don's name. Sentimental, the cop wasn't, but by his calculus Donato had done more by laying off the game than that crazy old bitch had done by terrorizing it. Also, he personally mourned for his departed downline. Otherwise, Deacon Franzetti was thoroughly delighted. This would be the biggest handle in at least three years.

With a big smile on his face, he strolled over to the priest and put his big cop arm around the callow young clergyman's shoulders and, with his other arm, panned the breadth of the packed hall. "Well, Father," he gloated, "I don't suppose your high-and-mighty computer could give you this."

The priest dislodged himself from the deacon's grip and looked him square in the eye.

"Mike, I don't know what your problem is with me, and I don't particularly care. But I am telling you this now: back the fuck off."

The cop, for once, was speechless. As Father Steve turned on his heels and headed toward the rectory, all the startled Franzetti could do was watch. He blinked rapidly as his gaze followed the priest out of the hall. Then, when the fire door banged shut, his smug smile resumed. Or, just this once, was he feeling admiration?

The priest headed upstairs to the sacristy, where he reached into a steel cabinet for a three-liter jug of O-Neh-Da sacramental wine. It was the haut sauterne, a pale, straw-colored vintage that tasted to him like actual straw, but which was slightly less repulsive than the chalice white that he'd also sipped a thousand times in the central sacrament of the faith. Consecration turned jug wine into the blood of Christ but did not do one blessed thing for palatability. Father Steve unscrewed the cap and quickly drained two glasses as if they were Hawaiian Punch. Not much of a boozer, he was surprised how quickly the warmth of the alcohol surged through him and how immediately the brain buzz took hold. He didn't care for that especially, so, before doing any more damage, he carefully rescrewed the cap, replaced the wine in the cabinet, and changed into street clothes. Then he fled Our Lady of Grace and stumbled toward the subway.

Five miles away, on the far side of Prospect Park, two goons sat in a 2002 Buick Lucerne waiting for a murder to get over with when they noticed a man walking in their direction with a shotgun.

"Fuck's with this bozo?" said Medium Marco. "He looks like your friend, the weirdo." Casper, who was busy texting Randy Black about his next Waldo's gig, didn't look up. "Yo, Casper, check it out. Dude with a shotgun."

"Shotgun?" Casper sat up straight. "Where?" Marco pointed across 4th Street, where a paunchy man in a panama hat was hurrying along with a twelve-gauge over his shoulder. "WHAT THE FUCK?" Casper was out of the car in a heartbeat to intercept him. He tripped on the tall curb and took a spill before righting himself against a leafy black tupelo in an earthen pavement cutout. Then he darted across the street between parked cars, narrowly avoiding exactly the kind of pedestrian tragedy all children are warned about practically from birth. A taxi screeched to a stop with its bumper six inches from Casper's torn trousers.

The Collector did not even acknowledge the near miss. He was fixated on collecting Larry Rizzo, who saw him approaching and made a sharp right at the corner, scurrying toward 5th and picking up the pace in a mincing race-walk gait. The barrel of the shotgun shimmied against his shoulder. Casper hollered at him, but the sandwich man kept jiggling his fat ass in the direction of the Russian's house. So the singing mobster used his vocal gift to share his thoughts more expansively.

"Larry," he crooned, "if you don't stop now, I'm going to empty my gun in your asshole."

Larry stopped.

Casper was only a short distance behind him, and the target he'd mentioned was a big one. "Now, gently put that shotgun down next to you and walk backwards toward me."

Larry complied.

"Now, sit down on the payment."

Larry did that too.

Casper then headed for the weapon, a Remington 870 pump-action with five shells jammed inside. Casper ejected and pocketed all the ammunition while Larry sat crisscross applesauce on the sidewalk. It looked like story time at loser kindergarten.

"You wanna tell me what you're up to here?" Casper inquired.

Larry replied with a shrug.

Casper replied to that by doing to the sidewalk with the shotgun exactly what he had done to Mr. Mattress with the baseball bat. The gunstock splintered, and Larry, startled, all but levitated from the concrete.

"Larry, next one is on your thick skull. What the fuck you doin' here?"

"I can't tell you, exactly," Larry said. "Top secret. Can't burn my controller."

"Fuck are you talking about, *controller*?"

"Handler. Can't burn him. He's an important asset."

"You high on something?"

"Roger that," Larry said.

"Where you going with that blaster?"

"A *negotiation*," Larry replied.

"Huh? What kind of fuckin' negotiation in fuckin' Park Slope?"

"Twep."

"Huh?"

"I've said too much already. I'm Larry Rizzo. I own J&L's. 273-73-4554."

"What?"

"That's my social, and that's all you're getting from me."

Casper believed Larry meant what he said, so he cracked him on the shoulder with what was left of the gunstock. It was a modest blow, but it still knocked Larry sideways, and he yelped in pain.

"Christ, Casper!"

"Twep that, Larry. You have five seconds to tell me what you're up to, or you die on this payment."

That offer slightly weakened Larry's resolve.

"I wasorderedbymyhandlercodenametheChiropractortoliq-uidatetheRussianandsoIlookedhimuponAnyWho.comandcame-heretotwephimandtheChiropractorisJackSchiavoneofthenewmat-tressstore."

"Jack Schiavone…Come again?"

Just then, Larry reached into his pocket and stuffed something in his mouth, trying to swallow it without being detected by the armed man scrutinizing his every move. Lacking any water, and with his throat parched by fear, Larry simply choked on the object and quickly coughed it up. The half-chewed Gas-X tablet shot out of his mouth like a projectile. The gagging stopped, but now he was reduced to sobs. "Just no waterboarding, I beg you!" he cried.

"Jesus Christ," Casper muttered to himself, "what a fuckin' retard."

CHAPTER 77

FACEBOOK FRIENDS

"IS HE OUT?" SHE ASKED.

Seth looked down at Smirdov in horror. Yes, he was out. It had worked. They had three to five minutes to finish the job.

"Come on," she said, "he'll wake up. Flip him onto the bed."

Still, he stared at the unconscious victim. The budget assassin's face had gone pale. He was biting his lower lip. And trembling.

"I can't do it," he said.

"Jesus, Seth!" she snapped, trying to keep her voice down so as to not alert any downstairs gunmen to the incapacity of their boss. "Snap out of it."

"I can't do it," he mumbled. "I can't murder somebody."

That one stopped Angela cold. *Can't* murder *somebody? He thought that?*

"Seth! Nobody's murdering anybody unless he wakes up before we get this done and shoots us both." Was it possible Seth didn't know the plan? Jack had been the one to lay it out for her. It never occurred to her that he'd held back on the Chiropractor. But here they were, at zero hour, and the guy was quivering like a toddler just out of the wading pool. So she took off her white coat, and then her pants, and then her underpants, and as far under her breath as she could, she barked out the orders.

"Get him on the bed!"

In something of a fugue state himself, Seth did as he was told.

"Pull off his shorts."

Seth did, exposing the taut Russian's extraordinarily hairy ass. Angela, meantime, removed her shoes, loosened her bra two notches, and stuffed the Nerf balls into the cups. The resulting bulge vastly rounded out her T-shirt, which she did not remove. As the chiropractor looked on, totally mystified, she pulled her makeup from her purse and began to work on her face. Eye shadow, eyeliner, mascara, lipstick—all in ninety frantic seconds. Considering her lack of experience in the art of face spackling, the results were impressive. She looked a little exotic, a little erotic, and a lot cheap. In short, just like her sister. Then, at breakneck speed, she bunched her hair back with elastic bands and inserted combs to pull the black silk straight back. Then she fell flat on her back in the center of the bed, her legs spread, revealing all. The chiropractor was too much in shock to even try to understand. "Now," she ordered, "get him on top of me."

"On top of you? What are you—"

"Hurry!"

What she'd asked wasn't easy. Smirdov was 144 pounds of deadweight at the foot of the bed, perpendicular to Angela. Rather than climbing next to her and pulling the stiff toward Nurse Porno, he tried leaning over from the side of the bed to drag Smirdov by the shoulders into her embrace.

"Oh!" yelped the chiropractor/not-murderer. He was frozen in situ, trying to breathe, but each gasp made him grimace.

Angela didn't understand. Was he shot? "Seth! What's the matter?"

His face was contorted, his jaws clamped, his lips peeled back, his eye squeezed shut. "My *back*," he gasped.

No, no, no. He was in sudden, agonizing, lumbar spasm. He could barely breathe, and he certainly could not move. Angela didn't know what to do. The Russian would wake up soon. There was no time to help the chiropractor. Everything, including their tomorrows, depended on getting these shots. She tried to drag the Russian closer to her, but it was no use. She may as well have tried to move the triple dresser. But wait. Maybe it didn't matter if the fucker was actually on top of her. So she jumped out of bed, fetched her cell phone, set up the camera function, and gave it to the frozen chiropractor.

"Seth!" she hissed. "I don't care if you never walk again, but get these pictures." She then commenced to rearranging her half-naked self around the deeply sleeping Russian's naked self. One pose, then another, then another. Each time she had to prompt Seth to snap. Each time, wincing and grunting and increasingly hyperventilating, he found the strength to comply.

The Russian began to stir.

"Hurry! MMS them!"

Seth didn't know what that meant. He shook his head slightly, through the breathtaking pain, to let her know that. So up she jumped again, grabbed the phone, and began madly to open, address and click, open, address and click. As the Russian began to shake his head, getting the cobwebs out, she hit SEND on the final MMS. She had dispatched no Russians, but four extremely graphic photos. As Smirdov came to, she made the conscious decision to clamber back in bed, with her bare vagina positioned as the first thing he would awake to see.

Worked like a charm, that did. The Russian opened his eyes to a spectacular view of Nurse Rachel's pussy, and damned if he could figure out why. He was still woozy as he turned his head to get his bearings. By the time he eyeballed the grimacing Dr. Seth, both men were, variously, half-erect. Smirdov could imagine somehow having bedded Nurse Rachel. He did not understand the chiropractor's continued presence, let alone that grotesque pose. Kids play "Freezing Statues" in Moldova too, but…

"Vat heppened?" he croaked, rubbing his eyes with his hands. "I fucked with you?"

"No, you scrawny little shit," Angela replied, "I fucked with you. Now pay very strict attention."

Smirdov was not easily intimidated, yet as he tried to wrest himself back into action, still a little rubbery in the limbs, he sensed that these people, whoever they were, at least momentarily had his advantage. He hadn't worked out exactly how, and by no means why. So he did not fetch any of his twenty guns and kill them.

"You know who you are fucking veeth?" he growled. "I say vun vord, you are dead."

"Well," answered Angela, "unless we save you, you are dead right now. Wanna see the last pictures ever taken of you?"

"Vat you are talking about?"

"Have a look, Romeo. Seth, where's the camera?"

The chiropractor was still twisted half-bent over the side of the bed, with one hand on the mattress to keep his balance. "Under the table," he said, through gritted teeth.

Angela hopped off the bed and bent down below the adjustment table for the camera, making sure to give the Russian a good show. Had she somehow channeled her sister? Had Nerf molecules leeched into her bloodstream, rendering her floozistic? She turned on the camera and sorted through the images until she found what she was looking for. "You're very photogenic for such a little asshole," she said as she handed him the camera. Smirdov snatched it from her and petulantly scrolled through the photos. He was shaking his head, muttering.

"*Nyet, nyet*. Ees not me. Look like me. Not me."

"Really?" Angela said. "I guess it isn't, but I'll bet anybody else who looked at those pictures would think, 'Why is Valentin Smirdov sitting there at Fiesta Travel counting money with half the Donato gang?'"

"Donato?" the Russian spat. "Vat?"

"Yep. There's Little Manny, my sort-of cousin, and there's Big Manny, my uncle. And there in your hands is a whole shitload of cash!"

"You are Donato?"

"Da, da, da," said Angela. "And you are fucked."

"Nobody think that me." The Russian shrugged.

"You know what?" said Angela, squinting as she looked over his shoulder at the tiny camera screen. "You might just be right. They're a little fuzzy and distant, aren't they? But these aren't."

Angela then produced the cell phone and handed it to the Russian, who was treated to very close-up shots, fresh out of the oven, of himself sleeping naked next to a spread-eagle Donato girl.

"I can't even see that tiny little penis of yours. Wait…Is that it?" She looked at his actual real-time groin. "Yep! It looks like a little mushroom cap! How cute? Can you find it there? The screen is pretty teensy-weensy too."

"I have phone now," he said. "You are stupid, and you are dead."

"No, Horshack," said Angela, "you are stupid, and you are dead. Those pictures have been e-mailed. They are at this very moment on a website. If I don't walk out of that door by nine p.m., the site goes live. And if I leave without a deal from you, the site goes live anyway. How long after that will you still be breathing?"

The Russian was silent. The chiropractor, meanwhile, managed to get himself almost straightened up.

"Doing business with another organization," Angela continued. "You know what that is? That is just plain disloyal. And sneaky. Here's a thought, why don't we call your guys up from downstairs and see what they think?" Angela, now playing tough guy even though she was frightened out of her skull, waited for Smirdov to process the available facts. Then she went pedantic on his skinny ass. "You know about the doctrine of Mutually Assured Destruction? That's what kept your fucking Soviets and our fucking Pentagon from blowing us all to kingdom come. Well, dude, you attack us, and you just watch the incoming. Also, you might want to see this nice picture too." Angela held out her hand.

Smirdov gave her the phone.

With a few thumb clicks, she found another image of interest and handed it back. "Don't I look pretty?" she asked.

The Russian looked at the screen and tried, unsuccessfully, to suppress a wince. It was a shot of her, unstuffed and uncosmetized, standing in front of Park Slope Realty, not five blocks away, next to Detective Sergeant Peter Vukovich, Deputy US Attorney Jeffrey Blatt, and ATF Special Agent Henry McWiggin. The image was a bit grainy, but everybody in it looked all business. "Those fellows look familiar to you? I'll bet they've been a real nuisance. I gotta tell you, they are parked around the corner and are soooo worried about me. Don't you just feel terrible for that nice Detective Vukovich? Poor thing broke his nose!"

"Enough! Vat you are vanting?"

"This: nobody in your organization sets foot in Ebbets Beach, ever. Ever. We see one of your goons on that boulevard, you read about yourself on SmokingGun.com. Anything happens to a Donato or one of our organization, you are on TruTV. That means murder. That means accident. That means a nut allergy. That means old age. Pray for our health, Peewee."

Seth cleared his throat and waved. "Rachel?"

"Oh, yeah. Him too. You're not allowed to hurt him."

The Russian didn't reply. He stayed in place, keeping himself balanced with both hands, working the situation over in his gradually less foggy mind. Obviously, if he shouted for his men, these intruders would be dead within twenty seconds. But then the compromising photos would go on the Internet, and, as the cunt said, his life would be over. Most likely very slowly and very painfully. At least if they walked away tonight, he'd be free to figure out a way to destroy them. Meantime, he was simply in no position to bargain. The stupid bigmouth he didn't even care about; he just wanted the fool out of his sight. The Russian looked Angela straight in the eye. Her father had been bombed to heaven in one loud instant. This one he would make suffer as nobody had suffered before.

"I agree this," the Russian said.

"Good, I'm just getting started. My father's funeral will be Monday. On that day, you and your people will not go out of doors. You will not go to your fur storage business. You will be under house arrest, in his memory."

Another long, glaring pause, as if he could murder her with his eyes. "I agree also this."

"And before Monday, you will bring us one million dollars in cash. This we will give to the owners of the barbershop and the car wash to cover their losses. What's left over will be donated to Our Lady of Grace Catholic Church. Someone will phone you with instructions. Seth, pack up."

"You are crazy."

"Probably. Gimme a sec, would you?"

Angela grabbed her phone and dialed a number. "Hi, it's me… Yeah, yeah, just fine. But he's feeling ungenerous. You need to go live with those photos…Sure, we'll wait." She turned to the Russian and gave him a sweet, obliging smile. "This is exciting! We're gonna be celebrities!" The display of vindictive smarm triggered something Valentin hadn't felt in a very long time. He was frightened out of his wits. "NO!" he interrupted. "I veel fuckink pay."

Angela feigned annoyance. "Ugh. It looks like negotiations have reopened. Listen, the Doc is on his way out right now. Please pick him up. He's a little worse for the wear. I'll be outside myself in five minutes."

The chiropractor gingerly gathered his things and very deliberately collapsed his table. "Don't worry about that, Dr. Seth. Our friend will carry that to the street for us."

Seth wasn't sure how to make his exit. This didn't seem to be an occasion for handing the patient a brochure, so he just said, "Really nice to meet you," and hurried out of the bedroom as fast as his severely hobbled gait could carry him.

Angela had not hung up with Jack. "OK, let me see," she said, and turned back to Smirdov. "So, by Sunday, right?"

"How I know you don't take money and steel publish photos?"

"Hey! Great question! I can see how a geek like you clawed your way to the top. So, the first thing is, if you get buried alive, we can't be absolutely sure your successor won't come after Ebbets Beach again. See what I mean? Also, there's the mortgage."

"Vat mortgage?"

"Oh, I might have forgotten that. Every month you don't want to be keeled by your own men, five thousand dollars for the Ebbets Beach Community Association, cash. OK?"

The Russian said nothing as he calculated.

Angela again spoke into the cell phone. "I think he's having second thoughts…Yeah, the monthly mortgage…OK, hold on." She turned to Smirdov. "Yep, I had it right. Five thousand. Should I say you agree, or…"

He nodded.

"Wonderful! OK, gimme four minutes…Bye."

For the next four minutes, while removing her makeup and getting dressed in her Ugly Betty outfit, Nurse Rachel moaned and called out Smirdov's name and did her best to approximate the sounds of ecstasy. Very loudly. For good measure, she added a borscht-curdling shriek and the words, "No, no, no! More! More! More!…Oh my God, yessssssssssssss!"

When she was finished, she grabbed her things, left the room, and walked down the stairs. The Russian followed, naked as a jaybird, hauling the ChiroPort. She could see the Russian soldiers peeking from the kitchen. She kissed the Russian on the cheek.

"My friend Tina was soooo right," she declared. "Valentino, you were fantastic!"

She then descended eight limestone steps to Jack's waiting car and headed with Mr. Mattress back to Mr. Mattress.

CHAPTER 78

INVENTORY REDUCTION, EVERYTHING MUST GO!

BIG MANNY HAD STAYED AT THE STORE. HE'D NEEDED TO. THE SALE didn't officially begin until Friday, but Thursday at 9:30, closing time, Mr. Mattress was still entertaining stragglers. Since 5:00, Manny and Jitnee had sold nine beds. Either they had tapped into an overflowing reservoir of pent-up mattress demand, or advertising really did work, or both. Jack had estimated nine beds sold through close of business Sunday. At this rate, including the Internet coupon discounts, the store was likely to take in $24,000 in profit over the course of the sale. Which, even after subtracting overhead and taxes, was more than the Donato crew was taking in every week. And Mr. Mattress never had to assault or extort anyone.

Anyway, almost never. When the phone call from Jack came in reporting, simply, "We did it. On our way," Big Manny felt certain his boss's days as a criminal mastermind were over. Now all he had to do was wait for a Mr. Spadafora to show up for the stamps. The hit man had been paid his half up front, only because Big Manny—unlike the actual remaining gang members—knew the combination to the don's safe. The chiropractor would receive the balance only because Manny came to the rescue. He was naturally pained to lose his prized collection, but if peace had been won for Ebbets Beach, and for Ralph, it was a sacrifice he was quite satisfied to make. As the don liked to say, and it made Manny laugh to remember it, "The only thing you can be sure about in life is death and Texas." Nothing in Manny's life had gone the way he, as a young man, had dreamed. Like the don, in the end, he harbored some regrets. He should not have been part of all that wrongdoing. He shouldn't have shamed his parents. He shouldn't have had blood on his hands. At least now he knew that chapter was over. Even the stamps were part of his previous life; they'd been lovingly amassed and studied entirely in his idle hours at the agency and the club. He'd hoped to spend the evening poring over his favorites one last time. Closure, they call it—and here one final regret. The only thing Manny was able to close Thursday evening was an unheard of number of sales. It was almost 10:00 before the last customer—sale number ten, incidentally—was finally off the premises. No trip down Philatelic Memory Lane for him.

With everyone cleared out, Big Manny took $200 of his own money and pressed it into Jitnee's palm. "Good work tonight, honey. From now on, you'll get a commission on top of your hourly. Now, get yourself home."

The first to return were Tony the Teeth and the chiropractor. Seth walked into the store as if he were wearing gravity boots, one deliberate and excruciating step at a time. At length, he managed to maneuver himself into a chair by the sales desk. It was clear to him that he had participated in a triumphant humiliation of Valentin Smirdov but couldn't quite make out how or why. What was that first set of pictures? He had heard the exchange in his office yesterday about an Arab vendor, who he surmised was the one seen posing with the gang. And the cash in the photo he figured to be the $16,000 Big Manny wound up advancing to him. He also gathered that the final picture Angela showed the Russian had captured her posing with policemen near the Russian's place, but for the life of him he couldn't figure out when or how. She'd been at his office since 6:25 p.m. and, as far as he knew, had arrived directly from Ebbets Beach. What he did know, however, was that the plan to which he had not been privy but in which nonetheless he'd been a critical player had gone off, as it were, like gangbusters. So, naturally, Seth being Seth, pain or no pain, he was itching to gloat. Assuming the shit-eatingest of shit-eating grins, he pointed to the black Thumper Maxi Pro carrying case, which Teeth had carried for him into the store.

"Hey, Tony, do me a favor, hand me that pouch," he said. When the hairy enforcer complied, Seth dug through it, feeling with his hand under the massager and producing a blue baseball cap, with the insignia *LA* embroidered on the crown. "My lucky lid! Once a Dodgers fan, always a Dodgers fan! Am I right?" He did not expect what happened next. Nor did Jack and Angela when they arrived upon a scene they themselves struggled to decipher. Really, who could? For what reason could anyone expect to see Tony the Teeth, without apparent provocation, in a place of retail business, urinating on a hat.

"Tony!" Jack barked as the puddle soaked into the industrial carpet and leeched outward. "What in the world are you doing?"

Tony did not answer Jack. Instead, he zipped himself up and turned toward Angela. "In other words, your friend here disrespected your dad."

"Huh?"

"Asswipe was wearing a Dodgers hat," Tony explained. "What should I do with him?"

What should I do with him? From irrational exuberance to that ominous question in the space of sixty seconds, Seth's mind reeled. Having no insight into the late don's lifelong feelings of betrayal at the hands of the Dodgers Professional Baseball Club, he was completely unable to make sense of this menacing weirdness, except to infer he'd been thrust right back into grave peril. The bizarre piss vandalism, so random and aggressive, had freaked him out. *What should I do with him?* made him quake. Now terror choked him. How greedy could he have been? His mind raced as he castigated himself for his stupidity and suffered for the fate obviously awaiting him. He had done the mobsters' work for them. Now, in order to leave no witnesses, they would return the favor—and not with a quick snooze. Tears began to well in his eyes and streak his cheeks. Trembling, he joined Tony—by pissing his own pants. Then after the longest five seconds of his dreary, compromising, corrupt little life, the chiropractor listened in disbelief as Jack answered the pregnant question.

"Pay him."

"Come again?" said Tony.

"Really?" squeaked Seth.

"Really?" volunteered Angela. "The guy's a train wreck. He never shut his mouth. Could've easily gotten us both killed. Come on, Seth, you started out good, but then you were out of control. I don't see how you can even ask for the rest of your money."

The chiropractor's eyes were closed, and he was panting in relief. Then he shook his head. "I'm good. You're right. I don't need any more money."

This seemed to satisfy Angela, but Jack was having none of it.

"No," he said. "Look, you get what you pay for. We made a deal. He took the risk. His brain freeze or whatever, that worked. It all worked out in the end. He can't help it if he's a schmuck. We pay him what we owe him."

"My guy's not here yet," said Manny.

"Well," said Jack, "Dr. Glick-Mermelstein will have to wait for him. Meantime, please give him the pickle jar cash. Seth, it's thirteen thousand dollars, give or take. Hang on, and you'll get the other eleven grand."

"Really, I can—"

"Seth!" Angela snapped. "Do you never know when not to run your mouth? You are getting another eleven thousand dollars. That's settled. But you have to be quiet. Is that something you can do? Be quiet?"

He nodded.

"Good. Do it."

Next to arrive were Marco, Casper, Leonard, and Little Manny, none of whom knew exactly what had transpired. But Casper and Marco had a story.

"You'll never fucking guess who we run into coming to help youse out," Casper says. "Stoned to his tits and armed to the teeth. Larry fuckin' Rizzo!"

"What?" Jack squeaked. "Larry? Armed with *what*?"

"Remington twelve-gauge pump. Said he was on a secret mission or some fuckin' thing. He said you"—he pointed to Jack—"was a spy or some shit. He was, like, babbling about twerps or twats. *Follia*. What the don calls—called—*follia*. He's in Marco's trunk."

"YOU KILLED LARRY RIZZO?" Jack screamed.

This made Casper laugh. "Get this guy. No, I didn't kill him. I what you call subdued him before he showed up at the Russian's place blasting away."

Big Manny addressed Marco. "He's still in your trunk?"

Marco nodded.

"And he's alive?"

"Medium," Marco replied.

"Medium? MEDIUM?" Jack shot back, still alarmed, for the point of the night's events had been to *not* harm anyone. "What's *medium* mean?"

"He was still breathing when we duck-taped his mouth," Marco explained, not quite getting what the fuss was about.

"Jesus Christ almighty," Jack gasped. "Get him out of there and bring him inside."

Marco shrugged. Seemed pretty dumb to him. The guy with the flowered shirt was obviously one outbound short of an itinerary, as they say at Fiesta Tours. He jammed a toothpick into his mouth, rolled it on his tongue, and headed out to the car to off-load the crazed gunman. It was a fresh moment of jeopardy for all concerned, so what a grand opportunity for the chiropractor to chime in!

"Such a putz," Seth sneered. "He could have ruined the whole operation."

Heads turned toward him—Angela out of shock that even through the panic and humiliation his inner dickhead shone through, and the newcomers because they hadn't even noticed him sitting there, by the desk, soaking in his own piss. Having as yet no news of the evening's results, Little Manny, Casper, and Leonard could only look on in puzzlement as Angela stepped purposefully toward the chiropractor and punched him hard in the right ear. Then she leaned over to the left one and shouted at the top of her lungs, "NOW SHUT UP!"

The boys, still in the dark, were now beginning to get curious about what led to Daddy's little do-gooder to go all Vice Principal Sister Bernadette on the chiropractor.

"So," Casper finally inquired, "the Russian...he's...?" He used the figurative stiletto of his index finger to slash the figurative Russian throat of his own.

Big Manny shook his head no.

"Fuck!" Casper said. "Doc, what'd you do? Fuck it up?"

"No," said Big Manny, "he didn't fuck it up."

"He sort of did," Angela said. "The guy's a serial douchebag— no offense, Seth."

Seth waved. His ears were variously pounding and ringing. A little name-calling he was fine with. Not that he had any kind of counterargument anyway.

Now Jack jumped in. "Angela and the doctor succeeded in a big way. They did not enter that house thinking to kill Smirdov."

Seth, of course, had absolutely entered the house intending for the Russian to die, but, at last, he was learning when not to chime in.

"We had another idea, and between luck and the heroism of the beautiful Donato sisters, it came off exactly as planned. Better than planned, really, because once she got the Russian in a compromising position, Angela did some ad-libbing." He turned to her. "What was that business about a mortgage? You called me about a 'mortgage,' but I couldn't follow what you were saying."

"Oh," Angela said. "That was just lawyer stuff. The other party seemed to be in a negotiating frame of mind, so I kind of raised the stakes. He's going to pay us five thousand dollars a month forever."

"Us?" asked Leonard the Calculator. "The crew? Five dimes?"

"Yes and no," Angela said.

"I don't felpin' get it," Leonard objected. "Is it yes, or is it no?"

"Be quiet," Big Manny said. "Jack is talking. Go ahead, Boss."

Here, however, Jack was obliged to pause as the door opened and profoundly tubby Marco backed into Mr. Mattress dragging a slightly tubby Hawaiian-shirted man bound in jumper cables and duct tape. With his arms tucked under the sandwich man's damp armpits, Marco scraped him along the floor to the Pillow Quilt Royale queen and then positioned himself to cradle the load. Larry was conscious and strangely acquiescent to the manhandling. He offered nary a peep as Marco lifted him and tossed him, like a sack of potatoes or Joey Sardines, onto the bed. The whole room full of conspirators gawked in amazement as Larry blinked his eyes, one more fully than the other. Was he trying to…wink? Jack considered freeing him, but rather liked the idea of Larry Rizzo speechless and immobile, an opportunity unlikely to present itself again. So he picked up where he'd left off.

"What I wanted to tell you was that Angela got that money on her own. All the plan called for was two hundred thousand dollars from the Russians to help get the barber and the car wash back in business. Now we have an extra five grand a month, thanks to her take-no-prisoners approach. Or take-one-prisoner approach, I guess."

"Two hundred thousand dollars!" Casper blurted out. "No fuckin' way!"

The chiropractor was also surprised.

"And he'll deliver two hundred grand to Little Manny by Monday, correct?" Jack asked Angela, who glanced sheepishly toward the chiropractor.

"Well," she said, wearing an expression of guilt and embarrassment, "yes and no."

"What's with the 'yes and no' shit, Angie?" Little Manny insisted. "Did you get the two hundred dimes or not?"

"No," she said.

"Fuck I tell you? Pop, how'd you let these civilians get into our shit?"

But Angela wasn't finished. "If I understand a dime is one thousand dollars...then it's...I guess, one thousand dimes. By Sunday."

"*What?*" Little Manny said.

"*What?*" Jack said.

"*Fuckin' what?*" Casper said.

"One million dollars," beamed Dr. Glick-Mermelstein. "Just the two of us."

Angela walked over to him and boxed his ear again. This time, he cupped it before she could much injure him, but he resumed being a nonentity and at long last kept his mouth shut. This would have marked a perfect opportunity for Angela to explain how she and Seth had a) entered a man's home under false pretenses, b) knocked him unconscious, c) temporarily enslaved him, d) alarmed him with pictures of himself exchanging cash with the enemy, e) stopped him cold with naked pictures of himself sleeping with the enemy, f) scared him over the edge with Jack's freshly Photoshopped composite of Angela, the cops, and a Park Slope storefront, g) finally blackmailed him for $1 million plus, and h) walked/limped out 100 percent not shot to death. It would have been a delicious moment—except that a policeman was standing ten feet from them. Sergeant Mike Franzetti had entered the store.

"Hello, criminals!" he announced cheerfully. "Rub out any rivals lately?"

Tony the Teeth looked at Big Manny, who subtly but definitively shook his head: *No, fellas, do not kill the police officer.*

Jack stepped forward. He at least knew that the cop knew something but was sure that the cop didn't know what he didn't know. "Hi, Sergeant. Jack Schiavone. We met at the hospital."

The two shook hands as Jack subtly maneuvered the cop away from a direct view of the bound-and-gagged restaurateur, who watched the choreography, but mystified everyone by making no attempt to get the cop's attention. On the contrary, it was as if he were trying to melt into the Pillow Quilt Royale. Jack subtly eased the policeman to a less incriminating vantage and addressed the officer's premise.

"I think you are working on some bad information."

"Like fun I am," Franzetti laughed. "Which one of these losers is the chiropractor? Is it you?" The cop looked right at the only man seated in the store, Seth Glick-Mermelstein, DC. Under Angela's threat, he was reluctant to speak. But he was too scared to ignore the cop. So he simply shook his head.

"Oh, really? So what's with that shirt...*Seth*?" Franzetti laughed. Nobody else did. The various onlookers didn't know how this would play out, but their triumph seemed to be evaporating before their eyes. On the other hand, how trustworthy were their eyes? Because the next thing they believed they saw was the policeman producing a manila envelope stuffed, absolutely stuffed, with twenty-, fifty-, and one-hundred-dollar bills. "Here ya go, sport. For the neighborhood watch. What do we owe you?"

"Sergeant," Jack broke in, "I don't understand."

"Like hell. Look, I know you took out the Russian tonight. And I know you were coming up short, cash-wise, and that dipshit Larry Rizzo tells me you hired some guy called the Chiropractor. So here I am to make the guy whole."

"Amway?" guessed Jack.

That struck Franzetti as hilarious. "You kidding me? I been in it for three years, and I ain't earned a fucking Atlantic City weekend. No, this here is a loan from the Our Lady of Grace bingo. I figure you mooks have done a good turn here, for the neighborhood. Plus, it's the least I can do for my downline. Plus, outta respect for your don, God rest his soul. I got twenty-two grand. What do you need?"

"You skimmed the bingo?" Casper asked. "Is that legal?"

"Fuck you, Eydie Gormé. Why don't you go sucker punch a fuckin' brick wall?" Franzetti turned back to Jack. "Like I said, it's a loan. I got you covered at least till next Thursday, all right. Meantime, I'll read the papers tomorrow."

"You won't see shimp," said Leonard the Calculator.

"Well, Mike, tell you what," said Jack. "Let us take you up on your generous offer. We need eleven thousand dollars to fulfill our obligation. You will have that back on Monday. I can't thank you enough."

Angela thought this was just too funny. She only wished her sister could be here to see the payoff. Before Tina broke her leg, she had agreed to be photographed pretending to blow the pretzel guy—or maybe not pretending. She'd further agreed to play Nurse Rachel and confront the piece-of-shit Russian with the blackmail photos. But Tina was still at Maimonides, in a thigh-high cast, receiving an after-hours sick visit—from a slightly giddy sick visitor who signed her cast *Steve Delewski*.

Meanwhile, as the crew watched dumbfounded, Franzetti began backing up to the Pillow Quilt Royale—whereupon the bound-and-gagged nuisance reacted by rolling himself to the far side of the bed. What the fuck was Larry up to? Impossible to know, but surely, if he fell over the side, the thud would be unmistakable, and the jig would be up. Franzetti edged backward, Larry scooched edgeward, underworld pulses raced upward. Nobody knew what to do because there was nothing to do. After a week of existential crisis, tragedy, desperate improvisation, and extremely strange bedfellowing, they were all about to be arrested, not for murdering the guy they hadn't murdered, but for preserving civil order by kidnapping a vigilante sandwich chef before somebody actually got hurt. In two seconds, Larry would go down, and the whole lot of them thereafter.

> *Quant'è laria la me zita,*
> *tutta fraricia e purrita !*
> *ritornello: ah laria è, cchiù laria d'iddra un ci 'nnè !*

Out of nowhere, Casper had broken into song. And it wasn't Waldo's repertoire. This tune was plucked straight out of Palermo.

> *Quant'è brutta la mia fidanzata,*
> *tutta fradicia e puzzolente !*
> *ritornello: ah brutta è, più brutta di lei non c'è nessuno !*

> *Havi la panza chi pari 'na utti,*

quannu camina fa ririri a tutti !
ritornello: ah laria è, cchiù laria d'iddra un ci 'nnè !

Sure enough, for several reasons, everybody's attention fell immediately upon Casper. For one thing, the spontaneous a cappella serenade was, like the ball cap golden shower, entirely unprovoked. Secondly, as Mr. Mattress had dutifully informed Casper to his face one short week ago, the store was a woeful venue for live music. Thirdly, and not least of all, Casper was not merely singing; he was foot-tapping and swaying and generally assuming the irrepressible personality of a Marsala-soaked wedding singer. Unaccountably, the sped had left the building. Yes, it was unnerving—like any other episode of musical Tourette's—but, shit, he was even snapping his fingers. Overhand! With both hands! And now he was dancing! It was a miracle. Someday there would be a shrine on the location, and weeping pilgrims kissing the industrial carpet. For now, though, more importantly, the attention riveted on Casper distracted everyone, especially the cop, from the drama taking place five feet from Franzetti's butt on the Pillow Quilt Royale. The cheerful bingo embezzler had frozen in place but now resumed his backward approach to the bed. As Larry teetered on the very edge. Casper commenced to belting. Not the cop with his fist, but the song with his larynx.

Ha la pancia che sembra una botte,
quando cammina fa ridere tutti !
ritornello: ah BRUTTA È, PIÙ BRUTTA DI LEI NON C'È
NESSUNO !

At "*c'è nessuno*," for the second time this evening, Larry Rizzo disappeared. Franzetti, now himself plopping *onto* the bed, noticed not a thing. The Donato crew 'n' friends hooted and applauded enthusiastically, as if the musical outburst were the most natural thing in the world—and well that they did, because the commotion obscured the muffled comment of Larry Rizzo from the floor on the far side of the bed.

"Ow," he said.

For his part, the cop somehow failed to process that the sequence of events made no sense. Perhaps he was just caught up in the festivity and cheer of a hit job well done.

"Not bad, dipshit," Franzetti offered. "You sing a shitload better than you gangster." Then he commenced to pulling bricks of cash from the envelope. Meticulously counting $11,000 to pay off the annoying and wet contract put-to-sleeper, he then rose, crossed the floor to the sales desk, handed the bundle to the Chiropractor, and slapped him on the back. He didn't know why Seth flinched and covered his ear with both hands. "Nice work, Doc. But now that I know who you are, better stick to spines or whatever, because I will put you away. *Capische?*"

Seth nodded vigorously. Quite vigorously. He took his money, stuffed it into his massager pouch, and, carrying the Thumper pouchless, soggily limped his way out of Mr. Mattress.

Franzetti followed him out the door and chuckled at the man wobbling to the curb and looking altogether disoriented. "Don't spend it all in one place, killer." The cop laughed, jumped happily into his Crown Vic, and pulled away.

Teeth had, in turn, followed Franzetti out the door. When Seth noticed the enforcer, it gave him yet another start.

"You wanna lift to your car? It's in front of the Russian's place. Or I could take you home."

Seth expressed gratitude, but he had definitely seen too many movies. "Thank you, sir," he replied. "But I have plenty of money for a cab." He hailed one, slowly climbed in, and got the fuck out of Ebbets Beach forever. Tony rejoined the victorious crew, and the carcass of stupidity slumped on the floor on the far side of the Pillow Quilt. He and the rest would have been enjoying a sigh of relief, if just then yet another character hadn't joined the *Night at the Opera* stateroom scene. Following Teeth inside the mattress store was a middle-aged, slightly stooped man with coarse hair dyed dully and impossibly black. This was a Mr. Spadafora, calling on a Mr. Aiala about a stamp collection. He too arrived bearing a bundle of cash.

Little Manny realized what was going on; this little bloodsucker was going to try to steal the big man's collection for peanuts. He approached the visitor menacingly. But Jack stepped in to intervene, keeping him as far away from the unlawfully restrained Shotgun Larry as humanly possible.

"Mr. Spadafora, I am very sorry to have inconvenienced you, but Mr. Aiala's collection is no longer on the market."

"Not on the market?" he protested. "I came all the way from Sheepshead Bay."

"Yes, sir. It was a misunderstanding, and I apologize. But here's how I can make it up to you: Any mattress/boxspring set in the store is yours, free of charge. Come by anytime this weekend, and we'll take care of you."

"I don't need a mattress," Mr. Spadafora said. "Free delivery too?"

"Yes," Jack said, trying to navigate the guy out of the store, "just come back by Sunday at six p.m."

"Could I have it shipped to my daughter in Paramus?"

"Yes, sir, but we are closed now. Come this weekend."

"But—"

"*OUT!*" Jack explained.

With the stamp dealer sent packing, Jack turned around to an odd tableau: Big Manny and the entire remainder of the Donato crew arrayed in a semicircle and a colorful, helpless prisoner wheezing out of view. Jack put his hand out in front of Marco, who dug into the deep pockets of his size fifty-two trousers and produced a knife. This Jack used to cut the tape around Larry's body. Thereupon he untied the jumper cables and carefully peeled the tape from the captive's big mouth.

And even then, Larry grinned. "We did it?" he whispered to Jack.

"Roger that," Jack replied. "Go home."

And then the most astonishing thing happened: without argument or delay, Larry did.

Through all of this, from the rest of the Inventory Clearance team, not a word. They were all entirely focused on Jack. As he'd struggled to eject Mr. Spadafora, he'd missed an important pronouncement from Big Manny. What the assistant manager had said was the following: "From now on, I am out of the Family for good. The Family is gonna change, a lot. A lot lot. There will be a new consigliere and a new boss."

It was then that Mr. Mattress resumed the group and noticed their attention to his presence.

Casper, who had only just yesterday terrorized the bed sales-man with a baseball bat, stepped forward and kneeled at Jack's feet. Bowing his head, he whispered, "Don Schiavone."

Nobody moved a muscle. Jack was silent. All he did in response to Casper was shake his head no as he made eye contact with Big Manny, who, in turn, whispered something in Ralph's ear. Then Little Manny stepped forward, touched Casper's shoulder, and gestured for him to stand. Casper, a bit uncertain, complied. Thereupon Little Manny turned toward Angela, took a knee, and bowed.

"Donna Donato," he said.

ABOUT THE AUTHOR

Photograph © William Neumann

Bob Garfield is a columnist, broadcaster, and author. He is cohost of *On the Media*, a Peabody Award–winning weekly newsmagazine produced by WNYC and distributed by NPR. He is also cohost of the insanely popular Slate podcast *Lexicon Valley*, a weekly conversation about language. An inveterate journalist, he is a columnist for both *MediaPost* and the *Guardian* and the author of three previous nonfiction books. Another book, *Can't Buy Me Like*, will be published in March 2013 by Penguin Portfolio. Garfield lives in suburban Washington, DC, with his film-producer wife, Milena Trobozic Garfield, and youngest daughter. He can barely locate Brooklyn on a map.